Traveling Ladies

Also by Janice Kulyk Keefer:

Fiction

The Paris-Napoli Express (stories)
Transfigurations (stories)
Constellations (a novel)

Nonfiction

Under Eastern Eyes:
A Critical Reading of Maritime Fiction
Reading Mavis Gallant

Poetry

White of the Lesser Angels

Traveling Ladies

stories

Janice Kulyk Keefer

William Morrow and Company, Inc.
New York

Some of these stories have appeared previously in *Canadian Fiction Magazine, Matrix, Country Estate, The Malahat Review,* and *Saturday Night*

These are works of fiction. The characters and situations portrayed are imaginary.

First published 1990 by Random House of Canada Limited, Toronto

Recognizing the importance of preserving what has been written, it is the policy of William Morrow and Company, Inc., and its imprints and affiliates to have the books it publishes printed on acid-free paper, and we exert our best efforts to that end.

Library of Congress Cataloging-in-Publication Data

Keefer, Janice Kulyk, 1953-
   Traveling ladies / by Janice Kulyk Keefer.
    p.   cm.
   ISBN 0-688-10284-0
   I. Title.
   PR9199.3.K4115T7   1991
   813'.54—dc20   90-19305
                                           CIP

Printed in the United States of America

First U.S. Edition

1 2 3 4 5 6 7 8 9 10

BOOK DESIGN BY MARIA EPES

In memory of Margaret Laurence

I would like to thank Ed Carson
for his generous and painstaking support.
I owe special thanks to
Michael Keefer, *compagnon de voyage*.

Contents

The real travelers are the ones who never arrive.
                                    —*Edgar Degas*

Prodigals

Anna came home because her grandmother was dying.

She'd been away for six years, and had never been a great letter writer. Because she so seldom had a fixed address, her family had abandoned all but the most symbolic communications: Christmas cards, which inevitably reached her by Easter, and birthday cards which, though mailed well in advance of June twenty-first, would reach Athens or Tangiers or Calcutta round about Hallowe'en. Anna was an English teacher, not attached to a proper college, but flitting from one fly-by-night language school to another. In Munich, where she happened to be staying in between jobs, a telegram reached her, forwarded from her last place of residence but one. It was from her father.

NANA HAS CANCER AND WON'T LIVE OUT THE SUMMER.

She'd been out on the balcony reading a book. It was Saturday, a midsummer morning, and her friend Dieter was home for a change. When she passed him the telegram he read it, folded it in two, and handed it back to her. "Nana?" he asked.

"My grandmother."

"I thought Ukrainians say *baba* for grandmother."

"They do. And grandfather is *Dyeedo,* but we could never manage it. We'd say 'Gigi,' instead—like the baby word for horse. *Baba* means old woman. She never wanted anyone to call her that."

"Shall I ring up about planes?"

"Please. I can be ready in an hour. And Dieter—"

"Yes?"

"She's only sixty-four. She isn't old."

Traffic was worse than terrible. They stopped and started so many times that Anna despaired of ever making her plane on time. Luckily, the flight had been delayed because of a bomb scare. "False alarm," said the woman at Security, and Anna gave her the most beautiful smile. It was an omen, she decided; things couldn't be as bad as her father made them seem. Perhaps Nana wasn't even ill, perhaps it was another ploy, the last, most desperate one, to bring her back to a place they called home. She wouldn't tell them she was coming. She would simply fly into Toronto, take a cab to her grandmother's house, and find Nana putting on the kettle for *chai,* or watering her garden.

When Dieter kissed her good-bye, Anna pressed her cheek against his and whispered, "Everything's going to be fine—don't worry," not even knowing she'd stolen his lines.

It was a midafternoon flight, filled with the less successful sort of businessman. The one beside her kept offering to buy her a drink, but when she pointed out they came free with the flight, he stopped bothering her. She lay with her head back, her eyes closed, fingering the key to her grandmother's front door. Years ago, Nana had given it to her; she had kept it hidden in a little Kashmiri box, under the silver charm-bracelet her parents had brought home for her after a trip to Europe. There was a tiny gondola, the Eiffel tower, a cuckoo clock with silver weights that swung back and forth, a silver crown for England. They had thought she would chain all those foreign places round her wrist, then marry a doctor, lawyer, or engineer, and stray no farther than the outer suburbs of Toronto.

When she'd announced that instead of completing her degree she was going to spend her savings and go traveling, her mother had wept for a week. "Whatever you do, don't tell your Nana—it will break her heart." Anna had promised she wouldn't. Instead, she'd spent an afternoon helping her grandmother weed the garden, then waved good-bye as if she were going back downtown, instead of to the airport. Once she'd reached Paris her parents gave out that she was studying abroad. That first year away, Anna had written only random postcards to her grandmother, keeping up the pretense that she had but one address, one country of residence. And then, when she'd started traveling in earnest, it had seemed simplest to stop writing altogether. She didn't know when her parents had broken the news that she'd gone for good. Perhaps after Jenny had married and had twins; when there'd been more than enough family to fill the empty place at Nana's dinner table.

She took the airport bus downtown, and then a taxi over to Dovercourt Road. Her grandmother lived in one of those handsome brick houses with chastely columned verandas, and narrow, prodigally fertile gardens. She recognized her father's station wagon parked in front of the house—curious that he should have hung on to it, with all of them grown up now and on their own. The last she'd heard, Jenny had moved to Fredericton, and their brother, Montreal. Unless, of course, they'd all come back to Toronto this summer. That would mean Nana really was dying, and this Anna would not for a moment allow. Her grandmother was as solid, as sturdy as the pillars holding up the porch roof. She'd survived diphtheria as a child, her village had been invaded by Russian soldiers during the First World War, and just before the second she'd had the miraculous good sense to get the family out of Poland into Canada. Her grandmother had done her own share of traveling, in carts and boats and trains in the night. Someone like that didn't just give over and die.

The house was exactly as she remembered it—even the lace curtains shielded the parlor windows with the same degree of starch. Someone was sitting in the living room; she could hear the drone of the TV as she tapped at the glass. Of course she could have used her key, but she hadn't wanted to startle the shape that was rousing itself from the sofa, parting the curtains. An old, gray face, like a letter that had been crumpled and then smoothed out. The curtains fell back into place. She heard a stumbling sound. Then the door opened and she recognized her mother.

"It's you, Anna? Really you? My God, why didn't you tell us you were coming? Your father would have picked you up at the airport. Let me look at you—oh Anna, Anna. You're all alone?"

Anna couldn't look for long into her mother's eyes; they looked as though they'd been stung. "I'm on my own, yes. I didn't want to bother anyone—I took a taxi." She wanted to ask about her grandmother, but couldn't. The house felt all wrong inside, but she couldn't tell why. It was spotless as always, everything in place except for a blanket rucked up on the sofa. Guiltily, Anna's mother shut off the TV. "I wasn't watching—it's just that I hate to be alone in the house. The noise keeps me company."

"No one's upstairs?" Anna didn't wait for an answer, but walked along the hallway into the kitchen. The electric clock buzzed over the window; the cow-shaped cream pitcher was in its customary place on a shelf over the sink.

"The apartment has been empty for the last six months. Alita got married in December."

"Alita?"

"You didn't know her. She's a nurse from Jamaica. She's been very good to Nana." Abruptly, her mother dropped down onto one of the kitchen chairs, spread her elbows on the scarred enamel table, and wept without making any noise at all. Anna bent down, as if to embrace her, but froze halfway. What was the proper etiquette for a prodigal? Kiss when the cheek is offered? Her mother hadn't so much as touched her hand yet. Anna straightened up and pushed her hair out of her eyes. She wanted to take a bath after the flight. And she was so hungry. Her stomach growled and she suddenly understood why the house felt so strange, so cold; there was no smell of baking.

Suddenly her mother stopped crying; she patted her hair into place, rubbed her mouth, and pushed herself up from the table. "You must be tired. I'll make some tea." Her voice was hoarse—she needed sleep far more than Anna did.

Before they'd finished the pot, there was a ring at the door. Anna's mother got up, disappeared down the hall, and came back five minutes later with her husband. He kissed Anna, and took the last cup of tea from her. It was as if his daughter had dropped in from around the block, instead of six years and an ocean away.

"When can I see her?" Anna asked. Her parents looked at each other, then her mother got up to rinse the cups in the sink.

"Tomorrow," her father answered. "You must be tired after all that traveling. Where did you fly in from?"

"But I've come all this way to see her."

"Anna—" Her father handed his wife his empty cup, and then straightened his tie before reaching for his daughter's hand. "We buried her last week."

Anna's mother ran out of the kitchen. They could hear the television start up; it didn't quite muffle the crying.

"She's tired," Anna's father said. "She can't get any sleep here, but she won't leave the house empty. She thinks someone will break in and steal everything. That's what she says, but it's—you know, white magic. She thinks that as long as there's someone in the house, Nana won't really have gone. It'll be all right once we clear things out." He paused for a moment, rubbing the top of his head with a handkerchief. "I'll take you to the cemetery in the morning. You'll need some sleep, too. What time is it back there? Midnight?"

"Something like that."

"Jenny was down with the children last week. I'll ring her up, let her know you're here. She and Ivan are in Winnipeg now. Stefan comes over the odd weekend, from Montreal. I'll put your suitcase in the trunk."

She had started shaking her head even before he finished the sentence. "No. I'll stay here, with Mum. Look, why don't I stay here instead of her? You can take her home with you, put her to sleep in her own bed. Wouldn't that be best?"

Her father shrugged, then nodded. He looked exhausted beneath his tan. How long had this been going on for them? And why hadn't they told her earlier? She could have come back and helped them. Or had she stopped writing home so that she'd never have to know how things had changed? She followed her father to the front door. Her mother kissed her good-bye, held her tightly, but Anna knew it was too late. She had shut herself out from her grandmother's dying—she had disinherited herself.

"Where's the fatted calf?" Anna whispered, peering through the lace curtains, watching her parents' car pull away. Her throat ached, as if she'd swallowed something hot and sharp.

Alone again, she refused to turn on the television or even the radio. She wasn't afraid, though she refused to go up the varnished oak stairs to the second-floor apartment. Not that there were ghosts, or any ghosts she wouldn't have welcomed. Her grandmother's tenants had always been kind to her, given her drinks of ginger ale, let her look inside their curio cabinets. China ladies with starched lace skirts, and parasols—that was Mrs. Buck. Sonia and Steffko had been the salt and pepper shakers. And much later there was the widow, Mrs. Roshko, who was always complaining to Nana about her "nerfs," and who'd scandalized the whole block by going off to sunbathe in High Park on Saturday afternoons. Mrs. Roshko had married again, a man much younger than herself. She'd even told Nana it was high time she found herself a new husband. Nana had shot back something so funny, so scornful that Mrs. Roshko hadn't known whether to laugh or cry. They'd been speaking in Ukrainian—Anna couldn't remember the words.

She sat on the stairs, in the cold, queer silence of the house, trying to recall her grandmother's voice, the exact tone. Strong and carrying. Except when she spoke to Yurko. Then her voice had been soft, coaxing. . . . That was why the house sounded, as well as smelled so strange—Yurko was gone. Anna ran into the dining room off the kitchen. The stand was there, but the cage had vanished. Perhaps it was outside—Nana would often take the canary into the garden to keep company with the jays and blackbirds. Anna rushed to the door that led from the dining room, past the cellar steps, into the backyard. The door had been bolted and chained. She rattled it open, and walked outside, along a path that wasn't much more than a cracked ribbon of concrete. She went past the flower borders, down three steps, along the vegetable garden until the yard ended in a high wooden fence.

Anna left the path to sit on the slope of grass for a moment. She felt dizzy, and closed her eyes, then opened them cautiously. It was as though she'd jumped off a speeding train, a train going so fast she hadn't seen anything but a blur when she'd looked out the windows. Wasn't this the hill down which she and Jenny had turned somersaults with their grandfather—oh, twenty years ago? Only a week before Gigi had died, her father had taken a home movie in this garden, with Anna and her sister wearing white organdy dresses, poking daisies in their hair. She had such a clear image of the movie, though it had been years since she'd last seen it. The film was so brittle it had bubbled under the projector light. She could remember herself watching her long-abandoned image dance and fall down. Why, then, couldn't she recall the feel of the grass as she tumbled over it, the precise clasp of her sister's hand? Near the end of the film she'd been crying—they'd asked her to do something, and she'd refused, lying down on the grass in a little ball, refusing to look at anyone. But what had made her so stubbornly sad?

Anna rose to her feet, brushing grass from her skirt. There was no going back, no forcing memory. All she had of the past was a picture of a picture. And tomorrow she'd be pushed from the house into a future she didn't want to know: her grandmother lying under freshly turned earth. A granite slab, inscribed.

Sprinklers were going in the neighbors' gardens. Anna walked up and down the borders, naming the plants she saw: hydrangea, roses, delphinium, phlox. And then runner beans; feathery clumps of dill; onions and rhubarb and carefully staked tomatoes. She went to the very back of the garden, next to the fence that bordered the alleyway. It was too late for strawberries, but raspberries were ripening on the canes. She broke off a few berries and ate them, though they were whitish, hard, more seed than fruit. Suddenly she felt as though she could drop onto the grass and go to sleep right there, just as she was. But she heard the telephone ringing from the house. Stupidly, she thought it might be Dieter calling, though she hadn't left him any number.

It was her mother, wanting to know if she was all right, whether they shouldn't bring her home after all. Anna said she was fine—she'd just gone out into the garden for a bit. There was a little pause, and then her mother spoke. "You're home to stay?"

Anna listened to the slight hum along the wire; it made her think of hairs standing up along an arm. "Really, I'll be all right." And then, too quickly, "I was wondering—what's happened to Yurko?"

She was afraid her mother might burst into tears again, or even shout at her. But all she said was, "Alita took him. Nana gave him to her, when she knew she wouldn't be coming home from hospital. She said Alita was the only one she could trust to talk to him enough."

"Oh. That's all right, then. You get some sleep. Good night."

Anna washed up in the new bathroom that had been installed just off the dining room. Before, Nana had had to go down to the cellar where there was a boxed-off toilet with a chain flush—Anna had never been able to reach it as a child. Had they got rid of the huge tub with griffin legs? Upstairs the bath was pink; there was a matching toilet and sink with gold-colored taps. Anna decided she preferred the griffin tub, though she was just as glad not to have to go down to the cellar tonight.

An hour later, lying in her grandmother's bed, windows open to whatever breeze could be lured inside, Anna listened to the ringing of crystal pendants on the dressing-table lamps, until sleep pitched her down like a stone.

"Jenny pushed me, she hurt my arm!"

"Anna started it. She kept swinging her foot and scraping my leg, even when I asked her to stop."

"Oh, be quiet, the two of you. I don't want your grandparents to hear you bickering. If you keep on like this we'll just turn the car and go straight back home. Right, Max?"

Their father is cursing the traffic under his breath. "Damn right."

"Max, I keep telling you not to use language like that in front of—"

The sisters move to opposite sides of the car. They know the threat will never be carried out, but it wouldn't be wise, just now, to push their parents any further. It's only another five minutes to their grandparents' house. Anna nudges the handle of the window with her thumb. It's so hot in the car—her dress prickles against her legs. Her mother never lets them ride with the windows open. She's afraid of drafts, drafts make her sick with sinuses and a stiff neck. But if the window were only a quarter of an inch, a hair's breadth open—

Quickly she looks at Jenny, to see if she would notice. But Jenny's already opened her window a good inch; she's holding her fingers against the gush of air. Anna gulps, tears scalding her eyes. It isn't fair, Jenny always does everything first, gets away with things that Anna never dares to try. Because Jenny is two years older and two years smarter, even if Anna has caught up with her in height, and wears a size larger shoes.

The car turns the corner. They have passed the Clover Leaf Cinema, and the Toreador Club, with its neon sign that says DANCING and its poster of a Spanish lady biting down on a rose. Anna's mother never mentions the Toreador Club, except to say that her daughters should pretend it isn't there when they walk past it on their way to the movies. Today is Sunday—there isn't even a matinee. The car slows down. Well before their father has taken the key out of the ignition, the girls are pushing open the doors. "Now remember—" their mother begins, but the doors have slammed shut before she can remind them to be good, to keep their dresses clean and their voices down.

Nana is already on the porch to greet them. Jenny runs up to her, dancing; she's a feather twirling in the air, thinks Anna, delighted, grudging. Jenny always gets everywhere first—what's the point of even trying? So Anna stops on the sidewalk, under the linden tree. She throws back her head, her hair tickling the small of her back as she breathes in the green honey of the linden flowers. Only when Jenny has waltzed inside does Anna come up to the porch and give her grandmother a long hug. She wants to have her all to herself, but her mother's beside her now, straightening the sash of her dress. And her father's lugging the movie camera up the steps—she has to make room.

"Where's Gigi?" she asks, and Nana tells her he's in the backyard. Jenny has come back out onto the porch, is doing pirouettes to show off the crinoline beneath her dress. Anna stomps down the steps, round the side of the house, and shoves through the high, narrow door that seals off the garden from the street.

Gigi is tying up runner beans at the back of the garden. Anna can't believe her luck—she has her grandfather all to herself. As soon as she calls out to him he drops his ball of string, steps back from the poles, wipes his hands on his trousers, and gathers her up, swinging her high overhead. She is big for six, everyone is always telling her that, but her grandfather lifts her just as if she were a feather, exactly like Jenny. Anna kisses and kisses him, smacking kisses that often miss their mark. Her grandfather laughs, puts her gently down, and holds his arms open to Jenny, who is flying down the path toward him.

"Shcho stabóyu?" Nana asks: "What's wrong?" She takes Anna by the hand, up the path and into the house. Climbing the stairs to the kitchen they have to pass the cold, dark throat that is the cellar. Once Nana had taken them down to the cellar so they could see her prepare the chicken she'd brought home from market. Jenny had sat on a high stool, swinging her feet, but Anna had stood back a little, with her hands clenched in her pockets. They'd watched the chicken drop from the brown paper, looking like a limp, pink bag with jelly dribbling out. The butcher had cut the head off—there was only an ugly, ropy-looking stump where the neck ended—but he'd left the feet. Nana chopped them off with a cleaver. One foot for each of them to hold—she showed them how to press the yellow, scaly part, so that the claws opened and closed, opened and closed. Anna had shaken her head and given the foot right back, but Jenny had kept hers, creeping up behind her when Nana had to go upstairs to get more salt. Jabbing, tickling her with the chicken foot... Anna had

screamed and screamed, and Nana nearly twisted her ankle rushing down the cellar steps to see what was wrong.

"*Hóchish pítih?*" Anna nods. She's suddenly very thirsty, and she knows that Nana has made strawberry juice for her from the syrup at the bottom of the preserving jar. The juice is cold; not pink but red like jewels. The froth tickles her nose as she starts to drink. "*Dyáhkoyu, Nana,*" she remembers to say. Jenny didn't learn English till she was five, but no one has taught Anna much Ukrainian. Her grandparents speak half Ukrainian, half English with her. If she doesn't understand every word, it doesn't matter. They don't make fun of her for not knowing, or make her feel ashamed, the way other people do.

"*Dóbreh?*" her Nana asks. Is it good?

"*Tahk. Dúzhe dóbreh.*" So good that Anna would like to put her arms round her grandmother and squeeze her hard, just as if she were a strawberry in her mouth. But Nana leaves the kitchen. Anna's mother is calling from the bedroom—she's lying down there, with the curtains drawn. She's always lying down these days, throwing up in the mornings, not being able to eat what she's cooked them for supper. Anna has asked her father if her mother is sick, and he says no, but it's not the truth. When Anna throws up she has to stay all day in bed with a bowl by her side; she's not allowed to go outside. Jenny says she knows what's wrong with their mother, but it's a secret, and she'll never tell.

Anna stares up at the little shelves on either side of the kitchen window. On tiptoe, she can just see the horns of the china cow. She listens for a moment—no one is coming up the back stairs or along the hall. So she pushes a chair over to the sink, stands up on it, and looks straight into the eyes of the cow creamer. She doesn't dare to take it in her hands. It is precious, it has roses picked out in real gold over its belly. Anna keeps hoping that one day when Nana makes *chai* she will take the cow pitcher down from the shelf, fill it with cream, and let her pour it into the cups. Just once—she wouldn't want it all to herself, she'd let Jenny have a turn—

"Anna Ipana!"

"Don't call me that. I'm telling..." But she can't, otherwise Jenny will tell about her standing up on the chair, stroking the cow creamer.

Perhaps Jenny hasn't noticed—she is jumping from tile to tile on the dining room floor; she can never keep still, not even for a moment. "Anna Ipana. Why don't you call me something back?" she calls out sweetly, without missing a jump.

"Because." Once she'd tried Jenny-penny but her sister had only laughed, and said she liked it.

"Anna Banana."

"I hate you—"

Jenny just skips sideways to the door; she sticks out her tongue and says, "I dare you to go down to the cellar."

"Dare yourself. You're such a coward—you'd never go."

"Scaredy-cat, stupid brat, peed her pants and never hit back."

Anna runs to slap her, but Jenny's too quick. Down the steps, through the door, and into the garden. Anna lets the door slam, even though she knows her mother needs some peace-and-quiet. Jenny's run all the way down the path and is scavenging raspberries while Anna's still standing inside, rigid with shame. It's true, she is afraid to go downstairs on her own. The cellar is dimly lit, and smells of mushrooms. There are old clothes hanging up in plywood wardrobes, and Anna imagines there are people inside the clothes, people waiting to spring out at her the moment she turns her back on them. The furnace makes roaring sounds in winter, and in summer there's a strange, underwater sort of silence that frightens her even more than the people hanging in the wardrobes. Jenny has told her that all the cellars on Dovercourt Road are linked by secret tunnels that lead up to the Toreador Club. There is an old man who lives in the Toreador Club; he only goes out at night, shuffling along the sidewalk, spitting into flowerbeds. During the day he creeps through the tunnels and hides behind the preserving jars in the cellar. One day he will be hiding there when Anna comes down to use the toilet. He will jump out at her and stuff a rag into her mouth, and pull her up through the tunnel, into the Toreador Club. No one will ever see her again.

Panicking, Anna slams the kitchen door behind her, and swims out into the summer heat. Jenny runs up with a handful of whitish raspberries, offering half to her sister. For a moment there is perfect peace between them. They cram the unripe fruit into their mouths, pretending they are horses snuffling up oats. But now their father is calling them from the kitchen door: "Jenny, Anna! It's time to make the movie. Come on, you two, hurry up!"

And they are suddenly in their mother's hands. She has come into the garden, wearing her dark-green cotton dress that ties round her neck and makes her bare arms look a million miles long. Anna can tell she's put some makeup on—her mother smells powdery and creamy, and her lips are as red as if she's been drinking strawberry syrup. "Stand still, Jenny." She is tugging the comb through Jenny's black hair, fluffing out her bangs. She licks her fingertips, and rubs out a smear of something on Jenny's cheek. "Now you, Anna. Oh, *what* have you been up to—look at your dress! And your hair—hold still, this is going to hurt, but we've got to get the tangles out."

Anna can't hold still. And she doesn't want a daisy in her hair, it will only make her look stupid. Her own hair's as white as the daisy petals. She would like to have brown, curly hair like her mother; she would like to have a long green dress like her mother's, and high-heeled shoes with little holes cut out for her toes to peep through. Her mother's toenails are red as her lips.

"There—that's the best I can do. Now for heaven's sake smile, but don't stare right into the camera. Just play. Daddy will tell you what to do."

"Okay, girls." Jenny and Anna stand holding up their stiff or-gandy skirts with the froth of crinoline below. Jenny says she feels like an eggbeater, and Anna starts to giggle, but she's not supposed to—her father wants a nice, steady smile. Now they join hands and skip across the grass to the flower border. Their mother bends down and breaks off a sprig of hydrangea for Jenny to give to Nana. She is about to do the same for Anna, but something has gone wrong with the focus on the camera. Everything stops. Anna is glad—she hates the sickly green tinge of the hydrangea. She wants to give her grandmother something much more beautiful, a bunch of red roses from the bush against the fence. Everyone's helping with the camera. They don't see her as she slips into the flowerbed, she doesn't even know she is trampling the forget-me-nots and sweet william as she wrestles with the roses that will not break off the branch, stinging and pricking her hands as her mother shouts at her to come out of there and for heaven's sake, behave.

Everyone's looking at her. Even the squirrels have stopped chittering in the branches of the pine tree. Anna looks back at the path she's trampled through the border; examines her hands, and the little smears of blood that have somehow transferred themselves to her dress. The worst of it is that she has nothing to show for herself. The roses she tried to pick flap sadly down from the stalk—she could bend, but not break it. Everyone thinks she did it just to make a mess, to draw attention to herself, to be difficult. And she can't explain. She opens her mouth but the words hang inside, and won't break off. Just like the roses.

"All fixed," their father calls. "Let's try another part of the garden, now."

"Why don't you do somersaults down the hill?" suggests their mother.

"I could do a handstand," Jenny pipes up.

"That's not fair," Anna complains. Even on two feet she always loses her balance. It wouldn't be right for Jenny to show off, and for her to look like a clown, or a cripple. Their mother agrees. "No handstands, Jenny. Just a somersault or two."

The camera begins to whirr and Jenny does three perfect somersaults, all in a row down the hill. Anna rushes after, but again, everything goes wrong. She keeps landing on her head—she can't curl over. Anna collapses into a little ball on the grass, hiding her face from them. "Get up, Anna, it doesn't matter. Just hop or skip or something." The camera keeps shooting.

It's her grandfather who saves her. He goes down on his hands and knees, and gently butts his head at her. She lifts her face cautiously, shielded by the bell of hair that's got loose from the bobby pins and daisy. Gigi is doing somersaults now—he curls over, but he looks so funny, he's so huge, his legs don't go into a ball the way they should. He doesn't mind. He sits up and shrugs his shoulders, laughing. Her mother and Nana are laughing as Anna sits up and brushes her eyes. It's all right, then. They can pretend it was a joke from start to finish. It's Jenny who's left out, Jenny who doesn't know how to play at being silly.

"Enough," Nana calls out, but the camera is turned to her now, coming out of the screen door with a tray of biscuits and glasses and strawberry juice. Then Anna's father puts down the camera, and they all have something to eat and drink. Anna sits on her grandfather's lap, and he strokes her hair. *"Dónyu,"* he calls her, which is a special name, a pet name. Anna nestles even closer to him. He loves her more than anyone, he is always there to help her whenever she's got herself into trouble. He knows exactly how it feels to be forever younger and clumsier; so knock-kneed that everyone is always telling you to stand up straight. *"Dónyu,"* he says, and she squirms round to hug him. She wants to say, "I love you." The words are a lump in her throat, she can hardly breathe for love, but all she can do is press her face closer against his clean white shirt. And then Jenny is worming in under his arm—he moves Anna to one knee, and puts Jenny on the other, and dances them up and down, up and down.

After supper the girls play a game of Crazy Eights on the dining-room table, while Nana and their mother wash the dishes, talking too softly for them to hear anything much. Besides, they are speaking Ukrainian, they are saying things children aren't meant to understand, though Jenny affects to know. She looks important as she slaps down an eight and switches suit: "Diamonds. Now they're talking about babies." Before, it had been husbands. Their father is watching baseball on the television in the living room; Gigi is reading a Polish newspaper across from them. He has a small glass of what Nana calls *veesky,* and into which each of the girls has dipped her tongue, shivering and hiccoughing, pretending to be drunk.

"Go get your sweaters, girls—they're on the bed." This means it is nearly time to go home. Anna and Jenny go as quietly as they can into the bedroom. They know better than to start a fight now. If they are good and don't disturb anyone, it will be another half-hour before their mother mentions that tomorrow is a school day, and their father jingles the car keys in his pocket. So the girls move down the hallway as though their feet are bound up in wool. They don't even whisper once they have, inch by inch, pulled tight the door, and shut themselves inside.

Jenny flops on the bed, pretending she's playing angels in the snow, sweeping her arms up and down the chenille spread. Anna goes over to the dressing table, sits on the low, faded pink seat, and moves the wings of the mirror so that she can see three of herself and only one Jenny stretched on the bed. She sighs, but not from tiredness. Once again she is met by the mask that someone's tied over her skin, so that her real face can't show through. If she could only pull off the mask, she would look beautiful. Everyone would love her, they wouldn't be able to help themselves. She would be so good and so clever, she would never complain, even about Jenny. . . . Anna lifts her fingers to her eyes and pokes tentatively at the corners, just to see if there isn't a little place she could start to pull from. But the mask is stitched tight and everything stays: her lips that are too small, her nose that's too big, her eyes with all the shadows and pouches underneath. Her teacher had made a joke once: "Going on a trip, Anna? I see you've got your bags with you." Anna had smiled, not knowing what else to do, thinking that she must have misunderstood—that a teacher could never say anything cruel.

Jenny springs off the bed and runs to the closet. The door is polished oak, with a glass part at the top. Inside hang Nana's dresses, all cool and dark and silky, and her fur coat, with the little mink clutching the collar, his eyes stiff and bright, his mouth snapping your fingers. There's a light you can switch on inside the closet, but the bulb has gone. Crossly, Jenny flicks the switch back and forth. Anna doesn't care. She is staring at the lamps on either side of the dressing table; they are hung with crystal pendants that make rainbows when the afternoon light comes through the windows, little broken-off bits of rainbows. It is still light outside, but the pendants hang dead and dull from the lamps. Anna can't bear for them to hang so leadenly there. She lifts her fingers, knocks the crystals one against the other, making random music.

When they leave it is almost night. The air is warm against their skins, plush with the smell of chocolate. That's the Neilson's factory close by. Anna sticks her tongue out as if she could lick some sweetness from the dark. She's too tired to give more than a little peck at her grandparents' cheeks. She will visit them next Saturday; Gigi will take her to a cartoon matinee. On the way home there is a brief fight as to who's taking up the most space in the back seat, and their mother whirls round: "Please, please be quiet—can't you see how tired I am? If you fight like this we won't ever take you back to see Gigi and Nana. So for heaven's sake keep still."

And they do. They fall asleep, knees up, heads back, their mouths slightly open as Anna dreams of the old man hiding in the cellar, and Jenny dreams of chocolate.

In two hours, Anna, still on Munich time, will wake. Though there'll be no need for her to get up, she will find it too hot, too close to stay in the house. She will pull on a housecoat that is hanging on a hook from the bedroom door, make her way to the kitchen, and prepare a pot of tea. She will start to pour out milk from the carton she'll have found in the refrigerator, but then she'll check herself; returning to the shelf over the sink, she'll reach up for the cow-shaped creamer. Wiping the dust away she'll remember how, as a child, she'd always wanted to make milk gush from the cow's gold-rimmed, eternally open mouth, and how she'd never dared to try. She will think of asking her mother whether she mightn't have this one thing from her grandmother's house—the cream jug in the shape of a cow, with the noiselessly mooing mouth and roses over its belly. And then she will set down her desire just as she sets down the jug, knowing she can make no room in her life for things that take up too much space; that could easily break when moved about.

It will be a few degrees cooler on the porch at the front of the house. No one will be on the sidewalk yet, so she'll be able to drink her tea, barefoot, in a housecoat much too short and wide for her. While sparrows and blackbirds peck themselves out of the shell of sleep, she will breathe in the swaying scents of the linden tree, and shut her eyes. On either side of her will be white-columned porches, in receding perspective, mirroring the porch on which she'll sit, cradling a cup of milky tea. Bits of a dream will flash in her head, the way a room's lights burn inside your lids long after you've shut your eyes. The dream will have been a long and jolting one, like a rickety train made up of mismatched carriages. But there is one part she will remember.

She is coming back to her grandmother's house, after a long time away. The front door has been taken off its hinges; none of the rooms are locked. She goes from room to room in the house, which has been picked clean as a bone. She goes down the hallway, past the dining room, and halts before the entrance to the kitchen, as if listening for something. At last she goes inside; the kitchen, too, is perfectly empty, perfectly still. She is about to turn and go back out the front door, down the porch steps, when she halts once more. For this time she has heard something—someone calling from beyond the kitchen, from the cellar steps.

In her dream she is not afraid, nor is she curious. In her dream she already knows that when she walks through the kitchen to the place where the cellar yawns, dark and cool and deeper than she's ever imagined, she will find her grandmother. Nana will look the same as she always has; she will not be eaten by pain and fear and the longing to die. And yet she will have changed. She will not come up from the cellar steps, but will stand halfway up and halfway down, offering something to Anna, gesturing for her to come closer. And as Anna approaches, she will see that what her grandmother is holding out to her is a basket of food gathered from her garden; food she has baked or preserved. And everything will be neatly, carefully packed: prepared for traveling.

The Gardens
of the Loire

In the dining room of the Hôtel du Balcon, Madame de Bèze polishes the bottles of spirits, liqueurs, and *eau de vie* arrayed in the corner cabinet—amber, emerald, gold, and the very silver of transparency. She sighs, and wonders whether it is time to ask the couple by the window whether they would like a *digestif;* the man is merely toying with his cheese, the woman has left half of her *sorbet au citron* to melt into a pale mess at the bottom of the dish. They have, perhaps, more appetizing items to anticipate? Madame de Bèze notes how lonely the pear looks in the bottle of Poire William, and sighs again. She has been a widow now for thirteen years. This young couple from Canada has been married for how long? One week? That, at least, is how long they've stayed at the Hôtel du Balcon at which, the young man has told her, his own parents spent their honeymoon. But that had been before the war, and under a different management. Madame de Bèze shifts her glance to the only other occupant of the dining room, her nephew, Georges. She frowns. There are perhaps three fingers of liquid at the bottom of the bottle—she could do worse, much worse, than offer it to these *Canadiens*.

She will be sixty-three next week; she will have to decide whether it is finally time to pass on the Hôtel du Balcon to Georges, who will run it into the ground, installing televisions in every room and video games in the lobby, creating special menus for the tour buses: sushi, sauerbraten, baked beans on toast, hot dogs with a side order of ketchup. Whereas now the hotel possesses an ambience, neither elegant nor homey, and the irreplaceable cachet of authenticity. A two-star provincial hotel with cuisine which, though it may not merit a detour, is not without its felicities, as the current author of the *Guide Michelin* agrees.

And this young *monsieur* here, with his correct if somewhat mothy French (he'd told her his family had emigrated to Canada in the sixties, when *Liberté* herself had been rampaging here)—this fair-haired bridegroom with the insignificant eyebrows and an alarming tendency to blush, had chosen the Hôtel du Balcon as the perfect setting for that old-fashioned kind of honeymoon which had suddenly become so popular again. No Club Med antics for him and his pretty, if somewhat bewildered-looking bride. It had to be admitted that there was a certain lack of harmony, an imbalance of proportions in the arrangement of this particular couple. The girl couldn't be out of her teens, and he must be thirty if he is a day—he has the unyielding habits of a man past his first youth, observes Madame de Bèze. But then, perhaps this couple could be seen as proof of a trend. In keeping with the new, cautious attitude toward things of the flesh, husbands were actively seeking out virginal brides—look at the future king of England! What could be more appropriate for such a pair than a honeymoon at a small, calm, out-of-the-way hotel. Video games indeed—Georges was a fool with his eyes on the moon. If he removed one grain of soil, bruised one peony petal in her garden—

Madame de Bèze is referring to the *jardin-terrasse* which her husband had created some years after their purchase of the Hôtel du Balcon. You walked out the glass doors from the lobby onto a flagstone square bordered by banks of peonies and roses enclosing artfully clustered tables and chairs. But the *pièce de résistance* erupted from the very middle of the square. It seemed, at first glance, to be the huge, hollowed-out trunk of a magnificent oak, bleached silver by centuries of mist and rain. You could walk under it from four directions, admiring the ivy cunningly twisted round outside, the mossy coolness the interior afforded even on the hottest of July days. Yet the whole thing was made out of concrete—sculpted by César's hands, of course, but concrete all the same. It would last, he had boasted, longer than the hotel itself, long after he and his wife had found more permanent lodgings under the ground.

In one of the dozen travel magazines to which he subscribed, her husband had once seen a picture of a garden—in Spain, or perhaps India—whose focal point had been a kind of raised grotto, the inside encrusted with shells, the outside heaped with flowering vines. For a long while he'd dreamed of visiting this grotto, and only when several profitless seasons had made it obvious that the hotel would never provide the wherewithal to transport him to the Alhambra, never mind the Taj Mahal, did César de Bèze decide to construct one of his own. His wife never understood what had fascinated him about the grotto, why he had been driven to build it. All that she had understood was her husband's happiness at his work, a happiness he'd never shown while setting tables or settling accounts. The problem had been that she didn't understand happiness. Or rather, that she was more at home with disappointment and something she might have called—if she hadn't tempered and mastered it—grief. Many times during her marriage and the long years of her widowhood had she woken out of shallow sleep with her arms stretched wide, the burden of their emptiness crushing her ribs. Though it had never prevented her from getting up to pour out *café au lait* and *chocolat chaud* for her dwindling clientele.

Madame de Bèze folds her polishing cloth, puts the bottle of Poire William and two glasses on a tray, and sighs once more, a sigh that's more a call to arms than an expression of defeat. Georges has made known his intention of removing what he calls "the eyesore" with advanced explosives that will not disturb so much as the hotel curtains. He hasn't offered any guarantees for her roses and the peonies. He also intends to string up colored lights and make a kind of outdoor disco, paving over the entire garden, with nothing to soften the effect but a tub or two of common geraniums. That was all most foreigners expected of a French garden, he'd declared—and look how much trouble it was to keep the garden going: spraying insecticide, putting down slug pellets last thing at night. People didn't go away on holiday to be poisoned, he'd exclaimed. "Besides—a lot of people these days are allergic to flowers. Hay fever, asthma—they wouldn't look twice at a hotel with a garden."

As if on cue, the man at the newlyweds' table lifts his head, shudders volubly, and gives not one but three volleys of sneezes. His wife reaches into her purse and hands him a whole packet of Kleenex tissues—the cellophane-wrapped kind designed for traveling.

At the exact moment that he began to sneeze, Felix had been rhyming off the number of châteaus left for them to visit. He has barely recovered from his attack when the lady who owns the hotel comes up with a silver tray, two crystal glasses, and a bottle with a small, skinned pear inside. *"A votre bonheur, Madame, Monsieur."* Felix explains to Teresa that they're being offered a complimentary glass of *eau de vie*—made from pears. Felix is always explaining things to her, especially now that they're in a country whose language he presumes she cannot speak. Her sister, Ellie, had cautioned her always to let her husband think he knew most, as well as best. So Teresa has never confessed that, having not only studied but excelled in French in high school, she understands a good deal of what is being said around her. And that she could, if pressed, go so far as to speak for herself in restaurants, cafés, and hotels.

"It's a little tribute from Madame de Bèze to the two of us, in our capacity as newlyweds." Felix nods at the hotelkeeper, who nods back at him, giving an almost sympathetic smile to Teresa before she pads off with the tray. He doesn't add that what the old woman has toasted is not their health, but their happiness, or at least their prospects in that direction. It doesn't seem worth translating, Felix decides—at any rate, it isn't of the essence, as far as he and his bride are concerned.

"In our capacity as newlyweds"—that's such a silly word, Teresa thinks. "Lovers," why doesn't he say? But then, that wouldn't be like

Felix, and if Felix weren't the way he was, she would never be sitting across from him here, with a gold ring tightly circling her finger.

What is Felix like? It is safest to say that Teresa's groom is Ellie's idea of the perfect husband. Not that Ellie has owned to any intention of getting married. She has spent the best years of her life picking up pieces after her mother ran off one winter morning with a Toronto-bound trucker, leaving a mildly alcoholic husband and six children, of whom Ellie was the oldest and Teresa the youngest, as well as being the only other girl. Ellie had managed to get her degree at Teacher's College and hold down a part-time job at the local high school, while somehow raising them all. As soon as the youngest boy had announced his intention of quitting school and lighting out for the oil rigs, Ellie had grabbed Teresa, left her father to his bottle, his TV, and his comfortably failing variety store, and lit out for Halifax, where she'd been offered a job at Immaculata High School. Ellie had always said she'd enter the novitiate once she'd got her siblings off her hands, but by the time she surrendered Teresa to Felix, she'd discovered that she really hadn't the vocation. As she'd told Felix's mother, "I'm afraid I'm just not good enough," whereupon Felix's mother had made Ellie another cup of strong coffee and proceeded to relate the trials she'd gone through with her husband—for whom, it also seemed, no woman could ever have been good enough.

Felix is clean-shaven, has gray eyes, a smooth, pink skin, and receding hair the color of winter wheat. Though tending slightly to fat, he has a delicate constitution—that's the first thing his mother told Teresa and Ellie when Felix took them home to meet her. He was asthmatic as a child, suffers badly from hay fever, and shouldn't be kept out in the rain or the mist. That's why he doesn't like the idea of walking in the hotel garden at night—even for five minutes, just before going into bed. Teresa can't help darting a glance at the double doors that lead out from the lobby into the garden. There's a man sitting at the table nearest the door, a youngish man with a short black beard, smoking a cigar.

Felix doesn't smoke. He keeps his nails clean and nicely pared. You can tell a lot about a man just from looking at his hands, that's what Ellie says. She'd approved of Felix that first time she'd seen him at the office. She'd met Teresa there after work—they were supposed to go on to the church bazaar, but instead, Ellie had Felix taking them out to a pizza restaurant. Within five minutes of ordering, Ellie had ascertained that Felix was not only a Catholic but also that he belonged to their parish, lived with his widowed mother, and had just been taken into partnership by the law firm for which Teresa was working as a temporary secretary.

At the church bazaar later that evening, Ellie met Felix's mother and was relieved to discover that, though born in Dieppe, she spoke excellent English. Ellie would never say at just what moment she was given to understand that Madame Leynaud felt it was high time her Felix married a nice Catholic girl and gave her some grandchildren to make up for the loneliness she'd suffered since her husband's untimely death (a stroke, and *not* hereditary). Felix, understandably, had been so busy writing entrance exams to law school—studying, articling, and working overtime to get his partnership—that he'd had no time for girlfriends, or any silliness of the sort. Though there was nothing wrong with Felix, there'd been none of *that* in their family, either, Madame Leynaud had promised Ellie. And indeed, once Felix had been brought to recognize that marriage was the inevitable next step for an up-and-coming lawyer, he had proceeded to pay Teresa the kind of attentions you would expect a marriageable young man to make to an exceptionally pretty, though shy and modest nineteen-year-old from Scratch Harbour. When Felix had first kissed her, Teresa couldn't help thinking of a fish sucking at aquarium walls. "Marriage," Ellie had countered, "is more than just kissing."

"A penny for your thoughts?" Felix smiles benignly at his wife, who is not, he's discovered, an accomplished conversationalist. Not that he minds—indeed, he has a horror of talkative women—in the professions, that is. He smiles even more intently at the girl across the table, wishing she were not quite so young and inexperienced; that she had—some more meat on her bones. He'd never admitted it to his mother, but he preferred large, comfortable-looking women to skinny young things with xylophone ribs and hip bones protruding at bruising angles. "Come now, Teresa, tell me what you're thinking."

"Oh, nothing—nothing at all." But he's determined to extract an answer, and he presses her again, exactly as if they were in court. "Badgering the witness, that's what it's called," Teresa tells herself. Nevertheless, she squares her shoulders, looks up at her husband, and invents a smile. "I was just thinking—how good the fish was at supper. You should compliment the chef, shouldn't you?"

"But Teresa—we ordered veal. You really must pay more attention, dear. You know, it's the small things that are most important in marriage."

Teresa drinks up her glass of Poire William. Felix is quoting Ellie.

Georges watches his aunt perform her little ceremony over the Canadian couple. *Tant pis*—it means he won't be able to finish off that bottle of Poire William as he'd intended. Each night of his stay, he'd come down to the dining room long after the lights were out and poured himself a glass of liqueur or *eau de vie*. He wasn't a thief by nature; he didn't consider it thieving, but rather a little game of tit for tat. He flicked the saltshaker with his finger, causing it to do a little dance over the tablecloth. A glass of aquavit or cognac was a mere drop in the ocean compared to what he was entitled to take—the whole damn hotel, if the truth be known. He was his aunt's sole surviving heir; she owed him the hotel, and here she was prepared to wait it out till Judgment Day, instead of handing things over to him and going back to her husband's hometown in the Dordogne. He wasn't going to kick her out—he'd pay her more than enough to secure a nice apartment with an elevator, and a bit besides—for rainy days. He would have it written into the deed of transfer—that he was prepared to look after her, and in no mean style, at that. So why wouldn't the old bat let go?

There she is, giving away his Poire William to a bridegroom who has all the appeal of a squashed bun—how had he managed to get himself a wife at all? That they are husband and wife, not lovers, is as obvious as the fact that they are foreigners. They lack that saturated look, the warm, salty scent lovers give off, even in the most respectable of rooms, even with their clothes still firmly fastened. Regrettably, the wife favors the style of dress that Lady Di (Georges pronounces it "Laddie Dee") has brought into fashion: kindergarten-teacher chic, all high, ruffled necks and closely-buttoned sleeves, wishy-washy pastels. In those clothes, her pale hair tied chastely back with a velvet ribbon, she looks as though she could be part of the kindergarten class herself. Georges shakes his head. Not his type, not his kind at all.

Yet there is nothing else to look at in the dining room except the overvarnished wainscoting, the bleached-out flowers on the wallpaper, and the menu whose specialties he already knows by heart. Every year it becomes more and more difficult to pay his courtesy visit to his aunt. She scolds him for his restlessness and prescribes the infallible remedy his own mother has proposed: marriage. Marriage to a practical, sensible woman—never mind the frills and furbelows; those can always be obtained on the side. The trouble is, as Georges concedes, that he's perfectly happy with nothing but the side and sees no need to alter his arrangements, now or in the future. What had marriage ever done for his mother except bestow on her a continually expanding irritation named Georges? What had it done for his aunt but saddle her with a failing hotel and a concrete monstrosity in the middle of a pest-ridden, overblown imitation of an English garden?

Georges sits back, stroking his beard, his eyes moving between the bottles mirrored in the corner cabinet, and the submerged-looking girl at the table across the room. Involuntarily, he drums his fingers on the tablecloth. One more week and he'll be able to take his leave with a clean heart, if not a clear head and, more importantly, with his aunt's promise to give him the deed of the Hôtel du Balcon by the close of the season. In the meantime, he will have to amuse himself as best he can. Tonight he'll make inroads on the *marc de Bourgogne* and then, who knows, go out into the garden for another cigar. Just to amuse himself, he might even throw a handful of gravel at the window of the couple's room. The bride, he's sure, will prove to be the lighter sleeper of the two. He smiles, thinking of how he could, if the girl were a little less limp and cloistered, entice her into a walk along the river. But then again—Georges strokes his beard, eyeing the saltshaker which has finally tipped over onto the table-cloth—there are all sorts of uses to which a simulated hollow tree trunk can be put.

Teresa waits till Felix falls asleep again, as he always does the moment he pulls away from her. Disentangling herself from the sheets, she steals into the bathroom, locks the door, and peers into the mirror. She wants to see if the signs are branded onto her skin, to prove to herself that she really is a married woman. A flush over her breasts and on her face; the smell and feel of salt between her thighs, as if she'd been wading through a warm, shallow sea. Quickly, quietly she washes herself, steals back to the bed, and lies down beside him. She has opened the shutters he'd insisted be fastened: Moonlight splashes the room. He goes on sleeping, so she raises herself on her elbow, pulls away the sheet, and looks at him, curled on his side, facing her. He doesn't look any longer like a man with a name and address and profession, but like an animal sleeping.

On his cheeks and chin she can see what the razor erases each morning—she'd like to tell him to stop shaving, that he'd look better with a beard. But it would hurt him to know she'd think he is any way imperfect. It's odd that he looks no handsomer here than he does at home—Ellie had said Felix needed to be seen on French soil to be properly appreciated. Yet it's true that when Madame de Bèze calls him *monsieur* there is respect in her voice; people on the street look at him as if he were a column of figures to add up: his clothes, the watch he wears, the accent with which he speaks. It all comes out to an even number, sufficiently high for the owner of the hotel to toast their happiness, for the waiter in the café to have given them a table by the window and not in the corner, opposite the toilets.

Felix has no hairs on the backs of his shoulders or his hands, for which she is very glad; her father has hair thick as a welcome mat

over his body. Once, when she was little and saw him stepping out
of the bath, she'd screamed, thinking he was a great, wet bear. Ellie
had slapped her. Felix has only a few strands of blond hair waving
down the middle of his chest and then thickening where his belly
starts. It's absurd that men should have nipples—flat, small as
pennies—what on earth are they for? She could never ask. He doesn't
like her even to look at him, and dresses with his back to her. He
will not kiss her on the street, though she has seen couples here
inside doorways or on park benches and they are doing more than
kissing.

That first night he'd been a madman; he tried to tear her open as
if she were an envelope. She'd wanted him to wait, to touch her as
if he were blindfolded in a strange room, his bearings always changing. But how could she have asked for that? She doesn't have the
right voice, never mind the words. He seems smaller now, lying
curled in sleep. Even with his pajamas on he lies with his hands over
his groin, cupping himself as if he feared someone would hit him
there. Do all men sleep that way? She doesn't think women protect
themselves like this, even though they are made to be slit open like
envelopes.

Halfway through their honeymoon, their nights have assumed a
much calmer aspect—now there is no great rush, no great anything,
to tell the truth. She would like to ask Ellie why you have to go on
being good, even after you've abstained and refrained, and had the
ring forced down your finger. But would Ellie know, never mind
answer? Could she explain to Ellie how, each time, it's as if she were
floating on the ceiling, face down, watching two strangers go through
a limited number of motions on the bed below? Sometimes he would
lie with his head between her breasts, though his hair tickled terribly—she had to force herself not to laugh, she was afraid her laughter would sound too much like crying. Then he'd kiss her and roll
away, pulling the sheets with him. Falling fast asleep.

Teresa lies watching the wind ruffle the curtains, the moonlight
stroking the walls. She knows she is lucky, very lucky—how many
girls from a background like hers end up marrying a professional

man, going off to Europe for a honeymoon, moving into a house of their very own? (True, there was a room set aside for Madame Leynaud, and there would even be one for Ellie when the time came. Felix had arranged to buy a large house on the outskirts of Halifax, where prices were cheaper and the neighborhoods were safe for children.) And Ellie had described, time and time again, all the pits into which a girl as pretty and frail as Teresa could fall. "Think of our mother," Ellie had warned when Teresa had wanted to go to a Friday night dance, see a movie with some neighborhood friends, accept a dinner invitation from the man who'd interviewed her for her first job. "Being as pretty as you are, Teresa, is like having a handicap, being a target. Until I've got you married off to the right sort of man, you'll be a cross I'll just have to carry." Ellie was taking advantage of her sister's honeymoon to go on the first vacation she'd ever had —two weeks at a religious retreat off the Cabot Trail.

Felix shudders in his sleep, rolls onto his other side, away from her. He is dreaming of bats or tigers, of the work he's left unfinished on his desk, of the cost of two weeks of food and drink and clean sheets in the Loire. Lying in the dark with her eyes shut tight, willing herself to sleep, Teresa hears an odd, scratchy noise, as if a cat were trying to get into the room. She opens her eyes—there it is again, coming from the balcony. She would like some company, even if it's only a cat, so she creeps out of bed, belting her dressing gown round her. She opens the glass doors that Felix insists be kept shut—he's afraid of drafts and mosquitos—and steps out onto the balcony. There is no cat, not even a mouse, just a small red glow coming from under the funny stump in the garden. Someone is sitting out there in the dark, in the perfume that roses are throwing impulsively through the night.

She sighs, and her robe slackens a little round her waist—it's not cold at all; she wouldn't mind sitting out on the balcony just for a moment, getting a bit of that fresh air against which Felix takes so many precautions. Suddenly the red spot under the stump begins to move in a slow arc, back and forth, like someone waving at her. Before she knows what she's doing, she lifts her own hand, waves back. She waits for a moment, and the person inside the stump waits, too. Then the small red light begins to move again—a different motion, as though she's being beckoned, invited. Uncertainly, she clutches the lapels of her dressing gown, pulling them closer together. Truthfully, she can't sleep—it's too bright, too hot. What if she were to slip on her dress and take a quick walk in the cool of the garden? Could even Ellie see much harm in that?

Suddenly there's a horrible noise from the bed—Felix is grinding his teeth again, gnashing away as if he had a ton of wheat to turn into flour by morning. Teresa forgets all about the moonlight, and the red star inside the stump. Turning her back on the garden she dives blindly back into the bed. So great is her haste that she forgets to fasten the glass doors behind her. Six hours later, Felix will wake up with congested sinuses and spend the half hour before breakfast inhaling menthol crystals over the bathroom sink.

Four days later Madame de Bèze asks them the most natural and innocent of questions: *"Avez-vous bien dormi?"* and the girl looks as though she's ready to burst into tears. Her husband blushes, answering *"Si, Madame,"* and hides behind *Le Figaro*. Now there are real tears striping the girl's cheeks, dribbling over her lips. She licks them away and tries to break off a piece of her croissant, but entirely without success. Madame de Bèze wants to lead her away to the kitchen, give her a bowl of *chocolat chaud,* stroke her hair, and say, "What's the matter, little one? You can tell *maman.*" If they haven't slept well, whose fault can it be but his own, this overweight and inattentive fool on whom that celebratory glass of Poire William had so obviously been wasted?

Madame de Bèze returns to the kitchen, muttering under her breath about the general stupidity of men. She includes Georges in her condemnation, Georges who is reading a *bande dessinée* and polishing off the last of the apricot preserves. Really, what was there to choose between the blushing husband in the dining room and this unblushing Don Juan devouring jam in the kitchen. What women had to put up with nowadays! Whatever could that girl's mother have been thinking of, marrying her child to a fussy old man like that? Now if she'd had a daughter. . . . But it's useless to think of things like that; she has her roses and her peony bushes, she has the Hôtel du Balcon, and yes, she has Georges, giving her one of his charming and perfectly hypocritical kisses before he rushes off to waste the day in a boat on the river, with a detective novel and heaven knows how many bottles of wine. Not to mention women—though whoever was silly enough to end up in a rowboat with Georges deserved whatever she had coming.

While Felix reads *Le Figaro* and sips a *thé au citron* to soothe his throat, Teresa prays for the fortitude and humility to forget the events of the previous three nights. But the more she tries not to remember, the more indelible is the image of herself, in her nightdress, standing on the balcony and staring out at a perfectly empty garden, while Felix shams sleep, curled away from even the impress of her body on the sheets. He'd refused to make love to her—or at least had managed, once again, to fall asleep before she'd finished rinsing out their underwear and hanging it to dry over the railing of the tub. If it happened again tonight, she would have to phone Ellie—if Ellie could be reached, that is. Though what she couldn't tell Ellie was that what most distressed her was not her husband's refusing her, but the fact that there had been no small, fiery light in the middle of the garden the last three nights; no signal for her at all.

Sometime between three and four this morning, she'd made a resolve never to speak to her husband again. It's no good—he doesn't seem to have noticed. Felix finally emerges from his newspaper shell, examines a page of the *Guide Bleu,* and reaches deep into his suit pocket. "I'll need change," he says. "Go to the desk and see if Madame can give us some smaller bills." Teresa flies out of the room to the reception desk, where she's suddenly seized by the desire—no, the need—to get some fresh air. Before she knows it, she's out the door, down the street, and around the corner into the pedestrian section of the town.

All the stores are having sidewalk sales, and Teresa finds herself ensnared by porcelain dolls, plastic replicas of the châteaus, stands of naughty and *Belle Époque* postcards, and, in a rather more dignified area, a dress shop with dozens of breezy, flimsy cottons, imploring the passersby to free them from their hangers. It is getting hotter every second—she feels like a pressure cooker inside all the layers of easy-care fabric appropriate for visiting the museum Felix has selected for today's outing. Surely it isn't good for her delicate vital organs to get overheated—surely it makes sense to dress for the weather, rather than to expect, as Ellie certainly had, that the temperatures in the Loire would be as bracing as those in Halifax harbor. And surely she has a right to some of the francs her husband had asked her to change. How could he begrudge her a souvenir, something to remember her honeymoon by? What better souvenir of France than a dress, something different from the sturdy polyester with which she'd filled her first set of Samsonite?

Ellie had helped her shop for the honeymoon, selecting the kind of apparel that would suit the wife of a lawyer and Knight of Columbus; avoiding the things that could only make Teresa look cheap and trashy. Ellie, of course, had no truck with the vagaries of style; she was a big-boned woman—certainly not fat, no one with flesh as firm and decided as Ellie's could be accused even of plumpness. But she had a certain amplitude about her; she reminded Teresa of a bathtub filled almost to overflowing, except that in Teresa's case, for Teresa's own good, the water therein had not even been tepid. "Think of our mother," Ellie had seemed to say every time Teresa had turned to her for a hug or a consoling word. And hadn't their mother—small-boned, slender, with hair exactly the same honey blond as Teresa's—been much too lavish with her affections, and not just to her children, either?

Teresa's suitcase is full of high-necked blouses and voluminous skirts, floor-length flannelette nightgowns, perfectly square white underpants innocent of bow or ribbon, and brassieres that could have been designed in an armory. "A man can lose his respect for you like *that*," Ellie had pronounced, snapping her fingers. "Especially a husband." Teresa hadn't been listening as carefully as she ought—she had, in fact, been fingering a bikini in the Sun 'n' Fun section of

Sears. "Don't forget, Teresa, you're going to be the mother of his children." And Ellie had taken her sister firmly by the wrist, leading her away from the offending swimsuit, as if some devious spermicidal substance had been woven into the Spandex. Felix, at thirty-three, expected children, the sooner the better. Felix's mother wanted grand-children, even Ellie was not averse to the idea of nieces (one of whom would surely be named after her). And nephews of course, who would turn out to possess vocations.

Teresa herself was not so sure that she wanted children—at least, not right away. She felt she'd hardly left her own childhood behind; certainly Ellie made her feel as though she'd never be able to make the kinds of decisions incumbent on anyone responsible for raising children. Why, she couldn't even make up her mind, right now, as to which dress to take—the one she knew Ellie would approve, a short-sleeved, pale-pink shirtwaist, with a Peter Pan collar—or this one she was holding up against herself, stroking the soft cotton, tracing the pattern of butterflies across the weave. You'd hardly know you were wearing anything at all, the fabric was so light. "Cotton lets you breathe," remarks a salesgirl who has come out to the sidewalk. Teresa nods at her, smiling, and follows her directions to the chang-ing room. Once inside, she reaches for the pale pink shirtwaist, only to find that she's taken the butterfly print, quite by accident.

They have spent the entire day tramping round the museum, looking at paintings, faïence, tapestries, plastered ceilings, embossed leather paneling, sixteenth-century bookbindings, and archeologically accredited pottery shards. Felix, understandably, is exhausted, with the beginnings of a migraine on top of his mild sinusitis. Teresa would have been just as happy to have spent the day in the Hôtel du Balcon, drinking *citron pressé* in the garden, or strolling along the river—you could even rent boats to take out on the water, but some-how Felix had never learned how to swim, and didn't appear eager to do so.

In his green and orange striped pajamas—a gift from his mother —Felix kisses her good night. His is the practiced, perfunctory manner of a man who has been twelve years, and not twelve days, married. Teresa has recovered from this morning's fit of nerves. Even though Felix, deep in the *Guide Bleu,* didn't seem to have noticed her protracted absence from the breakfast table, even though he didn't actually bother to count the bills she gave back to him, she had decided to hide her morning's purchase at the very bottom of her suitcase. She hadn't ever intended to wear it—that would, of course, be wrong. But to bring it back home, and occasionally take it out and even dress up in it, when she was quite alone—*that* she could manage without the smallest nip of conscience.

The impulsive acquisition of the butterfly dress, and the wholly unexpected event of her having literally run into Madame de Bèze's nephew on her way back to the hotel—her parcel had flown out of her arms on impact, and he had been kind enough to bend down and pick it up for her—have had the effect of resigning Teresa to the indefinite interruption of what Ellie refers to as "connubial encounters." Yet Teresa cannot help minding the fact that it's nine o'clock on a Friday night, and she can't even put on the light and flip through the magazines she's borrowed from the lobby. Inside there are pictures of models wearing the briefest of bathing suits, or sometimes nothing but their suntanned skins. Felix says it's a disgrace the way you can't walk past a billboard, or even look into a drugstore window in France without seeing naked bodies.

Had Felix chanced to waken on his wife's climbing out of bed, he would thus have been pleased to note that in pulling her nightdress over her head, Teresa reveals not nakedness, but a most respectable skirt and blouse, even if her legs are bare. Deftly, she locates her shoes from under the wardrobe, and even manages to pick up the key from the night table without making the slightest noise. As she steals out of the room and turns the key securely in the lock, Felix sleeps on, under the influence of the numerous objets d'art and antihistamines he has consumed that day.

She could have sailed right down the stairs, out the front door, and onto the streets of the town, but she is not looking for adventures. No, she only wants a little change, a change from all the things that Felix desires and Felix decrees. If, by some mischance, her husband were to wake up and miss her, rush to the balcony and fling open the glass doors, he would find her sitting calmly, quietly in the garden, counting the stars. If he happened as well to catch sight of a small red light glowing in the darkness—well, that is hardly her affair. She simply wants to sit out in the garden till she feels sleepy—can there be anything harmful in that? At the back of her mind she does not so much hear as see Ellie brandishing a finger more forceful than a ferule; her mother-in-law with her hands raised fearfully to her face, yet peeking through her fingers. Teresa hits a switch at the back of her mind, consigning Ellie and Madame Leynaud to the same fogged darkness as Felix.

It is a warm, even a sultry night—she undoes the top button of her blouse, and then, a moment later, the next one down, so that her throat, at least, is exposed to the random breeze that riffles the peony petals and wafts to her the lavish scent of roses. All the way round the border she walks, stopping now and again to bend her face toward the flowers, until she arrives back at her starting place. She pauses for a moment and then, as if it were the most natural thing in the world to do, she crosses the flagstones and takes the most direct route back to the lobby doors—via the arch under the concrete stump. As soon as she enters, the small spot of red, glowing like a magically arrested comet, falls to the ground and is silently stubbed out. Just as silently, a hand touches her face—perhaps it is no more than a moth's wing—and she feels, on the newly vulnerable skin of her throat, breath that is warm and fiery and sweet—doubtless the scent of roses.

Georges watches them from the café as they stand in the exact middle of the old stone bridge. The husband, he thinks, is like a parasol, keeping the sun off this wife he's just married, keeping her out of the sun. She looks different today, deliciously different—she's wearing a flimsy little sundress, and most of her hair has escaped from that stupid ribbon at the nape of her neck. He can only attribute this exposure of arms and legs and shoulders, this discovery, in fact, of her own flesh, to their innocent encounter in the hotel garden the night before. If only his aunt hadn't chosen that particular moment to put down slug pellets under the roses. No harm had been done— the girl had slipped back inside the lobby as quietly as she had come—but then, no good had come of their meeting, either. He stretches out his arms and smiles to himself, thinking of how a mere fifteen minutes alone together—even five, though that would have been rushing things—might have changed the girl's expectations, if not her life, forever. Well, that was the way things had happened to work out. If he hadn't chanced to argue with that German girl he'd picked up four days ago in the café, he wouldn't have bumped into the little *Canadienne* by chance that morning.

From here he can only see her back, but even that has its rewards. She's slightly knock-kneed, but her legs are long and slender, and the awkwardness gives her a certain vulnerability, which is a quality Georges prizes in his women. As for that pompous, provincial fellow in the linen suit—does she have any idea what she is in for with him? Thirty, forty years of starching his collars, trimming his mustache, going round to his *maman*'s for Sunday lunch. *Dégueulasse.* Still, there's no accounting for taste, or for necessity, and it would seem that this marriage had not been what you would call an *affaire du coeur.* All the same, Georges is a great believer in marriage; without it he'd never have found the opportunity to play his natural role— temporary *trois* without any of the bother of *ménage.*

Yet it was a pity—and a bother, too. Wouldn't his aunt laugh up her sleeve if she knew that she'd scotched more than the slugs the night before. His aunt's laughter—Georges doesn't relish even the thought of it. And he has to admit that his little scheme for a quick seduction has proved more than a matter of one-two-three. In fact, it shows signs of going into the hundreds and thousands. Mightn't it be time to admit defeat and cut his losses? Except that there is something undeniably attractive in the girl, the situation—stealing her right from under the nose of her plump and pious spouse. Stealing her like a thief in the night, and then, like a good constable, returning her none the worse for wear before her good man has shaken the sleep out of his eyes. Perhaps it is worth another try—how will he be able to face himself in the mirror if he gives up on this one after so many near-misses. And as if to strengthen his resolution, as if to mirror his intentions, the girl wheels round, and looks straight at him. Her face is flushed—her eyes and lips unnaturally bright. To his delight, to his astonishment, she lifts her arm and waves.

Madame de Bèze waves back, startled but pleased, at the little bride from the hotel. She wonders why the girl is gesturing in such a friendly way to her, while the husband, usually so correct, so intent upon appearances, keeps his back turned, and seems to be contemplating a dive into the river below. She simply cannot comprehend these North Americans. Are they in the middle of a lovers' quarrel? Except that anything less like lovers Madame de Bèze has yet to see. This morning, for example, the man had been sitting in the dining room over a croissant and *thé au citron* for a whole hour before his wife had come downstairs. She hadn't eaten anything, but had called him from the lobby—he had run to catch up with her as she slipped out the front door and into the street.

He had been unusually talkative with Madame de Bèze as she'd poured out his tea, telling her about the visit he planned to Chamfort that day; volunteering more personal information. It turned out that he was a lawyer in a city named Ollifachs. Madame de Bèze had never visited Chamfort, and she disliked lawyers; in her experience they wasted time and money to a degree that would never be tolerated in a chambermaid or bellhop. She had considered legal action when Georges had begun to press her about the hotel, but had given up the idea as unworthy of her. If she were already in her dotage, yes, but for a woman of sixty-three, with all her faculties, not to be able to handle a stripling of twenty-nine. . . . Oh, he had his airs and graces, Georges—she had seen him luring that poor innocent down to the garden last night. She pitied the girl, with her forget-me-not eyes and the kind of hair that would suit an angel in a nativity play.

How could she protect the girl from Georges, or even from the husband she had chosen? A husband who knew more about châteaus than what was going on under his own bedroom window.

Had Georges overheard the talk about Chamfort this morning? He had been defiantly eating cornflakes at the table next to the Canadians'. But he'd scarcely bother the girl during the day; châteaus and husbands are not his strong suits. Madame de Bèze sighs, and continues in the direction of the market. She'll get some perch for supper and pick up some liqueurs to replace the ones that Georges has polished off. On an impulse she stops, turns round, and cranes her head in the direction of the café where Georges sits out the mornings, watching the women go back and forth. He'd been there a moment ago, yet now he's vanished. So have the girl and her husband. Madame de Bèze purses her lips, tightens her grip on the handle of her basket, and walks on.

At the very moment Teresa had turned away from her husband on the little stone bridge, turned with tears blistering her eyes to wave helplessly at Madame de Bèze as if to prove to herself that she was not without friends in this strange country, Felix had been chastising her. Though it was at least eighty-five degrees in the shade, though she was feeling far from well, Felix was insisting they visit yet another château. They have already seen lovely Amboise, picturesque Sully, stately Chambord, idyllic Azay-le-Rideau, and romantic Chenonceaux. This last day of their honeymoon, Teresa had asked only to laze on the little beach behind the bridge—to read magazines and catch up on her sleep. Felix had accused her of being unfeeling and ungrateful, reminding his wife that since he was paying for this honeymoon, it was only natural he should decide how they would spend their time, and where.

Felix's mind is made up. They will go to Chamfort—she will like Chamfort, there are magnificent gardens there. How can she say he's only thinking of himself? Hasn't this whole honeymoon been designed to enlarge her cultural horizons? As for her feeling tired, *he's* the one with migraine—yet he's manfully swallowed three aspirin, and he advises his wife to do the same. Teresa says that aspirin make her throw up. She smooths the skirt of the sundress she has finally plucked up the courage to wear, this last day in the Loire. Their argument began over Teresa's dress. Felix was appalled by the fact that she bought it in secret and with his money. He distrusts the promiscuous whirl of butterflies—crimson, azure, chocolatey brown —over the bright yellow cotton. Not only did he accuse her of deceiving him, but he hasn't said a word about how she looks in the dress. He has, of course, let her wear it—it's too late for her to change and he can scarcely rip it off her here in the street.

Moving as briskly as he can—his head feels like a shattered teacup—Felix calls back to his wife, "Hurry up, Teresa, or we'll miss our train."

"I hope we do," she calls under her breath, a faint mustache of perspiration over her lip. She licks it away, reaches up to her hair, and yanks the ribbon out. It's even hotter like this, but she wants her hair to fall forward and cover her face—she will die if anyone sees she's been crying.

Once off the train, Felix takes his wife's arm and guides her through the white dust of the streets of Chamfort. He wishes she'd brought a sweater, a jacket, her arms and neck look so bare; it isn't difficult to tell she's wearing almost nothing underneath that dress. What could have possessed her to buy it? She usually dressed so sensibly. Already it's scorching outside, but perhaps there'll be a wind, a storm—that often happens; he doesn't want them both to return to Halifax with colds. His head throbs—the aspirin doesn't seem to be having any effect. He doesn't quite catch the remark she's making about the trees that line the main road: sycamores, pollarded so that they look like war amputees, she says.

"It's to ensure that their branches grow regularly, evenly. Next year they'll be all thick and full enough to shade the pavement."

"But it's this year now, and look at them—why does everything have to grow 'regularly, evenly'? Why can't they be left to grow as they please?"

"Because that's the way they do things in France."

"In France, in France—"

Why is she so irritable? Dragging her feet, pouting because she has to go and see one of the splendors of the civilized world. He doesn't like this mood she's put on with that flimsy dress—a sullen mood, most unlike the sunny, almost simple girl with whom he'd walked in the Public Gardens only a month ago. They'd fed the ducks, and she'd been happy as a child! It had been a mistake, bringing her to Europe, expecting her to share his enthusiasms. After all, it's not important that Teresa understand the intricacies of Renaissance architecture. She's still very young—and as her sister had pointed out, that was a definite point in Teresa's favor. Young and inexperienced and therefore good as gold, unlike all the other women he'd encountered at university and in his practice. He has to make allowances.

He notices that from time to time she rubs her stomach. Could she be hungry already? It's nearly eleven and the heat that's been drowsing in the dust has woken now, puts out heavy hands and burdens everything—the awnings over the grocers' shops where they stop to buy things for a picnic lunch; even the leaves of the trees, dull green bottles stuffed with sunlight. Neither of them says anything now—it's too hot to talk. Felix wonders, for one wild moment, whether Teresa's stomachache might be a precocious sign of pregnancy. If so he can forgive her anything. He takes a sideways look at her, noticing how her dress clings to her damp skin, how it sticks against her legs.

By noon his own shirt is plastered to his skin. They've entered the grounds of the château and are picnicking in a small patch of shade under some chestnut trees. The pâté he bought smells peculiar; Teresa's forgotten to bring a knife, so they have to use their fingers to spread goat cheese over their bread. Even after they've wiped their hands again and again on the grass, the smell of goat pervades the air. The apricots have got mashed together, and the plastic bottle of mineral water—heavy as a magnum of champagne in the carrying— is unpleasantly warm. Nonetheless, they polish it off and sit back on the grass. Felix shuts his eyes, sun branding his head; he'd forgotten to save some water with which to take another aspirin. Teresa lifts up her skirt to fan her legs—they've walked for what seemed like miles—she doesn't think she could move another inch. But just as she is getting ready to stretch out flat on the grass and doze, he leans over her, whispers in her ear.

"Of course not." She's as horrified as if he'd uttered an obscenity. "No, I couldn't be."

"All right, let's not make a fuss about it, Teresa. I just thought— you've been so peculiar this last little while." He stretches out a hand and pulls her to her feet. "Come on, it's time we toured the gardens —they're among the finest of their kind."

Of course they were fine—great care had been taken to replant them exactly as they'd been in 1653, Felix remarked, quoting the *Guide Bleu*. Rose gardens, herb gardens, kitchen gardens, yew mazes, flower clocks—everything that was ingenious and intricate and or- dered. To her it is the pollarded trees, over and over and over—she can't fathom what so delights him in all this primly patterned vege- tation. She tries hard not to remark that she prefers the Public Gar- dens in Halifax, the wildflowers growing in the ditch outside her father's place.

Right now he's pointing to a sundial made out of fifty different kinds of herbs. His voice sounds strained, yet still he goes on, dis- coursing about the various uses to which rosemary, garlic, and colts- foot can be put. To stop him, to make him close the book and keep from always talking, Teresa goes over to a hedge and picks a rose, a fat pink rose. He stares at her as if she's just thrown a brick through a jeweler's window.

"Teresa—what are you doing? Put it down, drop it—you know you mustn't pick things here, it's—"

"Forbidden. I know. Forbidden to walk on the grass, forbidden to pick a flower or hop over a fence, blow your nose, or even a kiss. Oh, I *know*." Her hair has fallen into her face, her cheeks are flushed, she looks to him as though she's been drinking, as though she's years, decades older than that little office temp who came into his office with a file folder one February morning. She comes up close to him, trying to pin the rose in his buttonhole, but he takes a step back. So she tucks it into the bodice of her butter-yellow dress, its skirt awhirl with butterflies. Round and round his head, warm, furred wings in his eyes and mouth as he grabs at her, snatches the rose, and tosses it away into the fountain.

"What did you do that for? Felix, how could you?" Teresa's voice rings out—there are tears in her eyes again. Cramps are rising, black and sour, in her belly.

"Sssh, don't make a scene—" He tries to take her arm, but she pulls away. There are a few people about—an elderly man with a homburg and an extremely elegant woman wearing a hat and gloves and looking like a sliver of ice as she crosses the gravel path in front of them. He wonders, suddenly, what Teresa will look like when she's that woman's age. Will she ever be able to carry off a hat and gloves? Teresa's eyes are twin comets with fiery tails: "I said, how *could* you?"

He's never heard her like this, her voice sulfurous. She whirls round and stalks off—to the very fountain in whose basin the pink rose floats, nearly drowned by its own voluptuousness.

"Teresa," Felix calls out—but not loud enough. He's afraid someone will hear. At all costs he must avoid a scene, and she can't be meaning to—yes, she is, she is hiking up her skirts and wading into the fountain, scooping up the rose. Doesn't she care what she looks like, her skirts soaked, clinging to her legs? If one of the guards should see, they'd be thrown out at once. He stares, mouth agape, as she comes toward him, trailing water as she goes, gravel sticking to the soles of her bare feet. She stops perhaps a foot away from him, the rose inside her dress, between her breasts. Can this distressing, dangerous woman be Teresa?

"It's no good, Felix. It's impossible. Why didn't she tell me? I want . . . you can't— Don't you undersand?"

What on earth has all this got to do with vandalism in a public park? Perhaps she has sunstroke, perhaps she *is* pregnant, perhaps—

"Oh, what's the *use*!"

Felix can only go on staring, the hammer in his head pounding his eyes, his ears, even his tongue. Suddenly, violently, Teresa blushes. She looks right through Felix, then turns on her heel and darts through one of the yew arches into the maze. What if he simply lets her go off in a huff? How can he run after her when his head is cracking into a thousand pieces? He should be lying down in a dark, quiet room; he should see a doctor. His father had died of a stroke —these things happen, there's such a thing as heredity. Doesn't anyone realize how serious this is?

Where is Ellie? She would understand. He must get back to town and call her up, that's the only thing he can possibly do. It's only a matter of walking down the road, and finding a phone, and getting through, at last, to Ellie.

Despite the heat, Georges has enjoyed playing shadow. Having overtaken them on the road to the château, he has trailed them all afternoon, at the most discreet of distances.

Now he waits round the corner of the yew hedge, just where he'd been when she'd finally glimpsed him over the roses. With his black beard and eyes he looks like a pirate, she decides—but she's not sure whether or not this frightens her. He's reaching out his hand and speaking to her in quick, friendly American English:

"It sure is hot out—why don't we have a drink? I've got my car right outside the château. We can drive into town and just sit for a while at the café. Then I'll take you back to the hotel."

Teresa cannot take her eyes off his face. He's shorter than Felix; in fact, he's not much taller than she is. No, she's not frightened, though Ellie's warnings about how men are all alike scuttle through her head. She feels for the return stub of her ticket in her pocket. She can always go with him to the café and make her way back on her own if need be. But what if Felix walks past them while they're sitting at the café? Even as she wonders this she gives him her hand and speaks.

"I don't even know your name."

He draws her beside him, as if he would like to kiss her. But doesn't. "Georges," he says. "And you're—?"

She waits a moment, and then replies, "Thérèse."

He lets go her hand and leads her out of the maze to the car. On the way to town she asks him where he's learned such good English, and he tells her that he lived in New Orleans for a while. It's so pleasant being able to sit back and just listen to him talk. He's not like Felix, who always has to be informing her about the history of culture, and who can never bring himself to say anything like, "It's a hot day," or, "I like the way you smile." Before she knows it, they are at the café. Georges is pulling out a chair for her and ordering two Stella Artois. Icy beer, rattling her teeth, hurting her tongue. He keeps talking to her, telling her he loves this heat—he's from Marseilles, and never feels at home except in such weather.

Talking on and on about the south, the way people live there, the long siestas from noon till four. She would like it in the south, he says—he can tell just from looking at her that she's the southern type. She never says a word but leans her face toward his, pressing her elbows into the wrought-iron table until the pattern's embedded in her skin. The beer anesthetizes her; she no longer feels the heat, or her cramps, or the slightest confusion. She even manages a few words about Cape Breton, how beautiful it is—just like Scotland, though she's never been to Scotland—but that's what people say. As she talks she twists her wedding ring round and round on her finger until finally she has worked it right off her hand and into her fist, where she feels it like a pat of butter, melting.

He signals to the waiter, who brings them each another beer. *"Santé,"* says Georges, clinking his glass against her own. After she has taken a good, long sip, he leans forward, stretching out his hand, his fingertips just grazing her bare arm. "Why don't we go someplace for supper, and then drive back to the hotel when it's cooler?"

She doesn't pull back so that he can't stroke her arm any longer —nor does she lean in toward him. She simply stays as she is, looking across at him, enjoying the way he plays his fingers along her arm. She feels so peculiar, she can't understand what it can be. And suddenly she knows. She is happy. She is herself, Teresa, nobody's wife, nobody's sister. And she is happy. Why, she wonders, is there nothing about happiness written into the marriage ceremony? About making each other happy? That was what she'd been trying to say to Felix, to herself, just before she'd run away from him in the garden. All she wants now, perhaps all she's ever wanted, has been to be light and free. To play.

Her head is whirling; she feels as if she were one of the butterflies on her dress, uncaged from the cloth and beating her wings just for the joy of it. Everything that has been weighting her down for as long as she can remember—Ellie's warnings and Ellie's ambitions, Felix's ideas and Felix's decisions—suddenly blow away, as if they're not great black stones at all, but flakes of burned paper. Hastily, Teresa lifts her glass to her lips and polishes off the Stella Artois.

"What do you say? Shall we have supper together and then drive back? I know a great country inn not far from here."

Teresa smiles, a little unsteadily. She doesn't drink—she's never had two beers before, not in a row. If only she hadn't felt so thirsty. But he's waiting for an answer. "I—I just want to wash my face and hands. I'll be back in a moment."

"Take your time," says Georges, smiling beautifully through his trim black beard. "There's no need to rush at all."

White dust turning his well-polished shoes into ghosts of themselves. Sky overhead cerulean: azure, cerulean—he says the words over and over, as if they're a kind of glue keeping the pieces of his head together till he finally arrives at the station. Curiously enough, the walk seems to have done him some good; he thinks he'll be all right if he can just get himself back to the hotel and into bed. The thought of Teresa stranded in the ornamental gardens of Chamfort buzzes for a second inside his head before he brushes it away—it makes his migraine worse. Dropping onto a bench, Felix rubs his fingers over his face. He will phone Ellie as soon as he gets back to the hotel, as soon as he's had some sleep. None of this trouble would ever have happened if Ellie had come along; why on earth hadn't they asked her to join them? Why hadn't she suggested it herself? It wasn't like her not to take all the precautions necessary. Ellie never left anything to chance. Except this—this possibly most significant, most important event in his life—his honeymoon. Oh, why hadn't Ellie come along?

A train pulls up at the station, the train for Beaulieu. Gingerly, Felix rises from the bench, shuffles over to the track, and finds himself a seat in one of the crowded compartments. He's astonished that the pain has not yet sawn his head in half. Light zigzags under his eyelids—as soon as he gets back to the hotel he'll crawl into bed and sleep until morning. He dozes as the train rocks him soothingly from side to side. Sleep is a compass drawing circles round him: Ellie, his mother, his wife, the office, his wallet, his keys. . . .

He's returning to the house on the outskirts of Halifax, after a long day at work. Opening the door, he's surrounded by a troupe of children who all have his face. *Maman* takes his briefcase and shoos the children away—he is hurrying effortlessly up the stairs. The bedroom door opens of its own accord and gently closes after admitting him. And there, lying on the bed, almost indistinguishable from the great fluffy duvet and the quilted bolster, her arms wide open, is his wife. Into her warm, ample, welcoming flesh he sinks, as she murmurs, "There there, my dear, there there." He lies with his head between her breasts, her breasts not small and hard, but large, warm, fragrant cushions enclosing him, hiding him from whatever hurts or disappoints. . . .

The train slows, stops—he jolts awake. Beaulieu. Everyone's shoving past him to get out. His legs won't move, he wants to stay here, rooted in the dream he's already losing, the feeling of being rocked and lulled and covered over. A whistle—shrill enough to peel the skin from his ears. "Wait!" he cries, lurching across the compartment and out the train doors just as the car is gently moving off with whatever it is he has lost or left behind.

Unsteadily, Teresa makes her way to the washroom, her legs moving most unlike a butterfly's wings. The room is tiny, grotty, odiferous—she has to squat over a horrible-looking hole on the two porcelain feet provided. This is one hallmark of *la civilization française* on which her husband has never held forth. Standing up again, she washes her face and hands—tugs the useless little comb in her purse through her hair, sticks out her tongue at the reflection in the glass. Her face is white, her eyes huge—a stranger's face. There's a hard little glitter in her eyes. Felix is waiting for her—no, not Felix, the man from the hotel—she forgets his name. He wants to take her for a drive. No, for dinner. He wants to show her the countryside, he wants to play butterflies—

"Jesus, Mary, and Joseph." A cramp wrings and knots her belly. On the far-from-gleaming tile underneath her feet she sees one, two, three great drops of blood, bright as the roses in the hotel garden. They seem to have no connection with her whatever, yet here they are, like a sign. "Oh," she moans to herself. "Oh no . . ." She will have to get to a *pharmacie* to buy some tampons. How would she explain to him? *Les règles,* wasn't that the word? "I'm sorry but I can't go with you—I have the rules." For how could she drive off with him now—she would stain her dress, the seat of his car, and Ellie would see.

A golden blur in the mirror. Outside the washroom is the back door of the café. It leads to a side street, down which a blonde girl in a brightly patterned dress is wildly running, praying she will get to the station in time to catch the train for Beaulieu.

All the journey long she sits with her legs pressed tight together. It isn't fair, it isn't right that this should be happening to her now, just when she finds her only chance. What had he said when she didn't return? Felix, Georges. What could she ever say to them? They would both go back to the Hôtel du Balcon. Felix would be sleeping in the clutch of his migraine, Georges, smoking a cigar in the garden. And Madame de Bèze? Where would she be, the one person to whom Teresa could tell everything?

Carefully, she rises from her seat as the train pulls into Beaulieu. She takes a quick look at the upholstery—thank God, nothing shows. There is no *pharmacie* in sight. Besides, she has no money. It's late afternoon, still bright, though the sun looks shriveled. Every man at every café table seems to be staring at her as she walks by. She can feel their eyes like eels down her back; she can feel a dark, sticky stain spreading down the back of her skirt, marking her out, a woman who has abandoned her husband, gone off to drink beer with a man who might as well be a perfect stranger. "Think of our mother!" Ellie would say. Of course she will have to confess to Ellie. And Ellie will patch things up, her stitches so tight and so precise that Felix will forget he ever took his bride to look at the gardens of the Loire.

Inside the Hôtel du Balcon Teresa stops short. Here is the staircase, and up the stairs, along the landing, third door to the left, the room in which her husband would be waiting. Does she really have to go up these stairs and round to the left, dragging her feet, not caring anymore if she bleeds all over the runners? There is nothing else to do but face the music, however loud or shrill, that's what Ellie would say. But Ellie isn't married to Felix. Ellie doesn't have to go back to Halifax tomorrow, to a house on the outskirts of town, a house in which Felix's mother is already waiting, waiting for grandchildren. . . .

"Jesus, Mary, and Joseph," Teresa whispers, halfway up the stairs. "I can't." She turns abruptly round, glancing fearfully down at the lobby. Suppose Georges should appear, furious at her having run away like that. Suppose Felix should have heard her on the staircase, suppose he's belting on his dressing gown, ready to come thundering down the stairs. Suppose he's called the police, suppose he's phoned Ellie, suppose they're all coming for her, all together. Is there nothing she can do but put one foot in front of the other—on and on and on, without ever finding her way out?

Under an evening sky still milky with the day's heat, Madame de Bèze points her shears toward a clump of peonies; she wants to cut some for the great glass vase at the reception desk. The flowers are a creamy white, with the merest flare of pink. They show up beautifully against the roses. But she doesn't get a chance to clip even one of the peonies because something quite extraordinary is happening. A fair-haired girl in a yellow dress, a dribble of blood down her legs, runs toward her, arms outstretched. Madame de Bèze drops her shears and basket and opens her arms. She draws the girl close and says, over and over again, "What's the matter, little one? You can tell me, you can tell *maman*."

Serenely, with just the right amount of pressure from her cloth, Madame de Bèze polishes the bottles of spirits, liqueurs, and *eau de vie* arrayed in the dining room of the Hôtel du Balcon. Amber, emerald, gold, and the very silver of transparency. She frowns, wondering whether Georges could have been into the cognac. It doesn't seem likely; his wife seems to have cured him of that indulgence, at least. Who would have believed that such a slip of a girl could have taken a man like Georges in hand? Not that he doesn't steal glances at the women who come into the hotel on the arms of their husbands or lovers; not that he doesn't disappear from time to time to look after odds and ends of business in Marseilles. His slips and slidings, reflects his aunt, may be due to the very ease with which his young wife has learned to manage her hotel. As though she'd been joyfully born to the work. It is Teresa who plans the menus, orders in the wine, draws up the ads for the tourist brochures, and turns a handy profit. Madame de Bèze can spend her time now polishing glassware, pruning roses, and hoping that Georges and Teresa will yet give her grandchildren; if not a whole brood, then at least a boy and girl whose names she has already picked out: César and Simone—her husband's and her own.

Madame de Bèze folds and puts down her cloth, and walks to the window overlooking the garden. Colored lights loop over the flagstones, and the tables and chairs have been pushed to the edges to make a small dance floor. That is the extent of whatever damage Georges once plotted. The concrete stump's still there, smack in the middle of the terrace, where César had built it one autumn. She draws the curtain with only a trace of a sigh. For eighteen years now, she has been a widow. Not once in all her married life had she complained to César about their lack of children. Nor had he ever reproached her for pinning him to her father's hotel, when all he had ever desired to do was travel. They'd found consolation for their separate griefs in a concrete stump within a flower garden. Happiness, after all, was nothing more than a gloss on contentment. Between them, they had not done too badly.

She rarely wonders whether Teresa regrets having stayed on with her here; having agreed to exchange a clean-shaven, responsible, undeniably respectable husband for one who's bearded, impractical, and undeniably *voyou*. She never considers whether Georges minds her having made over the hotel to Teresa and whatever children Teresa might produce by him. And she refuses to speculate on what might have happened if things had not worked out so fortuitously for Teresa, that last day of her honeymoon in the Loire. Nature intervening so that a mere hour of carnal pleasure shouldn't preempt a lifetime of the Hôtel du Balcon—well, why shouldn't it? Do not the most significant events, the acts that decide any number of fates, happen by accident, blind chance, slips of heart and tongue?

Neither Georges nor Teresa have ever confessed to being in love. Yet the real miracle, as far as Madame de Bèze is concerned, is that they can be happy. Not day in day out, but rarely, randomly—yet often enough for the hotel to go on the way it always has, and the peonies to keep blooming. For the roses to perfume the air under the colored lights, between the dancers' bodies as they sway to music—Madame de Bèze's own collection of the Hot Club de France—piped out from the lobby.

Sometimes, at the end of a summer evening, when all the guests have gone inside, Georges will fetch Teresa from the reception desk where she is going over the accounts, spin her out the glass doors, up and down the terrace. And then they dance together through the arches of the concrete stump, into which they disappear for such a length of time that Madame de Bèze pulls the switch for the colored lights, shuts off the music, and tells the boy at the night desk he can go to bed. *Monsieur* and *madame* are attending to the garden—they will lock up for the night.

Isola Bella

To celebrate her divorce, Collie rented half a house in a hillside village in the south of France. Nibs and Jetta came along for company. They would share the rent, electricity—such as there was—and groceries. Collie would write, Jetta would paint, and Nibs would look after them all. Jetta jumped at the idea because she had a show looming; any canvas oozing Mediterranean sea and sun would be sure to sell, even before the opening. Nibs came in spite of losing money on the deal—there was no way she could possibly sublet her apartment at such short notice. Collie kept telling Nibs that she owed herself a holiday, and that off-season was the only time to see the Riviera. She neglected to say that the village she'd chosen lay some thirty-five miles from shore.

St. Barbe de Bourgeon turned out to be one of those architectural still lives colonized by entrepreneurial esthetes. Dozens of dormant, crumbly buildings had been rapidly restored and rented out to potters, dried-flower artistes, painters of stones and pastel portraits, glass-blowers, restaurateurs, and innovative jewelers. In May, when the season officially opened, the tilting, narrow streets of St. Barbe de Bourgeon, or St. B de B, as Collie preferred to call it, would resound with the thud of espadrilles and the skittering of pretty leather flats, with the chink of crockery in cafés, and the incessant wheeze of tour buses. In March, however, there was nothing to be heard but Collie cursing the brackish water that gurgled out the taps, Jetta fuming about how her fingers were seizing up with the cold, and Nibs trudging back and forth to the well, filling up plastic containers with *eau de source*. It would have been more fun, Jetta had complained to Nibs, if the decree had come through in May. But nothing could be done about that now, and Collie's freedom was the main thing, wasn't it? Or so Nibs had ventured to reply.

Collie was supposed to be using her freedom to write a new Harlequin. Her third of the half of the house in St. B de B came from an advance her publisher had given her for *Love's Lady Lost*. Collie had struck a new vein in the genre—she set everything on the twenties Riviera, with acres of the beautiful and damned as a backdrop for her central characters. They, of course, discovered true love and salutary passion in each other's arms and more exotic parts of their anatomies. By throwing in allusions to F. Scott, Pablo, and the Ballets Russes, Collie attracted anyone who'd taken Introduction to Modern Culture in first- or second-year Liberal Arts, but who could still be caught leafing through *People* or *True Romance* at the supermarket checkout counter. Her editor had even talked of creating a "blue" series of Harlequins for Collie and her *consoeurs,* to capture the more cultivated portion of the market. Collie didn't care. If she slapped together three books over the next year she'd have just enough for a down payment on a lakeside house in Burlington. There'd even be the possibility, six or seven novels down the road, of a sabbatical to be spent writing a volume of short stories in the Munro manner. And should she need to spend a night in town she could always find a few inches of floor space in Jetta's studio.

Nibs wasn't doing anything in the way of art, so that she quite fell in with the task of "clearing a space," which Jetta and Collie had declared essential for their respective métiers. On the rare sunny mornings during which Collie lay almost clinically naked on the terrace, soaking up the skittish sun (Jetta painting her from the studio window, dropping cigarette ashes equally onto her palette and Collie's bare back), Nibs would wander down to the market with her basket on her arm to buy the day's bread and pâté and cheese. The studio was supposed to have been Nibs's bedroom, but Nibs had agreed to sleep on a couch in the kitchen—the warmest room in the house, Collie had pointed out to a temporarily and uncharacteristically remorseful Jetta. "Don't think she doesn't get the most *intense* pleasure out of sacrificing herself like this. She lives in an utter dump of a bachelorette somewhere near the end of the subway line, though she could afford to buy up half of Rosedale. She's the kind of person who sends off fifty bucks to every good cause that sails in through her mail slot—Energy Probe, Foot and Mouth painters, Oxfam, the whole deal. Look, when we were at school together she'd get positively *orgasmic* about doing without so that some kid in Asia Minor could have eyeglasses or a pair of rubber boots—though why you needed rubber boots in Asia Minor I never figured out. Believe me, Jetta, you'd hurt her feelings if you didn't let her give up her room for you. She wants to—it's just her way."

It was also Nibs's way to read through the postcards her housemates gave her to take to the *bureau de poste* in town. None of the cards with laundry-bluing sea and skies, bilious thickets of mimosa, or anemic-looking children in *costume Niçoise* said anything about the black tap water, the more than occasional rain and wind, the defective heating system, and the outrageous prices they paid for food (it all had to be trucked up from Nice). The bliss of life without cars or telephones or TV was dashed off in their different hands—Jetta's spiky, concise, Collie's looping and flooding. They both seemed to be writing mainly to women, though there were a few cryptic cards addressed to men, none of whom had, as far as Nibs knew, ever been married to either of them. Once Collie sent a thick white letter to her daughter, who was at school in Lausanne. Nibs was sorry Geraldine hadn't been invited to St. B de B—she liked children, though Geraldine was going through what her mother called a simply-frightful-bloody-awful stage. Jetta sent a similarly opaque envelope to Rudi, who wasn't her husband, but who managed her investments as carefully as if he had been. One evening when they were drinking coffee after one of Nibs's invariable omelettes, Jetta had leaned back in her chair, run her fine hands through her short black hair, and asked whether they'd think her a cretin if she did marry Rudi, after all. Collie had deliberated for a moment, polished off the rest of her espresso, and then pronounced, "Rudi is five inches shorter and fifteen years older than you. Oh yes, and half a million dollars richer." "If you think you really love him—" Nibs had been about to say, when Jetta closed off all further conversation with, "I'll bet he's like an overripe banana in bed."

Nibs sent only one postcard of her own, to the woman who was watering her plants while she was away. The card was a large purple blur which turned out, on closer inspection, to be a field of lavender in Provence. It was not a strictly accurate representation of where Nibs had found herself, but she let that be. She was used to practicing small deceptions. Her money, for example; there was far less of it than Collie supposed. Nibs had gouged her savings to cover the plane fare and her share of the house, but she couldn't have afforded not to. Her only capital, with a friend like Collie, was this notion that she was rich, and that eccentricity alone kept her from showing it. As for Jetta—she was simply the most alarming person Nibs had ever met. In the damp, cold house on rue Manette, Jetta fairly crackled; she painted houndstooth-check patterns on her fingernails, wore no underwear of any kind, drank prodigious amounts of cognac, and teased Nibs right to her face, Nibs who'd never been noticed by anyone before.

Out of the *bureau de poste* and halfway to the *alimentation,* where she bought canned goods and stale bread, UHT milk, and eggs that came as dear as hand-dipped chocolates at home, Nibs ventured a few steps beyond the entrance to the town. She put down her basket and sat carefully on the low stone wall lining the slope. In one direction, over the terraced hills, was a turquoise smudge she knew to be the Mediterranean. Coming into Nice, she'd been sure they'd crash right into the water—she had meant to pray, but hadn't been able to take her eyes off the shadow of the plane's wings over the sea. Directly under the turquoise, strange white plumes were waving. She supposed that if you were to get a mouthful of the Mediterranean, it would taste like the gassy mineral water she could never bring herself to drink.

They'd gone straight to a hotel in Nice and slept off their exhaustion, intending to spend another day in town before heading off to St. B de B. But the next day it had rained, and they'd decided instead to hire a cab and settle in at Number 7 *bis,* rue Manette. The house had no name, and the niche over the door held neither local saint nor Virgin and Child—there was wire over the empty space, so you couldn't even put a vase of plastic flowers there. These were its chief drawbacks, in Nibs's eyes. Jetta and Collie, on the other hand, were more bothered by the volcanic noises emitted by the toilet, which for some reason had been placed at the very top of the house, and could only be reached by a convoluted stairway. But they'd made the best of things—the *eau de vie* Jetta found in the wardrobe had helped enormously. And they all agreed that it would be ten times worse in the city; there had been pamphlets at their hotel advertising Nice as the Los Angeles of France; the very sight of the freeway to Cap d'Antibes had made Collie shudder.

Nibs shifted her not inconsiderable weight on the old stone wall so that she could find the other bit of water visible from her lookout. That was Menton, which Jetta wanted to see; there was a Jean Cocteau museum there. Collie had agreed it would make a nice change, and they were only waiting for the decent weather that would make it worth their while to walk all the way down to the bend in the road by which the bus to Menton was reputed to pass. Cautiously, Nibs lifted up her round, grayish-green eyes—speckled trout, Jetta had described them that very morning, over croissants and cigarettes. The clouds were definitely thinning—perhaps tomorrow they would wake to a clear sky, and make it down the hill in time to catch the bus. Nibs made a note to set her traveling alarm clock for six-thirty, just in case. She was on the point of rising from her seat and turning in the direction of rue Manette when she noticed a darkish blur on her hands. A pair of butterflies were overhead. She watched them flitter back and forth and then descend onto the stone wall.

Like many heavy people, Nibs could attain perfect immobility, and she did so now, hardly breathing as the butterflies alighted. They quivered their wings for a few seconds afterward, as if they were drunk on air and light and needed to regain their balance. As she watched them a word came into her mind, and she found herself repeating it, more for the sound than the sense. *Precarious.* It had something to do with her being alone here in a lovely little island of sun. Perfectly alone. Everything delighted her—the scentless roses drooping over the wall, the roughness of the stone on which she sat, even the crude color of the butterflies' wings, which were nothing but a shake of yellow powder over ribbed transparency. And then she thought of Jetta, whose hands were fans made out of the finest bone, just webbed with skin.

Jetta had asked Nibs to pose for her, peeling onions at the kitchen sink, and Nibs had agreed, until Jetta had insisted she take off all her clothes. "Oh, no, Jetta," Nibs had said, with a finality that Jetta had mistaken for embarrassment. "It's not something I can do." Jetta had roared, telling Collie, and both of them had teased her ever after. Neither of them knew that one of Nibs's huge and jiggly breasts was an affair of rubber and wire; that were they to stumble into the kitchen in the middle of the night they would see a different Nibs stretched out on the camp bed, a Nibs with only half of her bosom rising and falling under her rose-sprigged flannelette. But Jetta and Collie were sound sleepers, and Nibs was just as glad they didn't know. Sometimes people got upset with you for bringing certain things to mind. She didn't want to spoil Collie's celebration or Jetta's holiday. She was perfectly fit now; there was no reason anyone should ever know.

The butterflies looked slightly stupid with the sun they were sucking up through their queer black legs and feelers. Which, she wondered, was male, and which female? How could anything so delicate as a butterfly have anything to do with the pressing and shoving that was sex? Subways and streetcars at rush hour—that was Nibs's idea of copulation. She'd never liked crowds. Nor did the butterflies. So quickly that Nibs couldn't follow the strokes of their wings, they had shaken themselves off the ledge and were gone, leaving a tremor in the air. Nibs waited for a moment, perfectly still, hoping they might come back again. And then she collected her basket, maneuvered herself up from the wall, and returned along the dusty road. She walked as though she were swimming, as though the air were a sort of jelly through which she had to propel herself. Halfway home, Nibs stopped under a pepper tree, broke off a sprig, and crushed it between her fingers. She followed the tug of its scent all the way back to 7 *bis,* rue Manette.

It was a perfect day for the excursion—luckily Nibs had remembered to set the alarm, though Collie had cursed when she'd been jostled awake at seven, and Jetta had refused to stir out of bed for a full fifteen minutes. Nevertheless, Nibs managed to get the three of them down to the right bend in the road by eight-fifteen. She'd even brought sandwiches and a bottle of well water in her carpetbag— they could pick up fruit and patisseries in Menton. Jetta was insisting they stay on for a supper of oysters and white wine, even if they had to walk all the way back to St. B de B. Collie pointed out that in the kind of costume Jetta affected—a tight black tunic and patent-leather pumps whose toes and heels looked like they'd been shoved into a pencil sharpener—they'd be a good three days on the road. Collie was wearing mauve sandals, a long, wide, faded denim skirt, and a padded silk jacket over a lace camisole. Only Nibs had dressed at all sensibly for a long walk along a country road: canvas sneakers, jeans, and a sweatshirt. Yet as Collie joked, she still looked like the Queen Mum. It was the way she had of carrying herself, as though there were always an invisible handbag on her arm, a flowery hat plumped onto her hair. Nibs had laughed as much as any of them as they'd boarded the bus.

It was a milk run, calling at every conceivable habitation on each loop and knot of road, until at last they reached the sea. Palm trees, gently breaking waves, yachts with masts clinking in the breeze— this, sighed Collie, was finally *It:* everything the novels and movies and tourist magazines had promised. In her relief she lowered the handkerchief with which she'd been blocking the bursts of Jetta's perfume. Poison? Opium?—whatever it was, she stank like a civet cat. Over the last week Collie had begun to get irritable with Jetta, who, frankly, had been too bloody productive up in Nibs's surrendered bedroom. Jetta made all the money she needed from her paintings, and yet the paintings were good: bright, sparse, shadowless. She would admit it without any qualifications; Jetta was an artist while she was a hack, a hack who'd have to bang out three Harlequins a year just to keep afloat. It wasn't fair. Oh, fine, say that talent was something you couldn't just go out and get; say that it flocked to one person out of ten thousand, the way a bird lights on just one branch of an enormous tree; say that Jetta had it and that she never would, and yet—

And yet if she had the kind of independence, the endless free time that Nibs possessed, what couldn't she do? And what *did* Nibs do with all that money her father had left her? She lived on her own, had neither friends nor lovers, never went out except to the supermarket and the laundromat. But then, what could you expect from someone who hadn't even bothered with university? After St. Radigonde's, Nibs had gone back to Brockville to keep house for her doddering parents, sold their house once they'd both expired, and moved into that perfectly loathsome apartment on the outskirts of Toronto. Collie had quite lost touch with her old school friend until the divorce was pending, whereupon she'd made several swoop-and-seduce calls on dear old Nibs, who hadn't forked out so much as a nickel. Whatever could she be saving it for? Collie shrugged, then gave a little start. Why, she'd been perfectly stupid not to have let Geraldine come down for a week—they might just have hit it off. Was it too late to make Nibs a godmother?

Because they were three, they had to sit apart—Collie and Jetta together near the back of the bus, Nibs stranded beside a squat, severe Italian nun at the front. Collie and Jetta could see the familiar scarf (printed with horses' heads and shoes) pulled tight over the rusty-looking hair—they affected to hear the click of her needles, too. The fact that Nibs was knitting for her didn't dull Jetta's tongue. She had already explained to Nibs that banter and insults were forms of incontestable affection. "Besides, artists are never responsible for what they say or do—it's what they make that counts. Risk and be ruthless, that's my motto, Nibs. So don't mind my mouth, there's a darling." Nibs had smiled at this—she had very pink, rather squashy lips which always seemed to be smiling indulgently, even when Jetta had called her Moby Jane, or pretended to be Rubens, declaring that she "zimply had to paint ziss makkkniffficent vooman—zuch bowntivul vvvvlesh!" Collie had laughed till she'd cried, wondering, while she wiped her eyes, how far Nibs would let Jetta go, and if this was going to replace racquetball as their sport for the season.

But here on the bus Jetta didn't want to talk about Nibs. She too was irritable, but not toward Collie, who wasn't a worthy target for even the smallest bit of spleen. Jetta beat a tattoo with her thin black pumps on the metal floor; then, without lowering her voice in the least, she informed Collie that she wanted a man. "You know— the way you can want a beer. Just tilt the bottle, down it, and out the door. No games, no hearts and flowers, no caring and respect—just five minutes in a doorway, even. Christ, who ever thought I'd miss old Charlie like this. Charlie the tool."

Collie didn't join in the laughter. Charlie was eight years younger than Jetta, and had shared her apartment for the last three months. He had milky blue eyes, an endearingly broken nose (from minor league hockey), and even more endearingly, he thought of himself as a sculptor, though Jetta declared he'd be better employed on a construction site. Collie had fallen wildly in love with Charlie at Jetta's last party. She had sat on one arm of a huge black-leather wing chair, and he had sat down on the other, opened his mouth, and talked Jetta, Jetta, Jetta. Collie had invited him to St. B de B, even offering to pay his plane fare; when he'd refused, she'd asked Jetta and Nibs along, having got Charlie to swear he'd say nothing to Jetta—"it would hurt her too much." The silly sod had believed her. Charlie the tool, indeed.

"It's always like this when I'm painting—Jesus, if this bus doesn't get us to Menton in the next five minutes, I'm gonna leap through the window and fucking *fly* there." Jetta drummed with her heels on the floor, loud enough for the people ahead of them to turn round and glare at her. She looked right through them; natives poor enough to have to take public transportation were so many cubic feet of air to her. But now they were jolting into the heart of Menton, and Collie and Jetta had already leaped off the bus before Nibs had rolled up her knitting, secured her needles, and shoved the lot into her cumbersome, ugly bag.

They'd eaten their sandwiches in the bus, but Collie wanted something more than *eau de source* to drink, so they headed for a café on one of the main boulevards. Collie pinned her thick, tawny hair off her face, and Jetta began chain-smoking Gauloises, despite Nibs's anxious disapproval. "Yes, Nibsy, I know it can kill me, and you too, but hell, we all sucked in DDT with our mothers' milk, so what's the point of banning cigarettes?" Jetta had hiked up her skirt to show off her long, lean legs in their dead-white stockings—it wasn't fair that someone as short as Jetta should have such long legs, Collie reflected. The sun was directly overhead, like a great kettle boiling over onto her hair, her neck and nose. Of course she'd never even thought to bring a hat, never mind sunscreen. Jetta had slipped off her jacket, and was hunching her shoulders under the cut-out tunic, trying to look as tarty as she could. Heaven knew she didn't have to go to any extra effort. Nibs had her nose into her *citron pressé,* as if by doing so she could ward off the deleterious effects of secondhand smoke. "If I don't get away from these two, I shall have to scream," thought Collie. So she pulled herself up from the chair, marched off to the *pharmacie* across the road, and purchased a gross of sunblock and Lypsil that she stuffed into Nibs's bag, on top of the knitting. Nibs didn't mind the extra weight—what worried her was the man with whom Jetta had run off.

"He doesn't look at all nice, Collie—he was much too young. She wouldn't listen to me. I don't even think she knows what time we have to catch the bus back to St. B de B. And she can't possibly walk home in those shoes."

"Oh shut up, Nibs, and get out the map of Menton. Don't worry about Jetta, she'll swallow him whole—didn't she say she wanted oysters for dinner? Oh never *mind*. Now where's this Cocteau thing —I suppose we ought to see it, even if Ms. Post-Modernist seems to have lost her appetite for culture this afternoon."

The Cocteau museum turned out to be a toy fortress right on the promenade—there were some Picasso-ish things there, and a few interesting photographs, but it was hardly worth the bus fare into town, Collie complained. The lady at the desk thanked them for the largeish contribution to the acquisitions fund Nibs had felt obliged to make (admittance was free) and told them not to leave Menton without visiting the Salle de Mariage at the Hôtel de Ville—she even marked out the route on Nibs's map. Collie grumbled that it was in poor taste to drag a divorcée to a marriage hall, but Nibs insisted. She felt sure that Jetta would have come to her senses and be waiting for them there. Collie shrugged—it wasn't impossible that Jetta should be in the Salle de Mariage—five minutes in even the darkest of doorways would leave her with time on her hands.

Naturally, it was far more trouble than it was worth. First they had to find someone who would stop shuffling papers long enough to speak to them, and then they had to follow a troupe of tourists— academics on some sort of conference—into the marriage room. *And* listen to an English-language tape recording in which someone who sounded belligerently South African explained the symbolism of the décor. Kitsch, pure and simple, Collie decided, though she did approve of Cocteau's color scheme: blood red and pitch black. That leopard-skin rugs were splayed across the floor, and that the frescoes should depict Orpheus and Eurydice surrounded by stricken birds and brawling centaurs seemed in keeping with her own experience of matrimony. Stiltedly, the tape recording Englished the inscription: "Orpheus, turning his head, lost his wife and his songs. / Men became stupid, and animals, vicious." Collie couldn't help thinking of how she and Jack had accused each other of the most revolting things to try and secure sole custody of Geraldine, whom they'd ended up packing off to boarding school. She poked Nibs, who was staring stupidly at the ceiling as the voice bade her do if she wished to see Poetry astride a winged horse.

"Let's get out of here, Nibs. What does a faggot know about marriage, anyway?"

Jetta did not show up at the Hôtel de Ville, and Collie refused to let Nibs go off to the police to file a missing persons complaint. They went back to the café, where Collie had a Pernod and Nibs another *citron pressé*. "What *is* there to do in Menton?" Collie moaned, adding water drop by drop into her glass. "Don't you *dare* take out your knitting, or I swear I'll poke the needles up your nose. This isn't teatime at the Empress, you know!"

Meekly, Nibs put away her carpetbag. She suggested they go off and buy some postcards, but Collie hadn't time to reply before some twenty-five people—the same group with whom they'd shared the Cocteau—invaded the café. A gentle-looking man asked them if they'd mind sharing their table. He was British, by his accent, so Collie answered in English—"Help yourself. We'll be leaving any minute." The man and his companion, a woman who was Collie's age, but looked it, sat down at the little white table. They both ordered coffee, and the woman began to speak in a plangent voice.

"I wish we could have got into the house. You can't get any idea of what it was like from that miserable little cell downstairs. Besides, that was the servant's room."

"Yes, the old boy wasn't very accommodating, was he? I can understand that it's his home, and there *were* rather a lot of us—"

"And some of us come from New Zealand, chum. We don't get the chance to hop across to Menton every other week like you people."

The waiter brought the bill. Collie sat staring out at the bay, so Nibs paid. It was only three o'clock. What on earth were they to do with themselves in this dry, dusty, illimitably boring town? Collie was damned if she'd go for a walk on the beach. She was not an elderly Japanese or German tourist. And she'd left off work on chapter seven for this. . . .

The woman from New Zealand rose from the table: "That's the trouble with all this sun—you do nothing but drink and pee all day."

She had legs like sausages, Collie observed, watching her disappear behind a dirty glass door. Nibs was pouring another packet of sugar into her glass; her hair looked as fine as a baby's in the afternoon sun. Collie looked over at the faded, bearded man who was gulping down his coffee. Early fifties. Whitish, shiny band of skin round the fourth finger of the right hand. On his face, the unmistakably flattened look of the recently divorced. Perhaps it was an inexpressible relief at his companion's absence that made him turn toward Collie as she was adding up his firm mouth and bluebell eyes against the receding hairline and funny teeth she'd just subtracted. To her delight, he blushed. Collie shifted her shoulders so that the padded silk jacket revealed a fraction of the camisole underneath, leaned toward the empty ring in the table where a parasol should have been, and dropped her voice to its throatiest.

"Look, I hate it when total strangers barge in on my holidays, but I've simply got to find out, before I go mad. Is there *anything* to see in Menton besides that blood and thunder wedding room?"

The man blinked, as if unsure whether Collie was a mirage induced by the intensity of the espresso. At last he gave an undecided smile, and managed to reply. "I'm afraid there's very little, unless you're a Mansfield scholar. Katherine Mansfield, the short story writer."

"Oh, yes—a compatriot of that friend of yours with the weak bladder. I prefer Woolf, myself. Virginia. I wrote a perfectly unreadable M.A. thesis on *Between the Acts*."

"How very interesting."

Before long they were Geoff and Collie; Nibs had been ordered to get on with that damnable jersey and the New Zealander had cut her losses and joined another table. Geoff, who'd just ordered a double brandy, leaned in toward Collie, telling all about how Mansfield had spent part of a year at the Villa Isola Bella, just five minutes' walk away. She'd come, of course, because of her T.B. If she'd only stayed on she mightn't have popped off three years later in an unheated cow byre at Fontainebleau. The villa was sadly changed since Mansfield's time, of course.

"Isola Bella? That's such a pretty name. Our house hasn't got one—we're just 7 *bis,* rue Manette. I think houses should have names, if people are going to be happy in them. Don't you agree?"

This was Nibs's first sally into the conversation, which promptly died. Geoff coughed politely and made the motions preliminary to getting up, as though he, too, had to go off and pee. Collie swore under her breath, then asked Geoff whether he felt Mansfield really had influenced Woolf in the writing of "Kew Gardens." He settled back into his chair, and Collie's jacket slipped off her pleasantly tanned shoulders: Those chilly mornings on the terrace in St. B de B had been well worth it. Of course she'd sworn off men, men of all heights and weights and professions, the way she'd sworn off chocolate and red wine on account of migraines. But Geoff wasn't exactly howling at the moon, with his monologue on form and technique, and how Mansfield had transformed the very nature of the short story in English. Charming was the word for him, Collie decided; she would tell Jetta that she had met the most charming Englishman that afternoon, and that they'd talked about the art of short fiction over double brandies, under the most divinely scented pepper trees. Nibs would back her up—but then, that was the trouble. She had to get rid of Nibs, but without making Geoff think she was preparing the way for a pass. He wasn't the sort to make a pass, she felt. At the best they might manage dinner together before they got on their respective buses home. They might even exchange addresses; he taught at Cardiff, which wasn't exactly Cambridge, though Jetta needn't know. But what to do with Nibs?

Nibs, however, was shutting up the various scraps of jersey into her bag, smoothing and shaking herself in preparation for leaving the table. In what Collie would later describe as a miraculous access of intuition, Nibs asked the gentleman if he would be kind enough to point her in the direction of the Villa Isola Bella—she needed a bit of exercise.

"Eight-thirty at the bus stop across from the Hôtel de Ville," Collie shouted after her.

In her carpetbag Nibs had squashed the equine headscarf as well

as a windbreaker she had brought along just in case. She'd thought-
fully left Collie a tube of sunblock on the wrought-iron table. She
hadn't minded leaving the café—she had an excellent sense of direction; there was no worry about her not getting to the bus stop on
time. In fact, she'd been in a dither for the past half hour—was it or
wasn't it the right time to get away and start her search for Jetta?
She thought she'd been rather clever in making a visit to the Villa
Isola Bella an excuse for leaving the café. Collie would be furious if
she found out—Collie was jealous of anyone who cared more for
her friends than for her, and Nibs had had the devil of a time making
sure her attentions seemed balanced. Hadn't she just finished a car-
digan for Collie—hadn't she let them sit on the bus together all the
way up, instead of claiming a turn beside Jetta on the way to Menton?

Menton wasn't a big town, and it was such a beautiful day—who
would want to spend it inside? She went past all the outdoor cafés
and restaurants she could find, looking for a flash of white and black,
listening for Jetta's stiletto laugh. When she found them she would
go up to Jetta and pretend she needed to measure the jersey, see if
she'd made the back long enough. And she simply wouldn't go away;
she'd stick with them till it was time to get to the bus stop. She'd
never forgive herself if anything terrible had happened. Jetta, so small
and thin, so mushroom-pale in the mornings before she made herself
up. Collie had made a point of telling her just how old Jetta was—
not much younger than Nibs herself, if the truth be known. But Nibs
wasn't having a word of it—Jetta was a waif, a foundling, a stray—
she needed looking after, far more than Collie ever would.

In none of the cafés and restaurants was Jetta to be found. Nibs
walked part of the way down the sea front, but the sun hurt her eyes.
When there was no place else to go, Nibs found herself walking in
the direction of the Villa Isola Bella, the carpetbag heavier and
heavier in her hands, her stomach growling. She walked right past it
the first time—it was on a steep road next to the railway track, and
there seemed to be cars blasting up and down the hill every two
minutes, as if trying to frighten her away. Only when she had turned
round and was heading back to the center of Menton did she find the

place, her eyes caught by a plaque on a wall. Nibs crept up against the locked iron gate to read the inscription, but it was indistinct, too far away. She stood there, pressing her soft, scarred body against the railings, her eyes on the window, behind which there seemed to be nothing but an empty bookshelf. If only there were something to see, something she could describe to the others on the way home. But there was only a bookshelf, and cars roaring past, and the plaque whose lettering was too small to read.

It was Nibs who was late for the bus. Collie and Jetta, bless them, were keeping the driver from going off without her—though perhaps it was more for the fun of watching Nibs gallop, her bag banging against her thighs, her free arm waving frantically—like an ambulant octopus, was Jetta's description. Of course they ribbed and scolded her, and Nibs fairly basked in all the attention. She found a seat right behind them, and leaned forward to hear the account of how they'd spent their afternoons. Collie and Geoff had had supper at a marvelous little restaurant right near the Italian border; he was leaving for England tomorrow morning, but had asked her to look him up in Cambridge on her way back. Jetta, it turned out, had gone swimming. "Without a bathing suit?" Nibs couldn't help exclaiming. Jetta's shoulders shook. "Yes, my diddle-diddle darling," she'd replied, turning round to stroke Nibs's cheek. "In the Newd. Starkers. People do here, you know?" Collie asked her about her young *galant,* and Jetta had laughed. "Five minutes under a boat is worth fifty in a doorway," was all she'd say. Nibs sat back, relieved. Jetta was all right, Jetta was back safe and sound. Collie was smiling for the first time in weeks, and they'd waited for her—bless them both for waiting.

It was nearly midnight by the time the bus dropped them off. The women walked all the way up the hill in the light of a gibbous moon, Collie subdued, Jetta exuberant, Nibs lagging behind. One car passed them, but it was going in the wrong direction. As Nibs unlocked the front door of the house, Jetta declared herself exhausted. She went up to her room without another word, and just flopped on the bed—she didn't even bother to kick off her shoes. Nibs removed them so gently Jetta hardly stirred; she covered her with one of the scratchy blankets that came with the house, and then padded downstairs. Collie washed her face and hands carefully in a basin of well water that Nibs had hauled up that morning. Having already brushed her teeth, she refused Nibs's offer of cocoa, and fell asleep over chapter seven of *Love's Lady Lost*.

Jetta and Collie had peculiar dreams that night. In Jetta's, she had married Rudi after all. Tired of him, and missing Charlie, she had encouraged Rudi to have an affair with a plain, fortyish, muffin-headed acquaintance of hers. And Rudi had actually fallen in love with the woman—he walked out on Jetta and nothing could persuade him to come back. In the dream she tried everything; she was walking with him on a bare, heathy kind of place, pleading with him to return to her. Several times that night Jetta woke up in purest misery; her heart felt as though someone had hollowed it with a knife, scraped it clean inside. She would tell herself it was all a dream, only to fall asleep again into the same distress.

As for Collie, she dreamed that it was before the divorce; she and her husband were lying together in their double bed when Charlie had crept in. Her husband knew Charlie was there, knew that Collie was reaching out to Charlie, pulling him over her, but had said nothing. Then they were suddenly in Jetta's studio, Collie and Charlie, with Jetta gone, all her canvases turned against the wall. Charlie began to kiss her, and Collie was filled with the purest desire, as though her mouth were a sponge pressed into a pool of water, and could never soak up enough.

Nibs had no dreams that night. She drank her cocoa, and the mug she'd prepared for Collie, changed into her nightdress, and said the same prayer she always had, since childhood: "Please God, may there be no war and no fallout, and may everyone everywhere keep safe and sound, forever and ever, amen." To which she added, "Thank you for bringing Jetta back with no harm done, dear God." But when she got into bed she couldn't fall asleep. The moon kept shining in through the curtains, propping open her eyes with silver coins. Nibs lay back on the slightly damp sheets. She thought of Collie's daughter away at boarding school, unable to visit them here. She thought of Jetta's sunburned face and salt-caked skin, cocooned upstairs; she thought of her houseplants, cared for by her neighbor, Mrs. Trong. She had looked after them when Nibs had been in hospital, having the operation she had told no one about. She would bring back a little gift for Mrs. Trong—sachets filled with lavender and herbs, perhaps.

Her mother had kept lavender in the linen cupboard; all the years Nibs had spent at home she had slept not between sheets, but in a field of flowers. And here she was in France, where lavender grew like wheat, miles and miles of it. Lavender was not blue but purple; they had worn purple tunics at school—Collie said it made Nibs look exactly like a plum. Nibs befriended her because Collie was a new girl, from England; everyone else made fun of her accent. She had sold her parents' house to come and live in Toronto because Collie was there, but Collie hadn't bothered with her much, not until the divorce. She'd only come to France for Collie's sake. . . . But if she'd stayed behind, she would never have met Jetta. She knew Jetta would forget her once they all got back to Toronto—she knew that. She didn't expect anything of Jetta; she was just glad to have been able to look after her for a while. Except—she would have liked to have said yes when Jetta had asked to paint her, peeling onions by the kitchen sink.

Nibs sat up, threw off the covers, and pushed herself out of bed. She walked across to the sun-rotted curtains and tugged them apart, disclosing a smooth black square, like a brand-new blackboard. And then she drew her nightgown up over her head. Her body looked overly soft and abundant reflected in the window, like the flesh of a pear left too long to ripen. A pear with a brown spot cut out, a niche emptied, a lack. How could Jetta have painted that? Jetta didn't know. Jetta had run off the way she had because she didn't know the things that could happen—what could be taken from you, and never given back.

Carefully, Nibs attached her prosthesis and pulled on the jeans and sweatshirt she had worn for the excursion to Menton. Then she opened the kitchen door and went out onto the terrace. The mat on which Collie had been lying the previous afternoon had not been taken in; it still felt warm from the day's sun. Next to it a huge snail was tracing a glistening, sticky line. Light seemed to irradiate the shell, making it a replica of the moon itself: small, silver, lopsided.

Nibs settled herself onto the lumpy mat, hugging her knees and hunching her shoulders, as if she were protecting something hidden not very deep inside her. The word *precarious* came back into her head as she watched the snail spool and unspool itself across the stones; up and over the garden wall.

The Grandes Platières

It rained for the entire week the Kovacs had spent in the Alps, crammed into a one-bedroom apartment at the back of the resort. From their concrete balcony they had an unparalleled view of the giant parking lot, and if they cricked their necks and leaned out beyond the partition, they could just discern a bit of mountain. When Katie had memorized every article and advertisement in the fashion magazines that her mother kept threatening to incinerate, when her brothers were imitating fighter bombers, and her mother chipping calcified macaroni and cheese off the baby's highchair, Katie would pull on her raincoat and slip out onto the balcony for as long as ten minutes at a stretch. What she could see was a woolly mass of fog obscuring the edges of a sullen mountain pass. It looked like a smudged letter V out of a copy book. "You'll catch your death of cold," her mother would yell, hauling her back into the apartment for a supper of chicken noodle soup and liverwurst sandwiches—the only things they could afford, given the outrageous prices in the local shops. Katie would spoon up her soup and wonder just how you would go about dying of exposure, what it would feel like. It happened to people in Canada, of course, but not over here. Europeans were far more likely to meet their deaths outdoors because of lead poisoning—that's what her mother had said after their week in traffic-clogged London.

Intrigued by her mother's warnings, desperate for something even slightly out of the ordinary to happen, Katie would make regular sorties onto the balcony. And it was while staring out at the mountain pass one afternoon, rain dribbling down her glasses, that Katie heard the argument in the parking lot below. A tall woman in a white slicker with a blue and white polka-dot umbrella was standing by a car and calling to a girl about Katie's height. The girl was in the opposite corner of the parking lot, standing at the exact point where the asphalt gave way to a slope of sodden grass.

"Victoria Louise, come here! You will come here this instant!"

The girl's only response was to pull off her tam, which was woolen and couldn't be giving her much protection from the rain, anyway. She threw back her head so that her long black hair streamed almost to the pavement, then she opened her mouth as if to drink up all the rain that could ever pour down.

"I am not going to run after you—not this time. You will come here and get into this car, and when your father phones . . ."

Immediately, Katie recognized the admission of defeat. Hadn't she grown up hearing her own mother make the same threat, without paying the slightest attention? What, after all, could a father do, especially over the phone?

"Victoria Louise!" Katie could see the arm that held up the umbrella shaking, so that the polka dots began to blur. The girl at the extreme edge of the parking lot began unbuttoning her raincoat. Slowly she shrugged it off and chucked it down the ravine as though it were no more than a candy wrapper. Her eyes never left the woman's face.

"Very well, I'll leave without you. You can stand there in the rain. You can get pneumonia and end up in the infirmary for the rest of your vacation—or in a cemetery at Carrôz. Wouldn't that be a lovely ending to our little holiday?" The woman's voice had a lilt to it now, almost as if she were getting the same queer pleasure out of her words as the girl had had in pitching her coat down the ravine.

Katie flicked the rain off her glasses, using her index fingers as if they were windshield wipers; then she bent over the railing to get a closer look at what was happening. The woman was climbing into the car; the girl had turned her back. She had on only a cotton blouse and a pair of shorts. Both were slashed with rain.

"For God's sake, Katie, come inside—you'll catch your death out there. And it wouldn't hurt you to give me a hand, you know. Katie! Haven't you got ears? I said come *in*, can't you see I need help?"

"Okay, okay, I'm coming." But Katie kept on leaning over the railing, waiting. How could that girl be brave or stupid enough to just stand out there in the rain? Would her mother really drive off and leave her? But Katie never found out, because the woman's car, instead of revving up and whirling out of the parking lot, made a choking noise, then hiccoughed into silence.

"Katie, if you don't come inside this *minute*, I'll—"

The woman didn't get out of the car. The girl at the edge of the parking lot began shaking, not just shivering, and it was then that Katie made up her mind.

"Look, there's a lady down there having trouble with her car, and her kid's standing out in the rain. She looks like she's my age— couldn't we ask her inside to dry off?"

"People don't do that kind of thing over here, Katie—they're much more formal. Besides, the place is a pigsty—you still haven't picked up your pajamas from the bedroom floor, have you? Just come inside. They can get help from the garage, it's not far away. And it's a warm rain—"

"Then why did you say I'd catch my death?" Without waiting for an answer Katie shouted across to the girl, who was beginning to flap her arms to keep warm. When she heard Katie's voice, she looked up to the balcony, and waved.

Fifteen minutes later, Marjorie Kovacs was offering instant hot chocolate to Victoria Louise, who insisted she be called Vic. She was now dressed in a pair of Katie's jeans and a sweatshirt with "Ottawa, The Nation's Capital" in half-erased glitter over the front. The twins were thwacking golf balls off the bedroom walls, while Jimmy sat strenuously sucking the ear of a Gund rabbit. Allan Kovacs, down for the weekend from Geneva, was helping Sarah Carscallen to jump-start her car; by the time they'd climbed the five flights up to the apartment, so that Victoria Louise could be fetched and Marjorie thanked, Allan had discovered that the woman he'd rescued was none other than the wife of the man under whom he'd be working in two weeks' time.

Later, Marjorie and Allan would conclude that no one but Katie herself had been to blame for their curious acquaintance with the Carscallens. For the sake of retrieving a faded sweatshirt and a pair of jeans, all the Kovacs were asked to come for drinks next day at the Carscallens' chalet. "Of course it won't be any trouble," declared Mrs. Carscallen. Their chalet was perfectly equipped, even if they had decided to do without the maid this year. Two o'clock would be fine.

"Les Capucines" was carved into a piece of wood nailed over the front door of the Carscallens' chalet. "It means nasturtiums," Allan explained to Marjorie, who was emptying her purse out onto her lap searching for Jimmy's pacifier. He had started teething again this morning. Katie had been made to rub some medicated jelly onto his gums. Even without many teeth he'd managed to bite her so hard she'd had to have a bandage on her finger. Allan peered sternly into the car mirror.

"Stop picking at that Band-Aid, Katie—you're making it look as though it's been on for a month, instead of half an hour. And when did you last clean your glasses?"

"What are nasturtiums?"

"Katie, don't play dumb—you know how it annoys your father. Will you boys *please* shut up? If you're not perfectly polite during this visit you will lose your entire allowance for the rest of the month. And this time I mean it. Nasturtiums, Katie, are those red and orange flowers in the window boxes over the veranda. Oh, God, there they are—and underdressed, wouldn't you know it. *Jesus.*"

As they made their way toward the veranda, Katie hung back for a moment, imagining what her mother must appear like to the Carscallens. Marjorie was big rather than fat, and more than a little faded; her skin sagged from her bones. All in all, she resembled a sofa in urgent need of reupholstering. She wore clothes quite unlike anything Katie had ever seen in *Cosmopolitan* or *Chatelaine:* a white polyester blouse with frilled neck and sleeves; a bleached-denim skirt that had holes punched through the waist and laces pulled too tight, so that she looked like a domesticated Annie Oakley. Marjorie smelled of flour and milk, of Jimmy's sticky breath, and the Yardley eau de cologne the boys had given her for her thirty-eighth birthday the week before they'd left Ottawa for Geneva. In vain had Katie left her magazines wide open at the makeover sections so that her mother might pick up some useful hints. Marjorie remained resolutely "before," getting by with a splotch of blush and a splash of lipstick from a tube she'd had for as long as Katie could remember. Yet all the cosmetics in the world wouldn't have helped her today. For Jimmy had been up all through the night and the boys had woken early, complaining of sore throats. Dispassionately, Katie watched as her mother struggled up the veranda steps, Jimmy squirming like an octopus under her arm. She knew that Marjorie's feet, in their pointy-toed shoes, were, if not actually killing her, then applying some lingering form of torture to her toes—in the apartment her mother went barefoot or wore sneakers.

Allan was already up the stairs, greeting Vic, who was sitting curled up in a patch of shadow, her arms round her knees, and rocking gently back and forth. She was wearing denim cutoffs, an oversize T-shirt, and nothing at all on long and slender, positively dirty feet. Katie winced—Marjorie had made her wear a mock Tyrolean skirt and blouse. Mrs. Carscallen was sitting on the other side of the veranda in the uncustomary sun—she had on a bikini, cerise lipstick, and a pair of the biggest, blackest sunglasses Katie had ever seen. With her red hair knotted carelessly at the top of her head, tendrils like little tongues licking her cheekbones and the nape of her neck, Mrs. Carscallen could have been cut out of *Vogue* or *Elle* and pasted onto the veranda of Les Capucines. She didn't get up from her chair as Allan approached, nor did she invite him to sit down in the empty chair beside her.

Marjorie, the boys, and the baby remained huddled at the top of the steps. Obviously there had been some terrible mistake—all the more terrible because Mrs. Carscallen had made it, and didn't need either to acknowledge or correct it. Katie, who had joined her family at the top of the stairs, pushed in front of her brothers, and then stopped. Since coming to Europe her father had impressed upon her the criminality of staring or pointing at people. Yet it never entered her head to stop staring at Vic's mother. Imagine being the daughter of anyone as beautiful as this. Katie's sigh was audible—Marjorie poked her. Katie refused to step back. If only Mrs. Carscallen were her mother—she would bow to her slightest whim, follow her to the ends of the earth—

"Doesn't anybody want a drink? I'm *perishing* of thirst." This from Vic, who'd risen to her feet and was slopping—there was no other word for it—into the sunlit part of the veranda. "You'll have to help," she ordered Katie, who had no choice but to stop staring at Mrs. Carscallen and follow Vic inside. By the time they reappeared with trays filled up with tea things, a pitcher of lemon squash, several mismatched glasses, and a plate of biscuits, Mrs. Carscallen had thrown a white caftan over the bikini and moved her chair into the shade, though she kept on her huge dark glasses. Allan was in a wicker rocker, chatting, while Marjorie chased Jimmy up and down the veranda, trying to keep him from wedging his head between the slats. The twins had disappeared, looking for golf balls on the lawn. Vic took Katie, two drinks, and most of the biscuits to the back of the veranda, from which they had a view of Rossignol and the mountains beyond.

They sat leaning against the chalet wall, their knees drawn up under their chins. Vic's legs, Katie observed, were all muscle and bone, while her own were white and flabby, covered with fine dark hair that Marjorie had forbidden her to pluck or shave off. Vic's legs were bare and brown: her toenails filthy. "*She* wants me to put varnish on them," Vic said, observing Katie's glances at her feet. "I think it's stupid."

"Varnish? Isn't that something you put on wood?"

"Nail varnish, you idiot. She's always on about my looking like a lady—not that she knows anything about it. Look at her in that bikini."

"She's got a dress over it now."

"I wish I could throw a sack over her. I'd tie her up and dump her into the river. That's what Little Klaus does."

"Little Klaus?"

"In Hans Christian Andersen. You don't read much, do you?"

"I don't read fairy tales," Katie declared.

Vic stretched out her long, thin legs, and banged her knees together. "This is so stupid, sitting here. The first sunny day in two weeks, and here we are hanging round this rotten chalet, when we could be up there." She gestured with her empty glass to the top of the highest peak.

"Do you mean going up in that gondola thing?"

"Of course not—I mean hiking it. I've been climbing since I was three. I went up Mount Rundle in a backpack when I was a month old—my father took me. He's a fabulous climber—we're going to walk round Mont Blanc when he gets back from New York. You start off in France and walk right round the mountain into Italy."

"When's he coming back?"

Vic reached her hands up to her head, pulling her hair into a topknot. Long black strands escaped, curling softly round her face— for a moment she looked exactly like Mrs. Carscallen. Then she dropped her hands, letting her hair rush down over her shoulders. She spoke with a kind of violent indifference. "I was born in Canada, you know. I haven't been back since I was three. *She* says she'd rather spend home leave in Uganda than in Ottawa."

"Is she a model?"

"Do you mean a model bitch?"

Katie made no reply. She didn't like the way Vic talked about her mother. Frowning, she sucked in her cheeks, gathering them into folds between her teeth. Mrs. Carscallen had perfect cheekbones. Some models got their molars extracted so they'd end up looking as if they had the kind of bones Mrs. Carscallen had doubtless been born with. Quickly, she stole a look at Vic, who was staring up at the mountains again. She wasn't all that pretty, Katie decided. She wasn't so beautiful that you'd drop everything and stare at her the way you did at her mother. Vic had a sour, scowling look about her, and she was always slouching. She was terribly thin, even more so than Mrs. Carscallen.

"*She's* from Milwaukee, though she tells everybody she was born in Madrid. She says her father was a diplomat, but he was just in some boring old business—they rattled around all over the place. Just like us; we've lived in ten different apartments in the last six years. Are your parents sending you to school in Geneva?"

"I guess so. I mean, yes." Not that there'd been any choice; no one had asked her opinion about schools any more than they had about leaving Canada in the first place. At supper one evening her parents had told her they'd all be going off to live in Europe. They'd talked and talked about what a wonderful opportunity it was and wouldn't let her say a word until she took off her shoe and hurled it across the kitchen, denting the dishwasher. Then she'd been sent up to her room, and her mother had come in to talk to her. That was the worst part. Marjorie had said she didn't want to leave Ottawa any more than Katie did, but that it was Allan's big chance; if he passed it up he'd never be promoted again. Then her mother had hugged her so tight Katie hadn't been able to breathe. The whole thing had ended with Katie being led downstairs to apologize to her father and finish her cold spaghetti.

"You're lucky. It's not exactly brilliant, but it's better than boarding school. That was *her* idea. I only agreed to go because of my dad. He said he was counting on me. I hate it when he says that—it makes me feel like an abacus. One of those Chinese things. You don't know very much, do you, Katie? And how can you stand to be called

Katie—it makes you sound four years old. I'm going to call you Kate."

Katie had been going to say how she wished her parents would send her off to boarding school. She hated the confusion and crowding of her home, her brothers' Lego always underfoot, the continual panic about whether Jimmy had swallowed bits of this spaceport or that castle. She'd read books about wonderful English schools where girls named Miranda and Chloe spent endless hours riding ponies and sharing secrets in something called a study hall, which she pictured as being full of oak paneling, candle sconces, and stained glass. But she didn't want to contradict Vic. After all, she wouldn't know her long enough to be able to patch things up if they did start quarreling today.

Vic was drumming her heels against the weathered wooden planks. "She never lets me go up on my own—it isn't fair. I'm a better climber than she'll ever be; she hates the mountains, anyway." Abruptly, Vic drew up her legs, pulled herself round so she was looking Katie straight in the face. "I tell you what, you could come along. We'll go up together. I'll lend you a pair of hiking boots. What size do you wear? You can have Sarah's—my mother's, of course. They're brand new."

Even while Katie was mumbling excuses, Vic had run into the house, slamming the door behind her. Katie tiptoed round to the front of the veranda. Allan was perched awkwardly on a part of the railing free of nasturtiums. Marjorie was holding a fidgety Jimmy on her lap. Mrs. Carscallen—Sarah—lay back on her chair with her eyes closed. Katie found herself walking toward her, wanting to be near. But her mother called out to her.

"Where have you been all this time, Katie? Aren't the twins with you?"

"They're around somewhere." The back door slammed. Vic would be looking for her, hiking boots in hand. Katie positioned herself behind Marjorie's chair, holding tight to the wicker rim. "Want me to hold Jimmy while you get the boys?"

Marjorie smiled up at her, her mouth like a stitch pulled too tight. "That's okay, honey. I'm going to hand him over to your father— he needs a change. Badly. There you go, Allan. I'll get the diaper bag from the car."

Allan held Jimmy like a football under his arm. "As a matter of fact, I think it's time we got going. I'm sure you've got plans for this beautiful afternoon, Mrs. Carscallen." There was no answer, so Allan shifted Jimmy downwind, and tried again. "Isn't it grand to see the sun?"

Grand? Katie plopped into the empty rocker and stared at her sandals, examining the scuff marks. Since when did her father use words like *grand*? Maybe it was Mrs. Carscallen's influence; she had a British accent, even if she had been born in Milwaukee. Katie lifted her head to steal a look at her, only to find Sarah Carscallen staring back. Katie could feel her face burning; she was acutely aware of her glasses sliding down her nose, the lankness of her mousy hair, which she was trying to grow despite her mother's hints that a short perm would suit her best. Mrs. Carscallen's hair was gorgeously red and tumbled. When Marjorie didn't comb her hair it just looked messy, but Mrs. Carscallen—

"You two girls seem to be hitting it off."

Mrs. Carscallen was speaking to Katie. Singling her out. And then she did an extraordinary thing—she finally took off her dark glasses. Her eyes were emeralds: large, clear, not exactly warm, but—interested. Katie opened her mouth. No words came out.

"Katie's delighted to find a friend her own age, aren't you, sweetheart? There you are, Marjorie." Mr. Kovacs lodged Jimmy firmly into his wife's arms, from which the diaper bag dangled. "I was just telling Mrs. Carscallen it was time we pushed off. We'd better round up the boys, don't you think? Well, it's been—so kind of you to ask us round. Won't it be wonderful if this weather lasts? No more trouble with cars refusing to start, I hope."

"Here—try these." Vic had tramped round from the back of the chalet; she dumped a pair of hiking boots by Katie's feet. Then Vic saw Marjorie poised on the stairs, and Allan holding his hand out to her mother. "You're not going right now, just after I've lugged out these boots for her! Can't you leave her here? Oh please do—we're going hiking. Why can't she stay?"

Marjorie preempted Allan: "That's kind of you, dear, but we've imposed enough already. Besides, Katie's not dressed for mountain climbing."

"She can wear those things of hers I borrowed yesterday. Where are they, Mummy? Weren't we supposed to give them back?"

"How stupid of me—run and get them from your room, then." Mrs. Carscallen ignored Marjorie as if she'd never spoken. To Allan she remarked, "Your daughter's perfectly welcome to stay, you know. Actually, I was planning to get in some tennis later—I use the courts at Rossignol. I could take her back with me once she and Vickie have had their little stroll."

"Well, that's awfully kind of you. You're sure it won't be too much—"

But Marjorie was thrusting the soggy Jimmy into his father's arms, and clamping her hands on Katie's shoulders. "Sorry, Mrs. Carscallen, but it's just not possible. Our daughter's none too fond of heights, and she certainly isn't an experienced climber. Besides, I don't believe in letting my children run around strange places on their own."

"Then hadn't you better find those boys of yours, Mrs. Kovacs?" It wasn't so much the words, or even the tone of voice, but rather the slouch of Sarah Carscallen's body on the chaise longue, the carelessness with which she swung her dark glasses from her long, slender fingers. Katie could see how her mother was not only mocked, but utterly dismissed. She didn't know whether she felt more anger or embarrassment on her mother's behalf, but she did know she'd give anything to be able to learn this trick of standing people up against a wall and flicking knives to pin them there, exactly where you wanted them. Mrs. Carscallen uncrossed her legs, and leaned in toward the rocking chair. "What do you say, Katie? Would you care to spend the rest of the afternoon with us?"

Katie had meant to refuse. Her mother was right, she was scared of heights, and besides, she'd already seen as much as she wanted to of Vic. But Mrs. Carscallen had stretched out her hand and was gently lifting Katie's chin. All Katie could say was "Yes." And then, in the short silence that followed, "Please?"

"You *are* slow—I bet that baby brother of yours could walk faster."

"I didn't ask to come along—you practically forced me to."

"Oh, do shut up, we're nearly there. Want some chocolate to keep you going?"

"Yes—and a drink of water."

"You've already had far too much—this is supposed to last us for the whole day. You're supposed to take small sips, you know—*bouchées de montagnard.*"

The girls halted while Vic fished out the chocolate from her knapsack. "Here—it's melting, you might as well finish it. Oh, go ahead and sit down, if you want to. I'm going to scout on ahead—there may be a more interesting way up."

"More interesting" was sure to mean "harder." That first day— the afternoon of the tea party at Les Capucines—Vic had chosen an easy trail, one that led straight out into a meadow, where they'd found a small hut with writing carved onto its beams: *1822: Dieu Soit Loué: Jacques.* They'd sat on the sill, and dried out their boots; the grass, of course, had still been sopping with the last week's rain. Butterflies came to sun themselves on Vic's feet, wings yellow, azure, tiger-striped: taut as parasols. Katie had decided to pick a bouquet for Mrs. Carscallen. She'd gathered Queen Anne's lace, cornflowers, and a lily whose petals looked as if they'd been steeped in wine. It smelled horrible, but Vic wouldn't let her throw it away.

"That's a *Lys Madragon*—it's protected by law. You kill the whole plant just by picking the flower, so you'd jolly well better take it with you now. If you don't I'll report you."

Katie had known, then and there, that she and Vic were not going to "hit it off" in quite the way Mrs. Carscallen expected. The afternoon had ended as badly as possible. They'd taken much too long getting back to the chalet because of the blisters Katie had hatched from her borrowed hiking boots. Mrs. Carscallen had been cross—they'd made her late for her tennis—so Katie had stuffed her flowers into the garbage while Mrs. Carscallen was backing out the car. Vic hadn't seen; she was inside, fetching the bag with Katie's Tyrolean skirt and blouse. When she'd got back to the apartment she'd found that her father had rushed back to Geneva, that her mother had developed a migraine, as she always did after quarreling with Allan, and that the twins were feverish. The doctor had come round the next morning and diagnosed chicken pox. Marjorie had bought a gross of baking soda and spent the next twenty-four hours bathing the boys and waiting for Jimmy to come out in a rash.

When Mrs. Carscallen had stopped by next afternoon and offered to take Katie for a couple of days, Marjorie had capitulated. Katie, who'd had chicken pox when she was two, had offered to stay and help, but Allan, who had called, contrite, that morning, insisted his wife hire someone part-time from the Rossignol Children's Center. Katie, he said, was to get out into the fresh air and into more rewarding company. Later, her mother would stress how concerned and caring Mrs. Carscallen had seemed in her inquiries after the boys; how conscientious she'd been in describing the kinds of outings the girls would be allowed to undertake. So Katie had been packed off to the Carscallens' chalet with the warning that her father was counting on her to be polite and to do what she was told. That meant going for all-day hikes with Vic while Mrs. Carscallen played tennis at Rossignol or drove into Carrôz to go shopping.

Katie licked the last of the chocolate from her lips, leaned against a ledge of stone, and forced herself to look out over the gorge. She was standing on one side of that very V, all blurred with mist, that she used to watch from the apartment balcony. They'd begun this walk by going down from the Carscallens' chalet to a small lake; there were sheep and cows with bells tied round their necks making a dismal, disembodied sound as they wandered over the meadow. People were fishing by the rocks in water so cold it stung your fingertips. Vic had stopped to talk to one of the fishermen. She spoke

French as though she'd been born here. Katie came from Ottawa, but her French was terrible. It had come as an unexpected comfort to discover that Mrs. Carscallen couldn't care less about the language, according to Vic. "She won't even learn enough to be polite to people. When she has to speak French to the maid or a salesgirl you'd think she had something dirty in her mouth. I wish they'd just *spit* at her."

When Vic spoke like this, Katie would think of a gun firing at a mirror. She'd often grumble about Marjorie to herself; sometimes she even said angry things—but to her mother's face. What frightened Katie was that Vic and Sarah Carscallen never seemed really to speak to each other at all.

"My father's French is wonderful. He knows Italian, too. And he learned Cree when he was my age—he used to spend his summers up north. His parents had a camp in the Gatineau Hills. Of course I never saw it; my grandparents died before I was born. Now my father owns the camp—we're going to live there once I'm finished school. We'll go canoeing in the summer, and in winter we'll skate on the lake, and listen to wolves howling across the ice."

"There aren't any wolves in the Gatineau."

"There *are* wolves, my father told me. How would you know, you don't own a camp there, do you? You don't even have a chalet over here. All you can afford is that dump of an apartment—" Vic had broken off, furious. Katie couldn't think of what to say. Then Vic had bent to pick up a pebble, which she'd tried to skip over the lake. Katie had expected the stone to slide across the surface; the water had seemed cold enough. But it sank, after all.

Vic was grabbing Katie's arm, now—she started marching her up along a different path. "Come on, we've got to get moving or we'll never make it to the top by lunch. She wants us back for tea, but I bet you anything she'll be late—she always is. Stupid bloody tennis."

Katie stuffed the chocolate wrapper into the pockets of her shorts, and, turning her back to Vic, sat down to take off her sneakers, shake out the pebbles inside, and secure the laces with double knots. She was determined to waste as much time as she could. There was a scrabbling noise high overhead, and then she heard Vic calling down to her, urging her to hurry up and join her. Slowly, Katie lumbered up a zigzag path, finally reaching the place where Vic was waiting. There she sat, perched on a ledge jutting over the gorge, head thrown back to the sun. Over her shoulders hung the sweater that her mother had forbidden her to wear; tatty, miles too big, it belonged to Vic's father. Hair scraped back from her face, eyes screwed up, the clumsy hiking boots seeming to stub out her long brown legs—it didn't make any difference—she was unbearably beautiful.

Katie clenched her eyes as if they'd been fists. If she were to sit on that ledge and throw her head back into the sun—if she could get up her courage to crawl out onto a blade of rock and lie there, like Vic, as if she hadn't a care in the world—she'd still look like a lump of lard, a lump of lard wearing glasses. If only for an hour, for even five minutes, she could look like Vic, be Vic, she would happily die —yes, pitch herself into the glacier bed below. Vic didn't even care that she was beautiful—that was the worst of it. She didn't know what it was like to be locked inside a body you hated, a body that, however many pounds you carved off would never be anything but ugly. Beauty's only skin deep, her mother said, but it wasn't true. If you were beautiful the way Sarah and Vic Carscallen were beautiful, nothing could hurt you. You were singled out; you were born having already finished what everyone else spent their whole lives trying to begin. You were perfect, and powerful; you could do anything—

"Stop mooning about, Kate. Hurry up." Vic had leaped down from the ledge onto a steep path overgrown with weeds still slippery from the rains. Here and there a few madragon lilies rose up, fiercely conspicuous, as if daring passersby to uproot them. Katie opened her eyes, pushed her glasses back up to the bridge of her nose. It was no good. She would have to follow Vic, who was beautiful, who knew exactly where she was going and what was due to her. Katie stumbled going up the path—she wasn't allowed to stop and catch her breath.

"We're almost at the top," Vic called down. "Another half hour should do it."

Thirty more minutes. Katie knows she will die, she will choke on her own sweat, pouring down her face into the mouth she can't keep from flopping open. Vic has disappeared again. She hates Vic, hates climbing, hates the Alps, hates her father for making her mother send her off to the Carscallens', her mother for not being Sarah Carscallen. Hates herself for not looking like Vic.

Forty-five minutes later they had reached the top of the mountain—Vic dismissed it as a mere hill. On the ground lay an empty pack of Gitanes, the cellophane from a pack of biscuits, assorted bits of orange peel and tinfoil. "Stupid tourists," Vic complained, gathering up the garbage and squeezing it into her knapsack. "The French are beasts about littering. I can't wait till my father takes me climbing in the Rockies. We're going to Jasper and Lake Louise, where there are no people and no candy wrappers, just rocks and snow. I never want to go back to Mont Blanc. Millions of people, all crammed into this horrid room watching slide shows and waiting for the cable cars to take them down. The toilets are always blocked, so the whole mountaintop stinks. At least they haven't turned this place into a lavatory."

Katie merely looked away. Mountains ringed them, a stranglehold of rock broken by clouds no thicker than a feather.

"The *montagnards* used to think that angels lived up there." Vic gestured to the highest set of peaks. "And dragons, too. They thought dragons carved out caves from the snow."

Katie rubbed at a scrape on her leg; she was still panting from the climb. Vic took the water jug from her knapsack, uncorked it, and gave it to Katie. She sat down beside her, elbows like knives digging into her knees.

"I'd love to be a dragon, living all alone up there, with nothing but snow and rock, and mist frozen in the air. I'd have fights with the angels. They bleed differently from us, you know. Their blood's transparent; it's nothing but ice water."

She spoke so seriously that Katie put her hand up to her mouth —not to laugh, but to hide a gulp of alarm. She had a sudden image of Vic refusing to go back down; staying up here forever. She was afraid to look at Vic, she was stupidly afraid she might have changed into a frozen plume of cloud beside her. "Let's go—I'm tired," Katie forced out. Better not to say anything like, "Your mother will be waiting for us"—Vic would never come down if she heard that. So she tried again; louder, more clearly this time. "I'm cold and I'm tired, and I'm going back down."

Vic was lying spread-eagled on the ground, her blue eyes wide and still as autumn lakes just needled with ice. After Katie had spoken, Vic closed her eyes—for a moment, an hour, Katie could never remember how long. And then she'd shaken herself, sat up, and packed the water jug back into her knapsack. "I suppose I'll have to get you home," she said, jumping up, and without a glance at her companion, running down the path, all the way to Les Capucines.

"Victoria Louise, can't you think of anything but food?"

Vic was in the kitchen of the chalet, fixing a snack for Katie, who'd been starving at ten-thirty that night. But when Mrs. Carscallen came into the room, neither of the girls explained. Katie felt embarrassed about being hungry, and it seemed to be a point of honor with Vic to remain on the worst possible terms with her mother, even if it meant being shouted at for things she hadn't done. Except that Mrs. Carscallen never shouted; she used that clear, carrying voice Katie had first heard from the balcony at Rossignol.

"Bread and honey. Back to the nursery, is it darling?"

It wasn't fair. Not only was the bread and honey for Katie, but Vic hardly ate anything at all. It was Katie who wolfed down the sandwiches Mrs. Carscallen packed them every morning; Katie who ate a good three-quarters of the chocolate and oranges. Vic seemed to eat even less than Mrs. Carscallen, and Mrs. Carscallen lived mostly off a box of Ayds that was kept in the near-empty fridge. The only indulgence Vic allowed herself was the duvet on her bed—filled with swansdown, she told Katie; printed with gentians and edelweiss. A present from her father.

"I can't think how you're ever going to fit into your uniform. And you can't go back to school in shorts and a T-shirt, you know." Vic's face stayed perfectly blank; she kept lathering butter onto a slab of bread. Mrs. Carscallen stood watching as Vic took a huge bite, forcing it down a throat as slender as a flower stem. Katie blushed, the dark, splotchy sort of blush she'd inherited from her mother. Mrs. Carscallen didn't notice. She was addressing Vic.

"Your father called last night—I forgot to tell you. Something's just popped up at The Hague, something he says he can't get out of. He won't be able to join us at all, it seems. So isn't it nice that we've got Katie to share our little holiday?" Mrs. Carscallen turned to go back to the living room; she paused, and looked back at her daughter. "Oh, yes. He said to tell you he was sorry."

No response from Vic, who was letting honey drool down the spoon, back into the jar.

"Vickie? Did you hear what I said? Your father won't be back before you leave for school."

Vic picked up the honey spoon and put in into her mouth. She turned it round and around, till Katie thought she would twist off her tongue.

Mrs. Carscallen walked back into the kitchen, but not to Victoria Louise. Instead she came right up to Katie, who was sitting on a chair beside the kitchen table, trying not to look as though she was overflowing the small wicker seat. Mrs. Carscallen lifted her hand and just touched Katie's hair.

"You know, I'm so pleased that you and my daughter have made friends. You're such a sensible girl—you'll make sure that Vickie doesn't get into mischief, won't you, Katie? You will look out for her, I know you will." Mrs. Carscallen smiled down at Katie, her eyes like fields of green and glinting grass. There was a sharp, slapping noise. It was the honey spoon—Vic had dropped it onto the floor. Mrs. Carscallen bent down to pick up the spoon, gave it to Katie, and walked out of the room before the girl could begin to explain.

Next morning Vic was late for breakfast. When she finally lounged into the kitchen, Katie spluttered into her glass of milk. Mrs.

Carscallen looked up, registered the fact that Vic had cut off her hair to within an inch of her scalp, and returned to her magazine. The only sound in the room was the fluttering of the gas jet on the kitchen stove.

"I thought today we'd try the Grandes Platières, Kate." Vic drank half a glass of orange juice and nibbled at a triangle of toast. "You can see them from the veranda—come take a look."

Mrs. Carscallen spoke without raising her eyes from the page. "You're not going up there alone, it's much too dangerous. If you go anywhere, you'll take the trail to the lake and back."

"We did that yesterday," Katie ventured. She didn't want to go to the Grandes Platières at all; in fact, she would have preferred to lounge on the veranda, reading magazines. But after what had happened last night she felt obliged to stick up for this plan of Vic's, even though she agreed with Mrs. Carscallen.

"Oh, Mummy, I've gone up heaps of times before. You needn't worry, I'll make sure Kate's all right. We'll just look at the Platières —she'll be studying them in geography class, you know. At school in Geneva."

Mrs. Carscallen shut her magazine and frowned. For a moment, Katie could see the woman's skin not as an expanse of porcelain, but as something living, able to be scratched and scarred. Wires tugged the corners of Mrs. Carscallen's mouth. "Victoria Louise, do you understand? I am responsible for you and your guest. I said I'll not have you galloping over the Platières, and that is that. They're full of crevasses, and the last thing I want to have to do is pay for a helicopter to drag the two of you out. Do—you—understand!"

"Just as you like."

Three hours later the girls had halted by a ridge of tumbled rock on the verge of the Platières. They were looking down at Rossignol —Katie had her eyes on the reddish square that was the tennis court on which Mrs. Carscallen would be playing.

"Come on, Kate, don't just stand there."

Katie rubbed her forehead with the back of a sweaty hand. Mrs. Carscallen had asked her to keep Vic out of trouble—she would at least have to try. "I'm tired, Vic—can't we sit for a while before going down?"

"Who said anything about going down?"

"What else are we going to do?"

"We're going to cross the Platières and go down the other side —past the lookoff to Lac Vernant. There's lots of rhododendrons there, and gentians—you can pick as many as you like."

"But you promised—"

"I said, 'As you like.' Don't look like that. Can't you understand? Adults are such hypocrites. They keep telling us to act our age, but they can't stop treating us like babies. Don't worry, Kate, I'll get us across without a single slip. Just follow me—I've done it dozens of times."

Vic got to her feet and hoisted the knapsack onto her shoulders —Katie had offered to carry it once, but Vic had just laughed at her. The knobs of Vic's collarbones pushed up through her skin: each kneecap looked as big as a skull. She had refused the squashed ham sandwich Katie had offered her for lunch, and had only taken a square of chocolate, leaving Katie to finish the rest.

"Right, then," said Vic, stepping up and dislodging a few pebbles which rolled across Katie's primly crossed feet.

"I still think we should head down," Katie wailed, but more to a marmot that had appeared a few yards away than to Vic. Katie watched the animal for a few moments—it seemed paralyzed, but with watchfulness, not fear. Then it twitched its eyes, gave a warning whistle, and vanished.

The Platières were flat, the color of chewed-out gum. They looked, Katie decided, as though someone had sloshed a huge vat of concrete down the mountaintop. Every few feet the rock was fissured: sometimes a hairline crack, sometimes a gap of two feet or more. Vic would take running leaps over the largest, while Katie drew up short at the narrowest part of each crevasse. Taking a deep breath, she would step back and then shove her whole resistant body across. Vic could have crossed twice in the time it took Katie to pick her way over the Grandes Platières. She was beyond weeping or raging; all her energies were focused on this one thing, crossing each fissure, picking her way to the lip of the next, crossing that fissure, inching over to the next one and the next.

Some of them were deep enough to swallow you up entirely, or at least anyone as thin as Vic. She, Katie, would fall down and get wedged in a fissure, too ashamed to cry, while Vic skimmed over the rock, oblivious to what lay beneath. Katie shivered—there was snow all around them, and traces of ice in some of the gaps which they crossed. Unseasonable weather: all the rain that had turned the parking lot into a paddling pool had been blizzarding the mountaintops, burdening the wings of Vic's angels, icing the dragons' scales.

Katie clenched her fists and rocked a little on the edge of the last, and widest, chasm. She'd never make it—she knew she'd fall. Straightening her glasses or taking a few steps back didn't help; instead of heaving herself across the gap, she fell to her knees. Vic had warned her not to look down, but she couldn't help it—she had to know what it was she was expected to cross. Lying on her belly, gripping the edge of the rock, she peered down. For a moment she thought that if she looked long and deep enough she'd catch a glimpse of a horn or snout, the fire-flicker of a dragon's tongue. But the longer she looked at the fissure, the more it narrowed down to nothingness.

She knew she should get to her feet and jump across to where she'd be on safe ground. But she couldn't move. She didn't know anymore that it was possible to move, that there was any solid place on which to land. What if there was only this shallow, fissured rock over what wasn't even emptiness, since there was nothing with which it had ever been filled? Vic's angels and dragons—she wished she could believe they were here, fighting ice against fire, stopping up the holes in the rock with feathers and scales. But there were no dragons, and no angels, either—there was just this nothing.

A faint crack in the glassy air above her—it was made by someone calling out from the very end of the Platières. Still crouching, Katie turned her head and saw a small figure, no more than a stick drawing, wave her arms. And yet the girl was quite close—there was only this last fissure between them. Katie chewed at her lip and then suddenly heaved herself across the crevasse. Vic leaned toward her, holding out her arms. Katie felt her heart fizzling, a small blue jet, as Vic hugged her so tight it hurt. "You did it, Kate, you did it—I knew you could. You'll see, you can do anything now, anything."

Katie couldn't look at Vic—she stared down at her hiking boots instead. They were wet. She and Vic were standing, hugging, in a patch of snow. Katie shook herself free from Vic, crouched down, and made a snowball, pressing it tight so that she had a dirty, icy round in her hand. And then she leaped at Vic, scraping the snow over her face and down the back of her shirt.

Vic stood quite still as Katie did this—she didn't even reach to clear the snow out of her shirt, but left it there to melt against her. Suddenly, both girls began to laugh so hard they doubled over, gasping for breath. Until Vic grabbed Katie's hand, and the two of them lunged, shrieking and laughing, down the path to Rossignol.

Mrs. Carscallen was no longer on the tennis courts. The girls found her in the club lounge, having drinks with a group of people who were all speaking English. One of them, a tall, balding man, rose to his feet when Katie and Vic entered the lounge. He made them a little bow and called out, "Here are your poor lost lambs, Sarah. You needn't worry any longer." "Ugh," said Vic, not even bothering to whisper. "He's a Swede—they're the worst kind." "Worst kind of what?" asked Katie, but before she could get an answer, Mrs. Carscallen had collected her things and was marching them out of the lounge.

Katie had expected a tongue lashing, but all Mrs. Carscallen said was, "There's a good film on in town—I thought you two might like to get out for a change. We can have supper at the fondue place, if you like." They rode home in silence, Vic dozing off in the back seat while Katie concentrated on keeping her mouth closed and her knees together.

Once at the chalet, Mrs. Carscallen ordered them to scrub up and get decently dressed—"I won't have you looking like some goat-

kccpcr's child," she told Vic. Katie changed into her jeans and the
Ottawa sweatshirt, and her only pair of earrings, screw-on hoops—
her mother wouldn't let her pierce her ears. Vic wore gold keepers
in hers. She said they'd been done when she was still a baby.

Dinner was awful. Katie hated any kind of cheese except farmer
and Velveeta. She ate half of her salad, and managed to lose most of
her bread to the fondue pot, so that she wouldn't be obliged to eat
the gluey lumps. Vic barely touched her dinner. She sat back with a
frown cut into her face, and said nothing, leaving Katie to make up
a story for Mrs. Carscallen about how they'd spent their afternoon.
And as she told about the meadow they'd explored, the butterflies
and wildflowers they'd seen, Katie began to doubt whether she and
Vic really had crossed the Grandes Platières. Certainly the girl across
the table was not that Vic who'd held out her hands to her and helped
her across the last crevasse. And had she washed Vic's face with
snow—could she have dared? There was no time for dessert; all
through the meal, Mrs. Carscallen kept looking at her watch and
issuing warnings: they would be late, they'd miss the first ten minutes
and not have a clue what was going on. Perhaps that was why she
decided to drop them off at the door of the cinema, giving Katie the
money for their tickets. She said she'd be back to pick them up two
hours later. "Katie, I'm leaving you in charge—I want you to make
sure my daughter behaves herself."

Katie knew she was going to like the movie; it was an American
comedy starring an actor she watched all the time on TV at home. But
Vic shook her head at the poster inside the lobby. "I'm not wasting the
best part of the evening on that rubbish," she said. "Let's go."

"But your mother—"

"Don't be such a baby, no one will know. We can go to an
outdoor café and get back here for the end of the film. She won't find
out, and anyway, she won't care."

Katie persuaded herself that Vic was right. After all, nothing terrible had happened that afternoon; they'd been fine together. Once at
the open-air café, she even began to smile—it was a pretty place, a
square lined with what looked like toy trees, with a fountain in the

middle, and pots of flowers. Vic ordered ice cream with the money Kate should have used to purchase movie tickets. Their waiter looked at least thirty; he had a black mustache, and he swaggered with their tray, seeming to take twice as long to set down Vic's ice cream as he did hers. Katie couldn't blame him for trying to flirt with Vic. Even without makeup she looked older than fourteen. She'd washed her hair, or what was left of it—it framed her face like an inky halo. She didn't resemble her mother at all, Katie decided. Sarah Carscallen looked as perfect as a new sheet of paper; Vic, with the bitter blue of her eyes, her painful slenderness, was a match just rasping into flame. She refused to talk to the waiter, who lingered with the coins she'd slapped down on the table, speaking a French Katie was helpless to decipher. At last Vic crossed her long, brown legs under a skirt short as her hair. Fixing her glance on the fountain across from them, she said something in a tone of voice that even Katie understood: *"Va t'enculer."*

After that the waiter let them be. Katie polished off her ice cream while Vic sat looking out over the pollarded trees toward Mont Blanc. The last of the sunlight was playing on the stone, turning it gold and then pink, shades as delicious as those melting together in Vic's coupe de Cassis. Katie sighed and lay down her spoon inside her well-scraped bowl. It was time to get Vic back to the cinema. "Shall we go now—isn't it time?" Her words broke uselessly against Vic's silence. They sat there together, their little table like a patch of snow in the stream of talk and laughter running past them. When Vic finally spoke, Katie had to lean in across the table to hear her.

"Do you know the most wonderful thing I ever saw? I was flying from Geneva to my school in England—it was winter, and dark already on the ground. But up there, so high up you were above the clouds, and couldn't see a thing below—there was a whole other country. Chains of mountains, crusted over with snow, and such colors—you can't believe how beautiful they were. And you could have climbed them—they were frozen hard—if you stamped your feet against them they would ring like church bells."

Katie shifted in her chair. She felt fat and stupid after the ice

cream; she knew they'd be late if they didn't leave this instant for the
cinema. What would happen if Mrs. Carscallen arrived and didn't find
them? What if they had to walk back to the chalet—would Vic know
the way? Anxiously, she peered at the streets that bordered the café,
trying to decide which one would take them home.

On one of them, she saw Sarah Carscallen walking arm in arm
with the Swedish man from the tennis club, the one who'd called
them poor lost lambs. Katie couldn't say a word—she reached out
and touched Vic's hand, then pointed out the couple as they reached
the end of the square, turned the corner, and disappeared.

"What's happening?" Katie whispered.

"I don't know what you mean."

"Didn't you see them—"

"I didn't see anyone I know." Vic turned her face back to the
mountains, staring at the flush of evening sun over the rock. But
someone pulled a switch, and suddenly the mountains went out: gray,
dead, dry as old bones. Vic rose quickly from her chair. "We'll have
to get back now—she's probably on her way."

Katie was dreaming of angels racing round mountaintops as soft
and insubstantial as a coupe Chantilly when their voices woke her.
She'd been put in the guest room, across the hall from Mrs. Carscallen's room. Katie had left her door ajar, and a long stroke of yellow
light interrupted the darkness. Silently she padded to the door and
peeked around. She could see nothing but a similar stroke of light
arrowing from Mrs. Carscallen's door. But she could hear them all
the same.

"I'm going to phone him right now and tell him—"

"Tell him what?"

"You know what."

"All I know is that I'm stuck in this godawful chalet while he
flies off anywhere he damn well pleases. Oh, yes—I know that he's
the one who promised you we'd spend our holidays here. Why don't
you ever try blaming him—why don't you play your little tricks on
him for a change? Just what do you think he's doing off in The

Hague, or whatever's turned into his latest excuse? Do you really think he's reading reports all night in some embassy office?"

"It's your fault he won't come back, it's all your fault."

There was a small silence, and then Mrs. Carscallen began to speak: slow, sad, gentle-sounding words you could almost have mistaken for a lullaby. "I think you really work at being stupid, don't you, darling? Just what do you think would happen if you phoned him now—assuming you could get hold of him, that is. Do you think it would matter to him what I was or wasn't doing here? Do you think he'd drop everything and fly back—to rescue you? You care too much. You shouldn't, you know. It's best not to feel very much of anything. That's the only way to get by. You'll find that out before too long, if you haven't already. Your father—"

"Shut up about my father, shut up will you please—shut—up!"

Katie hadn't time to get back from the door before Vic ran past, but she needn't have worried. Vic had been in no condition to notice anyone.

Voices carry in the mountains; anyone could have heard Vic shouting out to Katie, discovered what the two of them were setting out to do, and tried to stop them.

"It's not going to get any sunnier, don't you understand? Come on, we can get to the top before the mist closes in, I know we can. Hurry up, Kate—you should be able to skip all the way up after that ice cream you polished off last night."

Katie couldn't help herself—she began to cry. Vic had started up the path, and was threatening to disappear. She'd announced, at breakfast, that today she was going to take Kate up Tête Pelouse. Katie had replied that she wasn't feeling well, that she wasn't in the mood for a climb, and that really, she preferred to go back to Rossignol—her mother would be wanting her by now. Katie had directed these words at Mrs. Carscallen, who'd been sipping black coffee out of a china cup and reading *Vogue*. She hadn't looked up from her magazine; she didn't seem inclined to recognize the existence of either girl, never mind their quarrel. Katie had decided then and there that she had better pack up her things and walk back to the Rossignol apartment, since no one was about to offer her a lift. But she knew that even if she could find her way home, her mother wouldn't know what to do with her. And her father would be furious when he learned that she'd behaved so badly with the Carscallens.

Here she was, then, at the foot of Tête Pelouse, after a long and shaky gondola ride. Vic had stopped ahead to let Katie catch up with her. You were never to go climbing alone, the guidebooks said; you might break your leg or be knocked unconscious, and how would you be able to call for help? Katie shivered and looked up into the sky. The good weather seemed to have vanished; the sun was just a silver disk, slicing in and out of the clouds. Clumps of snow lay on either side of the track—and here she was wearing sneakers and cotton socks. Mrs. Carscallen hadn't said a word about canceling this expedition—perhaps it wasn't supposed to be dangerous? Vic had grabbed her hand and was tugging her up; she had to follow her, or else. Or else—

They stopped at a bend in the path so that Vic could pull on her old gray sweater. That and a pair of woolen socks tugged up to her knees were the only concessions she'd made to the bitter weather. A party of hikers passed them by, returning to Rossignol—they called something out, but Katie couldn't catch the words. When she asked what they'd said, Vic replied, "They say the view's terrific from the top."

"What view?" Katie blurted out. "There's mist coming down over everything."

"Oh, it goes as quickly as it comes. You'll see."

Sure enough, by the time they reached a lookout point they could locate three different mountain ranges: white, calcareous, the way the moon looks when it's just a thin white rind over the morning sky. If you walked to the very edge, which Katie refused to do, you could see Lac Vernant, or so Vic insisted. They found a sheltered spot in which to picnic, in the overhang of a brute, black rock. From here there was a last bend in the path—after half an hour's walk they would reach the summit. "You'll be able to see Mont Blanc from there if it stays clear."

"And angels and dragons fighting it out on the very top, no doubt."

Vic shrugged. "You might. If your eyes were good enough."

"Aren't you even going to eat some chocolate?"

"I'm not hungry. Go ahead and finish it."

Katie shook her head. "You've got to eat something, Vic, it's not healthy. You'll get ill, starving yourself like this—"

"Shut up." Vic spat out the words, exactly as she had to her mother the night before. She curled her head down, so that her eyes were hidden by her knees; her thin shoulders shook under the awful sweater. Katie rubbed her hands miserably together, trying to warm them. Vic didn't move. Hesitant, Katie put her arm round Vic; it was more of a support than an embrace. "I'll have to watch it, Vic. I'm starting to sound like my mother."

She felt Vic's shoulders heave—she didn't know what she should do. Her mother always said that when someone got hurt the best thing was to take her mind off it, distract her—then the pain would go away, at least until she could handle it. So she withdrew her arm, and in the most commanding voice she could muster, asked, "Vic, will you tell me something?"

Vic didn't raise her head, but her shoulders stopped shaking, and at last she answered. "What?"

"When you—cut off your hair. How—I mean—What did you do with it?"

Vic pulled herself up, looked blankly at Katie. "I flushed it."

"Flushed it—?"

"Down the loo." Vic closed her eyes for a moment, then opened them. The shadows underneath made them look black-blue, like gentians. Vic smiled, and Katie thought of a glass with a long, curving crack through it.

"Listen, Kate. Shall I tell you a rhyme they say at school in Geneva? It goes like this:

Make friends, make friends,
Never, never break friends,
For if you do,
I'll flush you down the loo.

Now you'll know just what to say when you get there. Come on,
then—stir your stumps. We've still got a good climb ahead of us."

But even as they were packing up their water jugs and pocketing
the chocolate wrappers, the mist dropped again—exactly like a dirty,
sodden towel, shrouding the mountains, the nearby rocks, their very
faces. Vic shuddered. "I should have brought an anorak."

"Anorak?"

Vic didn't explain. "Bloody mist—look at it—if you can see to
find it. I suppose it wouldn't be the cleverest thing in the world to
press on—we can always try tomorrow."

Katie couldn't believe the good sense that Vic was showing—
now they wouldn't have to waste an hour arguing over whether or
not to go on ahead. They started down in the direction of the gon-
dolas, not talking much, moving as quickly as they could to keep
warm. There was a point at which the trail forked—they could go
back the way they'd come, or take the other way, a path Vic at once
declared a short cut, and besides, far more interesting. Of course,
Katie knew she should have insisted they go back the same way
they'd come up.

For years afterward, whenever her mother wanted to point out
her shortcomings in the area of common sense and basic prudence,
Marjorie would refer to precisely this moment of the expedition to
Tête Pelouse: "Katie, Katie, I'd have thought you'd have learned
something from that time in the Alps." And Katie would never be
able to say just what she had learned, climbing with Vic that day.
Could she have changed Vic's mind about trying a new path down
the mountain? Hadn't they crossed the Platières together, safe and
sound, in spite of everything? She'd known by Vic's eyes how tired
she was—she couldn't have slept at all the night before. Usually Vic

walked miles ahead, but there she was jolting along beside her. And it wasn't Vic but Katie who'd been the first to see the ice blocking their path, blanking the hillside down to where the track wound round again.

"We'll have to go back," she'd told Vic. "We'll have to go back up and come down the other way." She was certain she'd said this, and just as certain of Vic's reply.

"Rubbish. It's too late for that. It's going to snow—look at those clouds."

Katie had looked; they were almost black, where a moment ago they'd been the color of porridge.

"I tell you what. We'll slide down to where the path comes out below. It'll be easy—it'll be fun, Kate, like tobogganing. I'll go first —I'll catch you when you come down."

But in the end it was Katie who caught Vic, caught her up in her arms from the little gully to which she'd rolled after striking the path below. Katie had burns on her palms from where she'd clutched at the ice, trying to slow her fall, but Vic's hands hadn't a scratch on them. They'd kept on and on at her about what had happened, asking whether Vic had jumped or fallen off the hill, and whether she'd hit her head on the way down, or only when she'd rolled off the path against the rocks. How could Katie have told what Vic had meant to do, and what had simply happened? "She said it would be fun—she said she'd catch me," were the only answers Katie gave.

A doctor had arrived with the rescue party sent by the hikers who'd spoken to Vic on her way up Tête Pelouse. The doctor had said that Katie was in shock and that they should stop all questions till she got over the accident. Katie couldn't say whether she ever did get over it, since years later she still couldn't answer for Vic, at the top of that sheet of ice. She certainly hadn't been able to answer her parents or Mr. Carscallen, who'd flown in all the way from The Hague to attend to matters, as Katie's parents had phrased it. Marjorie didn't speak to Allan for a week afterward, except to say, "I knew we shouldn't have let her go off climbing like that. I told you it was dangerous. My God, it could have been our child, it could have been Katie."

As for Mrs. Carscallen, she was the only one who didn't ask any questions at all—not at the hospital, nor on the day the Carscallens closed up Les Capucines and returned to Geneva. They'd come to pay a formal call on the Kovacs, who were themselves in the process of packing up—Allan had finally found a suitable apartment in the city. The Carscallens stayed only for a moment. When Katie saw them together, standing side by side, she felt a tension between them, strong as the rope with which climbers lash themselves together, going up the sheerest cliffs. Mr. Carscallen wore a suit, as if he were attending a business meeting. His eyes were brown—Katie had thought they'd be black-blue. He said they knew Katie had done everything possible for their daughter—that they appreciated how brave she'd been, and what a terrible time she'd been through. He said, "Thank you," and then he suddenly stopped speaking, as if he'd forgotten language altogether. Mrs. Carscallen didn't say anything. Her face was blank paper; her eyes were glass.

Once they'd gone, Katie assured her parents that she was all right, just a little tired. She'd gone back to the bedroom and lain down on her bunk. Shutting her eyes, she'd tried to picture herself leaping across a plain of fissured rock, racing so hard she would at last spring off into the air, holding her arms the way a bird holds its wings, soaring. But always she stopped short on the lip of each crevasse, crawling forward, hanging her head down. And whether she closed or opened her eyes, what she saw was always the same: a vast gap, narrowing down to nothing.

The Amores

In her dream she is at a railway station, an old-fashioned place with a glassed roof and wrought-iron pillars, the kind she can just remember having known in Hungary. Only she isn't a little girl, but her present age, seventeen—which makes it all the stranger that she should be dressed in a child's tam, an embroidered woolen coat whose full skirt finishes high above her knees, and ankle socks with lace-up leather shoes. In one hand she is holding on to a small suitcase, much too small for the things she will need on such a long journey. For in her other hand she grasps, as firmly as she can, a ticket the size of a blackboard, bearing an endless list of the stops she will have to make before she arrives at a destination whose name she hasn't yet discovered. A conductor leans out from the train, urging her to board before she makes the whole party late. She tries to explain that she can't leave until her mother has come to embrace her and say good-bye. Her mother is always late, so in this dream it does not occur to her to think that Marta might have forgotten, or worse —decided not to come at all. Pigeons wheel under the metal rafters, making a noise like soft thunder as the conductor starts to shout at her, shouting and shouting. He reaches down to pluck at her arm; the train begins to push out just as she catches sight of her mother running, wearing only a slip and bedroom slippers, so frantic has been her haste to come to her. And then, somehow, Anyès has jumped aboard, slamming the compartment door so hard that the conductor, still reaching out toward her, tumbles down to the platform. Always, it is the scream of his whistle—furious, bereft—that wakes her as the train smokes away.

High on the walls of Miss Vance's classroom lay an ample cornice, on which lodged her pupils' monuments to their teacher's indestructible enthusiasm for her subject. A model of the Forum, columns manufactured from white-painted corrugated packing paper; papier-mâché replicas of shields and amphorae; plasticene reproductions of figurines and jewelry; and a copy, one foot high, of the statue of Caesar Augustus reproduced on page ninety-seven of *Living Latin*. Dust furred the replicas. The columns of the Forum had begun to crack under the Caesar's cross-eyed gaze and warning finger, but the effect of the whole remained inspiring from ground level, especially to the superintendents who came on their yearly rounds to assess what contribution the study of dead languages made to the acquisition of knowledge and school spirit.

You can learn everything you need to know in life from Latin and the Bible, Miss Vance could have told the inspectors—did tell each crop of students whose lot it was to learn every week a new declension, conjugation, item of vocabulary. To this day, many of those students who have gone on to become doctors, accountants, social workers, even school principals could, if ordered with the rap of a pointer to a blackboard, reproduce *bellum, belli, bello; amo, amare, amavi, amatum,* spurred into unwonted accuracy by the presentiment of Miss Vance behind them, Miss Vance with her short gray hair—clipped, not cut; her spectacles restraining the overbright, overround eyes that seemed like fluorescent tennis balls glowing in darkened courts. She wore straight skirts and tailored cotton blouses over breasts both enormous and flattened. Mannish, they had called her; an apparition of white and gray, with lisle stockings and lace-up shoes supporting legs that bore her up like pale, tapered columns under the massive weight of some temple roof.

Julia Vance, Anyès had learned from the flyleaf of a volume of the *Aeneid*—Miss Vance's own copy, through which Anyès had been allowed to leaf while her fellow students were still gnashing their pens over *arma virumque cano*.

"To my daughter Julia, as a reward for proficiency in her studies, with the hope that she may learn from the immortal Mantuan the sublime value of selfless service. Edward Archibald Vance." Miss Vance had often told her students about her father, his ministry, and the travels father and daughter had undertaken before the Reverend Edward Archibald had expired—not lingeringly, self-indulgently, but in his customarily efficient way—from a heart attack after Sunday service, lunch with the Missionary Society, and an afternoon spent reading *The Presbyterian Herald*. She had shown them slides of the Reverend Vance standing beside a Celtic cross somewhere in County Kerry, and next to Vergil's monument, the one erected in Mantua. He was a large man wearing a peculiarly rigid fedora and a dog collar that made you think of the spikes bulldogs wear round their necks, such severity of starch did it betray.

"We didn't care a hoot for Mantua," Miss Vance had said in her loud, eager, yet authoritative voice. "Or for Italy, if it comes to that." And she had left the image of her father—his hand outstretched to the verses engraved on Vergil's monument—imprinted on the screen while cautioning her students about the inevitable shock they would feel if they were ever unwise enough to try to travel to the land of Caesar and Cicero and Publilius Syrus. "The only ticket there," she'd bellowed, thumping a copy of *Living Latin*, "lies in these pages."

She had been looking at the entire class when she'd begun her peroration, but on pronouncing *pages* fixed her eyes on Agnes Sereny, who was sitting with her small feet primly together, her hands clasped on the desktop, her eyes fixed on Miss Vance's in an expression that might have been fear or reverence or perhaps just the desire to produce whatever it was her teacher wished to see reflected there.

Shining in Miss Vance's eyes was a mixture of encouragement, admonition, and something she would not name. Stern, solid, selfless was Miss Vance's life, as befitted the daughter of such a father, a daughter who had lost her mother and shouldered responsibility for her father's well-being at an age when most girls would have stopped playing with dolls and started to become them.

Yet in this, the fifty-third year of Miss Vance's life, the thirtieth year of her vocation, she had discovered herself capable of something she feared was love. Not the passionate obedience she had shown her father, but rather, his own need to seize and shape and control the beloved; a desire to possess, not the girl's affections, but her very nature. Had Miss Vance's knowledge of the classics ever flooded those watertight compartments into which she'd deposited the rules of grammar and the laws of style, she might have had second thoughts about the story of Pygmalion, or at least about Venus's role in the whole affair (Miss Vance could never remember the name of the marble woman come-to-life, but then you weren't supposed to—she was hardly the point of the story). As it was, she focused on the fact that Pygmalion had gotten everything he wanted—it was one of the rare myths that ended happily.

She had taken Agnes to heart from the very first class. Perhaps it was nothing more than that the girl's name and her appearance went so fittingly together. Agnes—Miss Vance pronounced it with a hard *g*, even though she knew the girl's mother said Anyès, the way the French do, turning the very softness of the letter into an endearment. *Agnus*; the kind of hair that was not blond but white, an impossibly pure shade that always looked as if it would melt should you touch it. A body not short (that implied a defect) but small, and skin fresh, full—as if it would spring back at your touch. Round, brown eyes; not deep, not dark, but light and clear. Sweetness, whiteness: "Lamb," Miss Vance would have called her, had she ever descended to endearments. There were aspects of Agnes's life, however, which obliged Miss Vance to treat her not as a pet, but as a child. Her own.

One of these aspects was the girl's undoubted ability as a Latinist. Whereas her classmates, however brightly they began their five-year

immersion in the Latin tongue, ended by balking at the endless ex-
amples and exceptions to be memorized before each class, Agnes
seemed to need them the way you do ground under your feet in order
to stand up. On her face would appear an expression of utter serenity
when she was construing difficult phrases. She didn't find Caesar's
accounts of the Gallic Wars at all tedious; she positively glowed
when they tackled Vergil in the senior grades, and she'd shown herself particularly adept at translating the few, rigorously selected passages of Ovid to which Miss Vance allowed her students access.
(Catullus and Petronius were, of course, so far beyond the pale they
didn't exist, even up on the dusty, distant cornices of Miss Vance's
classroom.)

But this unusual aptitude for Latin in an age when all but the best
schools had axed that subject from the curriculum was not the deciding factor in Miss Vance's adoption of Agnes. It was rather the necessity the teacher felt, faced with her pupil's background and
environment, to be more than an academic instructor. In the first
place, the girl was Hungarian. There were certain foreign races—the
French, the German, even, precariously, the Italian—which Miss
Vance could accommodate in her conception of society. Though of
pure Scots-Irish stock, she did not hold with those who would not
acknowledge the existence, never mind the virtues, of those who were
not Anglo-Saxon as well as white and Protestant. But she drew the
line at certain sure points. She warned her senior pupils against applying to University College, for example, because there were—so
many Jews who went there; an Oakdale student would be much better off at Trinity or Victoria. And when it came to ethnic groups who
didn't possess recognizable alphabets, whose language even the most
rigorous phonetics could not decode, Miss Vance proclaimed not defeat but disgust.

About the Serenys she had obtained all necessary information.
Agnes and her parents had escaped from Hungary after the uprising
—that gave proof of endeavor, fortitude, however distastefully dramatic to Miss Vance's eyes. The family had established itself in a
split-level suburban home some ten minutes' walk from Oakdale

School; this was all unexceptionable. But a few years before Agnes made the transition from junior to senior high school, Mr. Sereny— a pharmacist with his own shop downtown—had gone bankrupt and died in much too quick succession. The suburban house had been sold, Agnes and her mother moving to one of the new and crudely built apartment towers that were springing up at the extreme edge of the municipality, disfiguring a skyline that previously had only to deal with immature blue spruce and maple trees. The apartment tower smelled of boiled cabbage and suspicious spices, one of Miss Vance's junior colleagues had told her—he'd been there looking for accommodation soon after his appointment to the school and had wisely decided to lodge elsewhere. Not, however, in the low-rise, respectable apartment house in which Miss Vance lived—across from the shopping plaza, it is true, but screened by a high wall of impenetrable shrubbery.

That shrubbery protected Miss Vance from more than the sight of leather-jacketed, cigarette-spouting loafers at the plaza five-and-ten. It allowed her and the other tenants of Oakdale Manor immunity from the kinds of activity that went on in less reputable buildings than their own. For the same colleague who had rashly gone one Saturday morning to inquire about renting a bachelorette at Oakdale Towers had witnessed, right in the lobby, an embrace between a young, badly dressed, foreign-looking man and an older woman whose too-short skirt and whose hair—peroxide-platinum—gave her away as none other than Mrs. Sereny, whom the teacher had encountered only days before at a Home and School meeting. Luckily, Agnes hadn't been anywhere near the lobby—hopefully, might not even have been in the building, since the most scandalous thing about the whole episode, as Miss Vance understood it, was that the couple was obviously coming down from the apartment where they had spent time—perhaps the night—together. There had been a certain something about the way they clung together in that most inhospitable lobby, with its hard, narrow benches drawn up in a travesty of intimacy around a fake rubber plant. But at this point Miss Vance had silenced her informant with a look that went like a pin through a finger.

The next afternoon she had talked to the girl while everyone else was belaboring a tricky passage assigned as an impromptu translation exercise. Agnes, for whom the passage was no more difficult than the riddles on bubble-gum wrappers, sat at the long table at the back of the classroom, working on a papier-mâché model of an aqueduct. Miss Vance watched her silently tearing strips of newspaper and then abruptly asked whether she'd decided to which universities she'd apply at the end of the year. Agnes had neatly piled the strips of newspaper, tightened the lid of the glue bottle, and finally replied in her soft, unaccented, yet not quite Canadian voice, that she'd never thought of going on to university. There wasn't the money for that; she had her mother to think of; she would get work as a salesgirl at one of the shops in the plaza, and take a secretarial course at night, and with the two of them working they could afford a larger apartment. Miss Vance had smiled. Then the buzzer rang; obediently, Agnes went back to her seat and left the classroom with the others.

That evening Miss Vance had checked the syllabus of her alma mater, a small liberal arts college in New Brunswick that had the reputation of turning out excellent classical scholars. On page eighty-two of the syllabus she found, among a list of entrance scholarships, exactly what she wanted: the Charles Maltman Award for Classics, to be bestowed upon a student whose exceptional ability was matched only by his or her financial need. There were even provisions for the student's being given summer employment tutoring deserving high school children from the local town. Miss Vance had lain awake till nearly two, plotting a campaign that would remove Agnes forever from the stink of boiled cabbage and immorality in her mother's apartment.

The Serenys' apartment smelled most often not of boiled cabbage, but of chicken paprikash, poppy-seed strudel, brandied plums. For Marta Sereny, having sold the suburban split level to help pay her husband's debts, met the rent on the apartment at Oakdale Towers by acting as cook at the Hungarian Village, the plaza restaurant—overlarge and funereally underlighted. Anyès and her mother invariably dined off leftovers that Marta took home in aluminum baking dishes and small Styrofoam containers. The Hungarian Village was perpetually on the verge of folding, except that the owner, a Mrs. Lampman, who lived in Rosedale, operated the whole affair as a tax write-off and was rather fond of Marta Sereny and that sweet, small, pale daughter of hers, who waitressed on weekends, reading whole books between customers.

Mrs. Lampman occasionally came to lunch at the Hungarian Village; over coffee and dessert she would listen to Marta's fears and hopes concerning her daughter. It wasn't healthy, all this fussing with a dead language. Surely she ought to be taking something more practical, like typing and shorthand—things that would give the girl a chance in life, a chance at meeting the right sort of men—doctors, lawyers, businessmen, pharmacists. Worst of all, *that* woman was trying to turn the girl against her own mother, though it would never work; Anyès always told her everything, they were that close—and Marta had held two rosy fingers, pressed together, inches away from Mrs. Lampman's eyes.

Mrs. Lampman went on stirring too much sugar into her tepid coffee as she listened, thinking how old Marta looked. Her face was like a map that had been creased and opened far too many times; she looked tired in the same way as do small children who've been allowed to stay up far beyond their proper bedtimes, and in whose heavy eyes you read a reproach to grownups who should have known better. Marta's features, too, were exaggerated like a child's —her lips soft, wide, crisscrossed with lines like the palm of a hand; the blue of her huge eyes pale, as though the color had been carelessly scribbled in. Yet it was a face that seemed blurred, as though you were always seeing it through tears, which was curious, Mrs. Lampman reflected, since she could not once remember Marta having cried all the times she had recounted bits of her personal history.

That her marriage had not been a happy one, for example. Marta

would put one small, plump hand against the rise of her breasts—
she favored plunging necklines—as if to gesture to and yet conceal
the cause of her marital woes. It was no wonder there was only the
one child, Marta had sighed. Yet Anyès had always been so attached
to her father, though God knew he never had time for her. The end
he made hadn't interfered with her schoolwork, though; she was an
A student, the kind who worked so hard she had to excel. But in
Latin? Come to the New World and study Latin? And that teacher—
she was so masterful, so demanding, she had the girl staying up half
the night to do extra projects. Anyès worshiped her, just as she had
her father. It wasn't good for a child to worship anyone like that,
especially when she had her own mother to help her and teach her
things you didn't learn at school.

Mrs. Lampman listened without nodding or shaking her head. She
said that she'd heard of the teacher in question; she possessed a marvelous reputation, had been with the school for years, had helped
form the character of hundreds of children from the best families. If
this Miss Vance felt that Anyès had a future as a Latin scholar, that
her talents would be wasted with bedpans or carbon paper, why not
let things take their course? Without waiting for an answer, Mrs.
Lampman had pushed away the cold, sugar-saturated coffee, risen
from her chair, and told Marta in parting that she'd mention her name
to a Mrs. Jablonski who needed a caterer and waitress for a birthday
party she was giving in two weeks' time.

"Bitch," Marta had hissed after Mrs. Lampman closed the door,
but it wasn't clear whether she was speaking of Miss Vance or the
owner of the restaurant. She went back to the kitchen and began
packing up leftovers from that day's cooking. Tonight they closed
early—it was her evening off and Zoltàn would be coming. They
would eat the remains of the veal birds and poppy-seed torte, and
then Anyès would do her homework while Marta and Zoltàn took
the bus down to the subway station, and the subway downtown.
There they would walk, arm in arm, staring into lighted jewelers'
shops and the endless windows of department stores; or perhaps they
would see a Hungarian film at the Hall, and then have a beer in the

Blue Cellar Room. It didn't matter what they did, so long as they stayed out long enough for Anyès to have finished her homework, taken her bath, and fallen fast asleep in her bed—the foldout couch which had been moved to the spot farthest away from Marta's room. And then Marta and her lover, who had been at university in Hungary, but now worked at the Budapest Bakery and studied law at night school, would unlock the apartment door and creep toward the bedroom with such reverent caution that you would have thought there was a newborn asleep on the couch. Would lock themselves into the bedroom and make love so desperately that it would wake Anyès from dreams so full of loss and confusion she could hardly keep herself from crying out.

Between the time that Miss Vance had put into her pupil's hand a letter confirming that the Charles Maltman had been awarded to Agnes Sereny of Oakdale School, and the night that Anyès had finally confessed to her mother what the scholarship entailed—four years in a place far enough away that neither Marta nor Anyès would be able to afford telephone calls, never mind visits to each other—Anyès began to have a recurring dream. She would be at a railway station, waiting to board a train that always tried to leave without her. Unable to fall asleep again, she would switch on the lamp at the edge of the fold-out couch, pick up a book, and read, hoping that the very sound of the words would soothe her to sleep. *"Foelix qui potuit rerum cognoscere causas/Atque metus omnes et inexorabile fatum/Subjecit pedibus, strepitumque Acherontis avari./ Fortunatus et ille deos qui novit agrestes,/ Panaque, Sylvanumque senem, nymphasque sorores . . ."* But the more she read, the more distressed she would become, as if her very fluency were mocking her. She would put down her book, realizing that Pan, Sylvanus, and the sister-nymphs meant no more to her now than the plates she washed at her mother's restaurant. And then all the maxims and mottos she'd ever had to translate would pummel her: *Dum spiro spero*—while I breathe I hope—*Nemo timendo ad summum pervenit locum*—No man by fearing reaches the top—*Quod incepimus conficiemus*—What we have begun we shall finish. And she had had a vision of all the mottos at the headings of all the chapters of all the Latin textbooks in the world forming the bars of a colossal cage so intricately twisted that she was caught inside with no room to move even a finger.

The knowledge that she could leave the cramped apartment which had begun to seem even smaller once her mother and Zoltàn had started quarreling, and get onto an airplane to a beautiful place—Miss Vance had shown her slides of it—hit her like a fist in the face. What use—no, what good was Latin since it had nothing to do with anything that had ever marked her life? Or was that why she had loved it so much—because it made a marble labyrinth in which to lose herself, she who hadn't the slightest desire to find her way out again?

The conjunction *cum*, the present infinitive active and passive indirect statement—they had nothing to do with the young men she had seen being shot in the streets of Budapest, the young men her father had told her she was too young to have seen or remembered, even in a nightmare. Nothing to do with the last time she had seen her father—bruising her shoulder against the locked bathroom door, calling her mother, the two of them breaking into the room to find Anton Sereny in his business suit, with his hat on, stretched out in a tub of water pink as the roses on the wallpaper. Or, worse than all of this, the last quarrel, the one they hadn't tried to shut her out from by closing the bedroom door, so that she had heard, buried under the comforter on the couch, Marta accusing Zoltàn of watching Anyès when he thought she wasn't looking, of wanting to put his hands on her, touch her, and she only a child, innocence itself— The crash of his hand against her mother's face so that she wouldn't say any more, as if saying it, not thinking it, made it true. And her own silence, hot, smothered under the comforter, knowing that her mother was right and also that she was wrong—for Zoltàn had come an hour early that evening, knowing Marta to be still at the restaurant, and had stood over her as she worked at the kitchen table (consonant stems of third declension—*corpora, corporum, corporibus*) and put his hands on her shoulders and she had let him; and had slid his hands, which were large but finely shaped—she had studied them as often as she had her conjugations—light as leaves against her skin, under her sweater and over her breasts, and she had let him, having no language to ask, or refuse, or explain, even to herself, what she wanted to be happening. . . .

The night after all the nights Zoltàn had not come, Anyès had woken out of this dream of a railway station to hear, not the cries of lovers, nor the black hum of heating machines and electric wires in the apartment walls, but a sound she had heard only twice before: the night that her father had decided they must try to escape from Hungary, and the night before she and her mother had moved out of their house into the apartment. The sound of her mother weeping: not pleading or resisting, but as if she were mourning her own fate; as if she knew already what such travel would cost her, and that she didn't have the means to pay.

Anyès had pulled a sweater over her nightdress and gone soundlessly to her mother's room. The door was ajar, lamplight haloing its edges. Anyès walked inside. Dressed only in her slip, her mother was sitting on the bed, whose covers she had not even bothered to turn down. Beside her was a bottle of brandy, nearly empty, the stars on its label tarnished, forlorn. Marta had looked up at her daughter, rubbing the skin above her breasts as she did so, the satiny slip cutting into flesh which Anyès saw was too soft, too white, too full to be touched without hurting. Wordless, Marta held out her arms to her daughter, wrapped them round the girl's small and delicate shoulders, drawing her in as if Anyès were an infant to be put to the breast, fed and comforted; as if her daughter's tears were milk spurting from Marta's nipples, soaking them both. "Don't leave me. I have nothing, don't leave me, my darling Zoltàn—Anyès—Zoltàn."

Anyès gently loosened her mother's arms around her, lay her down, and pulled the flimsy blankets over her. Then she twisted the cap back on to the brandy bottle, turned out the light, and sat on the edge of the bed, holding her mother's hand until she heard the slow, shuddering breath of Marta, sleeping.

*   *   *

Miss Vance had proposed the presentation. Agnes had an obligation, she stressed, to mark the occasion of her winning of the scholarship with a demonstration, not only of her own intellectual capacities, but also of the intrinsic value of classics in the classroom. Agnes would speak during the last Latin class of the year on an author of her choice. The principal, the guidance counselor, the student teachers would all be invited to hear an exposition on the principal merits of the author in question, and a few well-chosen words of confidence in and gratitude for all that the Latin tongue could bestow upon its conscientious students.

Agnes had chosen Ovid—against Miss Vance's wishes (she favored Vergil, something from the *Eclogues,* perhaps). If it had to be Ovid, the *Baucis and Philemon* from *The Metamorphoses* would be the obvious choice, Miss Vance had decided. Agnes had agreed—at any rate, there was no further discussion, and so her teacher had permitted her to spend the last month of Latin class in the library, construing that one safe story from Ovidius Naso's libidinous pen.

The library was dimly lit—Mrs. Paulson, the school librarian, still had vivid memories of blackouts and rationing in her native England. Classical literature was shelved in a crepuscular corner which the school's architect had originally intended as a broom closet. And so Anyès felt for, rather than looked out, the volumes she needed for her exposition; and so she came upon the volume of Ovid that had somehow got squeezed behind the *Metamorphoses* and the *Tristia*—a different sort of book, with soft leather covers and a crested bookplate inside the cover: *ex libris* J. L. Stanhope.

Mrs. Paulson could have explained to Agnes that the book had not got lost behind the other volumes, but had been placed there deliberately. The library had received quite a generous donation of books from the late Mr. Stanhope, who had owned the farmland that was now the suburb of Oakdale, and whose large stone house, visible from the library's window, had become a Christian Science Reading Room. Among the books had been some texts in precarious, if not actively pernicious taste. Mrs. Paulson had not conferred with Miss Vance, whom she quite violently disliked. She couldn't bear the thought of throwing out books with perfectly good bindings, so had simply hidden them away. After all, they were printed in a foreign language, and she doubted whether the vocabulary lists to be found in *Living Latin* would permit even the most resourceful student to make much of this poet's dalliance with Corinna, that poet's address to Lesbia.

Yet in this one case—Anyès Sereny's happening to have chanced upon that supple, leather-bound version of the *Amores*—Mrs. Paulson had gravely erred. For the text was a dual Latin-English version, and the translations were lively indeed—so lively that Anyès sat for the length of each Latin class with them, and even returned at the end of the school day to devour the poems, oblivious to the rush-hour traffic returning faithful husbands from city to suburb; to the sunset's garish reflection in the windows of the Christian Science Reading Room; to the fact that Miss Vance expected her to help with repairing plasticene models, and that her mother was waiting for her to deal with dirty dishes and accounts at the Hungarian Village.

The afternoon of the presentation for Miss Vance, Agnes Sereny had taken her place at the podium in front of her fellow students, all of whom had by now the same repugnance for anything Latin as they'd have for objects in a mortuary. Yet as she began to speak they couldn't help but listen—not to Agnes's account of Ovid's life but to the excitement that beat wings through her words, carrying her into some higher, richer air. And when Agnes started to read what Miss Vance had announced as *Baucis and Philemon,* that tale of marital devotion and fidelity, they'd leaned forward in their absurdly child-sized desks as if following the flight of some exotic and endangered bird.

In a summer season, siesta time
I lay relaxed upon my couch.

One shutter locked, the other ajar
let in a sylvan half-light. . . .

And then, Corinna—her thin dress loosened,
long hair falling past the pale neck—

lovely as Semiramis entering her wedding bed,
or Lais of the many lovers.

I pulled away her dress: She fought to keep it
though it didn't hide much,

yet fought as one with no desire to win—
her defeat a self-betrayal.

Unveiled, faultless, naked
she stood before me.

Such shoulders and arms inviting my eyes;
Nipples firmly demanding attention—

Miss Vance, erect at her desk but gasping for breath as if something had been holding her under water for so long she thought she'd surely drown: "I think you've gone as far as good taste will permit. Sit down!"

On the girl's face an expression no longer somnolent, submissive, but open, as Miss Vance dismissed the class, requesting Agnes Sereny to stay behind. Yet when teacher and pupil were left alone with the array of peeling replicas, Miss Vance would not look at Agnes, but took off her spectacles and began rubbing her eyes with the heels of her hands, pressing them like a second pair of eyelids into her face. Watching her, Anyès felt the same shock of perception she'd had in seeing her father for the last time—knowing that it was the last time, that there was suddenly an immeasurable distance between them.

Miss Vance at last looked up unsteadily. Whatever she'd meant to say, the words came out as this:

"Once, only once, did I do something I knew was wrong. Some 'friends' at university dragged me off to a movie. *Ecstasy* it was called, or some such poppycock. It was supposed to be very daring. There was a woman, swimming in a lake. . . . But all I could think of was the work I should have been doing in class, of what my father would say if he ever found out. I hated every minute of it. And I never did a thing like that again. Ever."

Anyès made no answer. As Miss Vance covered her eyes again the girl thought of her mother as she'd seen her that night—disheveled, exposed. And knew, suddenly, that she was free of them both, that she could never again give them whatever they needed from her, and that they knew this, too. There was no call for any valediction. She picked up her papers, took the library copy of *The Amores,* and walked from the classroom as if out of a dream—in a hurry, as though she had a train to catch.

Bella Rabinovich/
Arabella Rose

Every summer, Bella Rabinovich boards the overnight train at Union Station, descends into the smoky dawn of Montreal, and hails a taxi to the *Empress of England*. Twelve days later she disembarks to strangled tunes from a small brass band at Tilbury docks, catches the coast train to Brighton, and takes a cab to Number 3, Montpelier Mansions. She walks up the pocked stone steps, raps the dolphin knocker on the huge front door, and, like a conqueror taking delayed possession of a kingdom, she steps inside as Arabella Rose.

But there's a ritual to be observed and rules to be obeyed, ensuring that her transformation is complete, that Bella doesn't infiltrate Arabella in the way that dye from crimson sandals seeps into the clean white socks of those foolish enough to step in puddles. Spells must be recited, confirmations given; silence must be kept. Between Toronto and Brighton lie more than two weeks of ocean.

Bella is short and dark and difficult. Arabella is tall and commanding; her eyes are diamonds, her hair bright as brass. Bella is Mendel Rabinovich's daughter and she lives in a pink-brick bungalow in one of the new, bulldozed developments that once were orchards or cornfields. Arabella is the daughter of her grandfather's house, with its turrets and lead-paned windows, its Oriental rugs and Chinese plates, its overgrown rose garden and its marble fountain.

No one at Montpelier Mansions thinks it odd that for July and August Arabella Rose should be living in a large room on the third floor, with a view of jangled rooftops and a splash of sea. Nor does anyone wonder that for the other ten months of the year she should abruptly vanish, leaving the attic silent, empty as an ice floe. It's obvious what Bella does those two lost months of summer: she rides round and round in a taxicab until it's time to board the *Empress* once again. But when Arabella vanishes each end of August, where in Montpelier Mansions does she go? Perhaps she fades into one of the family photographs, dead faces pitched like tents on the round tables and dresser tops. Most of the pictures are of Uncle Francis, who was killed in the war, or of Grandmother Esther. She died in the back garden. Minnie's a housekeeper, not a gardener. She lets the roses shrink and pucker, the weeds and thorns run riot: she hardly ever spends time out of doors. When Minnie's busy tending to old Mr. Rose, Arabella sits in the garden and reads the books her mother left behind when she ran away to marry. *The Secret Garden. The Little Princess. The Enchanted Castle.*

In front of the garden bench is a fountain that has long forgotten how to play. Once it held goldfish and water lilies, but now there are only dragonflies. They hover over the marble basin, their bodies thin blue pencils held by invisible hands. Sometimes they perch on the statue in the middle of the fountain: a nymph on tiptoe. Her face is distant and uncaring as the moon's. She has egg-shaped blanks instead of eyes, and moss growing in the whorls of her ears, so that she hears no one and sees nothing, not even the inscription at her feet: *In loving memory of Esther Rose: April 1896—June 1944.* Esther Rose died in the garden, dropping like a stone not two feet from the fountain. Heart failure brought on by sudden shock. It had to do with Uncle Francis getting shot down over Germany, Arabella's aunt explained. "You'll understand once you're older." The only thing Arabella understands is that the nymph inside the fountain is absent, like her grandmother. Under the nymph's blank eyes, locked inside her ears—perhaps it's there that Arabella disappears each end of August, when Bella comes back, at last.

"My mother said I never should—"

But it's not her mother, it's Aunt Audrey who's always warning Bella not to throw stones in the garden—they might chip the nymph, who is very precious and came all the way from Italy. Italy is only a little farther from Brighton than Toronto is from Montreal. Bella and her mother boarded ship in Montreal almost two weeks ago; they have already stopped at Halifax, St. John's, and Le Havre, and will dock tomorrow morning at Tilbury. Bella is tucked into her bed, which is itself screwed down into the stateroom floor. This voyage, however, the sea has been unusually calm; neither Bella nor her mother have had to miss a meal or even a cup of tea, a fact which has been duly inscribed on a postcard to be mailed back to Toronto as soon as they land. Everything is in order for disembarkation; the trunks are packed and tomorrow's dresses have been ironed. They hang stiffly from the closet door, too white, too flounced and frilled for traveling by train, but there are appearances to be kept up. Sally will not have it said that she and her daughter have gone native. At the vanity she searches out a pair of earrings—in the mirror at the back of the jewel box, Bella can see the little ballerina who used to pirouette to "The Blue Danube" each time the lid was opened. For three years now her mother has been promising to get the spring fixed once they get to Brighton.

One of the earrings is lost. "You haven't been dressing up in my jewelry again, have you, Poppet? Those are real pearls, you know. Daddy *will* be cross."

"He'll rap my head with a teapot lid." It's not an answer—Bella's just muttering to herself again. Her mother sighs, shrugs her shoulders and decides on a pair of opals. She is off to the captain's farewell reception in the first-class lounge. All the passengers with staterooms have been invited—all save Bella, who is only eleven and much too

young for champagne and chestnut meringues. She watches her mother make lazy circles over her head with a can of hairspray. In the lamplight, Sally's hair glows, a soft red cloud around her.

"Oh, Poppet, I *wish* you could have had my hair!" Her mother has said this to Bella for as long as either of them can remember. Bella has a vision of herself bewigged with glossy auburn curls, her mother bald as a full moon beside her. *"Naughty girl to disobey/Your hair shan't curl and your shoes won't shine/You gypsy girl, you shan't be mine."*

It is the first summer Bella can remember. Her mother is leading her down strange, narrow streets, past the coal-black tower of St. Nicholas Church, past endless terraces of white houses, down to the lanes. They enter a maze of pubs and jewelers and booksellers, then halt before a shop with gold letters scrolled over the glass. ISAAC ROSE: WIGS, HAIRPIECES, AND APPURTENANCES. She is pushed into a warm and musty cave, lifted up to a countertop for the shopgirls to admire. "Oh, Miss Sally, *hasn't* she grown! And you've come all the way from Canada"—they say "Carnarda." "Let's see if we haven't got something nice to give the little pet." They turn to rummage for candy in a drawer filled with dirty rubber bands and rusty paper clips. Bella doesn't want them petting her; she doesn't want their stale rock candy. What she wants is the golden crown, glowing, almost sizzling, like a lump of butter in a skillet, the wig of tight yellow curls stretched on a wire stand on the countertop beside her. Goldilocks, Rapunzel, the miller's daughter spinning gold from straw—if she can have it for her own she'll turn into a princess, the shop's sour gloom will become a magic forest. Her mother, who has never, ever hit her, slaps her hand away, hisses, "Don't touch—*lice,*" just as the women finish rummaging in the dusty drawer. She smiles as if nothing were wrong; she even scolds Bella for refusing the present these nice ladies have brought her. Bella puts the candy in her pocket. Once they are down the street from the shop her mother stops, empties Bella's pockets, and throws the linty chunks of Brighton Rock into a rubbish bin.

"Be an angel and do up the buttons at the back. Be careful now

—and hurry, darling." Bella's fingers are clumsy—she leaves little damp marks on Sally's silk dress. As she buttons, she starts her muttering again. This time Sally can make out the words of a nursery rhyme: *"The woods were dark, the grass was green/Along came Sally with a tambourine."*

"Oh, Poppet, you *promised* you wouldn't—" she says, more discouraged than displeased. "What *will* Aunt Audrey think if she hears you talking to yourself? And besides, you're far too old for nursery rhymes—remember what Daddy always says." Bella lies back on her bed and stares at the circle of sky inscribed by the porthole on the cabin wall. She refuses to remember what Daddy says, just as she's refused to keep any image of the ballerinas on her bedroom wallpaper, the child-sized desk and chair her mother's painted white and gold. Arabella is never scolded for anything; she is away and free from maiden aunts and meddling fathers. But Arabella isn't ready yet. In the narrow bed screwed into the cabin floor there is no one but Bella, limbo'd between Rabinovich and Rose. She pulls the bedclothes up to her face and breathes deeply into the sharp, starched linen.

Her mother pulls at the sheets and starts a plaintive scolding, wringing the words instead of her hands. "You *mustn't* pull the covers over your head like that—you're *sure* to smother. How can I *possibly* go off to the lounge—I'll be worried *sick* about you. If *only* you'd listen and do what you're told—then I wouldn't have to *worry* so. But you *never* listen: I've *told* your father, I can never do a *thing* with you, not a blessed *thing*."

Yet during the twelve days it takes to exchange the St. Lawrence for the Thames estuary, she manages some sort of transformation in her daughter. Bella's hair, for example. At home it's shoved back from her face with a stretchy nylon band that torments her with its ceaseless slipping and sliding. But first thing after boarding ship, Sally takes out a comb and brush and goes at her daughter's head as though it were a terrier that had passed an entire night frolicking down rabbit holes. The nylon noose disappears into Sally's square and sturdy makeup case, to reappear eight weeks later when the overnight train is pulling into Union Station. One hundred strokes through Bella's straight, black hair, and then a tortoiseshell band rakes to the middle of that head that Mendel always says needs to be vacuumed out, so full is it of fluff and lint and wool.

Her father doesn't mean anything unkind by this. He manufactures vacuum cleaners; in fact, he has a factory outside Toronto that turns out a special line called New Age Appliances—there are plans to produce a dishwasher before too long. Bella wonders if he'll soon start telling her that her brains need to be scoured, rinsed, and dried. Nothing unkind. Her father is concerned for her well-being—he wants her to be studying useful things, the solar system and the chief exports of the Americas. At her age he was all alone in the world, responsible for himself—he didn't get through by mooning about, reciting nursery rhymes, and telling fairy stories.

Bella's father never spends the summers with his wife and daughter in the south of England, but instead camps out at his factory on the Airport Road. "Mendel is *so* sorry, but the summers are his busiest time. He takes his holidays in the winter, we go south. . . ." Sally Rabinovich's voice always trails off at this point. It's not that she hasn't been telling her sister the whole and perfect truth, but that she knows her listener's Britishness to be knit like chain mail over her mind. How could Audrey entertain even the possibility of a south where flamingos parade on sugar-sand, not egg-sized rocks; where one gets burned from the sun, not razored by a North Atlantic gale?

Bella knows that an Ontario summer is hot and muggy in the same way she knows Ulan Bator to be the capital of Mongolia. Invariably, it rains for a good part of the visit to Brighton, and even when the sun sticks out its tongue through clouds or Scotch mist, they must never be rash enough to unbutton their cardigans. "Brisk and bracing," is how Aunt Audrey describes the Sussex summer. "Wonderfully fresh," Sally agrees. When Bella goes back to school on her return to Canada, she listens as if to the Brothers Grimm as her schoolmates read out their essays on what they did during the summer holidays. To their pageant of cottages, canoes, and summer camps with magical names (Wichimagoumi, Kanakawaka, Oppinogon), she could have opposed woolies and lollies, rock candy and the

Royal Pavilion, or Volks Electric Railway that runs a whole quarter mile between Palace Pier and Black Rock.

Could have, but never does. Her back-to-school compositions are never more than a sentence long: "This summer I went to visit my maternal grandfather, Mr. Isaac Rose, who lives in Montpelier Mansions, Brighton, West Sussex, England." She never mentions that her grandfather is more than a little crazy; that when Minnie is not opening tins of custard or trying to stretch the jerseys she's managed to shrink in the last week's wash, she is declaiming passages from Jeffrey Farnol or Sir Charles G. D. Roberts, while the venerable Mr. Isaac Rose struts up and down the drawing room, decked out with lace fichus and brandishing a smallsword. No one in or out of Willowvale Public School knows Arabella Rose at all. And Bella makes sure to keep it that way. Share no secrets, that's one of the rules; tell no stories, speak no lies.

It is lucky that Mendel stays behind in Canada, that his wife spends most of her summer holiday in London, going to the shops and the theater, and that Audrey only comes up on weekends to her father's house. Sometimes she takes her niece to the seafront. They walk a bit along the Promenade, but Audrey's legs aren't good for much, so they end up spending hours on the verdigris'd benches, gazing out to sea. Beyond the horizon is France says Aunt Audrey, and beyond France is another sea, and then Africa and then another sea and Australia, and then the South Pole, where the Eskimos and penguins live.. Bella knows perfectly well that Eskimos live only in the Arctic and that their real name is Inuit, but Arabella sits and nods and listens to Aunt Audrey. *Naughty girl to disagree.* If she is lucky, her aunt will keep to geography and not ask questions about her mother and father, whether they argue, whether they have separate rooms.

"You remember how to call the steward?" Bella lets her mother kiss her forehead, her nose and chin, the way you'd kiss a baby. As soon as she hears the lock click she burrows under the blankets so that anyone who does break into the stateroom will never suspect there's anything more than a bolster in the bed. In the warm dark

she hears her heart pounding too much; she tries to say over the end
of the rhyme. *"I ran away to sea,/No ship to get across./ I paid nine
shillings for a blind white horse—"* Whenever she is lonely or fidgety or
bored, Bella whispers rhymes. Her father goes white around his lips
and nose; the rest of his face turns brick red when he hears her. Aunt
Audrey thinks she's ninepence to the shilling. They don't know Arabella Rose, who is ravishingly pretty, wonderfully clever—they only
know Bella, a little small, a little slow for her age. But then, her
mother always says, it's not her fault; she was born prematurely.

She was born Bella Rabinovich—not Arabella, Isabella, Dora-
bella, but just Bella, as if, as soon as they looked at her, they'd decided something was missing. "Bella after Daddy's sister," her
mother told her once. "She died before you were born." Why can't
children choose their own names? It seems too important a decision
to be left to anyone else. When she's in Brighton Aunt Audrey makes
her name into a question, calling "Bella" with a little rise at the end
of the word, as if she doesn't expect her niece to be paying attention.
To her mother she will always be Poppet. It was her grandfather
who gave her her English name, taking it from the book Minnie was
reading to him on one of Bella's earlier visits home. When Minnie
takes her down to St. Nicholas, she introduces her to the vicar as
"Arabella, Mr. Rose's granddaughter from Canada." It isn't that Minnie doesn't know how to pronounce Rabinovich, making it sound
irresponsibly foreign, the way Aunt Audrey does; it is just that she
sees no need for last names, the way she doesn't need to append
"Jesus Christ" to "Our Lord."

Cautiously, Bella pulls the covers down from her face and moves
her eyes around the empty room. Satisfied, she gets up and peers
through the porthole; the closer they get to England, the bluer the
sky becomes—that's what her mother says. Bella pictures their arrival tomorrow at Montpelier Mansions, Minnie waiting for them on
the front steps—sturdy, smiling, dignified—she never hugs or kisses,
but her voice is soft as a hand stroking your hair. Minnie used to be
Arabella's nanny until Arabella disobligingly grew up. Minnie had
once bathed and burped her, braided her hair, shined her shoes, kissed

her forehead after tucking her into bed. Arabella Rose was Minnie's baby.

Sally admits that she's not much good with infants—she's always preferred being the baby of her own family, adored by her brother Francis. Yet once her mother died and her sister went off to London, she was left to her own devices, while her father shut himself up in his library in the company of cavaliers and lace-draped ladies. Sally's devices were rash, reckless. "Wafted away by a rich Canadian" is how Audrey describes Sally's fate to anyone inquiring after pretty little Sally Rose, once engaged to Oscar Landy, whose father owned the Grand Hotel. And when Sally Rabinovich comes back to Brighton every summer, sporting linen suits and silk sundresses, she looks just like the bride of a rich Canadian who might be something in gold or furs or hydroelectricity.

Whereas her daughter, Bella, despite the tortoiseshell hairband, the smocked dresses and leather sandals that have taken the place of shorts and saddle shoes, looks exactly who she is—the daughter of Mendel Rabinovich, who was himself the son of a tailor and born in one of those eastern European villages that do not exist anymore. *Shtetl* was the word he'd used in explaining his past to Sally. She had shaken her head until he translated it into *village,* and she'd immediately summoned up ivied cottages and ruddy-faced farmers in gleaming Welly boots. "So you see," she'd explained to her daughter, "we came from different worlds." She had met Mendel at the home of Oscar Landy's aunt, who was being especially kind to refugees who happened to find themselves in London after the war. Sally Rose and Mendel Rabinovich had gone for a long walk together in Kensington Gardens because Oscar's aunt had asked her to be nice to him. "He was so *insistent,*" her mother explains. "Oscar just expected me to marry him. Mendel *asked.* He pleaded, Bella—and you know your father's not a man to beg." "Two different worlds," Bella had repeated to herself, but nothing her mother said could explain why she ran off to Canada with Mendel Rabinovich instead of running the Grand Hotel with Oscar Landy. And why, since Bella is her mother's daughter instead of her father's son, she should look so much like

Mendel. Wasn't she called after his sister, the one who had died in the war like her uncle Francis?

During that walk in the park, Mendel had told Sally a story that she had finally passed on to Bella, so she'd understand why her father was sometimes "that way," and how he didn't really mean the things he said to her. When he'd been a child—no more than a child—there'd been trouble in the country where he lived, and his family was made to leave their village. There were men with guns making them march to some faraway place. When the men weren't looking, Mendel's father had whispered to his son and daughter, "Run into the woods—run as fast as you can, and don't come back." Mendel had run so fast that he'd reached the safety of the trees just as the shots were fired. Mendel was quick enough, but his sister turned to look back at her father and mother. "What happened then?" Bella had pressed, and her mother went on to describe how Mendel had lived in the woods like a wild animal, and then joined a kind of army, and then later walked all the way to England. But what Bella had meant was, "What happened to his sister?" And all Sally could say was, "Oh, Poppet— You'll understand when you're older."

It's not the sort of story she's used to reading in the fairy tales she hides under her mattress where her father won't find them. It's not, she decides, something that's meant to be understood. What Bella does understand is only this—that her mother made a wrong decision, and that she, Bella, is the consequence. Bella, whom her father reprimands and rails at because she's not the son he wanted. Bella, whom her aunt regards with a dislike as permanent and as incorrigible as a stutter.

"She certainly doesn't take after our side of the family." This is what Audrey says each time she greets her niece after the ten months' absence. Audrey is long and thin as a licorice rope; she is somebody's secretary in The City. She has never married, but not for the reasons one might think, Bella's mother once confided. "Audrey turned down proposals the way some girls do hems. She just got into the habit of saying no—it's a kind of addiction, like cigarettes. Don't hold it against her if she gets cross with you—she's not used to children, you see."

Bella doesn't see. Minnie has never been married, either, but she doesn't peck and prickle at her the way Aunt Audrey does. Audrey wears cashmere cardigans and smartly pleated skirts. Minnie's lisle stockings always droop. Audrey says her dresses look like crumpled paper bags—never in front of Minnie, of course, but to Sally, whom she treats like a piggy bank into which she stuffs all the year's complaints and accusations: "He should be in a nursing home. It costs a fortune to keep the house going. And why, for what? So she can have a home—so she can trap him into marrying her, the old fool. It's not my fault that I can't stay here and keep him—I've my work to do. I support myself and always have. God knows on what she spends the grocery money when all she can cook are beans on toast. She probably gives it all to that church of hers—she simply reeks of incense."

Arabella loves Minnie because Minnie smells of bread and milk. Her skin is smooth and pink-and-white as rose petals. She lives for her church, St. Nicholas-on-the Hill, and for old Mr. Rose, to whom she was sent by an agency after Sally ran off. Minnie has held the fort these past ten years, never taking holidays and needing no time off except for churchgoing. Arabella loves Minnie because Minnie expects nothing from her but that she should appear each summer at Montpelier Mansions and take tea with her grandfather. Minnie does not shout during the day and wake up screaming in the night so that the whole neighborhood can hear. She does not drag her round to hairdressers' and dressmakers' shops, or sit her down and talk, talk, talk at her, as if she were no more than another cushion on the sofa. Minnie does not lament that Arabella wasn't born a boy, or that she doesn't have blue eyes and curly auburn hair.

And best of all, Minnie takes Arabella Rose to church on Saturday afternoons, when she goes to change the flowers. She lets her walk up and down the aisle and stare at the skulls and hourglasses carved into the stones. She tells Arabella the names of all the stained-glass saints and martyrs, with their swords and spears and wheels. Even the women look fierce, implanted rather than painted on the glass. No one can knock them down, their rigid faces say—they will not be moved. Bella worships them. In their blazing silks, with their haughty eyes, they remind her of the cavaliers and ladies in her grandfather's books, the ones Minnie reads aloud to him at tea. Next to the saints, what Arabella likes best is the great brass eagle on the lectern, clutching a huge brass ball, filling the half-lit church like a great oath: I will not let go, I will hold on here for ever and ever. Amen.

The church stays damp and dim, even after Minnie switches on the light. Sometimes she lets Arabella put tuppence into the brass box, take a thick white candle, and fix it into a holder above a tray of fine white sand. Arabella loves the scrape of the match, its little blue blurt of flame. "For the Dead," Minnie whispers as the candle catches fire, but Arabella has no dead, just her grandfather and Minnie. She thinks of them as she watches the candle's one, small, winking eye; she listens for the soft drop of the wax onto the sand below as Minnie polishes the communion silver, singing all the while. Her voice is low, melodious, and warm, even when the words are about taking up the cross, walking through Death's Dark Vale. Minnie's face is always patient and gentle, but here, alone in the dimness of the church, she looks like the faithful servant at the end of the fairytale—as though her heart would burst for joy.

When Minnie calls her to help arrange fresh flowers for the altar, Arabella knows it is nearly over. They go to the little storeroom off the vestry where Minnie chucks out the dropsical roses and the spongy gladioli. She pours the brackish water down the sink, while Arabella plants a garden in the green sponge at the bottom of the vase. She has a way with flowers, says Minnie, for whom they merely droop or snap their stems. And then it's Arabella's turn to watch as Minnie carries the vase to the altar, sets it down, and prays. Then they switch out the lights and lock the door with an iron key that Minnie keeps at home in a kitchen drawer among bits of string and scraps of paper.

Once, when they were walking home up the steep streets on a

windy summer afternoon, Minnie began to talk about Our Father's House, and how there was room for everyone there—little yellow children in China and little red children in America and people of different faiths who had come Home to the Truth at last. She talked about how Our Lord had suffered all the little children to come unto Him, and how much Our Father loved His only son. Arabella will never know how or why but suddenly, stubbornly, Bella had interrupted.

"I hate my father, Minnie."

"Oh dear, no—you mustn't say what you don't mean."

Minnie had clutched her handbag tighter, slackened her step, looked earnestly at Bella. "If you dislike someone, dear, that means you've only looked at their outside—you haven't tried hard enough to find the good within. It is the soul you must try and see through to, the soul that withstands all suffering, that triumphs over death itself, and flies straight up to God. No one is entirely bad—"

"The devil is."

"The devil isn't a person."

"Wasn't Jesus a person?"

"*Is,* dear, Our Lord *is* a person. Why, He's here right now, walking down the street with us. He's inside us, around us, like the air we breathe. And if we follow His teachings then we learn to love what is good, even in the people we think we dislike. We can make those people good by loving them. Your father—"

"But I don't dislike him, Minnie. I hate him. Not because he's bad, but because he's my father."

"Then you must pray to God to take your hate away and give you love instead."

"Why can't God just take away my father?"

"Because God is a God of love."

"My God isn't. My God smote the people He hated. He smote the Amalachites and the Philistines in their thousands and tens of thousands."

"*My* God," Minnie repeated, tucking her handbag further into the crick of her arm, "is a God of love."

"And my God's your God's father, Minnie. Doesn't that make us cousins?"

"No, dear—no. I'm afraid it doesn't work quite that way. I can't explain. But always remember, you must never give in to your feelings, good *or* bad." Minnie had started walking then, faster than before. She never spoke to Arabella again about Our Father's House.

Minnie is an educated woman of good family—that is how Bella has heard her mother describe her. A lady who has fallen on hard times, "a distressed gentlewoman," Aunt Audrey sniffs. Once Arabella overheard an argument between the sisters:

"It's not as if I could take him back to Ontario, Audrey—surely you see that. I agree that Minnie's not quite what one would like in a housekeeper—still, she's as honest as the day, even if she does get the accounts all muddled up. Besides, it won't be forever, will it?"

"It's already been too long."

"Leave be, Audrey—Father will hear."

"Father? He hasn't heard anything we've said since nineteen forty-six, ever since *you* ran off and *she* came into the house. If you'd known where your duty lay, Sally, if you'd thought for even one moment of the consequences of your actions—running off with your Mendel Rabinovich when you might have had Oscar Landy—and what have you got to show for it?"

"I've got Bella, Audrey."

"Quite."

It's Minnie who finds her eavesdropping outside the morning room, who whisks her off to the kitchen for lemon squash and ginger creams, pretending there's been nothing at all to overhear; talking instead about the book she's reading to Mr. Rose. "You see, the castle is besieged by Roundheads, and young Lady Lavinia holds them off —her husband's away with the king, of course—with only a handful of soldiers and a faithful servant at her side. They have to bind up the men's wounds with lace tablecloths." Arabella chews on her ginger creams and downs her lemon squash. She looks at Minnie with love so carefully disguised that no one will ever find it out and take it from her. She wonders whether her grandfather looks at Minnie this way, too; wonders what Minnie hides from her grandfather's gaze.

The blue eye darkens in the cabin wall, becomes a lid blanking out the day. Bella's head sags on the pillows; she burrows down again into the securely fastened bed that rocks her up and down, back and forth as the engines thrum against the music from the lounge. Pulling the blankets up to just under her nose, Bella dreams of a "later on" in which Arabella Rose won't need to hide inside a statue at the summer's end, but will lodge year round in Montpelier Mansions making Floating Island Pudding, while Minnie reads aloud from *The Gallant Cavalier.*

"I ran away to sea, no ship to get across/I paid nine shillings—" Bella can't remember the rest. It doesn't matter. Their dresses are creased and Bella's is soiled. Her mother has read the latest copy of *The Lady* and Bella's devoured a packet of Jaffa cakes while staring at a blur of tiny kitchen gardens, houses with flint or pebble or flaking stucco faces. They are nearly at Brighton now; she must prepare herself. Arabella Rose does not recite nursery rhymes or make up stories— she has no need of that. She lives inside a story, she and her grandfather—and Minnie too, polishing communion silver in the empty church, singing her hymns.

"I wonder how we'll find him this time," Sally says to her reflection in the window, a transparent face gliding over fields and sidings. She sighs, examining the chips in her nail polish—it is impossible to board a train these days without some violence occurring. And then she turns brightly in Bella's direction. "We're so *lucky* to have Minnie—no one else would have been able to put up with him for so long. That's what people mean when they say, 'It's very Christian of you.' Being able to manage someone like your grandfather. Heaven knows how Mummy managed. But then he didn't begin to go funny till after she died. Maybe it was the war. I wish I could remember what they were like together. But I didn't know what to notice then. You don't until you're married, and then it's too late. Still, Minnie's a darling. I wonder if she's a little in love with the old silly? Audrey thinks she's after his money. I shouldn't think there is any, what with that house to heat and repair. I wish you could have seen what it used to be like, when Mummy was alive. Flowers in all the rooms, the windows gleaming, everything neat as a pin. Daddy had a whole room of armor, but he sold it just before the war. He's got some lovely little pieces still. And then there's the furniture—I do covet the little Regency sofa and that pier glass in the hall. *Such* treasures—they'll be yours one day, Poppet, isn't it wonderful?"

Her mother talks as if soliloquies were the usual mode of address, and conversation something only heard upon the stage. Perhaps that comes from having lived with Mendel Rabinovich so long. There is never company in Mendel's house—Aunt Audrey won't cross an ocean to visit the sister she can see in Brighton every summer, and Sally has stopped inviting her Willowvale friends to the house, because they would always say, "You and your husband must come over for dinner," and Mendel never will. So she's become accustomed to talking to herself, to the walls and the carpet, the mirrors and the windows. "You're getting more and more like Father," Audrey cautions whenever Sally's chattering goes on too long.

Sally doesn't see much of her father on her summer visits: this is partly because he keeps calling her Esther, and partly because she finds it disconcerting to be in the company of a man who wears his dead wife's maribou-tufted, high-heeled slippers under a scarlet silk kimono. Minnie had once dug out the sensible woolen dressing gown (black watch plaid) and felt carpet slippers Sally had sent him all the way from Canada; they were neatly stored in tissue paper in Mr. Rose's wardrobe, moth-holed, never worn. "It never seems to get cold enough for him to want to wear them," Minnie had apologized. "But they're lovely quality." When she added that he never wore Miss Audrey's gifts of hand-knit ties and woolen socks, Sally had brightened. "The important thing," she'd told Minnie, "is that he keeps on seeing a bit of Bella—she's his only grandchild, you know. Perhaps at teatime. She's old enough to learn how to pour—we never get around to things like that in Canada." So every day of every summer visit, except when Aunt Audrey comes down, or when her grandfather's indisposed or out of sorts, Arabella takes tea in the study with the Master of Montpelier Mansions.

He is very old; his skin is like paper, his voice high, cracked, like a schoolboy's. He has only a few tufts of hair, white and wavery, and his brown eyes have a film over them, which makes Arabella think of fat hardening over a jug of gravy. She would be afraid to look at him if it weren't for the dress-up clothes under the silk kimono which he tugs off as soon as Minnie signals that she's found the right chapter in their book. In his black velvet jacket with the lace tucked up the sleeves, in his glittery silver pantaloons, with his smallsword at his side, he teeters round the room on his high-heeled shoes, in and out the thickets patterned on the Turkish rug. He is splendid, he is like the King in a fairy tale, setting impossible tasks for the princes come to claim his daughter's hand. Every so often he will shake his sword at one of the paintings on the wall: portraits of women with sweet faces clamped inside enormous ruffs, or scenes of battle, smoke, and ravaged castle walls. "Huzzah," he'll shriek, or "Villains, dastards, I will be avenged!"

Now, after all her visits, after all the stories Minnie's read aloud, Arabella knows exactly what and when and how to do. Behind the Oriental screen that divides her grandfather's bedroom from the study is a large wooden chest with curious rough carvings: birds and beasts from some Eastern kingdom? Enchanted letters from an unknown alphabet? Inside the trunk are heaps of cloths, some satin and velvet, some mere rags of dirty lace. Arabella doesn't bother with fashioning herself a dress; what she wants she has to burrow for. Finally she pulls up from the tangled sea her heart's desire, sets the yellow wig upon her head. In the black-spotted mirror over the wooden chest she finds at last the Lady Arabella, perfectly reflected in the sun of her hair.

Though it's midsummer, the curtains are drawn; the room is warm and slightly smoky from the fire always lit there. Minnie's voice changes as she reads, rattling and dashing the words whenever a duel is fought, becoming soft and stroking when the ladies bid their lovers farewell. Arabella climbs onto the enormous leather armchair by the fire as if she were getting on horseback, half closes her eyes, and watches. It is Sir Geoffrey or the Duke of Cranleigh whom she sees pacing up and down, his slippers snaking through a meadow jewelled with flowers. He brandishes his sword beneath ruined castle walls and wanders through enchanted woods. But from her charger, from her tower it is she who looks down and commands: Arabella Rose with blazing hair and eyes as cold as stars.

"Come on, Poppet, let's brush the crumbs off you—oh, *look* at your hair. We're coming into Brighton, you *have* to be presentable."

Bella throws the empty pack of Jaffa cakes between the seats while inclining her head toward her mother's comb. What does it matter if its teeth scrape her scalp, if her mother rips out the tangles in her fine, straight hair. She will soon be at her grandfather's house; she will soon be Arabella Rose. There is a whole summer ahead of her, sure as the rails on which their train glides to the station, certain as the litter strewn across the platform.

As Sally leads a line of porters to the taxi stand, Bella walks ahead into the straight, sharp, English rain.

At the end of the usual journey, on the customary steps under the eternally peeling portico, Minnie waits for them, though not quite in the manner Bella has expected. Sally is too busy paying the cabbie and fussing over the luggage he is carrying up the front steps to notice, as her daughter does, what's wrong with Minnie's lips. They are jagged, quivering with information she does not know quite how to give. It is not with words, but with her body that she finally speaks. She simply stands and blocks the taxi driver's progress up the thick stone steps.

"Minnie, you'll have to get out of the way. We can't get into the house."

Minnie shakes her head, slowly. "I'd hoped— I meant— Oh, I'm no use at this kind of thing, no use at all. You see—I'm sorry—there is no house anymore."

"Don't be silly, Minnie. The house is right here, where it's always been. And I'm going to get out of the rain and go inside."

But it is Bella who darts up the steps, dodging round Minnie and pushing open the door. A quarter of an hour later, the three of them are sitting round a pot of tea in a kitchen denuded of copper saucepans and jelly molds. To be sitting at all is no mean achievement, since there appears to be only one chair left in the house. Sally sits gingerly on its sagging seat, while Minnie makes do with the dented lid of a rubbish bin. Bella perches on the edge of the table, swinging her feet up and down. She is waiting for Minnie to speak, to make some way out of the upset. But the only one who says anything is Sally.

"She might have *told* me, someone might have cabled the ship. It's a *terrible* thing to have happen unannounced. At least they could have delayed the funeral till our arrival—what *could* she have been thinking of? What *will* people think? And what are we to *do* for the rest of the summer? We can't camp out here like gypsies. We're not expected *back* till the end of August, Minnie. Our crossing's booked for the end of August—doesn't anyone understand?"

Sally's voice has gone all wobbly—her face is white as the scarred enamel of the tabletop. Some kind of hospital instinct comes over Minnie, making her brisk, efficient, sensible. She forces the shrunken tea cosy down over the pot, gently arrests the swing of Bella's feet, and leans across the table, till her face is close to Sally's. "You'll want to speak to the solicitor, of course, though I'm afraid everything's been done correctly. It's all above board—the will was perfectly legal. The furniture was removed yesterday—I marked down the address of the warehouse where it's being stored. Miss Rose went through the things first, of course; she took hardly anything, just that old pier glass, and the little sofa in the morning room. She let me have some odds and ends—tea cloths and runners—for the church jumble sale. Let me pour you some tea. I'm afraid there aren't any biscuits."

It isn't until her fourth cup that Sally registers a fraction of what has happened—that somewhere in the strait of Belle Isle her father had died. Halfway to France he'd been cremated, and the ashes dug into the rose beds behind Montpelier Mansions—a gardener was hired for the occasion. In sight of Ireland the will had been read and Audrey, the sole beneficiary, given the keys to the kingdom—the mahogany and walnut, crystal and silver, gilded frames and Oriental rugs which are now neatly tagged and awaiting disposal in some warehouse in Brompton. And that very morning, when the brass band had trumpeted them off the *Empress of England*, Minnie had received instructions to remove her own belongings and to hand over the house keys to the estate agent who'd be coming within the week to put up a notice.

"But what of *us*? What's to *become* of us?" Sally whispers with the voice of an exhausted child.

Minnie's Head Matron manner suddenly gives way. She blushes, clasping her hands so tightly together that Bella can see white spots on her fingernails. "Miss Rose telephoned to say that she's reserved a room at the Grand in your name—she's sure you'll find the weekly rates to be quite reasonable. And she left you a letter—I have it here—at least it was here—unless I put it away somewhere for safekeeping. Dear, dear, how stupid of me—I know I had it just a minute ago—"

By the time Minnie locates the letter, Bella has slipped out of the kitchen and is making her way upstairs. Even the runners have been removed from the steps. The front hall has been stripped of its banjo clock, the semicircular inlaid marble table, the elephant-foot receptacle for sticks and canes. Bella pauses before the door leading into her grandfather's study; rubs her palm over the handle; finally pushes inside. The room is perfectly empty. There is not even a shadow on the bare wooden floor to show where the costume chest had been.

The doors to all the rooms are closed. She's never realized before how many doors there are, how securely they all fit into their frames. With all its belongings gone the house seems like an emptied cage, one bar indistinguishable from another. She can't tell, anymore, which is the room where Arabella sleeps each summer, the room with a crooked view of the sea.

On the telephone, which hasn't yet been disconnected, though the little table on which it used to rest has been removed, Sally tries to ring through to her sister. At last she starts to speak; from the third-floor landing Bella hears an anxious buzz, like a fly caught between windows.

"But he *can't* have done that, no matter *how* potty he was. But *why*, Audrey? There was no money? Then what was he living on all these years—how were we paying Minnie? *Debts?* But you never asked for help—I could have spoken to Mendel— Yes, I *know* it's been difficult. But you might have telegraphed—you didn't know which boat? But I—oh, I can't remember whether or not I wrote to you—things are always so *busy* just before we leave. But Audrey, even so, why did you have to empty the *house?* What do you mean, it belongs to you? Don't you *see*, we might have had one last summer—You've no idea how upsetting it is for Bella. At least you might have let me choose something. For a *memento*. What do you mean, I have a husband instead? What? Oh I *see*. Then tell me, what am I supposed to tell Bella—that she's been *disinherited*? Don't you see that her feelings will be hurt? I'm not even talking about *me*, what *I* feel—what Mendel's going to say. He'll get his lawyer onto this, there'll be trouble, Audrey, and I won't be— Audrey? Audrey? Oh, Minnie—she's hung up. What shall we do, Minnie, what shall we ever *do?*"

Her cries are muffled now. Bella peers down from the stairwell; sees a child-sized mother hugging onto Minnie, who is patting Sally's head and murmuring, "There, there. Now, now. You have a good cry—it will make you feel ever so much better." There's no sofa on which to flounder, so Sally buries her head against Minnie's soft, shapeless front, as if trying to smother some bad dream that's tigered through the dark. Bella doesn't say a word, but Minnie hears her anyway. She looks up to the top of the landing but only stares as if she doesn't recognize the figure standing there: as if it were a perfect stranger and not Arabella Rose at all.

Slowly Bella tiptoes to the very top of the house and walks toward the fire door. She waits a moment before pushing it open and stealing out onto the little balcony. It has stopped raining, but the small, high metal steps are slippery. Her sandals have polished soles; they get no grip. She might easily fall if she isn't careful.

What would happen if she weren't careful? Why is it important not to fall? *The woods were dark, the grass was green.* Down into the garden, down into the roses, down into the fountain she cannot see from where she stands. It is blocked by a large gray rock, a rock with arms gesturing slowly, steadily up to her.

"Come down, dear, do. Come down—and be careful, please. Hold on tight to the rail, you mustn't fall."

It's no good—she can't make herself let go of the railing, run away forever to the dark, green woods. Bella descends, step by slippery step. Her hands are sore from where she's gripped the railing; flakes of rust and paint have scraped her palms. She stands on the last stair, waiting for Minnie to move so that she can see the fountain behind her, the nymph with her calm, blank face, her hooded eyes. But Minnie doesn't move.

"Your mother's called for a cab. Come now, dear—your shoes are soaking wet."

But Bella stands, arms folded, face set. "Where is he, Minnie. Where's my grandfather?"

"My dear, you know that Mr. Rose has died. That's why the house is up for sale. Now do come along, your mother's waiting."

"Where is he, Minnie? Where is his soul?"

Minnie blushes, a great lunge of red across her face. "He's at rest, dear. That's all that matters."

"No it's not, you said it's a person's soul that matters. You *said,* Minnie, don't you remember? Is he with God, Minnie? Which God —yours or mine?"

"There's only one God—"

"Yours or mine? You said His house was big enough for everyone. Then why isn't there room for my grandfather there? Or my grandmother—where is *she,* Minnie? Or Uncle Francis, or Aunt Bella, the one who was shot? For running away—how could you shoot someone just for trying to run away?"

Minnie lifts her arms from her sides, holding them out, awkward, empty. "Please—I don't know. Oh, Arabella, he's dead. That's all I know. And I wasn't even with him when he died—he didn't call out; it was night and he was alone. I wanted to—but he's dead. And God—"

"I hate your God."

Minnie drops her arms and bows her head for a moment. Then she turns to lead the way back to the house, and Bella sees what has happened. The fountain has been drained, the bronze plaque unscrewed, and where the nymph once stood with dragonflies brushing her eyes, there is nothing but an ugly metal spike.

On Mendel Rabinovich's decree, Sally and her daughter are boarding a Viscount Turbo-Prop for the twelve-hour flight from London to Toronto. There will be a lengthy stop at Gander for refueling, and Sally's already shivering in anticipation.

During their week at the hotel, Bella had refused to go any further than the lobby, or to do anything but stare at her hands clasped in her lap. Nor would she say a word to Aunt Audrey when Sally rang her up again. "You ought at least to say how d'you do, Poppet. Oh do, please do, you're her niece, Poppet, her only relation after me. Speak to her for my sake— No? You're getting to be more and more like your father, do you know that, Bella Rabinovich?"

Minnie came to the hotel to see them off, but Bella wouldn't say good-bye, or put out her cheek to be kissed the way her mother did. Minnie was staying with the Plymouth Brethren till she got another post. It was quiet there, she said—restful. Sally didn't ask her to send on her new address when she had one; Minnie didn't ask her to write.

Once they board the plane and fasten all the straps about them, locate the air-sickness bags, and read the pamphlets about emergency measures, Sally closes her eyes and clenches her fists, unwilling to open anything until the plane is up and over the clouds. Bella looks out the window smaller than a porthole at the tarmac and the green fields bumping by. She holds on to the strap above her as the plane lurches into the air, and fights down a yellow, sour snake that is trying to crawl from her belly up into her mouth. The higher they rise, the more she can see of an England that is no kingdom of ruined castles and rose gardens, but a checkerboard too small and far away to set up any pieces. And then the checkerboard falls away, and they are over the sea.

Her mother is airsick all the way home, but Bella keeps her face turned squarely to the window. She will not concede defeat by any foe so inconsiderable as a stomach. Just before they land at Gander she remembers the last lines of the nursery rhyme that had eluded her on the crossing over. She whispers them now as a charm against the night and the unknown place to which their plane is gliding:

I ran away to sea, no ship to get across;
I paid nine shillings for a blind white horse.
I was up on his back and off in a crack—
Sally, tell my mother I will never come back.

The Lesson

When Mrs. Dupont first began to run short of money, someone had suggested she give English lessons. You earned a minimum of fifty francs an hour, had no overhead, taught in the privacy of your own front parlor, and most important of all, you needed no other training or credentials than the ability to speak your mother tongue. A woman like Mrs. Dupont would have no difficulties in acquiring a reputation as an English teacher; in that section of the town where she lived, she was known simply as *l'Anglaise.* No hostility was intended by the good people of the *quartier,* and Mrs. Dupont knew this; it was not that she regarded with any secret pride her position in the town as a monument to the *esprit Britannique* (Mrs. Dupont was wont to feel contempt, not pride at the admiration of her inferiors), but that she accepted it with that coolness and assurance that had become the measure of her character.

She had married, at thirty-two—by which age her sister, comfortably settled with an ascending bank clerk, had produced her two children and was coasting into matronly middle age—a Frenchman several years older than she. He was an engineer, on contract to supervise a hands-across-the-Channel project with the firm in which his future wife was employed as a secretary. Two weeks before he was due to return to France he proposed to, and was accepted by, Miss Deborah Briggs, who accepted her translation to the higher spheres of matrimony and parts abroad with a tight-lipped disinterest which had infuriated her sister. They had remained on blank terms until four years before Mr. Dupont's death, by which time Mrs. Foster was fancying a little trip to the Continent in order to recover from the increasingly exigent demands made on her energy, good humor, and humility by her husband and two adolescent children. Mrs. Dupont had replied to that first ingratiating letter with a succinct invitation for her sister to come and spend a week with them at their home in the northwest of France. It had been, Mrs. Foster fretted, calculatedly unfair; one didn't spend that much money on one's fare only to come and, almost immediately, go. Nevertheless, she reasoned, one week in France was infinitely preferable to yet another week in Wembley; she would go and be prepared to make the best of it.

On her return she told her husband that Deborah and Jacques—for that was his name, and there was nothing so very distinguished about it—seemed to be reasonably happy. Their house, or rather, their *appartement,* was—here she stopped for words—was furnished to Deborah's taste, which hadn't changed over the years. It was extremely clean, as you'd expect, knowing Deborah, and there was a charming view out the bathroom window. But it had to be said that the exteriors of all French buildings looked distressingly dirty. You simply could not believe the amount of grit in the French towns; why, they had special machines to lay down dust on the pavements. It got into your shoes and all over your stockings. You simply wouldn't believe—

"Of course I would," her husband had snapped. "That's why I'd never be fool enough to go there on vacation. With the whole of England for holidaying, why waste your time in a nasty frog pond?"

Nevertheless, Mrs. Foster decided to be satisfied with her excursion. She had bought herself a frock in one of the finest shops in town—it was not too French-looking, so she could wear it to her Women's Institute Wednesday afternoons. She had eaten well

(Jacques did most of the cooking) and she had insisted on taking the two of them out for an expensive meal in a three-star restaurant. She had not thought about her own home or family for nine full days—and she had seen her sister.

"They seem to get on as well as could be expected," she continued to her husband over a cup of tea on the evening of her arrival home. "You would not believe it," she sighed, cradling a delicate china cup in her hands, "but there's no decent tea to be had in that country—or if there is, it comes as dear as champagne here. I don't know how Deborah manages. She admitted to me that she *does* miss it—a nice cup of tea." That had been the only thing she *had* admitted, reflected Mrs. Foster, watching her husband help himself to a large piece of the heavy Dundee cake that had been lying about since Christmas. And she sighed again as she thought of the pastry shops that mined the streets on the way to and from Deborah's flat. How on earth did her sister keep so thin, she wondered, refusing a slab of cake and nibbling a stale biscuit instead. Suddenly she put down her teacup, crammed the rest of the biscuit into her mouth, and exclaimed through the crumbs, "Of course! What a really lovely idea. I'll send Deborah a few packets of tea every so often—she'll be delighted, and it won't cost much."

And so, for a good many months, until the price of postage went up prohibitively, Mrs. Foster had sent brown paper packages of English Breakfast tea and plain Orange Pekoe to Mrs. Dupont. She had always intended to return and visit her sister, but then the husband had died, and she reversed her project. Deborah must come home, at least for a visit. It must be dreadful for her, alone amid the alien corn, mused Mrs. Foster, waxing unaccountably poetic. Deborah never mentioned either her emotional state or her sister's invitation in any of her letters. They were entirely factual, and usually so short that she never filled two complete sides of a piece of paper. The weather, the price of food in the markets, comments on the behavior of this or that member of the Royal Family, followed by an invariable "Yours, Deborah Dupont." Out of spite, Mrs. Foster signed hers with a curlicued and sweeping "Ever your loving Beryl." After reading one of her sister's communications she would sigh and give a little involuntary look down at her lap, now padding itself in preparation for the grandchildren who would in good time be deposited there. "Really," she would say, "Deborah ought to have had children. It's such a shame."

"Rubbish," her sister would have said. "We had barely enough money to look decently after the two of us. How could we have had children?" For the truth was that Mr. Dupont had, two years after their marriage, lost his job with the electronics firm that had originally sent him to England. The firm had collapsed due to some dishonesty on the part of its directors, so that there had not even been severance pay. At this point, Mrs. Dupont had begun to check the little advertisements in the local paper; someone might, after all, have need of an English secretary. But within a month, and just in time at that, her husband had found another post, this time with a much smaller company, and at half his former salary. Things could be worse, his wife had said to herself. They sold some furniture and wedding gifts; they moved to an apartment in one of the more rundown sections of the town. She made all her own clothes—she had brought an entire pattern book with her from England—and in the end they managed without her having to go out to work. On the channel steamer out from England, she—a bride of no more than twenty-four hours—had made two great vows: one was not to be seasick and have her husband fussing over her, and the other was never again to go out to work. She had loathed every one of her fifteen years spent as a badly paid, unnoticed secretary, and had flown to the first chance that had come her way to avoid yet another fifteen. The first vow she broke when they had been two hours out on an unusually choppy sea; the second she had kept, always.

Or at least till now. Her husband had died before his life insurance could amount to anything, and the payments from his pension plan had not, for the last six months, floated her over the current rate of inflation. Before, she had lived meagerly but decently—now she could barely afford to live. She was in her middle fifties; she supposed she could buy a book on commercial French, train herself to use a

French typewriter, and do shorthand as well. Her sister, lately widowed, had written yet again, pleading with her to return to England
where they could share the house she'd been left in Mr. Foster's will;
she supposed she could always go and live with her sister. And to
do either of these things would be to acknowledge that the one in-
dependent action of her life had been, if not a failure, at least its own
undoing. This was a lesson she would rather not appear to have to
learn. And so, on the casual advice of a dropped acquaintance, she
sat down one evening with six small squares of cardboard and a
ballpoint pen. *Englishwoman, highly qualified, offers lessons in commercial
or conversational English. Contact Mrs. D. Dupont, #6, 33, rue Emile Zola.*
In the morning, as she did her shopping, she left one card each at
the baker's, the butcher's, the news agent's, the shoe-repair shop, and
the launderette. The last card she carried home with her and taped
very neatly on the concierge's window. It was three weeks before
she received any replies.

There was one reply—from a family who lived two floors below
her, an excessive family with both parents going out to work while
the grandmother stayed home with the children. Mrs. Dupont had
never got on with any of them—they put on airs, had tried to establish a kind of condescending intimacy with her, and she suspected
that the mother laughed at her behind her back. This Mrs. Dupont
would not tolerate, and she had paid the woman back with a comment, in her correct but misaccented French, that people who couldn't
afford to look after their children—the grandmother drank, and kept
the ones too young for school indoors all day—shouldn't breed like
rabbits. The woman had glared at her, then fired off a round of aptly
phrased obscenities. From this point on she no longer talked to Mrs.
Dupont, who took to staring right through her as if she were a
smudged pane of glass.

All of this notwithstanding, the father came up to Mrs. Dupont's
rooms one evening with a short, moon-faced girl of thirteen. He
introduced her as his oldest daughter; her name was Clothilde. She
was not doing very well in her English classes—in fact, the professor
had advised them that they must try to find help for her outside

classes or she would never make her year. "She's not stupid," the man insisted, "she just doesn't understand." Mrs. Dupont looked at the girl: Clothilde—just the sort of name people like that would give to their first child, an aristocratic-sounding name to suit their over-weening social ambitions. She looked at the father's well-worn but nicely tailored coat, and then she named her price: fifty francs an hour was the going rate.

Father and daughter looked doubtfully at one another. The girl whined, "But Marie-Claire, she gets lessons for forty francs from a student at the lycée—" Mrs. Dupont stared the girl into silence and this must have impressed the father, for he nodded his head gravely and said, "Very well, fifty francs then." "I suppose she can start to-morrow afternoon—if it's convenient," said Mrs. Dupont in a delib-erative way, as if to suggest that she had any number of pupils, and that she would have to squeeze Clothilde into the one vacant spot in her schedule. It was convenient—it was to be hoped that the arrange-ment would work out to everyone's satisfaction; they were lucky to have found so highly qualified a teacher for little Clothilde, someone who lived in the same building as well. They shook hands good-bye, Mrs. Dupont laying her long, cool hand in the father's for so short a space that it made the man think of a fish flipping over in his palm.

And so Clothilde came every Wednesday afternoon and sat for exactly one hour at the worktable in Mrs. Dupont's parlor. She looked down at her hands, or up at the lampshade, and most often at the square clock in its oak case that Mrs. Dupont had brought with her from England. Clothilde never volunteered any English, not even "Hello!" or "How do you do?" and she required all her teacher's questions and remarks to be translated into French. If forced to an-swer in English she would sit there, a thick line furrowing her fore-head, or else wobble her lips over sounds too stupid even to be guesses. It was impossible. After three sessions the child was bored, not to tears, for she was incapable of any irregularity from her bovine norm—but to an even weightier opacity. There were certain signs of a straggling consciousness: sighs, head-scratchings, the occasional torpid nod when absolutely necessary, but nothing that could even jestingly be called progress.

Mrs. Dupont could be forgiven for the resigned hopelessness with which she regarded her pupil. It wasn't her fault that the lessons went so badly, or rather, didn't go anywhere at all. At last she requested the girl to show her the books she used at school, texts desperately designed to appeal to the inert imaginations of their readers: comic-strips, crossword puzzles, brain-teasers, the most obvious and repetitive of jokes and slogans. But this girl, it seemed, had made no other use of her book than to draw schematized daisies and stick figures in the margins. At the front of her book she'd written her name in obese letters with elaborate capitals, curlicues, and scrolls. At the back was a pocket in which were collected the girl's weekly tests. Mrs. Dupont lifted them all out and sifted through them, looking over at Clothilde as she did so; the girl's face did not flush or darken. Four out of ten, two out of ten, zero, zero, zero—she had at least achieved consistency. On each test some comment or other was scribbled; they increased in sarcastic exasperation until finally an "EXCELLENT!" was recorded beside a mark of one out of ten. Then they ceased altogether, with only the mark, invariably minimal, recorded. The idea had obviously been to humiliate the child into some sort of reaction, and the teacher had done his best until presumably the task of finding some new verbal stiletto had become too much for him. Or perhaps his words had never wounded, perhaps the girl's skin or her sheer indifference had been so thick that the man, demoralized, had laid down his shafts in total surrender.

Mrs. Dupont stared openly at her pupil, attempting by the intensity of her gaze to force some crack across that smooth, white, not wholly unattractive face. Was Clothilde secretly assaulted by anxiety and fear, did she detest her classes with the same attritive hatred that had kept Mrs. Dupont so gritty, spare, and glacial during her years as a secretary? If so, the woman could have felt some covert sympathy for the girl, might have abandoned her accustomed indifference to try and really help the child get by. Alas, who could tell? The girl was pale enough, whey-faced, but that might simply be from consuming too much starch and sugar—she was decidedly too plump for a thirteen-year-old. Yet with unaccustomed charity, encouraged by the fact that she was relieving the girl's father of fifty francs each week, Mrs. Dupont gave her pupil the benefit of many doubts. Accordingly, she set aside her plans for extensive martial drills in the fundamentals of English grammar and composition. Instead, teacher and pupil sat down for the hour with an exercise book that had belonged to the late Mr. Dupont. *Teach Yourself English* was its title, but Mrs. Dupont was confident enough in Clothilde's intractable stupidity to produce the work without misgivings. And indeed, they made progress of a sort, thanks to the stick-figure illustrations of unabashedly simple sentences in which the one word left blank would be laboriously filled in in Clothilde's ornamented script, on her teacher's dictation. It may have done little for the girl's ability to speak English, but it did impress her parents and, all in all, Mrs. Dupont began to feel a certain satisfaction every Wednesday afternoon from four to five o'clock. And she even developed—it may have been due to nothing more than the regularity of the lessons—a noncommittal form of acceptance, even commiseration with the child, who was, there could be no doubt, unfit for academic work of any kind.

At the end of each lesson Mrs. Dupont would make conversation in her stiff, accurate French: what was Clothilde's favorite subject at school, what did she like to do in her spare time, what did she want to be when she grew up? The answers to these questions were always variations of "I don't know," or "nothing." But at least they were given with slight shifts of expression which Mrs. Dupont interpreted as signs of a bewildered gratitude that someone was taking an interest in her as an individual rather than as an object to be improved and instructed. It was something of a triumph when, four months after the lessons had begun, Clothilde was brought to the admission that she liked watching television, and wanted to be a *speakerine* when she grew up; they looked so pretty, she said, even when they announced international disasters and catastrophic Acts of God on the evening news.

When the Christmas holidays approached, Mrs. Dupont spent a great deal of time considering whether she ought to purchase a small gift, connected, of course, with the English classes, for her pupil. Finally, she decided on an attractive Christmas card instead. But when the time came she felt that such a gesture would disturb the tenor of their working relationship, perhaps embarrass the girl. And so with a certain relief, Mrs. Dupont put the card back into her desk drawer—she had, unfortunately, inked in the child's name, so that the card could not be reused. Not that she had so many people in the small town where she lived, or for that matter, over the Channel, to whom to address Christmas cards.

It was long after the holidays and the midterm break, it was actually approaching Easter that Mrs. Dupont received one Wednesday morning an unusually tactful letter from her sister, inviting her to come and spend at least the long weekend with her in Wembley. A certain indisposition was alluded to, nothing too serious, but enough to make Mrs. Dupont drop the sheet of paper and sit staring at her oak-cased clock.

It became as plain to her as the numbers on the dial that she had come to count more than she liked to admit on the presence of her silly, snooping younger sister in her life. Not as a major figure, nor yet as a familiar, but as someone against whom she could define and justify herself. No matter what her present circumstances, she hadn't married a mean and stupid man who'd prescribed everything about his wife's existence from the brand of marmalade she spread on her toast to the cost and color of her stockings. Her own husband had never intruded upon her independence of mind—body, of course, had been a somewhat different matter. At least he hadn't burdened her with inconsiderate and scheming children. And she had, at least, got out of England, that sepia-suburban part of England that was all that Beryl knew. Poor Beryl. Were she to fall gravely ill, were she to die—and the possibility had hovered in the margins of her letter—it would make a difference to Mrs. Dupont. She would feel—left alone, rather than willfully solitary.

Inconsiderate and scheming children. Mrs. Dupont started in her chair, as if the clock had just chimed thirteen. Inconsiderate they undoubt-edly were, but scheming? Why had she so described them to herself? She pondered for a while, letting the minutes seep out of her tightly planned and packaged day. For the first time she realized that when Beryl died, the overfurnished semidetached in Wembley would be-long to the children, children who would never even think of inviting their expatriate aunt to come and spend the Christmas holidays, or even Whitsun weekend with them. Of course she would, in any case, refuse, but as long as Beryl was still round and about, so was the possibility of receiving offers of that house to which Deborah could come and, in Beryl's phrase, "make herself comfortable." Comforta-ble. Mrs. Dupont looked across her tiny parlor, and at the doors that led to the smaller bedroom, bath, and kitchen. If she could just scrape by with the money from this teaching—and other pupils must surely come, one day—her needs would be met. As for her wants—well. That was all.

She looked again at her English clock for some assurance that she had done right, done the only thing she ever could have done, given her strict and niggardly circumstances. But all she saw was the ar-rangement of the hands for three-thirty. Three-thirty, and she had not finished any of her cleaning. Mrs. Dupont had arranged her days according to an intricate schedule, cross-hatched with the minutiae of things-to-be-attended-to. It was her one unassailable satisfaction to adhere to this schedule, with cooking and cleaning, letters to Beryl and lessons with Clothilde totting up a regular if meager sum of day-to-day reality. Yet here she was, dreadfully behind—she would have no time for the afternoon walk which the doctor had prescribed as essential exercise for a woman of her years. And she would have to rush out after the lesson to do her marketing, an expedient practiced by the careless housewives and working women she detested. If she hurried, she would just have time to finish tidying the flat, then wash and change. She was wearing a shirt, trousers, and pair of socks that had belonged to her husband—she couldn't afford to wear her own clothes for cleaning, they'd be worn out in no time.

When the doorbell rang Mrs. Dupont was still working on the

bedroom; had she omitted to wax the kitchen floor she might have been ready on time. The bell rang again, and again. Finally Mrs. Dupont understood that it was her pupil, that she had to go to the door. She took a quick look at the parlor as she came out—it, at least, was perfectly tidy. She was about to open the door when she realized that she hadn't changed, that she was still dressed in her husband's clothes. She couldn't greet Clothilde like that—but she had to open the door before the girl traipsed off with her fifty francs. She would just let her in and excuse herself for five minutes to change. And this she did, reappearing in a clean blouse and well-pressed pair of woman's trousers—she hadn't the time to fiddle with stockings and a skirt.

As they sat down at the table Mrs. Dupont examined her pupil's face; it retained the gelid smoothness of old custard skin. She obviously hadn't noticed or thought anything of her teacher's unusual appearance when she'd first been let inside. Mrs. Dupont asked for the exercise book to be produced. Clothilde bent down toward her satchel, and immediately her face contorted, she was making sobbing, choking sounds. "Whatever is the matter—are you ill?" asked Mrs. Dupont, rising a little from the table to see her pupil's face. Clothilde shook her head, hiding it in her hands, shuddering in her straight-backed chair.

It must have been the delayed impact of receiving Beryl's letter, for in a contagion of fear and worry that spread helplessly to sympathy, Mrs. Dupont leaned across the table and took her pupil's face, firmly yet almost tenderly, into her hands, "If you are ill," she began, "we must help you, find a doctor—" She stopped; the girl was looking straight into her eyes, and the teacher saw that it was not pain or grief but silent laughter that had twisted her expression. Mrs. Dupont dropped her hands as if, in some dark corner of her flat, she had touched the rank fur or scrabbling feet of a rat. Instantly she rose to her feet.

"You find something amusing, Clothilde? Can you tell me what it is—if you can muster the English—or even the French—to do so?"

The girl at last controlled herself, but a smile fluttered along her lips as she shook her head, no, at her teacher. For a moment she looked almost attractive—older, too, than her thirteen years. Mrs. Dupont sat down again; she spread out the exercise book on the table, and the lesson began at last. Yet every so often Mrs. Dupont would notice the girl glancing under the table—each time she did so, a phantom of that smile flared her lips. Whatever could she be laughing at, she wondered, trying to imagine herself from the girl's perspective, to discover what she saw as she bent her head down.

And suddenly, she understood—she put her own head down to confirm the vision she'd so abruptly attained of her own shoes and socks. For there had been no time to change them, she had thought they wouldn't be noticed. For the first time she registered the ludicrous, diamond-patterned heliotrope of the socks Beryl had sent to her brother-in-law many Christmases ago. She witnessed the ugliness of her dead husband's flat, pointed, lace-up shoes. Immediately the teacher raised her head, but it was too late; her pupil had seen her and given up all camouflage, her eyes and mouth swimming in voluptuous waves of laughter. Mrs. Dupont could only stare at her, feeling her whole body sour and sharpen.

"What is it," she asked, this time in English. "You really must tell me, so that I can properly share the joke. What—can't you answer? Are you too stupid? You idiot, you fat, stupid fool, you can't speak even three words of English, you can hardly spell in your own language, you've no more brains than a pig, a cow—and you think you can sit there and laugh at me?" She pushed her face so close to the girl's that she could see her own reflection in Clothilde's gooseberry-colored eyes. "Stupid little bitch," hissed Mrs. Dupont. And then, her voice sliding up into a scream, "Stupid bitch. Stupid, stupid, stupid bitch!"

The girl only knew that something had gone wrong with the old Englishwoman's head—she was crazy; shouting like that, she looked like a mule braying. Stolidly Clothilde got up, the smile draining from her face like water from a sieve. She packed away her pencils and pens, leaving the workbook behind her on the table. But as she opened the door to leave, she turned to Mrs. Dupont with an altogether different sort of smile and said, *"Stupide bitche—c'est bien, ça. Je m'en souviendrai. Adieu, madame."*

Mrs. Dupont waited at the table until she heard the girl thump down the stairwell. She listened for a moment to the silence of the corridor, then locked her door. Calmly, with an admirable degree of self-control, she went into her bedroom to change her shoes and socks, then sat herself at the work table with a box of writing paper, a straight pen, and a bottle of black ink.

"Dear Beryl," she wrote in a careful hand. "Your letter of March twelfth, with its regrettable news of your illness, has finally made me change my mind about coming to visit you. I feel that I should be with you at this trying time. Obviously, the children have their own lives to lead, and cannot be expected to look after you in the manner you would wish. My obligations here do not make it either a simple or an advantageous matter for me to come to you. But then, I hope I know my duty and have not forgotten how much thicker blood should be than water.

"Ever your concerned sister, Deborah."

Accidents

It was not the house she would have chosen. It was on a street named after some particularly obscure member of the *Académie Française*—whenever Alison walked past the street sign, she thought of nonagenarians in black tricorne hats with gold cockades. Her daughter, Jill, was far more interested in the cat that came with the address, and her husband had little interest in such things as dead, minor academicians, though he was well on the way to becoming one himself. No, Douglas's main concern was his cleverness in having actually secured the house. Wasn't it within walking distance of the university at which he was spending his sabbatical year? And wasn't it only a short hop to the nursery school in which Jill would become fluent in French?

He'd never even thought of mentioning a garden in his letters to the real estate agent, though he'd made it clear that proximity to a park was a necessity. The closest park turned out to be a sandy square with a roundabout, a rusted slide, and a fountain in the shape of a lion's head; water dribbled over its tongue in a sad little stream. The square was called Creux d'Enfer—a cheerful name, though as Douglas pointed out, Jill need never learn that the words meant something like "hellhole." Their own house in Toronto, a coach house converted by Alison and duly photographed for *City Living* magazine, had an ornamental pool instead of a backyard. The front lawn had long since been paved over, and there was barely room for window boxes. Alison had given up planting anything there but foul-smelling marigolds, since passersby had formed the habit of decapitating anything showy, like tulips or daffodils. Besides, she hadn't the time to potter about with seeds and watering cans and trowels.

It was Douglas's dream to buy some land in the country north of Peterborough. A small farm, where Jill could have an acre each of flowers and vegetables, and keep a pony. "A tax write-off," declared Alison, and Douglas, looking wounded, had countered with, "Since we're only having the one, don't you think we ought to do everything possible to give her a perfect childhood?" It was Alison's decision that Jill should be an only child, as she herself was. But Alison had declined any guilt in the matter; she loved Jill, and she loved her job, and she couldn't handle any more on her plate than that, thank you very much. Lots of couples had only one child, particularly when their funds were somewhat limited. At this point Douglas had had to shrug his shoulders and surrender. Alison made slightly more money than he; though his family had contributed the hutches and spool beds and hooked rugs with which their home was furnished, it had been Alison's parents who had given them the down payment for the house itself. And besides, ever since the accident Alison had been so strange about Jill that Douglas had decided to drop the subject of another baby altogether.

Accidents happen to other people. When they happen to you, they're not accidents anymore, but violent illuminations.

Alison had been taking Jill to her parents' house for the weekend. She'd strapped the child into the back seat with her teddy and some books, buckled herself into the driver's seat, looked both ways, and then pulled out into the street. It was March; there'd been a storm during the night, but the roads had been cleared, even if the pavement was still a little slippery. The car had snow tires, and Alison was driving only as fast as the limit allowed—in short, she was not to blame. No one was to blame, nothing could have been prevented. That was what had made it so terrible. She was driving north; the car in the opposite lane was heading south, and it happened that there was an icy patch on which the other car skidded, spun, and crashed into hers.

Crushed up against the steering wheel, blood trickling down her chin, Alison had thought one thing, over and over again. "This can't be happening; accidents happen to other people, not to us." She could hear Jill screaming—not a cry for help, not Mummy or Daddy, just a brute, hurting noise. She couldn't say anything to comfort Jill—her mouth was full of blood. Unable even to turn round to see what had happened to her daughter, Alison could only listen, and imagine. Not until the police arrived did she find out that Jill hadn't been badly hurt, though the shock, of course, had been extreme.

They were kept in the hospital overnight for observation. Jill had bruises; she cried off and on for a good twelve hours, Douglas holding her, while she held on to her teddy bear. Alison had whiplash, of course, but the most painful thing had been the cut under her lips— somehow she'd managed to bite through the skin. Her whole chin was bruised, but the doctor had assured her it would fade; as for the cut, there'd only be a tiny mark, not worth bothering about. But she'd insisted on a plastic surgeon. Not until he'd erased the scar was she able to speak at length to anyone. Even her family; especially Jill.

Douglas was at a loss how to explain it. Alison had always been a copybook mother, taking a full three months of maternity leave, expressing countless bottles of milk to be frozen for the baby and defrosted by the nanny, taking turns with him at bathing Jill each night and reading to her. Sometimes he'd find the two of them asleep, side by side, in Jill's bed, Alison still clutching *The Wind in the Willows* or *Stuart Little* in her hands. Yet after the accident she'd made all kinds of excuses to have as little as possible to do with her child. Jill, thank heavens, seemed to have settled back into her usual routine: Nanny, Montessori, Sunday lunches at her grandparents' house. "Amazing how they bounce back," Douglas had commented to a friend who'd been visiting a few days after the accident. "Liar," Alison had said, staring out the window at the frozen flowerboxes. He and the friend had pretended not to hear.

She'd taken time off work, as was only natural after such a physical and mental shock. They might all have been killed—Alison and Jill as well as the driver of the other car, who'd been quite seriously injured. But the week's absence from her office became a fortnight, and then a month's official sick leave, until Douglas had met with her partner to suggest that a full year's break might be the best solution. Alison didn't care. She spent most of her time at the desk in her study under the eaves, filling huge sheets of blank paper with drawings of houses falling down, their roofs bashed in, walls buckling. The consequence of natural disasters, to which category she'd now added childbirth.

What a lie it was, giving birth, raising children; a lie in the child's face, over and over again. This was the illumination that had happened to her one winter afternoon, driving the few miles north to her parents' house. It was the equivalent of that scar on her chin for which, months after the surgery, she was always checking whenever she passed a mirror or a darkened window. Sketching collapsing houses, hotels, apartment towers in her white-walled study, Alison had only to shut her eyes to hear Jill screaming. Wordless, shapeless screaming, nothing like the cry she'd given when, annoyed, surprised, but ultimately trusting, she'd been pushed out of the warm, wet dark into her life. Jill's screams in the car—that had been the shock not of pain, but of betrayal.

Now, when Alison crept into her daughter's room at night, she couldn't even pass her hand over Jill's hair without fear of the child waking up, accusing her. "You brought me here, you told me nothing bad would ever happen to me." The lie that every parent croons to every child, pacing the floors at night or charming a nightmare away. "Don't be afraid of the dark, of ghosts, of little humpbacked men hiding in the cupboard. We're here with you, you're safe and sound, forever." The same lie her parents had given her, backed up by the large house full of flowers, the new cars in the garage, all the pretty dresses in the closets. And she'd believed every word, had moved right into it: the university degree, a profession, marriage, a baby. Until the bomb went off in her face.

Of course she was overreacting. Think of what other people go through, people whose children are dying of leukemia, people fighting civil wars, people made to disappear in the middle of the night. But the fact that others had suffered infinitely more than she— wasn't it obscene to suggest that this could somehow make her own hurt better? This new knowledge that her child had been in danger of her life, and that she hadn't been able to lift a hand to help her—didn't it erase her previous certainty that she would enter a burning house, lift away steel beams, expose herself to gunfire, all to save her child from harm? And how could it be excessive to recoil like this when her own case was but one of millions, infinitely more grave: deaths by accident and by design, deaths for which there had been no help, parents and children under equally intolerable sentence? Auschwitz, Hiroshima, Vietnam, Argentina, Lebanon—surely the doctor could continue the list without her help?

The psychiatrist to whom she'd been referred had had no answers to her questions, and so the sessions hadn't lasted long. Alison had been controlled, competent enough to finally say the things that would release her from a stranger's surveillance, allow her to be considered well on the way to recovery. Douglas had been brought to agree that there was nothing so very extraordinary in her wanting a bit of space around her, ample time to get over the scare she'd had. He'd even smoothed things over with her parents, and with the friends whom Alison refused to see. And he took up so much of Jill's time that the child could barely have noticed how her mother had withdrawn herself from any real relation with her.

Douglas was so good. Alison's complement: the model husband, father, son. Sometimes, when he was being exaggeratedly good-natured, he reminded his wife of a big, beautiful golden lab, allowed, as a mark of special favor, into the passenger seat of the family car. On and on he rode, ears pricked, tongue out, an expression of nobility and forbearance in his eyes. Her parents adored him, praising his wonderful patience with poor dear Alison, who only needed a change of scene to get back to her clever, sensible, affectionate self. Jill had thrown her arms around him, letting her father carry her off all the way to France. And Alison had had to follow. For Douglas had moved heaven and earth to get this sabbatical—and hadn't it already turned out to be the very cure they'd all been counting on?

For once her mother and Douglas had started packing away valuables, interviewing prospective tenants, arranging for visas, and negotiating with shipping lines, Alison couldn't help but be infected by all the confusion and flurry. From her invalid's room at the very top of the house, she'd listened to disturbances like picks and shovels breaking through to her. By deciding to take them all away for the year, Douglas did not order, but merely expected his wife to get back to normal. "Lightning doesn't strike twice in the same place," he'd reasoned. "Of course you've had a bad scare, but don't dwell on what might have happened. Just think how lucky you are." Douglas was a sociologist; he dreamed of people spending long and happy lives in clean, well-ordered cities full of parks and museums and general bonhomie. And it was to establish the definitive economic advantages of such a vision that he was going to France, to co-author a book with a like-minded colleague.

What could she do but go with him? After certain kinds of accidents you realize that the roof over your head is held up not by walls but by the flimsiest latticework, and that there's nothing to keep the wind from smashing it all in. Either you throw everything open and live on pure risk, or else your fear closes you tight, buries you under. Alison decided to exchange one burial site for another. She came down from her study at the top of the house, from which she'd spent the whole morning watching her daughter ride a tricycle in circles round and round the paved-over yard. She helped to pack away precious and breakable objects; she phoned up the utilities and telephone people and stowed winter clothes into an old steamer trunk.

She learned how easy it was to restore appearances, to dress herself in a false self, a skin that grew over every orifice, sealing off eyes and ears and mouth. Her child, her husband, her parents and friends —she performed all the necessary attentions, while giving them nothing. When she kissed Jill, her lips brushed over her like dead leaves across a pavement; when her husband made love to her she lay still, sealed, her real self growing more and more inward, as layers of blank, dead skin cocooned themselves around her. Nobody knew, no one could ever tell how deeply she had hidden herself away, the self that could give neither help nor shelter. By the time they boarded the plane for France, she'd stopped feeling even her own fear. She had become entirely enclosed, invulnerable. Nothing could happen to her again.

Now that they'd arrived and installed themselves, it seemed the crowning piece of luck that the house should be surrounded by a sea of pebbly earth. Jill would be able to muck about there to her heart's content, while Douglas wouldn't have to even look at a lawn mower, nor Alison lift a watering can. Of course there were drawbacks to both house and garden: diesel fumes from the boulevard that fronted the house, racket from the railway line a stone's throw from the bedroom windows, hideous wallpaper, threadbare carpets, and a bathroom as large and cold as Mont Blanc. Nothing, however, that they couldn't live with, or so Douglas decided. In fact, these very inconveniences would jolt his wife back into those habits of coping and contriving she'd not so much lost as abandoned after the accident.

So far they had settled in nicely, unpacking the trunk of books and clothes they'd sent ahead; taking down the calendars of Alpine cows and children, the repro of the Mona Lisa, which turned out to be the grease-spotted lid from a chocolate box. While they'd sorted out and put away, Jill had played in the garden, counting the wild pansies that struggled up in front of the house, and chasing after the cat that belonged to their landlady, Madame Boulez. Douglas had pasted Jill's room with photographs of people and places from home. He'd bought a potted azalea to put on the dining-room table and stocked the cellar with bottles of Nuit-Saint-Georges and Clos de Vougeot. He had also procured, and left prominently displayed on the telephone table in the hall (there was no telephone), a rash of booklets put out by the tourist bureau, the municipal office, and the *quartier* association, listing the town's cultural, athletic, and aesthetic activities in which all residents were urged to participate.

As for Alison, she appeared to be making the best of it. Jill had been enrolled at the local *maternelle,* and though she didn't appear to be learning any French, she didn't fuss at being dropped off at eight-thirty every morning and fetched in the early afternoon. Douglas spent every day in his office at the university, the house being dark and the lighting poor except for Jill's room, the bathroom, and the kitchen. Saturdays they did their shopping. The wonderful little places in the old town turned out to be wildly expensive, so they ended up going to a *hypermarché* on the outskirts of the city, a kind of barn the size of three football stadiums selling everything from artificial fingernails to prefabricated bathrooms. On Sundays Alison was allowed to sleep in—Douglas and Jill would fetch a brioche and some patisseries from the bakery round the corner, and they would all drink *café au lait* out of the huge, chipped bowls that had come with the house. Then they'd stroll in the park on the Roman road out of town, Jill riding her bicycle under the avenues of giant chestnut trees or feeding stale bread to the baby goats and sheep kept in enclosures there. They hadn't yet found a sitter, so there wasn't much of a chance to go out, even if Alison had wanted to.

For Alison wanted simply to shut herself up inside the garden walls. She stored the pamphlets of things to do under the mattress, and spent the month of September sitting out in the garden reading *Le Monde.* She had a craving, now, for news. Ten times a day she'd turn on the radio and listen to what was happening in Israel, Pakistan, Brazil, El Salvador, as if it were all some huge, interlocking serial. She was afraid that if she didn't keep reading and listening everything would end; she felt like those nuns she'd once heard about, some enclosed order in Austria or Belgium, who spent their lives on their knees praying for the remission of the sins of the world. If once they stopped praying, the whole globe would smash up, the very air turn poisonous, like the atmosphere of Mars.

And while Alison read about atomic tests or earthquakes or guerrilla wars, Madame Gaudet, their landlady's housekeeper, would be out hanging up the washing—mainly sheets. Madame Boulez, bed-ridden in the top-floor apartment, appeared to be incontinent. The real estate agent had told them the old woman was moribund, blind, barely able to speak. It was very sad, yes, but she'd reached a ripe age; it was something they'd all have to face, sooner or later. At any rate, they wouldn't even know that she was living on the floor above them. And it was true; except for the presence of Madame Gaudet, Alison would never have suspected the existence of Madame Boulez. Each morning, Madame Gaudet would smile at Alison from the laun-dry line, and she would smile back, unabashed, from over her news-paper. She and the *femme de ménage* were both busy about their work, and who was to say which task was the more important?

The house was fenced off from the boulevard by a black, iron grille. And the ropes of ivy throttling the grille were, Alison decided, the vegetal equivalent of boa constrictors. A stone wall shut off the other three sides of the garden, and there was a metal door that let people in and out on the side street named after the academician. The only time Alison opened the door and let herself out was at two in the afternoon, when it was time to walk down to the *maternelle* and fetch Jill. They'd buy an ice cream or a raisin bun on the way home, and stop at the Square du Creux d'Enfer for Jill to whirl on the roundabout. Then they'd go home, Alison unlocking the metal gate at the side of their house and shutting them back inside. Jill would spend the rest of the day in the garden, digging and scraping with sticks she'd collected, or else beating the rosemary bush and the rose beds for signs of the landlady's cat, while Alison got supper. Douglas would come home, they'd eat, watch the news, read Jill to sleep, and then fall into bed.

"How was your day," he'd ask her, returning with a load of books at five or six and pouring himself a drink. "Oh, the same as usual." "What did Jill get up to? Did she have any friends over?" "No, not today—she fooled around in the garden instead." Douglas insisted that she find friends for Jill. He was convinced their daughter would become autistic without the company of children her own age.

Alison never argued with him now. She knew that Jill was happy with shovels and a pail of water, rakes and trowels and odd rotting sticks with which she marked places in the soil. Was she digging for treasure, burying prizes? Alison couldn't tell. But she let her dig and haul the earth about—there were no flowers to be hurt except for a few moribund roses that seemed to beg to be put out of their misery.

"Any mail?" was Douglas's next and last question, and here her responses were bound to be more satisfactory. Both sets of parents wrote copious letters, with a frequency that seemed to exhaust the postman, an old man who lugged a wheezing bicycle up to their gate each morning. Douglas's parents were immured in Montreal—they couldn't comprehend why their son had bothered to go away to France when he could have had all the French he wanted in Quebec. Alison's parents were planning to come over and see them at Easter. They could all just nip down to Provence and see the lavender in bloom, or so Alison's mother suggested. Alison hadn't answered that letter yet. Her mother's confidence that there would be a new year, never mind a reenactment of the resurrection, seemed a trifle premature. The series of articles Alison had recently been reading in *Le Monde* had dealt with the poisoning of the biosphere, the insoluble and escalating problems of Third World debt, the lack of any failsafe disposal for nuclear waste. In spite of which Douglas rode off to work each day on a three-speed bicycle, and Jill kept digging up bits of old bottles in the garden or stalking the cat.

None of them knew what its name could be. It certainly didn't answer to Jill's "Here, kitty, kitty," or Douglas's "Minou, minou." Asleep under one of the deck chairs or gliding between the railings at the front of the house, the cat disdained any of their attempts to win it over. Douglas even suggested they get a kitten for Jill, since the old cat was so unforthcoming, but Alison had put her foot down. It would get run over on the boulevard; this was a disastrous place for an animal of any kind. So Jill went on unsuccessfully trying to make acquaintance with the cat, who might as well have been called Rumpelstiltskin, for all the names with which she beseeched it.

But one hot autumn afternoon, Alison heard a brittle, piercing voice call out, *"Nénette, ma Nénette. Viens donc, ma p'tite chérie Nénette."* At first she'd thought someone's grandchild must have got lost along the boulevard. When she realized that the voice was coming from the shuttered windows overhead, she took off her sunglasses and peered up. Jill stopped digging in the rose bed and sat down on the stones, watching her mother watch the window upstairs. Suddenly the cat sprang out of a rosemary bush and froze in the middle of the court-yard. *"T'es méchante, Nénette, je ne t'aime plus."* The cat meowed, spurted up the pear tree, then leaped from the lowest branch onto and over the wall. Alison stretched for a better view of the face be-tween the shutters; to her dismay, it wasn't the housekeeper, but an old woman who obviously wasn't bedridden, or blind.

"Bonjour, madame. Bonjour, ma petite fille. Je suis vieille. Je ne peux pas descendre."

Tentatively, Alison called back, *"Bonjour, madame—je suis désolée,"* and then explained to Jill, who was now leaning against the deck chair, that the old lady was crippled and couldn't come downstairs. Even before she'd finished her explanation, they heard the window bang shut. Jill went back to her digging, but Alison couldn't concen-trate on her newspaper anymore. The sudden appearance of Madame Boulez overhead at the window had startled, unsettled her. She felt as helpless as a child. It was as if the witch in the fairy tale had suddenly materialized at the edge of her bed while her parents went on, oblivious, reading out a mere story. She dropped the newspaper to the ground and got up from her chair. It sounded ridiculous, but she needn't tell anybody— she was going to do a little tour of the garden to spy out whatever dangers were concealed there.

Purple splashed along the top of the wall, not far from where Jill had been playing. "Clematis," she reminded herself, needing to keep a hold on names, even if she were using the wrong language. She turned toward the house itself, examining the massive walls, their dirty stucco interrupted by peeling shutters, the bare wood rubbed away by dust and wind. Geraniums licked at the stone within reach of their tongues; across from them lay the vegetable bed with its low tracery of weeds and grasses, rotting onions, and the skeletons of runner beans still clasped, like death and the maiden, round the trunk of a rose bush. It had a few reluctant buds; unpruned, its branches exhausted themselves in trying to touch the plastic roof of the porch over the kitchen door.

Now she turned the corner, taking a narrow path past a wall held in place, it seemed, only by a web of Virginia creeper. Its leaves softened on their stems, shrieking from green to red, then limping into heaps in the gutter below. She turned away from it and noticed, for the first time, a bed of tomato plants fenced in rusty barbed wire. No one had bothered to stake the fruit; it lay distended, hopelessly unripe, yet the stems put forth new flowers in the idiotic push of their cycle. It was worse than the ivy in the front yard, splurging on the walls, hugging the stones till the mortar cracked. She turned to the house itself for some defense against all this false fecundity, and observed, also for the first time, the canopy of stubbled glass over the sealed front door. Long fissures in the glass, erupting from what looked like bullet holes. She examined the ground at her feet for signs of shattered glass—Jill would have to be warned not to play here.

Where was Jill? The front yard was perfectly quiet, much too still. Perhaps she'd wandered out into the street? Alison called out her daughter's name, and suddenly sounds came gushing in—trucks groaning, the whine of mopeds, speeding cars, and finally a voice wearing a small groove into the familiar roar. Alison wasn't sure whether she first heard the words or saw the mouth shaping them. The child was below her; she seemed to have fallen down a well—but no, it was only the short stairway, a crater filled with leaves and sticks at the bottom of which was the iron grille and a locked door that once had opened out onto the boulevard. "I'm here—" That's what the child had been shouting. She crouched at the door, listening to the voices and footsteps passing by on the sidewalk. As if she were a prisoner plotting escape, listening for signals.

"Come out of there," Alison called sharply. "You're not allowed to play there, it's bad to be breathing in all that exhaust." And then, angry, afraid, she lost her temper, began to shout. "I said, come out of there. Anything could happen to you, you're never to play here, never—do you understand?"

Alison reached down to haul the child up toward her. She even shook her, to enforce the point—and then suddenly kneeled down beside her. Their faces were so close together that they seemed to be sharing the same skin, but their eyes—there were miles between them. Alison shivered. It was too cold to be out in the late afternoon without something woolen on. Woolies—that had been the nanny's word. "Do you miss Jeannie?" It was on the tip of Alison's tongue to say this, but she checked herself.

"Do you like it at school?" she asked, instead.

Jill turned away, hooking her fingers into the iron grille, counting the leaves on the screen of ivy. "I can't stand it," she said after a while.

Alison didn't know whether this meant that she couldn't bear, or simply couldn't understand, what went on in the classroom. She tried again. "Are there any friends you'd like to invite over to play?"

Jill touched one of the leaves with her finger. "Not specially."

"Are you frightened?" Alison didn't know what possessed her to ask the question; it came out as inconsequentially as a remark about the weather. Jill didn't respond. She was concentrating so hard on the pattern of ivy over the iron fence that Alison could see the tip of her tongue between her teeth. And then, because it seemed a logical progression, Alison asked, "Are you sad?"

Jill turned so that her eyes met her mother's. She simply looked at her, without smiling or frowning, and said, "I'm cold." Slowly, painfully, Alison got to her feet, while Jill ran off into the house. As she walked round to the back of the garden, past the open shutters of her daughter's bedroom, Alison could hear the child singing to herself; reciting a fairy story she knew by heart. Alison reclaimed the red deck chair, tried to finish the article she'd been deciphering, but gave it up, lay back, and closed her eyes. She must have fallen asleep, for the next thing she knew, the sun had gone—she was in a well of shadow and cold. There was a metallic taste in her mouth as she rose to go inside and start their supper.

* * *

It wasn't a knocking at their door, but the buzzer of the metal door giving onto the street. She wondered whether it was Douglas, whether he'd decided to come home for lunch and had forgotten his keys. But she opened the gate to a strange face, smooth, polite; a voice that had little arches of superiority in it. *"Madame?"*

"Oui, monsieur."

"Madame—?"

She understood at last that he was inquiring after her name. She supplied it, and he made a sort of bow. Then, stepping in and closing the metal door after him, he began his bombardment.

"Pardon, monsieur, plus lentement, s'il vous plaît, je ne comprends pas."

He smiled and recapitulated, speaking just as quickly. This time, however, she caught certain phrases: "Madame had been greatly inconvenienced; the door must be locked, yes, but never bolted."

"La porte?"

"Oui, madame, la porte."

And he bounded off again, leaving her to chase the ball of his words over hilly ground, until she shook her head, the idiot's smile of incomprehension on her face. And then Douglas did arrive, whereupon the stranger began all over again while she retreated to the kitchen to make coffee. She heard someone climbing the stairs. Douglas joined her.

"It seems the old lady's housekeeper couldn't get in this morning. Did you have to bolt the door? Didn't you hear her ring?"

"There must be something wrong with the bell—I didn't hear anyone. Unless it was while I was in the tub. It must have been then. What happened, was there some kind of accident?"

"No. But there might have been—Madame Boulez can't be left on her own for very long. Look, Alison, I don't understand why you've started locking yourself in like this."

"It's for Jill. So she doesn't wander out on the boulevard."

"But Jill's at school all morning."

"I forgot. That's all, I just forgot. Do you want some lunch?"

"No—oh, all right. I came for a library book; damn thing's a month overdue."

He was spying on her. He had arranged with that man to bother her like this. What was all the fuss about, if not a means to test her, keep tabs on her?

"Since you're staying for lunch, do you mind going out for some bread?"

"Why don't you go, Alison? I'll bet you haven't set a foot outside the yard since Jill and I left this morning."

"I was having a bath—"

"All morning? All right, okay. I'll go get the bread."

He returned an hour later, with Jill. He'd gone to the *boulangerie* down by the nursery school; had watched the kids playing in the yard and lost track of time. He kissed her, but didn't say sorry. They ate soup, and bread and cheese, and tomatoes they'd bought at the *hypermarché*. They tasted as green and hard as the ones Alison had discovered in the garden.

Douglas was pulling on his coat to go back to the faculty when there was another knock at the door. The incomprehensible stranger again, only this time he came into the kitchen, informing him that their landlady would like to make their acquaintance. It seemed she particularly wanted to meet the little girl who played with her cat. Douglas said yes for them all before Alison had a chance to run out of the room. She was furious. This stranger had first humiliated, and was now insulting her. And the old woman, who was supposed to be dying, she'd lecture her for letting her daughter chase the cat, for letting her hide by the fence, and listen to strangers passing outside their gates.

Jill held tightly to her father's hand as they all went up the narrow stairs, Alison first, so she couldn't turn back at the last minute. Halfway up there was a queer little niche in the plaster. It looked conspicuously empty, as if it should contain a vase of flowers or a statue of a saint. Above them, Madame Gaudet had already opened the door. She nodded at Alison and Douglas, and smiled at Jill, saying something intended to disarm and please a child. Whether Jill understood it or not, it worked, for she went right over to the old woman who was sitting in a brocaded chair, like one more bibelot in a room already crusted with china, photographs in silver frames, faïence, and filigree set out on innumerable small, heavily draped tables. To Jill, Madame Boulez handed a pack of dominos—not plastic, but ebony and bone. She told the child to go and play on the table by the window, and she did as she was told. Douglas looked quickly at Alison, who had told him Jill didn't appear to be picking up any French at all. Alison refused the look—she knew Jill and Madame Boulez were conspiring together, speaking the secret language shared by the old and the very young.

But then, when they were all settled in various chairs and Madame Boulez decided to recall Jill to her side—*"Viens, petite chérie!"* —the child refused even to raise her head. She was piling up dominos, making houses and bridges, brooding over their construction and exulting in their fall. "Jill," Douglas called out, "Madame Boulez would like you to go over to her." But Jill paid no attention. As the old woman saw the man rise from his chair to fetch his daughter, she appeared to change her mind. *"Non, non, ce n'est pas grave, monsieur. On ne force pas les enfants."*

"Ni les adultes." But Alison hadn't meant to say anything, sitting there straight-backed, feeling no older than her daughter, compared to Madame Boulez. She couldn't quite look the old woman in the face; she was afraid she might see flesh in the process of decomposing, retracting from cheekbones and eye sockets. So she stared down at her hands in her lap as Madame Boulez complimented her on how well she spoke French. *"Et votre mari aussi."* Douglas was deep in conversation with the social worker who'd knocked at their door. Reassuring him about the bolted gate, perhaps; excusing his wife's irresponsible behavior.

"Il est beau, votre mari." At this Alison had to look at the woman's face, or at least into her eyes. She saw a mask of pure age, pure infirmity. Except for the eyes. They were a joke on the rest of that

face; they were the alert, insistent eyes of a child. *"Si, il est beau, bien beau. Ça fait quarante ans que je suis veuve. Quarante ans, madame."* She swooned on the syllables, like a mother of sorrows in a Flemish pietà. *Qua-ran-te- ans, ma-da-me. "Ah oui, c'est triste. Et je n'ai pas d'enfants. Mes amis sont tous morts. Je suis seule."* And then, with a wicked little smile, *"Je souffre comme une martyre. Comme une martyre, madame."*

"Bien sûr, madame." Alison shifted in her chair, wishing Douglas would look at his wristwatch and announce that it was time to go, that Jill would have a temper tantrum with the dominos, anything to extricate her from this conversation with a corpse. *Triste, seule, morte.* The old woman's words were like the last few teeth in her head: present, stubborn, useless. Forty years a widow. No children, not even any friends left to keep her company. Was this supposed to make her listener feel guilty for her own good luck, consoled by the thought that things could be so much worse? Ah, Madame Boulez, if I could tell you what I know, the things I can't stop from happening to my beautiful child, my handsome husband.

Douglas was standing over them now, with Jill in tow, thanking Madame Boulez for having asked them up, explaining that he had to get back to his office. The old woman didn't appear to hear him. She called Madame Gaudet, who disappeared into the kitchen and then reappeared with a huge brass box which Madame Boulez took, opened, and shoved under Jill's nose. *"Vas-y, ma petite, vas-y."* Jill reached her small hand in and took one of the bonbons. There was no *"Merci, madame,"* not even a "Thanks," despite Douglas's cajoling. *"Elle est timide,"* he offered as his daughter simply stood there, not even eating the candy, but holding it so tightly that the sweat from her hand soaked through the flimsy wrapper. Was she afraid, embarrassed, suspicious? Jill was looking Madame Boulez straight in the eyes, as Douglas thanked everyone again, and wished the landlady a pleasant afternoon. As Madame Gaudet led them to the door, they could hear the old woman's voice, surprisingly clear and strong: *"Il m'a souhaité un agréable après-midi—moi qui est vieille, qui vais mourir. Il est fou, ce monsieur, il est complètement fou!"*

* * *

That evening they had a fight about what had happened at Madame Boulez's. Douglas waited till the child was asleep; then he switched off the news program to which Alison was listening, saying it was time they talked about Jill.

"What about Jill? You're not upset about that silly candy, are you?"

"I'm upset about the fact that Jill was rude to the old lady. That she doesn't know how to act in front of strangers, to speak. . . . In fact, she doesn't say much to anybody."

Alison yawned—she was ready for bed. "It's just the language thing—it's a shock for children to learn there are other languages in the world besides their mother tongue. She'll get over it."

"She plays too much by herself. You should have seen her on the playground today. Standing there all alone while the others were chasing each other, jumping around. And Jill not even looking at them, just standing staring at the fence."

"Maybe she was looking at the flowers by the fence."

"The point is she wasn't with the other children. She's missing out on socialization."

"Oh—socialization. Douglas, I'm tired and I want to go to bed."

"Tired? For Christ's sake, you don't *do* anything all day. I thought you were going to be working on a project, doing research—isn't that what you promised Murray?"

"I didn't promise Murray anything. This year is a holiday for me, remember? I'm not supposed to be working."

"Then why can't you take proper care of your own daughter?"

Alison got up from the sofa and walked into the bedroom. By the time Douglas followed her she was lying with the covers pulled up around her face, her eyes shut tight. *"Il est beau, votre mari."* And what of it? He was also superficial, commonplace, obsessed with appearances. Witness his overdone manners, his dress—correct, careful to the point of vulnerability. You had only to smile when Douglas came into a room and he'd immediately check to see whether he had a soup stain on his tie or if there was lint on his lapel. *"Bien beau."* Had the old witch been trying to make her, if not jealous, then a little more watchful of this desirable husband of hers? They'd been married a fraction of the years that Madame Boulez had been widowed, and Alison had never once wondered whether her husband was, as the saying went, faithful to her. It simply didn't occur to her to care. It seemed to her now that she'd married him precisely because he was the sort of man who would never make her unhappy. As for her own fidelity—there'd been no time to test it, not with her work and their child.

"Je n'ai pas d'enfants." That had been one of their landlady's laments. And she, Alison, could have all the children she wanted, merely by throwing away a package of little pills. But there was no room anymore; she had curled up so tight inside herself that there was hardly space for the child she already had. Alison fell asleep thinking of Jill that day in the garden, her face so close to hers, her eyes looking out from an immense distance inside. Yet how, clutching the bonbon in her small, sweaty hand, refusing to speak Douglas's language to Madame Boulez, her daughter had stared straight into the woman's fierce, old, child's eyes. As if she'd had nothing to fear from them, at least.

Douglas returned early the next afternoon bearing three red roses, not for Alison, but for Jill to take as a peace offering to Madame Boulez. Alison had made it clear that she wanted nothing more to do with the old woman; she wanted to grab the roses from her husband's hands and shove them into the garbage. But Jill was enchanted with the flowers, insisting they take them up straight away to Madame Boulez. Douglas had to rush back for a meeting at the university, so it fell to Alison to accompany the child. Jill held the roses reverently in their cellophane coffin as she climbed the stairs. Even so, one of the buds was crushed by the time the housekeeper answered the door.

"She's telling you to come in," Alison explained, pushing Jill gently toward Madame Gaudet, who was crouching down to talk to the child.

"Que c'est beau, tu es mignonne, ma petite. Viens, viens voir Madame. Tu vas voir la chatte, la vielle parasseuse. Nénette, viens 'ci Nénette!"

At the sound of the cat's name, Jill crept forward, the animal's curved tail luring her deeper and deeper into the drawing room where Madame Boulez sat in a chaise longue. A box and a magnifying glass were in her lap. The roses were presented all over again. Alison repeated how sorry they were to have inconvenienced Madame the other day, explaining that they'd bolted the gate so that the child wouldn't run out onto the street. The old lady merely waved her hand. *"Ne vous en faites pas, madame, asseyez-vous. Mais allez chercher un bonbon pour la petite, Madame Gaudet."* Alison frowned. This was supposed to be the merest courtesy call; she wanted to have Jill present the flowers and be done with it. But when the housekeeper came back with the brass box of bonbons, Jill shook her head and asked for the dominos instead. Soon she was seated at the little table by the window, laying out walls and bridges, and looking stealthily for the cat.

Madame Boulez had motioned Alison to take the chair beside her own. She was beginning again with, *"Comme il est beau, votre mari—."* Pointing to the photograph of a young man with curling mustaches, Alison forestalled her with *"Et le vôtre aussi, madame."*

"Ah oui, madame—cela se voit!" Thus it was settled that both husbands were handsome. Some extra gesture seemed called for, however, so Alison moved her hand to another photograph spread out on her hostess's lap. A hazy oblong, in which the pale, square face of a young woman detached itself from all the others and hooked into Alison's eyes. *"Et vous aussi, madame—très belle."*

Madame Boulez seemed offended, not by the familiarity, but by the obvious untruth. *"Madame—je n'ai jamais été jolie. Pas du tout!"* And then she stopped and softened, shrugging her shoulders in a creaky way. *"Moi—je plaisais. Je ne sais pas pourquoi, mais je plaisais. Un peu d' élégance, un petit brin de— Je ne sais pas, Madame. Mais—"* and here she brought the magnifying glass to her face, as though it were a mask. *"C'est fini. Je vais mourir. Je n'attends que la mort."*

She said it simply enough, this woman who had once been elegant, agreeable. She announced her death without pity or even dread; in fact, with a certain dramatic satisfaction. Alison looked over at her daughter, somehow playing dominos at a table crowded with furred plants in earthenware pots and a huge brass box. Jill was abstractedly sucking on sweets, swinging her feet under the tablecloth. The cat crouched silently below her, watching, waiting to spring. Waiting for death, or for a target—what was the difference in this overheated, overfurnished room? Alison remembered the blood filling her mouth when she'd been trapped behind the steering wheel of her car; she remembered how hot and red the blood had felt, and how it would never stop running, just as Jill would never stop screaming, accusing her.

A cry, and the cat diving past her under a cabinet.

"Mais qu'est-ce qui se passe? Nénette, t'es méchante, tu lui as fait mal."

Jill came running, throwing herself not at her mother, but at Madame Gaudet. "She scratched me, she scratched me." There were delicate crimson lines over the child's leg, just above the place where her socks ended. Madame Gaudet took her off to the kitchen, put iodine on the cut, praised Jill loudly for not crying about the sting, and gave her something sweet to drink. Alison had gone to the doorway to watch what was going on. Jill's eyes never left her mother's face as she drank up the glass of grenadine. But Madame Boulez was calling out to her, so Alison returned to her chair in the stifling room.

The old woman was tugging at something caught at the side of her chair. Alison bent and disentangled it for her: a long, thin bamboo cane. Madame Boulez leaned forward and shoved the cane with surprising force under the cabinet where the cat still hid. *"Nénette, vieille salope, Nénette,"* she hissed, so viciously that Alison understood why the cat fled to the garden whenever it could. Suddenly the cane struck home, the cat squealed, and Jill came running from the kitchen, the glass still in her hand. Madame Gaudet got down on her hands and knees and drew out the cat, placing it, quivering, on its mistress's lap. It made no attempt to claw or bite, but resigned itself to the leathery grip of the old woman's hand. She did not stroke the cat, but grimly held her down.

"Nénette, ma Nénette, pourquoi es tu si folle, si polissonne, mon adorable petite Nénette?" Her voice caressed the animal—Alison looked away, as if she'd caught herself eavesdropping on a pair of lovers. But then there was a hissing noise once more. *"Alors, va-t-en!"* Madame Boulez had shoved the cat off her lap; it thundered past them down the hallway. Madame Boulez again leaned forward in her chair so that her face was close to Alison's.

"C'est imbécile. Un chat, ce n'est pas un enfant, évidemment. Mais que voulez-vous, madame? Voilà ma mère, qui avait cinq enfants. Et ma grand-mère qui avait dix—si, dix!" She pressed the point home by flicking the empty spaces between her bottom teeth with the tip of her tongue. *"Et moi qui n'ai personne. Personne."*

All Alison could find to say were the phrases her grade-six French books had taught on the subject of commiseration: *"Quel dommage, madame. Je suis désolée."*

Madame Boulez sank back in her armchair, making a little motion of disgust with her fingers. Alison had said good-bye and was on her way to get Jill, when Madame Boulez clutched at her sleeve.

"Mais vous savez, madame—" And she motioned for Alison to sit down again beside her. She opened her olive-wood box of photographs and rifled through them, searching furiously—bending edges and tearing off corners—till she found what she wanted. She drew a photo out, then shut the box.

"Regardez, madame. Comme il était beau, mon pauvre mari." And she handed Alison the picture of a young soldier with a bandage round his head, sitting in a wicker chair beside other convalescent soldiers. When her guest had examined it long enough, Madame Boulez explained. Her husband had suffered a severe head injury in the first war. He had never been right after. Oh, he was clever enough at his work, but he got into violent rages. He would frighten the parlor-maid, he would frighten everyone but her. Sometimes it took her a whole night to calm him down. It had been unendurable during the

second war. The city had been occupied by the Nazis—they had shot
young men in the courtyard of the ducal palace. Young men and old.
There were spies everywhere—in this very house. Her husband had
died a year before the end of the war, but at least he had died in his
home, and not in some German prison.

Alison didn't know what to say. "And you took care of him all
that time? You must have loved him very much—*vous l'avez bien aimé,
madame.*"

The old woman pursed her lips. *"C'était mon mari, madame."* Just
that: "He was my husband."

Alison returned the photograph to the box. As she got up from
her chair, Madame Boulez asked her to come back again, another
afternoon. She enjoyed her visits, it made the time pass less slowly.
Alison stammered something about not wanting to intrude, but the
old woman cut her short. *"Mais vous reviendrez, madame. La petite
s'amuse bien chez moi."* It was simplest for Alison to nod her head: yes,
certainly they'd come back for a visit. Now that she'd seen Madame
Boulez, spoken with her, let her daughter eat sweets out of a brass
box and drink grenadine, what else could she do? She'd been com-
promised, helplessly exposed—she and Jill and Douglas, too. It was
as if the ceiling had been taken off their own rooms, as if their lives
were open to the old woman's scrutiny, to the flick of that bamboo
whip with which she chased her cat from its hiding place. And Alison
hated the overheated rooms with their clutter of memorabilia. She felt
as though she were stepping into a greenhouse where not plants but
the past itself lay under glass, neither dead nor alive, but in some
viscous state of in-between.

As they took their leave, Jill said a proper good day to Madame
Boulez. Her words seemed to please the old woman. But as Madame
Gaudet opened the door to let them out, the cat slid through. All the
way down the stairs they could hear fierce cries of *"Imbéciles! Nénette,
ma Nénette—reviens, sale bête."*

Because the weather continued fine; because she refused to spend
any more time in the house than she had to, now; because she some-

how felt more protected from Madame Boulez outside than in, Alison got into the habit of gardening. You could, after all, read only so many newspapers a day. And besides, it was something she could do with Jill, who played feverishly with sticks and twigs, or dug up snail shells and shards of pottery which she carefully washed, then placed along the edges of the carpet in her room. Douglas wasn't enthusiastic about this arrangement. He felt Alison should be going into town, joining him for lunch with some of the acquaintances he'd made, or at least taking Jill to play in the Creux d'Enfer. But as Alison pointed out, Jill didn't want to go anywhere. She was much happier digging in the garden and visiting Madame Boulez. If Douglas didn't approve of *that,* he shouldn't have begun the visits in the first place.

The time of day Alison liked best was the moment when the sun jumped over the wall to the front to the house, where the garden was wildest and darkest. She had started with her bare hands, loosening tufts of grass from the flowerbeds. Then, when the dirt worked itself under her fingernails, blackening and roughening her skin, she searched out a pair of gloves. They didn't help—she needed to feel the earth in her hands, and so she threw the gloves away and began again. She spent hours crouched down under the shattered glass portico, the traffic noises growing fainter and fainter, as if the ivy had swallowed them. It was curious how attached she felt to the garden now, as if there were a cord linked to the self she stored so far inside, a cord fastened to a place deep in the earth, miles under the soil and rock.

Jill worked at another bed, gathering up leaves, raking the pebbles on the paths. Sometimes she would dig up a bulb, or break off a piece of an iris root. She would bring them over to her mother with a sick look on her face, as if expecting to be punished. Alison told her just to dig them in again, and when she had, would call her over to look at the wild pansies, or a long, tough cord of root ending in a bit of flame. "It's scarlet pimpernel," she'd say, explaining how the flower opened in the light, and shut when rain was on its way. Jill would listen, painfully attentive, sometimes asking a question. It was a new kind of language they were trying out between them without even knowing; a language that they spoke together, even in silence, through the dirt scoring their hands, and the cramp of their legs as they crouched down under the straggling lilac bushes.

Even as October advanced toward November, they spent whole afternoons in the garden, a thin finger of sunlight on their backs, warming them in the regretful way that autumn light will do. It tumbled through the last leaves, brushing the new bareness of trunks and branches. One afternoon Alison called Jill to help her pull away the arms ivy had sunk into the ancient lilac bush, or round the sycamore and beech. They really needed a small axe—all she'd been able to find had been a rusty pair of secateurs in the kitchen cupboard. So Alison used her own hands to lug the creepers down, with Jill tugging at stems and leaves of ivy. The trees, so cleared, looked cheated, shamed, as if they'd been shaved in secret places.

Sometimes Jill tugged off bark with the ivy suckers, and then she'd try to pat the severed pieces back into place. But the ivy had an easy time of it—next autumn, when new tenants were in the house, the ivy would have repaired whatever damage the two of them so clumsily inflicted. Yet Alison wasn't disheartened. She couldn't tell, anymore, whether it wasn't the very air of abandonment, of sure, deliberative decay, that drew her to the garden. She remembered a children's book she used to love, and how she'd hated the part where the hidden garden is finally tidied and brought to heel, so that boys can run races over the grass. She had always liked it best when the sullen little girl had been alone with the blind push of bulbs and shoots into the air.

She would look out the book for Jill to read when they were home again. Except that she knew she wouldn't. It didn't sound real, that phrase, "home again." There was no garden for her to dig in there. She would be back at work, and Jill in school all day. And perhaps that was best, perhaps it was perverse to be out with a child, disrupting this dark, sour earth, which yielded, now and again, small corpses of birds and cats, as well as weeds and stones and broken glass. Then Alison would feel disgust at the feast of ivy on the light and air, think Douglas was right—she would be better off hauling the child to some bright, airy museum, to look at pictures of wild-flowers, slices of stone under glass. But then Jill would suddenly grab her arm, and point to the cat crouched inside the ivy, glaring at a blackbird perched on a twig. The bird always seemed to know just when Nénette was about to pounce; would beat its wings and be off at the last moment. Or at least, this was how it seemed to work in the daylight. Whether Jill lay awake at night worrying about prowling cats and sleeping birds, Alison wasn't about to ask.

Even in mid-November they had work to do—more than ever, since the days were shortening, and they had to be continually moving to warm themselves under the stiff, gray sky. Alison had collected a heap of red Virginia creeper against one side of the house. Jill would run up to it and fling herself down, stomping, flattening the leaves, scattering bits that Alison would patiently rake up again. And the next day more leaves would have wilted from the vine, leaving a stubble of naked stems on the walls, like burned-out matches. Even the convolvulus looked sickly, clutching at the throats of rosemary and sage bushes.

At times Alison felt uneasy about creating spaces where before there had been stones and glass and dead leaves; spaces needing to be filled with something before the weeds and ivy choked them again. She could trust herself to cut back dead branches, but to make something desirable come up, to plant a dead-looking bulb in the expectation that something would uncurl itself, exchange earth for air, and bloom—that was beyond her abilities. Or rather, it wasn't for her to do; she was just a temporary tenant of the house. Once, when they'd worked until dark in the garden, Alison had stood for a while, alone, while Jill put the tools away in the cellar. Watching the birds drawing together in the branches of the trees, and then, as the light diminished, the branches themselves coming together like the fingers of a hand, she'd felt as if her heart were a stone, and someone were scraping a knife over it, striking sparks. There'd been a noise, then, that had nothing to do with the cars pouring past the boulevard. It was her husband, standing at the parlor window, his hands tapping the glass. He was signaling them to come in—but she couldn't see his face, he hadn't put the lights on. They had stood there for a moment, the two of them, on opposite sides of the darkening glass—and then she saw him move his arm again. The house lit up and still she couldn't see him, just the glare of the bulbs in an empty room.

It had become a habit of theirs, Jill's and Alison's, to spend an hour or so every week in Madame Boulez's apartment. Madame Gaudet prepared coffee and hot chocolate and platefuls of small, dry biscuits. Jill had lost whatever shyness she'd had before Madame Boulez. She would stand gravely before the old woman, and let her hands be held in that tight, hot, leathery grasp that had imprisoned Nénette. And she would say *"Bonjour, madame,"* and *"Merci, au revoir,"* which even Douglas conceded to be major progress, though he had too much work ever to be able to attend the afternoons with their landlady. Jill would play dominos while the women talked, or else she'd do drawings with an ivory-handled pencil on watermarked paper supplied from Madame Boulez's desk.

Alison tried to hide her unease during these visits. The old woman spoke so quickly, and used such unfamiliar expressions that she couldn't be sure of the sense of what she did manage to pick up. Once she had made the mistake—if that's what it could be called— of telling Madame Boulez that she was an architect. The old woman had grabbed at her hand then, telling her that she, too, had some knowledge of that profession. Her husband had been an architect, she said; the part of the house that she now rented out had once been his office. They had worked together, she and her husband. What else could she do, a woman with no children? She'd done drafting, as well as accounts and correspondence. Then Madame Boulez had asked Alison her opinion of the buildings in the town—had she seen all the churches and the town houses? There were some particularly fine ones dating from the eighteenth century.

It was a magnificent town, Alison assured her. Had Madame Boulez pressed her as to just what buildings she had seen, she would probably have lied. To admit that she'd been here for three months or more, and had barely gone outside the garden gate, and she an architect—

"Oui, c'est tout changé, la maison, le jardin. Vous savez, madame, il était une fois . . ." And Madame Boulez went on, talking about how beautiful the garden had once been. Thick with roses, dark, red roses—and lilies, too, for contrast. The borders had been full of jasmine—the scent had been so strong on warm summer nights. She had met her husband in this very city—she'd been a mere child, but that was how things were done in those days. They had lived their whole lives together in this house. Her parents had stayed on with them—they'd had to fill up the space somehow. She gestured to a photograph framed in silver on the table where Jill was drawing, asked Alison to fetch it. As she did, Alison looked at the sheet of paper her daughter was covering with fine, slanted lines, like rain. Jill didn't seem aware of her standing there beside her; in fact she never acknowledged her mother's presence if she could help it, except when they were alone together in the garden.

So Alison returned, and gave the old woman the photograph, sitting down beside Madame Boulez to have things pointed out to her. A party in sepia, at a wicker table in what could not be, yet obviously was, the garden where Jill and she spent afternoons tugging down ivy chains. Two couples: an old woman seated, with her husband standing over her, hands grasping her shoulders, and on opposite sides of the table, a sad-looking but handsome man and his elegant wife. *"Oui, madame—c'était le jardin. C'est triste, maintenant—si vous l'aviez vu du temps de mon père . . ."*

It was more difficult than she could have foreseen, admitting the lost reality of young and unencumbered trees, a mere spray or two of ornamental ivy on the walls. She knew, looking at the photograph, how the benches the couples were sitting on would rot, the table disappear. How the very fields beyond the gate would become boulevards, asphalted over for trucks and tanks and ambulances. The lilac bushes were frail and unsupported even then—the young woman's arms looked empty, and there wasn't even the shadow of a cat within the frame.

Madame Boulez tapped at the glass over the photograph; she muttered something. Translated, it sounded like, "He would never hear of it. Though it was his fault, not mine." Alison stiffened, guessing that the old woman was talking about the children she had never had. She was so tired of hearing that particular refrain. And if she had had children, that elegant, shrewd-looking woman in the photograph, she would no doubt have pined for her lost freedom. For a lover with whom she might have run away except for the six little boys and girls, hugging her round like ivy.

"I want to go home now." It was Jill, tugging at her arm. Alison pulled away—she hated to be grabbed. "I don't *feel* well." And then Alison put her hand on Jill's forehead. It was papery, hot. She made her excuses to the two women, and led Jill downstairs, to her room. By the time Douglas came home from work, Alison was sponging off a delirious Jill, who kept asking for *la chatte, sale bête, la chatte.*

It turned out to be nothing—penicillin, a few days in bed, and a week off school, the doctor advised. His name was Raoul Jeunet. She would never be able to pronouce his first name properly, but then, would she ever have occasion to? He couldn't have been more than forty-five. He was dark; his hands were beautiful. He reminded her of someone, and she couldn't quite place whom, until she remembered Madame Boulez—her photograph of the sad-looking man in the garden.

While Jill was convalescing, she and Alison spent as much of their time as possible outside. After a few days of rain, the weather had again turned warm and fine and bright—more like August than November. After Douglas left in the morning they would go to the cellar, collect all the tools they had piled there the day before, and simply occupy themselves out of doors. Pointing, barely speaking, they shared observations about the things most near to them, the varied shades of the falling leaves, the exact manner in which the magpies and blackbirds flew down from the trees, seeming to fall, but skidding up into the air a foot from the ground, then settling themselves quite safely on the gravel.

All that week Alison didn't even go into town to buy a loaf of bread; she was perfectly happy to stay inside the garden walls with Jill. Toward the end of Sunday afternoon, when Douglas was off at a colleague's house, and Alison was stripping away the ivy from the front of the house, there was a sharp crying-out from the back of the garden. Running round to where the noise had broken, Alison found Jill sprawled within the vegetable plot behind the shed, her leg caught in a tangle of barbed wire that had been put there long ago to protect the tomatoes. The wire was netted with convolvulus—Jill had been trying to tear it away, and she'd lost her balance, fallen down—her leg was badly scraped. Alison, blood pounding in her ears, disentangled the child as calmly as she could. Jill had put her arms around her mother's neck, was holding so tight that Alison thought she'd be strangled. Lifting Jill up, she carried her inside the house and into the bathroom, where she washed the scrapes and poured on iodine. Tetanus shots—had Jill had her shots recently enough? She would have to get her to a doctor, but it was Sunday afternoon, and Douglas had taken the car. She couldn't even remember to whose house he had gone—she wouldn't be able to reach him, that was clear. And she couldn't even call him—there was no telephone. Then she remembered Madame Boulez—she ran up the stairs, rang the landlady's buzzer and started hammering on the door. Luckily Madame Gaudet was in. She called a taxi for them and, after Alison had scribbled a note for Douglas, they made for the nearest hospital.

It turned out that Dr. Jeunet was on call that weekend. He remembered their names; he was so polite, so assured examining Jill's leg with a gentle gravity, acknowledging that it hurt, and that of course he would make it better. She didn't cry out when he gave her the needle, but instead dug her small fingers into her mother's arm, so that Alison thought she was taking the pain of the occasion away from her daughter, bearing it for her. The small jab of the needle, the puncture it left, seemed to be made in Alison's skin. She was so astonishcd at what she felt that she hardly paid attention to the instructions Dr. Jeunet was giving her about changing the dressing on Jill's leg; she had to ask him to repeat them.

In the taxi on the way home, Jill sat on Alison's lap, sucking her thumb—something she hadn't done for months. But her mother didn't scold her. She held her loosely on her lap, as though she were afraid of choking her should she press her arms too tightly; she hummed a lullaby she'd sung when Jill was still a baby. Douglas's car was parked in the drive by the time they got home. He was outside in a moment, taking Jill from her mother's lap, carrying her inside, mindful of the bandages. Once Jill had been put to bed—she'd been half asleep in the taxi—Douglas poured out two enormous shots of brandy. They drank them down in silence, looking at one another across the corner of the dining-room table.

And then Douglas stretched out his arm toward her. She saw the sleeves of his crisp white shirt, and then seemed to see the null-colored skin underneath. And under that—a parcel of nerves and blood and bone. What did it have to do with him, or with her, either? Why wasn't he someone with whom she could have the simplest, most essential of dealings; why wasn't he Dr. Jeunet? What would she do if Douglas were to have some terrible accident, or fall ill so that he needed constant nursing? Would she stay by him, bandaging his head, calming him down as Madame Boulez had done with her husband? What if Dr. Jeunet called at the house, and packed up Alison and Jill into his black bag, spirited them away? And why was she even thinking about the doctor with his sad, fine face? He was no more real to her than a dead man in a photograph. Was it because dead men didn't hold out their hands, didn't admit pain and confusion and need?

There was Douglas's hand, reaching out to her own, which held the glass of brandy. She looked up at his face—he seemed to be in shock. It was as if what she had learned during that first accident, he were only discovering now. That it was only too easy for the worst to happen; that it was only by fluke or random miracle that it hadn't happened yet. Alison looked down at her fingers, still curled round her brandy glass. She imagined herself stretching out her hand, touching her husband's face. It was as though her fingers were bandaged together, tied to the glass. "There wasn't any danger," she said at last.

"No," he answered. "Everything's all right."

But she lay awake a long time that night, imagining things. Jill enmeshed in barbed wire, Douglas's face when the taxi pulled up. And Madame Boulez with her husband's photograph, sitting in the overheated apartment, calling for her cat and when it came, lashing at it with a bamboo cane.

Soon afterwards, the weather changed for good. Alison had to give up her afternoons in the garden and find something else to use up the time. She wouldn't stay in the house; she couldn't help thinking of Madame Boulez and her husband working together there, enduring forty years' unhappiness side by side. And so she spent her mornings taking walks to town, dodging umbrellas down the narrow lanes. When the cold and damp slid under her coat, she would go to a café or library or museum, or else sit inside a church, listening to an organist playing cold, columnar music. She didn't mind the wintry stillness of the church; it revealed all the more the very structure of the building—load-bearing walls under embroidered hangings, buttresses tolerating saints and angels carved at their extremities.

Sometimes she took Jill with her, on rainy afternoons when they couldn't go to the park. She would sit with her child in this cool, gray shelter while women mopped the floors around them, and solitary worshipers slipped on or off a prie-dieu under some obscure statue. Once she gave Jill a coin to go and light a candle. They were for the dead, but she told her daughter you could make a wish for someone dear to you, instead. Jill, obedient yet disbelieving, had taken her coin and dropped it in a serrated brass box, rather like the one in which Madame Boulez kept her bonbons. She took a long, spindly white candle, lit it at the wick of one ready to drop into the sand below the tiers, and fastened it in place. Alison didn't ask for whom she'd lit the candle, but Jill volunteered the information once they'd left the church. "It's for Madame Boulez," she said. "And Nénette."

"Would you like to go up and see her today?" Alison asked, and the child nodded. They hadn't paid a visit to the old woman since Jill had fallen sick. So on the way home they stopped at a florist's shop. Alison chose a small pot of bronze chrysanthemums, but Jill ran across to a huge pail of Michaelmas daisies and returned with her arms full. "Can we have these?" she asked. "I want these ones— they're better." And they were, so much so that Alison was reluctant to take them. She preferred the small, subdued glow of the chrysan-themums to that odd mix of sun and night in the daisies Jill had chosen—the petals looking as though they'd been drenched in wine, the centers a hot, pungent yellow. She looked sternly at her daughter, willing the child to put the daisies back, but Jill would not be budged. "All right, then, we'll take the whole lot of them." Alison dug out every centime in every pocket she could find, and they walked out of the shop with their umbrellas hooked over their wrists, arms full of flowers, and the small rain beading their hair.

Once Alison had unlocked the metal gate, Jill ran inside, up the stairway, past the empty little niche in the wall, till she came to the metal plate with *Mme. Boulez* inscribed upon it. Jill rang and rang— Alison had to take her hand away from the buzzer. She was afraid the old woman might be ill, and not want visitors at all. Just as they were turning to go down the stairs again, there came a shuffling sound behind the door, a weary, *"Attendez, attendez!"* Madame Boulez opened the door at last, or rather, not Madame Boulez, but a string of bones in an old leather pouch, shoved in a thick red dressing gown. Dark red, almost black, like the roses they'd given her that first time.

"Mais ce n'est pas possible! Vous m'apportez encore des fleurs? Elles vont mourir—moi aussi, je vais mourir. Et vous, madame, et la petite—"

Alison put her arm round her daughter's shoulders. Jill was crush-ing the flowers to her as if they were a doll to be comforted.

"Come on, Jill. Madame isn't well—we'd better go downstairs. *Nous nous excusons madame. Au revoir.*"

The door shut as they were going down the stairs. Jill half-turned as if she expected to see at least the cat come gliding by. But there was nothing. Halfway down she paused by the niche in the wall, deposited the unwieldy bundle of daisies.

"They'll die there—they need water," Alison chided, gently.

"I don't care—I don't want them anymore," Jill said, running the rest of the way down the stairs and then out into the damp, dark garden.

Alison waited for a moment, then gathered up the flowers and took them to the kitchen, where she stuck them in a pail of water behind the door. Jill wouldn't see them there.

That evening, at the supper table, Jill put down her spoon and asked, "Why is Madame Boulez so old? Why can't she walk properly? Is she going to die?"

Alison began to choke on her soup, but Douglas immediately replied. "She's very old, and things aren't working well in her body anymore. She's tired, and lonely, and she just wants to close her eyes and go to sleep forever. Maybe she'll wake up someplace beautiful."

"With Nénette?"

"Oh, yes, she'll have Nénette with her. Now eat up your soup, it's getting cold."

After supper, they made a point of playing with Jill: card games, and checkers, and finally hide-and-go-seek, which set the child laughing in a contagious, frenzied sort of way. They talked about how when they got back home to Toronto, she could have a kitten of her own. Jill was enchanted with the idea—she went quite happily to bed, and didn't stir all night. She seemed to have forgotten her questions about Madame Boulez. Instead, it was Alison who had the nightmare.

She dreamed that she'd become a nun—taken vows in an order in which the chief task was to prepare oneself to die. Life and the living had no importance here; all experience was just an accelerating readiness for death. She had her own room, gray stone walls with windows, equally gray, patterned and incised, so that she could not look out. She was divested of her clothes, her hair, the very smells of her body; her skin became like parchment, a plain, sexless envelope in which her soul was folded flat. And she lay in that cell for a long, long time. Then, abruptly, someone came for her. She was taken to another cell. On a bed an old woman lay dying, in the greatest pain. To the priest by her side the old woman cried out, "Must I suffer in silence, or is there some help for me? Can't I cry out?" But the priest turned away from the old woman, and came to Alison, instead. He took a scalpel from his pocket and slit open the blank envelope from head to foot. And what came out was a child, pressed flat like a dried flower, falling down through a floor which opened into nothing.

She woke reaching out in the dark for something to break the fall. It was her husband who caught her.

The next day Douglas didn't go to work. He stayed at home wearing his oldest clothes, hanging up the wash on a labyrinth of lines strung in the bathroom. When he'd finished, he put on a pair of old gloves and persuaded Alison to help him with a final session in the garden. How could she refuse him, though it felt unnatural for him to be about the house at all? Last night he had mistaken her act of reaching out, had pulled her under, held her down, all the time calling her name, kissing her face. And he'd woken this morning with so clear a conviction that everything was back to rights between them that she could only nod and take her cues.

Douglas performed all the tasks she had never bothered with, clearing away heaps of dead, soaked leaves that were clogging the eaves and drainpipes, collecting dead twigs and branches from the paths. They rarely spoke, and yet there was a sense of complicity between them; a solidity, as if each time they moved the rake through the leaves or tied another bundle of branches, they were putting up a supporting beam under a roof that had been threatening collapse. At lunch, Douglas declared they should spend Christmas in the country. They could rent a chalet in the Jura, go cross-country skiing—it was something Jill could manage. They could book for one week or two. Would she be bored after a week of snow? Did she think it might work out?

He was watching her as she drank her coffee. He wanted her to say, "Yes," to praise him for being so clever, so thoughtful for having hit upon the perfect plan. She took another sip of coffee, and looked back into his eyes. Madame Boulez was right; her husband was beautiful. But he was beginning to age—she saw, for the first time, the way his hair was thinning at the temples, the little lines nicked at the corners of his eyes. And she thought, "I'm looking into a mirror; I'm looking into my own face six or seven years from now. What does he see when he looks at me?" She put down her cup and leaned in toward him.

"Jill will love it. How do you go about renting the chalet?" And he was off and running, giving her the pamphlets he'd gathered, showing her the map of the Jura, pointing out the *station de ski* that looked least commercial, while all the time she looked at his face, memorizing the changes that were taking place in it, as though it were some terrain that the wind was hollowing out, changing beyond recognition. *C'était mon mari.* And she knew she could stay with him just for this, the length of days they had already known each other, the knowledge she would have of him as he moved through his life, beside her. Knowledge, not hopes or illusions. She thought of Madame Boulez unraveling so openly the griefs of her life: an arranged marriage, the children she could not have, the wounded man she could not heal, but only just control. It was the merest chance, pure accident that her own life was so much less ravaged.

Alison touched her cup against her husband's.

"I think it's a wonderful plan. Let's go for two weeks."

The day before they were to leave for the Jura, Alison took Jill into town to choose a small gift for Madame Boulez. She had been bedridden for the past week, or so said Madame Gaudet, whom they'd met at the gate on their way out. Rheumatism, arthritis, hardening of the arteries, a whole catalog of ills and pains. It was a wonder how she still held on when she could so easily let go. Perhaps in her sleep one night she'd just loosen her hands, and— "Yes," Alison had nodded, excusing herself, hoping Jill hadn't caught the drift of the woman's words.

All the way into town, Alison had talked about the skiing they would do, how clever Douglas was at handling hills and turns, how much he would teach her. But once they got into the street of fine old shops, Alison wandered in a panic from window to window. What could she buy an old, deathbound woman—what gift was there that didn't have some promise of time or health built into it? Madame Boulez had all the candies she could possibly want and she didn't eat chocolate. Hardly a calendar, nor yet another pot of flowers. A scarf, for someone who never went outdoors? Finally, she found a shop that sold bath oils and perfumes. They settled on a tiny flask of eau de cologne, which Jill chose for the picture on the package—impossible clouds of doves and roses.

Alison meant simply to give the present, with its embossed paper and curled ribbons, to Madame Gaudet, to offer to Madame Boulez on Christmas Eve. But the housekeeper insisted they come inside the apartment. Madame was feeling better today; she had missed their visits. She wanted to wish them *bon voyage*. And so Jill and her mother wiped their shoes on the mat and walked through into the parlor, where everything—the potted ferns, the curtains, the china cups on their saucers—seemed to tremble in a suffocating haze.

Madame Boulez was propped up in her usual chair, in a night-dress and quilted dressing gown, her cane at her feet. Alison gently pushed Jill forward, so that she might present the gift she'd chosen. Jill refused to move without her, so they both proceeded toward the ancient woman in the old, brocaded chair. Her eyes, as she took the gift, were impatient, and yet amused as well. She thanked them both, but made no move to open the gift. Madame Gaudet tried to prompt her, but the old woman simply shook her head. "Save it for yourself, for after I'm gone," was what her eyes were saying.

Finally, she spoke, addressing her words to Jill.

"Et tu joues toujours dans le jardin, ma petite?"

Jill didn't reply.

"She says, do you still play in the—"

"I know," Jill answered her mother. And then to Madame Boulez, *"Il fait trop froid."*

"Ah oui, bien sûr, il fait trop froid. Et comment, je me demande, comment va-t-on m'ensevelir dans une terre si froide?"

Alison looked quickly at her daughter's face. Did she understand what had been said? How could the old woman have talked about that in front of a child—being put into the ground? What sort of nightmares would Jill have tonight? But her daughter didn't seem upset—she couldn't have been listening. Jill was plucking at her mother's sleeve; she wanted something. Not dominos, but the cat, she wanted to stroke the cat, Alison explained to Madame Boulez. *"C'est permis?"*

"Ah, oui! Mais il faut l'attraper d'abord." And Madame Boulez pointed to where Nénette had settled—on top of a curio cabinet, the only place the animal knew to be safe. *"Nénette, ma Nénette,"* she crooned, without even lifting her cane, only caressing the handle with the palm of her hand. The cat did not respond; she lay sideways, an expanse of fur and startled breathing forming a sort of footstool for the feet of a lachrymose Christ that hung above her. The cat would not come down, any more than could the Christ. Alison wondered whether Madame Boulez abused them both from her armchair. What comfort could either afford her? What sort of prayer could you address to a God who had always given you the opposite of what you wished for? Alison looked into the eyes of the clever, wretched woman who so didn't want to die. She couldn't bear it, she wanted to say something that would give Madame Boulez some pleasure, if not comfort, but she could think of nothing. Finally she leaned forward, and lightly pressed the old woman's hand with her fingertip.

"Mais comme elle est belle, votre chatte. Et intelligente, n'est-ce pas?" Madame Boulez nodded the way someone lolling into sleep jerks up her head in a shocked recall to wakefulness. There was a sudden vivacity; the voice leaped up, *"Bien sûr, madame, bien entendu. Mais sa mère, sa mère . . ."* And she began to tell the story of a tortoiseshell cat that had come from Spain, a cat that had been a paragon, *tout à fait exceptionelle.* She had lived for seven years with Madame Boulez without once producing a litter, and then had disappeared one night. They'd found her next morning in the garden, under the rosemary

bush. She had given birth to seven kittens, seven, all of them alive when they came out from her belly. Madame Gaudet would swear to it—she was the one who'd helped to pull the last one out. And she, too, who'd forgotten that the kittens would need to be wrapped in cotton and wool against the cold. So they had all died, except for this one, Nénette. They had given her vitamins—that was why she had grown so strong and so clever.

"Seven kittens?" The voice came from the table by the window, where Jill was sitting, chin in hand. She stared up, eyes wide as saucers, and repeated the question in French.

"Oui, ma puce. C'était extraordinaire. Mais viens ici."

Jill leaped to her feet, but instead of coming to Madame Boulez, she ran to the cabinet, climbed up on a rickety cane chair, and reached over to where Nénette was lying. She stroked the cat's leg, which was all she could reach. It permitted the caress for a moment or two, then drew back. Alison ran over to her daughter, and started whispering.

"Come down from there, Jill. You mustn't climb up on the furniture. Come down at once—and say good-bye to Madame Boulez. Tell her *Joyeux Noël."*

Jill crept down with exaggerated care, as if she'd been perched on a high wire, but hadn't the least idea of how she'd got there. And then, to Alison's amazement, the child ran over to Madame Boulez, seized the woman's spotted, twisted hand, and as quickly, let it go. *"Au revoir, madame,"* said Alison, for both of them. Madame Gaudet showed them out the door, as the old woman tapped her cane on the floor, calling in her sharp, cracked voice, *"Nénette, ma Nénette. Viens, ma petite, ma polissonne."*

The very morning they were due to leave for the Jura, Douglas took Jill to the *hypermarché* and came back with a trunkful of assorted bulbs and a sheaf of indecipherable instructions. They all ended up on their hands and knees, scratching away at the hardened soil, pressing the little, naked bulbs under the earth. The sun shone weakly—there hadn't yet been a frost. Alison had her doubts about the skiing, though snow had been predicted for the holidays. It was foolish to be putting in bulbs so late—perhaps nothing would come up at all, and Jill would be heartbroken. But still, they let her dig wherever she wanted, not caring about light or shade, soil mixture or weeds. Alison took half a dozen hyacinth bulbs and lodged them in the planters on either side of the staircase leading down to the barred door, the boulevard. Perhaps they'd simply rot in the tubs—she didn't know, she didn't care anymore. All she wanted now was to get away from the house, and the shuttered windows behind which Madame Boulez was clutching her box of old photographs, her bamboo cane.

They did have snow for Christmas. The chalet was unromantic in the extreme: sunny, well-heated, ultramodern. They skied hard all day, ate huge amounts of cheese and bread and smoked ham, fell asleep by seven-thirty every night. Douglas had bought a small tree in town at an extortionate price. They spent Christmas Eve making decorations, and went to the village church for midnight mass, Jill falling asleep in her father's arms, Alison feeling bogus, foolish, and enchanted by turns. The presents they had chosen for one another were perfectly suitable—hand-knitted sweaters, chocolate and oranges for Jill, and a special, child-sized knapsack to wear on their skiing expeditions. Not once did anyone mention Madame Boulez. Alison didn't even think of the old woman until their car pulled into town well after midnight and she saw lights leaking through the shutters of the upstairs rooms. Nénette was at the metal door, crying to be let in; Jill, thank heavens, had fallen asleep in the car.

"Do you think she's dying?" Alison didn't actually say the words, but it seemed to her that her husband had heard them, so carefully did he gather up the child from the back seat, carry her into her room, and cover her so that she shouldn't wake and cry out. Madame Gaudet was in their kitchen by the time Douglas reemerged from Jill's room. They learned that Madame Boulez had had a seizure four days ago, had been in a worsening stupor ever since, and wasn't expected to live out the night. The doctor was with her now. If they wanted to come upstairs and—

"No," Alison cut her short. "No thank you," Douglas added. He remonstrated with her after Madame Gaudet had left. The woman hadn't meant to be ghoulish, he explained; it was just that death was a more public thing here, especially for people of that generation.

It was two in the morning by the time they'd dragged in all the suitcases and put things away; before the brandy started working and Alison could fall asleep. Neither of them heard Jill wake up early the next morning, make her own breakfast, and run outside to see if the bulbs they'd planted just might have come up, after all. As she bent down to poke at the earth she felt something thin, soft, rubbing up against her knees. It was Nénette, wanting to be let inside. Jill put out her hand to stroke under the cat's chin, scratch the top of her head. Nénette backed away for a moment, then returned, accepting the child's endearments. *"Nénette, ma Nénette,"* she called, trying to imitate Madame Boulez. The cat's fur was wet—she must have spent the night outdoors. Carefully, Jill gathered up the cat into her arms, holding her awkwardly, one leg hanging down. She could feel how frightened and fast the cat's heartbeat was; she could feel the body tensing, ready to leap out of the warm, unsteady circle of her arms. She would take it back to Madame Boulez. She would ring at the door, and if she were offered a bonbon from the brass box, she'd refuse—that would make it all right.

But before Jill even reached the top of the stairs a door flew open and a man came out, a man wearing a shiny black dress, with something glittering on his chest, like a star atop a Christmas tree. He passed her on the way downstairs, his shoes making no noise, but his skirts sounding like a bird's wings, rustling. The cat waited for a moment, then jumped from Jill's arms, darting past Madame Gaudet's feet into the apartment. *"Viens,"* said Madame Gaudet, and because the stairway was so dark and still, and her parents still sleeping, Jill followed the cleaning lady into Madame Boulez's rooms. They went into the kitchen, where Nénette was rubbing up against the legs of the big wooden table. Madame Gaudet poured some milk out of a saucepan into a little blue dish, which she placed on the tiles. They watched in silence as the cat stretched her head forward, ears alert; she drank stealthily, lifting her eyes from time to time. Madame Gaudet began talking in a sad, singsong voice. *"Pauvre dame, pauvre vieille dame,"* until Jill interrupted her, pointing to the blue bowl, which was empty. Madame Gaudet poured out a few more drops of milk, then sat back on her heels and looked up into the child's face. The woman's eyes were pinched with tiredness.

Suddenly the buzzer rang and the housekeeper went down in her carpet slippers to open the metal gate outside. She didn't come back. Jill waited in the kitchen until Nénette had finished preening herself, and then followed the cat into the hot, shuttered room where the dominos were kept. No one was there. Jill tried to switch on a little lamp by Madame Boulez's armchair, but nothing happened. She peered up under the parched shade and saw that the bulb had been unscrewed. So she walked over to the window, and pushed at the shutters. They hadn't been properly fastened—a little bar of light swung across the carpet. Nénette jumped at it, batted it with her paw as the sunlight swayed and then settled over the faded carpet. Then she lifted her paw and began to wash herself, scrubbing at her ears, screwing up her eyes. Jill crouched down at a little distance from her, watching.

And now everything goes wrong. Thumping up the stairwell comes her mother in a dressing gown, her hair every which way. Madame Gaudet is gasping for breath behind her. Suddenly Jill is being grabbed by her mother, held tight in her mother's arms, the way she hasn't been held since she was a baby. Nénette springs up to her favorite place of refuge—the top of the curio cabinet, under the crucifix. "Jill, oh my poor, poor Jill," her mother is crying, and then shouting at Madame Gaudet, "How could you let her inside, how could you let her come here, it's cruel—" while Madame Gaudet wrings her hands and cries, *"Ce n'était pas méchant, Madame, elle m'a rapporté la chatte, et c'est tout. J'ai fermé la porte de la chambre à coucher— je ne lui ai rien dit, vous n'avez rien à craindre—"*

"—letting a child see a dead person, it's indecent, it's—"

Her father in the doorway; she sees him looming behind the two women and finally she understands. She runs to him, shrieking,

"She's dead. Madame Boulez is dead." At last there is silence in the room.

No one says anything as Madame Gaudet shows them out of the apartment. As they descend the stairs to their own part of the house, Jill knows that her parents are angry with her. Her father pours her a bowl of hot chocolate—her mother has disappeared. It's only after she's finished her chocolate and her father has started his second bowl of *café au lait* that Jill tries to speak.

"If Madame Boulez is dead, who will look after Nénette? Can I have her; can you ask them to let me have her? I'll take good care of her, I promise. She won't be any trouble. Please ask them—Madame Gaudet would let me keep her."

Her father groans, and leans back in his chair. He lets his head fall back, then swings it in a slow half-circle. Finally he opens his eyes, and looks, not at her, but at the tablecloth.

"Jill— Everyone's very upset right now. I can't just barge up there again. We'll have to wait a little while. And I'll have to ask your mother. Tell you what, after I get shaved we can go down to the park, have a turn on the swings—"

But his daughter scrapes back her chair and runs out of the kitchen into the garden before he can finish.

Later that afternoon Douglas tried to speak to Madame Gaudet, but she had left the apartment. She must have taken the cat with her, for they never saw the animal again.

Alison had insisted they go off somewhere until the body was removed, but Douglas refused. He argued that it would make things worse, that Jill had to see what a normal, natural part of life death was. So they'd quarreled again, and Jill had ended up spending most of the day in her room, or walking round the garden, calling under her breath for the cat. Alison made sure Jill wasn't outside when the undertaker's men arrived, or when they departed, carrying a coffin that seemed to weigh no more than a packet of matches. There was no problem maneuvering it down the narrow staircase because of the niche in the wall. She ought to have seen from the very start that it was not intended for saints or flowers.

Yet curiously, after the first great shock, everyone seemed able to accommodate the death of Madame Boulez. Jill gave up calling for the cat; her parents patched up their quarrel, and things settled back into a tolerable routine. Snow fell all one January afternoon, muffling the outlines of the trees in the garden and hiding the scarred glass over the front door. Jill returned to the *maternelle,* and Alison began inviting her schoolmates home to play. During the day, Alison went into town, visiting museums and various public buildings or spending time at the university library, looking up architectural treatises she needed for a project she wanted to start once they got back to Canada.

Douglas decided that he'd been right, after all, in having taken his family to France for the year. Not only had Alison survived the shock of Madame Boulez's death, but she also seemed to have completely recovered from the accident. She was perfectly natural with Jill, taking her for walks, noticing when the child needed a new pair of shoes or gloves, reading her stories every other night at bedtime. And she was more and more like her old self with him. They found a babysitter and began to spend evenings at restaurants or cinemas; they even contemplated a weekend in Paris on their own, when Alison's parents came to visit.

And then, one night toward the beginning of March, Jill woke screaming in her bed. Douglas was the soundest of sleepers, so it was up to Alison to stumble into her daughter's room and comfort her. For a long while Jill couldn't say anything; she couldn't tell her mother what had frightened her. But, as Alison sat in the room with her, the little desk light on, Jill began to talk. She'd been floating through the dark, unable to see or feel or hear or touch anything. And knowing she never would, anymore; that she would never stop hanging in the dark, with no one beside her, and nothing underneath or overhead. Just black all around. "Is that what happens when you die? I won't die, will I? I won't go to sleep and never wake up again?"

Alison stroked her daughter's hair. She hesitated, but only for a moment. Then she bent down and kissed her daughter. "Of course you won't. Daddy and I are here, we'll protect you. No one's going to die tonight, or any night, for a long, long time. Now close your eyes, and I'll tell you a story." And she recited some tale of three brothers who each find a golden ring, and make various foolish or wise wishes. It took until the third brother had set off to seek his fortune for the child's eyes to close, for her to stop shuddering in her sleep. Alison pulled the covers up to Jill's chin, and crept out into the hallway. She stood for a moment at the one unshuttered window, looking out into the garden. She could hear trucks rumbling past, the chuffing of a train. If the bulbs were still alive they made no noise, stretching and turning over under the earth.

So here she was, having to start from scratch again, with no clear road ahead. She didn't know whether Jill had believed her promises or only in the desire that had prompted them, love's need to soothe, to help, to build a shelter against the cold and dark. As for herself, she didn't know what she believed anymore. That no illumination, however violent or gentle, lasts forever. That you could never perfectly enclose yourself, protect yourself or anyone else from grief and pain and loss. That there was nothing for it but to endure, as Madame Boulez had endured, with her photographs and bric à brac, and the cat she'd alternately petted and struck. And that even these beliefs, of which she was now so sure, would last only as long as a match struck in the night. Soon she would unlearn them; she would have to find another match to light if she wanted things to go on at all. Her whole life would be measured out in small flames and burned-out matchsticks, laid end to end along an uncertain line.

She went back to her bed, creeping in between the sheets. She lay on her side, her back against her husband's back, as if their two bodies formed a set of low, warm walls that couldn't stop anything from breaking through, on purpose or by accident. Walls which would have to hold, at least from one moment to the next.

The Gray Valise

The photographer had no difficulty whatsoever with Mrs. Fanshawe. Granted, it was only a passport picture, but some women of that age got as flustered about the response of customs officers to their recorded image as a girl of sixteen sitting for her first studio portrait. He'd had ladies requesting a diffused lens to turn all creases, hollows, bulges into haunting shadows and pearly gleams; insisting that profile shots, or at least, three-quarter views would produce a much more faithful likeness. Mrs. Fanshawe, however, had voiced no objections to the truthfulness required for the occasion—or at least, the degree of truth a passport photo could vouchsafe. She hadn't been to the hairdresser's, but had simply twisted her unabashedly gray hair into its usual tidy coil at the back of her head. She hadn't bought a new dress, but wore a plain white blouse with no jewelry. And she disdained to arrange her face into a smile; what the camera recorded was exactly what the customs officer at Rome International Airport saw: a thin mark, like a blank waiting to be filled in, cut short at either end by a parenthesis of strict, deep lines.

Faces set in the same way custards do, observed Mrs. Fanshawe, accepting her passport back from the official, and acknowledging his *buon giorno* with a slight inclination of her head. Those curving lines on either side of her mouth, when had they first solidified? Long before Digby's heart attack, long before he'd started stocking up the medicine cabinet with nitroglycerine tablets and making his little jokes about possessing an explosive temper—Digby had been renowned for his exceptional good humor, the mildness of his response to events that should have provoked, indeed, demanded, something in the line of black and brutal rage. When Caroline, for example, had refused point blank to enter university, and had run off to Mexico with a potter. Or when Richard had settled for pharmacy after having failed his entrance exams to medical school. No, the lines had set much earlier than that, had first been etched on Digby's return from the war, so that they could be traced even in her wedding portrait, fine as the pleating of her white chiffon: little lines of disappointment and containment, like a sigh or a cry suppressed in the very act of utterance.

Buon giorno. Nothing on earth would induce Olive Fanshawe to speak more of the language than she absolutely had to. It wasn't that she hadn't an aptitude for languages—she'd learned German in high school; she'd have majored in the subject at university if it hadn't been for the war. Instead she'd switched to General Arts and become engaged to Digby, who hadn't waited to enter law school before enlisting and shipping off to Italy. She'd wished he could have done officers' training in England, instead; she'd wished he could have done his fighting in France. When all those films came out after the war—*Open City* and *Two Women*—Olive had felt a squirm of distaste at the memory of those letters Digby had sent her from Pisa and Ancona and Naples. It wasn't the memory of their contents that had upset her, but rather the remembered feel of the paper, the fact that they had come from that country she now associated with coarse-haired women in tattered dresses; bare, dirty legs and staring eyes.

The Italian women she saw greeting relatives at the airport were not quite what Mrs. Fanshawe had expected. To begin with, they were dressed with what she could only call an overweening elegance. Settling herself with her handbag and gray valise in the Holiday Inn limousine, she pulled the edges of her sensible, no-crease raincoat tighter together. Her skirt was stained where the stewardess had managed to spill a Bloody Mary right into her lap an hour out from Gander. The woman hadn't even been contrite—she'd spent all her time chatting up the businessmen and flogging duty-free wrist-watches and perfume. Mrs. Fanshawe had refused the latter, just as she'd refused the offer of a free drink to make up for the clamato juice sloshed over her new seersucker. At home she'd occasionally take a glass of sherry or dry white wine, but journeying to a totally foreign country, suspended for hours in black midair, who but the most abandoned of fools would willingly intoxicate themselves? If the plane had been forced to land in midocean, as the precautionary pamphlet she'd been urged to read gave every sign it might, how could a bunch of hiccoughing, lolling boozers ever remember to take off their spectacles and shoes, and not inflate their life preservers until after they'd slid down the rubber chute?

Prego, signora. She had purchased an Italian phrasebook for the journey; all that she'd managed to memorize so far had been, "I do not like highly seasoned food," and "I do not wish to speak to you." She wished, for the briefest of moments, that she'd told Richard; requested he come with her. Richard could be here now, assisting her to get out of the limousine, giving the man instructions about being very careful with the valise and not, on any occasion, to drop it. Or at least, Richard could have seen to their bags, leaving her free to flip to the section of her guidebook entitled "Tips, the use and abuse thereof" and fish the appropriate amount of lire from her purse. As it was she stuffed the only coin she could find—a conspicuously shiny dollar-loon—into the insolently outstretched hand of the driver, who let it roll onto the marble floor of the Holiday Inn lobby as he lounged back to his cab. Mrs. Fanshawe deftly retrieved it on the way upstairs, after she'd checked herself and her one suitcase into the hotel.

She'd insisted on carrying the valise herself, even though the bell-hop spoke perfectly good English, and might indeed have hailed from Toronto rather than the Eternal City. Mrs. Fanshawe's sister lived in Toronto, and had had to move from what had once been a perfectly good neighborhood, now inundated with Italians brewing wine in their basements, and creating multicolored brick façades for what had once been a passable imitation of half-timbering. Caroline (who had returned from Mexico minus the potter, waitressed her way through Osgoode Hall, and was now making no money to speak of defending immigrants fighting deportation orders) had snorted at her mother's description of the current Italianization of northwestern Toronto. "That was fifteen years ago, Mother. Nowadays, to be Italian in Toronto is like being *ancien régime.*" At which point it had been Mrs. Fanshawe's turn to snort. All of which had distressed Richard immeasurably, this conversation taking place on the way to the chapel where Digby's coffin, draped with a regimental flag, was waiting to be prayed over and incinerated.

Richard, naturally, had been upset at the idea of cremation; Mrs. Fanshawe herself had been astonished at the clarity and decisiveness of Digby's instructions, to which his partner alone had been privy. In fact, due to Richard's getting all in a flap over his father's fatal attack—he had been told the news in the middle of the preparation of a particularly complicated prescription, and had lost hundreds of dollars in smashed bottles, spilled fluids, and hopeless dispersed powders—Mr. Deveau had been the first to break the news to her. It is difficult to be rude to someone who phones to tell you that your husband's heart has just stopped beating. Thus, though Mrs. Fanshawe had never approved of her husband's choice of partner; had, in fact, hounded him to stay on with Gilbert, Crocker, and Goodridge rather than sticking out his neck for a parvenu Acadian, she'd answered Mr. Deveau with a perfectly civil, "I see," "Naturally," and, "Of course, if he left written instructions . . ."

Once she'd scrubbed the clamato juice out of her yellow seersucker skirt, taken a bath, and unpacked what little her bag contained—she would be gone from her home for a total of five days—she lay down on the bed for a nap before lunch. She looked at her wrist and did some mental calculations (only with the greatest reluctance had she altered her watch to Italian time). It was eight P.M. in Fredericton; Elva Rogers would be starting the meeting of the Historical Association at which Olive Fanshawe had been supposed to speak—would have spoken, with great eloquence and iron conviction, against the necessity for raising funds for the restoration of what had once been the city's most flourishing brothel. Her arguments would have touched upon the dignity of women, the dubious architectural value of the site, the existence of more pressing objects of concern—i.e., the disintegrating glass in St. Elfrida's-on-the Hill— and the ethical implications of historical conservation. Almost certainly the committee would go ahead and vote for restoration without her there to point the weaker, undecided members in the right direction. Mrs. Fanshawe pulled the sheets higher over her bare arms and shoulders, took a deep breath, and gave a small, relieved sigh—this hotel used the same brand of detergent as she did at home. She didn't bother setting the alarm—she'd acquired the knack, during her long and vexing marriage, of being able to waken from no matter how profound a sleep, at whatever hour she chose, whether to administer a dose of medicine to a feverish child, prepare last-minute income tax returns, dispatch Christmas, birthday, or sympathy cards for the early post, or check to see whether the basement was flooded. Digby, of course, could sleep through anything, including his law practice, which explained the bulk of his wife's vexations during the forty-odd years of their marriage.

Another of Mrs. Fanshawe's acquired talents was the ability to dismiss her dreams immediately upon waking. Her nightmares were always the same; she would find herself back at university, about to take her degree (with highest distinction), when she'd be summoned to write exams for a course in which she'd never enrolled, on a subject she had never studied. It was, on the whole, an unexpected sort of nightmare for someone as self-assured as Olive Fanshawe seemed to be. She had matured into that kind of matron who'd reached her apogee some sixty years ago: large-bosomed, sturdy-legged, she could have carried off a pince-nez, shoulder pads, a black felt hat and a pug dog with the greatest aplomb. In fact, as Caroline had more than once pointed out, Olive and Digby had grown into the sort of couple associated with old-fashioned cartoons—Jiggs and Maggie, that sort of thing. Except that Digby had never had the wherewithal to deck his wife with pearl pendants, diamond necklaces, and dinner rings. No, if Olive exuded an air of absolute certainty and control, it had been to make up for the vagueness and ineptitude, the milky human kindness that leaked out of Digby like water through a patchy roof. So perhaps it was quite natural she should have recurring anxiety dreams, as a kind of surtax on a rather too insistent superego.

What was less understandable, to Olive at least, was that she would have the other sort of dream, the kind that carried her, this Roman morning, over unfamiliar smells and sounds into another sort of morning altogether, no less foreign to her for the past fifty years than Italy could be now. She was walking in the marshes on the outskirts of Sackville, long, wet grass lapping her bare legs like a green silk skirt. Still enough to hear the cows tearing off hanks of clover and buttercups; still enough to hear gulls mew through a fleece of fog. Air soft and vague and smelling of salt; a warm, slow rasp of salt against her skin as she walks barefoot over the flushed and silvery soil, through the clinging rustle of the grasses . . .

Mrs. Fanshawe woke with the taste of salt on her lips in the susurrant darkness of her hotel room, The air conditioners and purifiers whirred and whispered; according to the luminous green dial on the television set it was three o'clock in the morning. Olive sat up, clutching the sheets to her breast, shook the dream out of her skull with the mental equivalent of a straw whisk, and switched on the lamp beside the bed. She was in a room no different from those of the Holiday Inn in Halifax, except that there were prints of the Colosseum and not of the Citadel on the walls. Were she to open her curtains she would merely look into the spotlit atrium with its potted palms and replica ruins. Caroline would have laughed at her for reserving a room at the Holiday Inn, instead of some dirty *pensione* in which she could see the real Italy. With a practiced glance, Mrs. Fanshawe withered an imaginary Caroline. She had not come all this way to see the real Italy, or any Italy, for that matter. She had come to discharge a duty, divest herself of a burden. She loathed the whole idea of traveling—all her married life she had chosen vacations that had taken the family no farther afield than Cavendish, Prince Edward Island, and, one regrettable summer, Toronto, to visit her sister Beatrice. She'd seen all she wanted to of the great wide world in Toronto—street signs in Chinese, Indonesian restaurants, turbaned bus drivers, billboards in Portuguese. How could Bea, born and bred in Fredericton—not that Fredericton itself hadn't changed, over the last few years—and of course there had always been the French. . . .

It was no use babbling on like this—she might as well face the fact that for the first time ever, her internal alarm hadn't sounded. She had slept, not only through lunch but dinner as well (having prepaid for both). And no matter how she tried to scatter her thoughts she couldn't shake off the fingers of the dream she'd had, which she could still feel brushing up against her. Walking in the marshes, as she'd done when a child. No omens, portents, symbols —just the simple pleasure of walking barefoot in the marshes through the long and dewy grass. . . .

Mrs. Fanshawe willed herself to sleep—long, black, serviceable sleep—but with no success whatever. Three thirty-seven, the severe green digits proclaimed; her stomach gurgled. She threw back the covers and walked over to the desk; retrieved from her purse the bread sticks, roll, and packet of Colby cheese she'd saved from the flight, and washed it all down with a few sips of bottled water. Then, on a reflex, she checked the contents of her purse: her traveler's checks all crisp and still unperforated; her passport, its photograph neatly affixed, the customs stamp violating the purity of its pages. "Olivia Lucinda Fanshawe, née Crawford." The man had read her entire name aloud, in his peculiarly sonorous accent. She had been Olive ever since her fifteenth birthday, on which she'd decided it was high time to correct her mother's regrettable lapse into literariness. (Mrs. Crawford had been a founding member of the Sackville Shakespearean Play-Reading Society, and they had reached *Twelfth Night* the year of her daughter's birth. Olive could only be grateful it hadn't been *Troilus and Cressida* or *Hamlet*.) In fact, the issuing of her passport had been the first time, since the filling out of Richard's birth certificate, that she'd had to acknowledge herself as Olivia. She

couldn't help entering it as one more item on the list of her griev-
ances against Digby. For the hundredth time she asked herself, if
Digby hadn't been Digby Fanshawe, one of the Fredericton Fanshawes, however spindly an offshoot of that august trunk; if his name
had been Joe Allen, Frank Maclean, Steven Green, would she have
married him at all?

That was hardly the sort of question to be asking oneself at three
forty-nine on an Italian midsummer morning, Mrs. Fanshawe decided, tidying up the wrappers from her impromptu picnic, and
spreading out the map of Italy she had purchased at Coles only the
week before. She had given the travel agent a good run for his
money—he had written out everything: the time of the train, the
name, if not number of the bus, the address of the only hotel the
village seemed to boast, and in which a room for one night had been
reserved for her. Albergo Rustico. She shivered in apprehension—
straw mattresses, no doubt; rusty water, greasy cooking. Well, no
matter how primitive conditions were at present in the town of Fermio, they would have been a hundred times worse when Digby had
passed through. After all, he would have had Germans—or would
they have been Italians?—shooting at him; no doubt there'd been
lice, rats, all sorts of horrors that would surely have been eradicated
now. Lots of people, she assured herself, went to Italy for their holidays, though just why they would do so she couldn't fathom. Of
course if you were taken with paintings, sculpture, that sort of
thing. . . . Mrs. Fanshawe located Fermio on the map, folded it up,
carefully tucked the schedule into the inner pocket of her purse, and,
removing the yellow seersucker suit from the small but shining bathroom, took a long and forceful shower.

It was all ridiculously easy. The clerk at the desk had called her
a taxi to the railway station after breakfast; she had purchased her
ticket from a quite pleasant and respectable-looking lady at the station, had even managed *quanto fa biglietto andata e ritorno* with the aid
of her phrasebook. There was, of course, no direct train to Fermio;
she would have to bus the last little bit. Yet fresh from her triumph

at the railway station, Mrs. Fanshawe felt confident enough to sit back and enjoy the scenery out the window: wheat fields in which dribbles of red—poppies, she presumed—alternated with blue bits (cornflowers? chicory?) with only the occasional tractor to interrupt the pattern. The compartment, being first class, was nearly empty, the only other occupant a lady of about her own age, who seemed no more disposed to acknowledge Mrs. Fanshawe's presence than that lady was to admit the Italian's. From time to time Mrs. Fanshawe directed her gaze to the gray valise overhead—in it she had her packet, and necessaries for an overnight stay at the Albergo Rustico. She had taken her plane ticket and passport in the handbag she clutched tightly in her lap—she knew better than to leave valuables at any hotel, even a Holiday Inn. From her bag she drew out the envelope containing a photostat of Digby's instructions; for the last time she read it over.

I, Digby Horace Fanshawe, being of sound mind, do hereby bequeath the sum total of my estate to my wife, Olivia Lucinda Fanshawe, née Crawford, on condition that . . .

The very idea of imposing conditions. Mrs. Fanshawe fanned herself with the envelope—the compartment was becoming rather stuffy, but she supposed there was no way of opening a window. Digby Horace Fanshawe . . . His father had been a prominent judge, his uncle a federal MP, his grandfather a provincial cabinet minister; until Digby there had been Fanshawes in the New Brunswick legislature ever since there had been a New Brunswick at all. She had corresponded with members of the New Hampshire Fanshawes, descendants of that faction of the family that had not seen fit to honor king and mother country at the time of the Rebellion. There had even been plans for an across-the-border reunion of the Fanshawes; in fact, if Digby hadn't neglected to take his nitroglycerine tablets, she would be heading for Concord, New Hampshire, instead of some inglorious little Italian town in which Digby happened to have been billeted at the end of a war in which he'd done nothing whatsoever to distinguish himself. Except, of course, not to get shot. But then even that had been the accomplishment not of Digby, but of that tarty little miss whose photograph she'd found in Digby's filing cabinet, slipped in with T-forms and bills for office cleaning.

"Well, Digby? Don't you think you might explain yourself? You could at least have found a better hiding place—you knew I was going to fill out the tax returns this year—you made such a muddle of it last time. Speak up, Digby, who is she? Or did you even know her name?"

She'd surprised herself at the viciousness of her tone, and the turn her questions had taken. It was not, after all, the photograph of a naked woman: just the head and well-clad shoulders of what could only have been a peasant girl, no more than eighteen, with fair hair and black eyes. She wasn't even attractive; that is, she was no Anna Magnani or Sophia Loren. She had a slightly simple expression— perhaps because she was smiling so artlessly and so openly at whoever was holding the camera. One couldn't make a fuss over the snapshot of a girl who could have been an adenoidal younger sister; one couldn't interrogate one's husband over a harmless souvenir of the hard-fought Italian campaign. And yet Olive had proceeded to upbraid and harangue her husband, hardly caring whether or not she woke the children.

Digby hadn't protested. He'd only smiled at her, in his usual tenuous way, and said the girl was the daughter of a farmer who'd hidden him at Fermio just before the end of the war. Being Digby, he'd managed to get separated from his patrol one evening, found himself lost in the hill country, and drawn by valley lights into a village below. The farmer had hidden him in the hayloft of his barn, along with the other valuables he hadn't wanted snatched by the Germans: his watch, a photograph album, and his daughter Maria. Olive had known at once that it wasn't her real name—Maria was to Italian women as Rover was to dogs. She'd pressed Digby for details, but all he could tell her was that he'd left before dawn and managed to rejoin his patrol that afternoon. And that the girl had given him her photograph for good luck.

"Have you written to her since? I suppose she wouldn't know how to write, or to read, for that matter. And no doubt you'll tell me she means nothing to you. Nothing at all—is that right, Digby? You have nothing to say on the subject? Then I suppose you'll have no objection to me disposing of this worthless souvenir from a time you'd obviously prefer to forget?" And, with a precision and control astonishing even for Olive Fanshawe, she had taken the photograph to the kitchen, dropped it into a roasting pan, lit a match, and burned it up, while Digby watched, wordless, from the doorway.

He hadn't said anything at all afterward. Digby wasn't a talkative man, but a gifted listener, particularly with his clients, most of whom he undercharged—he was at once the busiest and most down-at-heel lawyer in Fredericton. She'd felt oddly aggrieved for the rest of the day after the photograph incident—she hadn't slept well that night. It wasn't that she was sorry for—she supposed—having hurt Digby's feelings, or for having caused him some pain over the loss of an item which he obviously cherished, however forgetful he'd been in storing it away. It was that she'd stooped to an act of passion—she couldn't see it as anything other than that. It had been a mean thing to do, a passion of meanness—and spite. Spite that he'd kept a secret from her, spite that this Italian girl had managed to share something with Digby, something other than a house, two children, and a precarious bank account.

When he'd courted her before the war, Digby had been a little vague, a trifle absentminded at times, but ready enough to be guided and directed by those he acknowledged as masters of those arts—not the least of them Olive Crawford. The Crawfords and the Fanshawes had been marrying each other for generations—all during the war, old Mrs. Fanshawe had been grooming Olive for the role of Digby's wife. And she would have made a perfect political hostess and helpmeet; she had a genius for organization, a devotion to duty, and an infallible ability to carry out assigned responsibilities, no matter how peculiar the situations in which they placed her—look at her here, now, in an Italian railway carriage, with Digby's instructions in her hands. He knew he could count on her for this—just as his mother had known she could count on her to pull Digby up to the mark, to make Digby what a Fanshawe ought to be.

And so she would have, had it not been for the war, the war that had turned Digby from a dreamy but malleable youth into a perfectly hopeless blank. Oh, he was adequate enough as a lawyer—honest as the day, and he seemed to know all the necessary legal procedures for the modest sort of practice he carried on. But he ventured no opinions, held no beliefs; he would make no statements of any kind. Any plan for launching Digby into politics had had to be abandoned. The kindest, most generous of friends (the mourners at his funeral had testified to that), the most indulgent of fathers (Caroline and Richard had adored him, especially at the moments of the Mexican escapade and the med school entrance exams), and the gentlest, most faithful of husbands. After all, he'd still been a single man, though engaged to Olive, during his escapade at Fermio. And all through their marriage he'd never given her cause for even a spasm of jealousy—or anything else, for that matter. Perhaps that's why she'd been so enraged about the photograph. If only he could have shown some passion, snatching the photo from her hands, bursting out with all the fear and rage that must have filled him coming home from that war, surrendering all that was left of his life to the bride his mother had chosen for him, the town in which he'd grown up and gone to school. Digby hadn't proved much of a one for traveling, any more than she had—Digby wouldn't have been able to ask for a ticket in a Roman railway station, wouldn't have been able to cope, as she was now, with finding the bus depot without losing either purse or valise, with boarding a hot, dusty, antique vehicle filled with fat old women in black dresses, holding chickens under their arms.

One of these women could be Digby's Maria, thought Mrs. Fanshawe, as the bus rocketed out of town, raising a fog of dust that turned the cypresses bordering the road into dark and dirty phantoms. *"Fermio, si, si,"* the conductor had said, punching her ticket and moving on to chatter with the women at the back of the bus. She understood it to be the last stop—she understood that the bus would pull up right in front of the Albergo Rustico. The yellow seersucker skirt was riding up—she wriggled in her seat, tugging the material down as best she could while still maintaining a firm grasp on the handle of her valise and the strap of her purse. And the lines around her mouth cut a little deeper with each kilometer jolted through on the way to Fermio. Now that she was actually approaching her destination, she would have to prepare herself—gird up her loins, that's what St. Paul said. She wondered for a moment exactly what was involved in such an action, and how it could possibly apply to women. And then, in a last spurt of speed and dust, the bus pulled up in front of the Albergo Rustico, and Mrs. Fanshawe followed the crowd of black-clad women and cackling hens out into the scalding clarity of an Italian afternoon.

Non intendo rivolgerle la parola was how you said, "I do not wish to speak to you," but Mrs. Fanshawe could not quite come out with it—partly because the phrasebook's guide to pronunciation was hopelessly complicated, and partly because the Italian seemed rather severe for what she intended as a simple, "No, thank you very much, I'm quite happy as I am."

She was seated at a wooden table covered with a plastic cloth, trying to keep bits of geranium petal from drifting into her water glass. She was feeling rather faint—she'd had only a few rolls for breakfast, and some rather milky coffee—she'd missed lunch because of having to catch the bus to Fermio, and had decided to put off her errand until after the earliest supper she could contrive. So she was sitting in the breezy little garden at the back of the hotel, waiting for soup and pasta, and chewing bits of bread. She had just finished her second roll when the man appeared at her table, asking, she assumed, for permission to join her, and then, oblivious to her *"Non parlo italiano"* (no doubt she hadn't pronounced it properly), ordering a bottle of wine and two chilled glasses from the sulky girl sweeping out the courtyard.

Non intendo—but she couldn't finish. He was a small man with neatly combed hair bearing not a trace of pomade, and dressed in gray trousers and a spotless white shirt with the sleeves rolled up. He smiled at her and poured out a glass of straw-colored wine. She shook her head, but he pushed the glass gently toward her all the same, clinked it with his own, and, offering a toast, downed it. For politeness's sake, she lifted her glass to her lips, moistened them with the wine, and set it down again. *"Non parlo italiano,"* she said this time as deliberately and authoritatively as she could. If she weren't weak with hunger—and here he was offering her wine!—she would have left the table immediately, called the hotelkeeper, and mustered as much of her phrasebook Italian as she could to explain the precise nature of the offense this man was committing against her. A simple excess of hospitality, complicated by the fact that the man at her table, pressing her to drink up her wine, was, in fact, the owner and host of the Albergo Rustico, Signor Bertelli himself.

"Inglese? Americana? Canadese? Buono, canadese, eccelente, canadese— Good morning, good afternoon, good night. *Guardi, Claudia, parlo canadese!"* And he beckoned to the girl with the broom, who slip-slopped over to their table and received lavish and rapid instructions from the man—hopefully about her soup and pasta. Mrs. Fanshawe sighed. She took a sip of the wine—safer, she assumed, than the brackish-looking water in the speckled glass, and leaned in across the table to catch the words of the hotelkeeper.

"Vous parlez français? ¿Habla español? Sprechen Sie Deutsch?"

"Ein bisschen." It must have been shock—otherwise, how could she have summoned the words—it had been some forty years since she'd even heard any German spoken. She couldn't account, either, for her sudden readiness to open a channel of communication with her overfriendly host. She drew back from the table, pulling her skirt farther down over her knees, pulling those knees in, away, like a tortoise retracting its head into its shell. But it was too late—the man was speaking to her in a German that was all the more comprehensible to her because it was halting, awkward, and incorrect. At the very moment when he was asking what brought her to Fermio, the soup arrived, and she busied herself with blowing on the steaming, fragrant broth before answering. *"Meine familie,"* she said—half of that was German, at least. And then she preempted any further questions by asking the man where he had learned to speak German—*Wo haben Sie Deutsch gelernt?* That was simple enough, it was ridiculously like English. And then she cursed herself, thinking of the war; he'd have

been a collaborator, his speaking German must mean all sorts of terrible things, the things Digby had refused to tell her, or anyone else, when he came home. But Signor Bertelli hadn't bristled at her question: indeed, he'd smiled in return and explained that he'd worked in Germany in the nineteen sixties. *"Einer Gastarbeiter: neunzehn hundert und sechzig."* He said he'd made enough money there to come back to his native town and buy the Albergo Rustico. There had been much trouble between the Italians and the Germans during the war. Partisans, he explained; much fighting, burning, shooting—he mimed, here, the action of a machine gun. But all that was over now—people were friends again, the whole world was trying to be friends. Look at her, coming all the way to Italy from Canada, coming to a little village like Fermio—and did she really have family here? She would pardon him for making such a personal remark, but she didn't look at all Italian.

"Mein Mann," said Mrs. Fanshawe, cutting into the steak that had followed the pasta. Signor Bertelli seemed to have added to her order—he opened a bottle of red wine to accompany the steak. She lifted up her head to watch something that had caught her eye—a group of swallows scissoring the air over the pond behind the garden. She spent a moment with her knife and fork suspended in the air, admiring the concision of the swallows' wings. Her host caught her eye; they smiled at one another. *"E molto buono,"* said Mrs. Fanshawe, tucking back into her steak, not even needing to reach for her phrasebook. Her pronunciation must have been correct this time, for the man beamed at her, and gave a little bow. *"Grazie,"* he said, and then, switching back into German, asked her how an Italian could have the name of Fanshawe?

She blushed, as if she'd been caught out in a lie, instead of the inadequate possession of a foreign language. *"Mein Mann ist nicht aus Italien. Mein mann hat in Italien"*—how did you say fight?— *"gekriegt.* My husband fought in Italy, *in neunzehn hundert, fünf und vierzig—in dem Krieg. Verstehen Sie?"*

"Und wo ist Ihrer Mann, signora?" Where is he?

Of course she should have answered, *"Tot."* But what with the wine and the swallows, and the unwonted effort of speaking German, she simply pointed to the gray valise under the table and blurted out, *"Hier."*

As they were walking up the hill, Mrs. Fanshawe noticed that the swallows sickling over the ponds and fields had given way to furry, fumbling creatures that, miraculously, never managed to get entangled in her hair, or to collide with the walking stick Signor Bertelli was brandishing to signal various points of interest. Fermio would have been no more than a hamlet, except for the fact that it possessed a small, squat church, bare of any embellishment except a lopsided tower. The chief grace of the town was, indeed, the Albergo Rustico, which, Signor Bertelli assured her, did a thriving business during the market season and on St. Livia's day, when there was some sort of procession to the church, which was, in fact, named after the saint. *"Es gibt ein schönes Bild darin,"* he said. *"Ein Bild von Sankt Livia."* Mrs. Fanshawe murmured something polite about taking a look at it in the morning, if there was time before her bus came. Although she wasn't terribly interested in paintings. But she wanted to show her appreciation to this kind, this most sympathetic and understanding man, who, once he'd got over his little shock at her gesture toward the gray valise, had listened to her explanation of what it was she'd come to Fermio to do, and even offered a suggestion as to where and how to go about it.

She wondered, as they gained the brow of the little hill, what Caroline and Richard would say—especially Caroline—if they could see her now, and in such company. "Oh, Mother—you're so closed off to everything," Caroline had once said—and a great number of other things, much less polite. "Of course I am," Olive had replied. "How else do you think I could get by at all?" "Get by" meant holding up her end of things, fulfilling her part of a bargain that Digby, coming back from the war, seemed to have entirely forgotten. She had known, the very day of his return, that something extraordinary had happened to him, changing him beyond all recognition.

She could have braved Mrs. Fanshawe's displeasure and broken off the engagement—left town, gone to Halifax, even joined her sister in Toronto. But she'd felt herself obliged to stick by Digby, consoling herself with the hope that, even if he never climbed to the heights of QC or MP, he would at least confide to her all that had happened to him in Italy. He had been silent as the grave. Why, if she hadn't found the photograph—

"Ecco." Signor Bertelli had stopped before a funny, wizened little tree rooted in a heap of stones. He made her understand, through a rough mix of German and Italian, and some expressive gestures, that this was a kind of holy spot, the site of a former church or pagan shrine, she couldn't decipher which. And that the peaky-looking bush had something to do with the patron saint of the church to which Signor Bertelli was pointing. You could see the whole village spread out below them, the houses and the farms, the courtyards with their terra-cotta pots of oleander and geranium, the precise little trees dividing crops so neatly planted they seemed to be painted onto the earth. *"Ecco,"* he repeated, with another flourish of his walking stick upon the dry, sweet-smelling breeze that rustled Mrs. Fanshawe's skirt against her legs. And then he handed her the gray valise, which he'd carried for her all the way up the hill, and took several steps back, turning in the other direction, so that for the next few moments she would feel herself entirely private, though not alone.

Olive bent down and unlocked the case. She lifted the packet into her arms, as if it were a difficult child that no amount of cosseting could quiet. Signor Bertelli believed that the saint's influence, the holy, or at least magical, ground on which she now stood, would ensure that Digby's ashes found their proper home as she cast them on the wind. Certainly, it was a good spot to release them, if only for the fact that the evening breeze would blow them away from her and down over the fields below—that had been her gravest concern, that she might end up with Digby's ashes in her mouth, ground into her hair and eyes. She unfastened the wrappings and drew out a large plastic bag; she undid the bag and, stretching out her arms, emptied it on the wind. And as she watched the ashes scatter and fall—some on the ground beside the bush, some on the hillside, some skirling right up in the arms of the breeze, to be carried far, far below—she felt peculiarly as she had that morning, waking from her dream of walking barefoot in the Fundy marshes on a misty summer morning. A sense of intimate connection with an unrecoverable past; a sense of the present as infinite loss.

What a fool she'd been. She, with her flair for languages, never being able to learn what Digby had to say to her. How many times had he tried to tell her, with the press of his body at night, and the drowning clutch of his hands; with the photograph he'd brought back all the way from Italy and planted in his files for her to find. And now, with this last message, printed out for her not in the instructions listed in his will, but in the bundle of ashes blowing from this hilltop overlooking Fermio, down into the fields and courtyards of the farms below. What if it was simply this—that he hadn't wanted to come back to her at all—hadn't wanted the war to end, or at least, had wanted to disappear into the arms of a peasant girl from Fermio and end his days sitting in a dusty courtyard, pungent with the odor of geraniums. What if he had come back only for her, for the sake of Olivia Lucinda Crawford, who had written him letters and knitted him socks all through the war, and whom he had promised to marry in the innocent way that children promise their parents to be good when they go off to a neighbor's house to play.

It didn't matter that Digby, had he asked for and been given his freedom, would have been no more capable of leaving Fredericton and returning to Italy than of turning his arms into wings by the simple expedient of flapping them. Just as it didn't matter that she didn't know the precise farm that had sheltered Digby forty-odd years ago; that she couldn't pick out which, if any, of the black-clad, mumble-toothed grandmothers was Digby's Maria. The ashes would sift down on all alike, finishing as no more than dust in somebody's yard, a mote in someone's eye. The thing was that finally Digby had spoken to her in a fashion she could understand. And that by coming here she'd made him a more eloquent response than the simple burning of a photograph.

Signor Bertelli gave a little cough, and Mrs. Fanshawe quickly folded up the plastic bag, wrapped it back in the cloth that had sheltered it, and locked it up in the gray valise. On the way down, Signor Bertelli offered her his arm and she accepted it gladly—she felt as weary as if she had walked all the way up the hill on her knees.

Mrs. Fanshawe returned to Rome the next morning after a brief visit to the little church Signor Bertelli had gestured to the night before. She spent that night at the Holiday Inn near the airport, and rose up early the next morning, with ample time to pack her nightdress and change of underwear into her strong and capacious handbag; the gray valise she left in a large wastepaper basket by the elevator. She flew to Fredericton without incident; she'd been away no more than the five days she'd allotted herself, and immediately took up the round of activities and obligations she had so briefly interrupted. She told her friends that she'd been to Halifax to visit an old school friend. And she mailed a letter with no return address to the Albergo Rustico; it was made out to Signor Bertelli, and bore only the briefest message: *Grazie per l'ospitalità*. She signed it "Olivia."

The only memento of her trip to Italy was a postcard Mrs. Fanshawe tucked inside the frame of her dressing-table mirror. On the bottom was printed *Chiesa Sta Livia, Fermio*, and a title that translated roughly as "St. Livia in the Miraculous Burning Bush." In it a young girl with an open, almost simple-looking face, with golden hair and a golden gown, crackled in a three-alarm fire. The flames were a bright, clear red—red in the way children imagine blood to be. A man with a sad and gentle face holds out spindly fingers, as if to tousle the flames. The landscape is a desert: bald and shadowless rocks, and a sky devoid of any trace of blue. The sky is gold, like St. Livia's hair and dress, like the exposed roots of the burning bush and the vegetation underfoot; leaves caught in the updraft of the fire. What little grass there is, is blistered, black.

Yet at night, when Mrs. Fanshawe dreams, the lines holding her lips so tight and thin relax. Her mouth goes slack, falls open as if she were slightly astonished at something, or as if she were about to utter some exclamation—whether of pain, or pleasure, or some shifting mix of both, it would be impossible to tell.

The Dark

What can I say that will be of any help to you at all? You see, I
hardly knew her. Our offices were next door to each other; once I
gave her a lift home when we'd both been working late. That sort of
thing. So I have no idea why I was sent for, or even why I ended up
going to that place. I came back as soon as I could, and I've never
mentioned that trip to anyone. That's what it was, a trip: something
necessary, quickly over. Not a voyage, certainly not a holiday. A trip
to a place I've never wanted to visit, not under the best of circumstances. Really, I've forgotten so much—none of this information will
be useful to you. It certainly hasn't been for me. I try to forget what
happened, I would have forgotten, if it weren't for you, always asking,
never letting me be. I get so angry at being forced through all of this,
again and again, when we weren't even friends. We weren't enemies,
either, in case that's what you think. We just happened to share a
corridor; sometimes I'd mistake her office for mine, or vice versa.
That does happen—it's not a criminal offense, you know. It means
nothing.

On this trip—this journey, if you'd prefer—I went alone, and not
in the usual fashion. You see, I don't use airplanes—you could say I
have a phobia about them. Lots of people do, it's not such a freakish

thing. She would have known about that, when she sent for me she would have realized there'd be certain delays, that she'd have to make allowances. Yes, of course—you've asked about the journey, and I'm trying to describe it to you as meticulously as I can. I didn't, of course, keep a journal, but I did jot certain things down in a notebook after I came home. If I spent a few hours, a few days—I don't know how much time I'd need—I might be able to turn up that notebook. It wouldn't be much use. It would be like coming across a story in a magazine, one that you could pick up or put down, just as you like. Whereas I am concerned—at your request—with memory, with what litters the floor of the mind. Or what falls through. Sometimes I imagine the past as an enormous and ornate room—a pantheon or rotunda. The floor has given way, you can't cross from one side to the other except by going all the way round, stabbing footholds into the walls. And even then you never reach the end, you just go on groping and pulling yourself round and around, grabbing onto ornament, excrescences. Perfectly nonsensical details—a hole in a door, a dried-up spider plant, perfume spilled on the bathroom tiles. . . .

Nonsensical. Because we've agreed; you must reconstruct that floor, you have no choice if you're to take any steps at all. You must be practical, deliberate; you must find your material and stick to it, no matter what questions are asked. And I've told you all this before; the only way to put the past behind you is to create a space ahead of you, paved with earth or wood, or, best of all, concrete blocks, one after another and another, for as far as you can imagine. That is the only kind of journeying that's safe—on condition that you don't stop, that you don't look back, or around you. But this is not what you've asked me about—you want to know about a trip I once took; you want to know about the train.

It left at five in the afternoon; it would deposit me in W—— at eleven the next morning. We would cross the border at ten-thirty, which meant that there was no point in unpacking the berth and trying to sleep until the customs officers had visited my compartment. I had brought a new biography along—that's the only sort of book I read these days—but I found it impossible even to turn the pages.

It was partly the jolting of the train, partly that I could not concentrate. I hadn't been able to eat lunch or supper that day. My stomach felt like an empty bag, flapping against my ribs, a paper bag the wind was trying to blow away. I couldn't eat, and I couldn't read, so I looked out the window as long as I could—it got dark at that time of year round about six, six-thirty, and the area through which we were traveling was hardly worth looking at. I have always observed that railways show people the very worst side of a city. Imagine the people who live in the tenements that back onto the cuttings; imagine the soot that settles in the clothes strung on the sagging lines, the whistle always moaning in their ears.

But perhaps you already know this about houses along the railway line. What is there that you don't know by now? In which case it doesn't matter if I leave things out of this account. Though I shall try my best to be complete, concise—I know you must be losing patience with me. It's the way I am, methodical, even fussy. And to use an old-fashioned word, prudent. A stay-at-home and stick-in-the-mud, as some would say. Nothing at all like her. But I am never jealous; I wouldn't want you to think that. I think it's small to resent people simply for being different from you, and I must insist on this, there is no resemblance between us, none whatsoever. She was always flying off places, making discoveries, taking risks. Especially with other people. What I'm trying to say is that she wasn't the settled and anchored sort. If it matters at all, she had lovers. Not that that has anything to do with what happened; not that it makes it any less terrible, or her the more to blame. As I've said, I don't care one way or the other, none of this really concerns me, except that somehow I've got mixed up in all of it. I don't know how—because of a name she'd left scribbled in her passport, or a letter they found on her desk. I was a name, an address to contact. Someone to be dragged here, by hair and heels, and made to answer.

It wasn't an eventful ride. We left the last of our cities behind, the last interruption before the border, at which point the train loops round and heads in a southerly direction. The land was flat, the light crepuscular—we passed a large lake, I remember, but it might have been empty for all that I saw of life on that water. Even the lights across the way didn't make any sort of reflection. Or perhaps I'm imagining this, because that couldn't be true; aren't lights always mirrored on the water? At any rate, I drew the curtains of the compartment, and tried to set my mind to something practical, immediate—not the tasks I would have to accomplish once I arrived in W—— (I'd rehearse those later, when I knew the train was approaching that city). No, I decided to concentrate on what I would tell the customs inspector. This was more of a game than anything else—not a sociable game; something more like solitaire, something to distract me till I could turn out the lights and crawl up into my bunk.

I would tell him—inspectors, in my experience at least, are always men—that I was going south for a family wedding. Most people are buoyed up by the mention of a wedding; they think of flowers and cakes and wine and confetti. I would say that my cousin, no, my niece was getting married—I could be old enough to have a sister with an eighteen-year-old daughter. I would look a little indulgent, a little anxious, as relatives of the bride are bound to be. And the inspector would be satisfied; he'd even tell me to enjoy myself, and give his best to the happy couple. But this is not the sort of thing you want to know—I only bring it up to show you in what sort of a state I was, to be thinking of deceiving a border official, even in so trivial a way. I didn't want him to know what sort of business I was on—how could I have explained? He might have thought I was going in order to make trouble, to set up a hue and cry, when all I was doing, at considerable trouble and expense, was to answer a summons. From a stranger like you.

As things turned out, when we did reach the border the customs officer didn't even ask to see my passport. He wasn't in uniform, but was wearing a nylon windbreaker. He had a baseball cap on his head. When I told him the name of the place to which I was going, he said how lucky I was. "It's real pretty there this time of year. Summer's already started." I smiled and nodded until he left the compartment —I am always nervous, slightly false with officials. Then I locked the door, got into my nightgown, and lowered the sleeping bunk, well before we started moving again. I'm happiest in bed with the covers pulled up high and close about me, all doors and cupboards and drawers shut tight.

I'm not ashamed to admit that I said my prayers, asking to be kept safe from all harm, and to get home again as soon as possible. And that I prayed for everyone else on the train to arrive safe and sound wherever they were going—it seemed selfish to be praying only for my own well-being. But then I began to wonder whether I shouldn't take into account all the people who were traveling anywhere, by plane and car as well as train—to all sorts of places and for any number of reasons, some of which may not have deserved a blessing. I couldn't help thinking, then, of the ones who'd traveled to her apartment—by bus, or car, or most likely on foot. And decided it was foolish to start in on that again when I was so close to sleep, and when I'd double-checked the lock on my compartment.

You may find it curious, but after that I began to enjoy the traveling, really enjoy it. The sensation of keeping still and yet moving, of doing something quite different from what I usually did; of leaving behind all those houses in which people were only sleeping, or watching television, while I was heading out into the night. I lay back on my bunk, rocking from side to side, thinking of cradles, of boats on the water, lulled by the clackety-clack, clackety-clack of the wheels. Silly things went through my head. I found myself reciting bits of poetry I'd memorized years ago, slivers working out from under the skin. "Down, down, down: we all go down to the dark." Who wrote that—and is that the way it goes? I don't know, but that's what the rails seemed to be saying, and it seemed appropriate, considering that we were heading down south, and it was pitch black outside, and that the note the whistle blew was slow and inexpressibly sad. Wait—did you notice? It's happening again. At the time, I certainly did not think those words—it's only in the remembering that I say "inexpressibly," a term I never use ordinarily. In fact, it's something she would say; she did use many romantic turns of speech, that's partly why people were attracted to her. Though it didn't help her very much. I mean, she may have tried to talk them out of it. But it didn't work, and that's beside the point—I was talking about the train.

I can't say when I fell asleep, but I know that I woke up from time to time—whenever the train stopped at a station, I suppose. But I'd sleep again as soon as the wheels began to turn. The conductor had to bang twice on my door to warn me it was the last call for breakfast in the dining car. I had brought some muffins with me, and a carton of orange juice, so I stayed put. I was so hungry that I didn't wait to dress, I sat there devouring muffins with the door locked, the curtains closed, filling myself up as if I were a bottle with a crack or a hole in its side. By the time I was ready to look out the window we'd passed all the pretty countryside: we were going through an unbroken chain of slums, then gullies choked with abandoned appliances and furniture and cars. There was even a small lake in which garbage floated as naturally as lily pads. The only person I saw was a boy, about ten years old, black, playing basketball with a ring that had lost its net. He didn't seem attached to anything, just as the basketball ring wasn't attached to a garage door, a pole, or post. As I remember it, the ring was just there, suspended in the air over a sea of cracked asphalt through which not even a dandelion sprouted. Even though, for the last eight hours, we had been heading into the sun, down into the blossoming trees and heat she wrote so much about her first weeks away.

I'd thought I'd have been able to assess, from the look of the leaves, the lushness of lawns and gardens, how advanced their climate was compared to ours, but soon even the gullies petered out, and we were passing through another tunnel of tenements. I closed my eyes and went over my list—it was time; the conductor had already come down the corridor, announcing W—— as the next stop. The list was quite short—I think I can recall it in its entirety:

1) taxi to house
2) go through apartment
3) bus to Bridgeford and back
4) taxi to train station.

It occurs to me, just now, that you may not understand, you may even laugh at my need to make lists and check off items, but I can assure you there are situations in which numbers and lines are the only defense against collapse of time and place and mind. What had happened to her was a blank space, a page without edges, the white spreading out and erasing everything. Until I got out my pen and ruler and set down a design. No design on heaven or earth could possibly undo what had happened, but with my list I could isolate her; draw a bottom line and turn the page. I could even shut the book, and that's what I've done, except for this conversation we always have. I want you to know that I make an exception for you. Normally I don't talk of this to anyone. I go about my business and people respect me for it. They know I have nothing to say that can change anything or anyone.

When the train pulled into the station I steeled myself—literally, I stiffened. I thought the city, the whole country a monstrosity, compared to the place I'd come from—I don't see how she could have chosen to live there in the first place. The taxi ride was shorter than I'd expected—I'm afraid I can't remember the name of the street. It was not an unfashionable part of the city; she got the house from a professor who was on exchange in Africa, I believe. I don't know why I should have been expected to visit it—but that's what was written down on my list. I had that item to cross out. I took the key from my purse, climbed the stairs, and let myself in. Immediately, I fastened all the bolts and chains and tested the peephole that shaped a little fishbowl image of the street outside. It was innocent, of course, as it must have been every time except once. She must have got out of the habit of looking through; she must have become too trusting. Or perhaps she was expecting someone she wanted to see too much —someone for whom she couldn't wait to open the door. I don't know—that's something about which I couldn't even guess.

There was nothing of hers left in the house—whatever jewelry, cash, cameras she'd had would have been stolen. All the same, I drew the curtains, just in case someone might look in from the street and watch me picking up certain things, turning them over in my hands, and putting them down again. I was looking for some trace of her, something that you might have been able to pick up with one of those hospital machines that turn different chemical paths in your body crimson or emerald or that queer electric blue. But it wasn't dark enough for that. I gave it up then—I wasn't going to stay until nightfall. There was nothing to tease out of a corner or closet; nothing had been overlooked. Except a spider plant in the kitchen—it was quite dead, the leaves withered, bleached to an ugly yellow. Odd that someone would have cleaned up the remains of the supper she'd been preparing, rinsed off the chopping board, washed the dishes, but not have watered the spider plant.

Did I say how stifling it was in that city? It was so much hotter than where I'd come from, miles and miles to the north. Perhaps that's why there was that smell on the way upstairs—I had to hold my handkerchief against my face, the odor was so strong. It was as if someone had smashed a hundred bottles of perfume, and the scent had leaked into the carpets, souring like milk. Except for that, everything seemed just as it was when she'd first moved in. A perfectly ordinary bedroom, still; the sheets stripped and the blinds pulled down. But I switched on the light and opened the blinds, so that I could make sure. There was no marker of any kind, and I remember I chided myself a little—you know the way you talk to yourself when you've done something more than usually stupid? What had I been expecting—bloodstains, bullet holes, some permanent sign of struggle? But they'd stripped the bed; nothing remained. The whole place looked ready for another tenant, you could tell by the way the sun came in, even after I'd pulled down the blinds: blades of light, hacking their way in.

What else do I have to say? That I took the bus out to Bridgeford, a suburb of W——. That was where the cemetery was. Nothing unusual about the marker, unless it was the lack of a message of any kind; just a name, the dates, and then space taken up by stone. What else could have been inscribed? That kind of thing happens in huge cities to the south, where people carry guns as casually as we do handbags. Perhaps that's why she reacted as she did—she wasn't used to the idea of a gun, someone aiming a gun at her. She should have panicked, and all she did was freeze, uncomprehending. She might even have said, "I beg your pardon?" Or maybe she looked right through the peephole and didn't even see the gun. There were three of them; one held the gun right up to the little glass eye, so that the muzzle was covering it entirely, so that all she could see was the dark inside what she didn't know was a gun.

You're curious as to whether I lost control—broke down, that's the expression, isn't it? Not in the house, and not while reading the name and dates on the stone, but strangely enough, when I got back on the train. That was when I started to cry, in my roomette with the blinds drawn down, and the train rolling back through the night and the day, I can't remember which. I don't want you to think that I became hysterical in any way. It's just that suddenly there were huge, soft tears rolling over my lips, into my mouth. I licked them away, and all the time I thought of how I used to catch snowflakes on my tongue when I was a child, when it was still safe to open your mouth to catch falling snow.

And that's the whole of it, finished with. She's dead. I've seen the empty house, the stone. I've gone there for precisely this reason— so I can sit here and tell you that she's dead, and I'm alive. And that we never knew each other to speak of. Perfect strangers, now. I can't think of anything I've left out that you would want to know. What is it you keep trying to make me say? That I sometimes have, not a dream, but an extended image of that afternoon, like a bit of film that's broken off the reel and got lost, mislabeled? That it goes like this?

She comes back from a day's work, and begins to make supper. There's a chopping knife, onions, a pound of stewing beef in the kitchen. And a glass of red wine, nearly empty. She's tired, but her face is flushed, expectant. The doorbell rings; she brushes her hands against her apron, pushes the hair out of her eyes, and runs to the door to let him in—thinking he's early, thinking that while dinner cooks they can go upstairs together. And so she opens the door, calling out his name, forgetting all about the peephole, the chains.

She sees the gun the way she'd notice a birthmark or a scar—pretending not to see it, so as not to cause offense, focusing instead on their dirty windbreakers, the baseball caps shading their eyes. And then there's the moment when she knows exactly what is happening, a moment clear and yet already wavering, as if it were glass turning to water, pouring down a floor that has collapsed, fallen away.

They push inside; bolt the door, jerk the blinds shut. And force her up. Always. Into the dark.

Going over the Bars

Breathe out, breathe in, breathe out, breathe in. In must always follow out for the whole business to go on at all. Even if it feels like rubbing your lungs back and forth along a grater, even if you have to throw yourself into the effort, the way you once threw yourself into an office assignment or a piece of housework. Out, in, breathe out, breathe in

For a moment, it feels as though she's swinging, abandoning her body to a plank of wood, ropes burning the palms of her hand—a surge of air. *Oh I do think it's the pleasantest thing/Ever a child can do.* An old rhyme, misremembered. Once she knew it by heart, once she'd spent whole afternoons swinging at the park, hanging her head back till her hair swept the ground; the whole world upside down as she aimed her toes at the sky. *Up in the air and over the trees/Till I can see so far.* Words going back and forth, in and out of her head, as if she were eight years old and swinging so high she gets dizzy. Never so high that she loses control, sailing over the bars. Some mornings she'd find the ropes of the swings wound crazily around the crossbar—someone's gone over, she'd think, and back away, avoiding the swings for the rest of that day, and perhaps a whole week after. *Byrd Ellen went widdershins around a church, and no one caught sight of her again on God's good earth.* Going over the bars she'd fly right off, and never come back at all.

Breathe out, breathe in, breathe out, breathe in. Dizzy. It's because of the medicine, fraying the links between nerve and brain. But how can it stop her from feeling the scrape of their feet down the thinning tunnels of her blood, jostling against her bones? Her bones, bitten to harsh lace. There are holes under the scars that were her breasts, yet still they keep on, voracious, racing from one watering hole to another. But they are nearly done for, those insatiable travelers. Soon they'll find themselves without a destination, never mind a road to take them there. Her blood and bones will suddenly give out, like a bridge suspended over a gorge, swaying, snapping as they rush across. *Breathe out, breathe in, breathe out, breathe in.*

Who decided it was best for them to bring her here? Her husband has arranged for her bed to face the window; he's arranged for the window to look out onto a garden, but when she does manage to open her eyes she can only stare at the ceiling. At home she'd look up to find rivers crackling an endless plain; the canals of Mars were there, and bruises from the Moon's sallow face. A map, a reassurance, like her doctor's jokes, the press of her husband's hand, the trusting incomprehension of her children. But here the ceiling is a mirror showing skin like lumps of powdered ivory. The travelers themselves are white, devouring her with stiff, colorless lips. She thinks of plagues passing over the face of the land: locusts, sirocco winds. There is a drought inside her; arteries, veins turned into skeleton leaves, a fringe unraveling.

Trees, she thinks, have the best of death, their flesh compact, burning clear and dry. She remembers them in winter, black-haired skeletons against a blank of sky. Or well and truly dead, branches polished beyond all possibility of bud or leaf—petrified lightning against blue summer air. And the way the leaves slough off—the leathery smell, the not unpleasant sourness of their decay. Flesh is a nicer word than meat. Once she'd felt shamed by its sheer sickened sprawl inside of her; now there is almost nothing left of it, they have worn it down with their rats' feet, rats' mouths, rats the size and speed of tigers. *Breathe out, breathe in.*

It's this shifting an iron bar from one hand to the other, the weight of air that makes her lungs ache. It's the funeral scent of the flowers; iris still clogged in its caul, tulips reeling on worm-soft stems. Today he's come in unexpectedly; he should be at work, should be with the children. He's here now because he knows the flowers make it impossible for her to find her breath, to throw it out again, lift up her hands to catch it back.

He takes the flowers and the vase away. Now she won't have to hear the noise the tulips make as their petals distend; the hiss as the iris shrivels. Now she will be able to hear her breath coming in, going out, the slow, unsteady creak of a swing. . . . It takes him a long time to get rid of the flowers and return to her bed, his waiting. Once he'd waited for her at airports and hotels; waited for her to finish dressing the children or undressing herself. Now he waits for the moment when a line fine as a hair will sever his life from hers; her dying from death. *Out, in. Breathe in after out, out after in, or the swing will stop altogether.*

Death may be an accomplishment of which we're all capable. Dying—at least, her kind of dying—is another matter. It is loss of control. Not surrender, but loss: progressive, irreversible, absolute. Out of an infinitude of cells all perfectly ordered and obedient, one becomes malignant, *disposed to rebel, disaffected, malcontent.* One cell deserting the ranks, changing itself, creating another in its own likeness. And that other spawns another, and another. Functions not so dissimilar to her own: to eat, to reproduce. To journey: *metastasis.* Her body an unknown continent discovered, devoured by travelers who burn so many bridges that there's no road back, nothing to go on to. They trespass on the routes of her blood and brain; they tunnel her bones. And her body answers back by closing shop, boarding the windows, locking the doors of whatever's left unvisited. They call it failure—her kidneys are failing, her liver and spleen. Her body an examination paper with X's piling up.

At first she'd dismissed the disaffected and rebellious cells. "I'm not giving an inch, not half an inch—you think you can do as you please, change as you will, but I'm not letting even one of you get your way." Her friends had applauded her spirit; she was a fighter and a winner; she wouldn't walk but swagger through the shadow valley. But something—not her friends, not her family, not even her own bravado—let her down. She'd had to switch tactics, lecture them the way she might have lived to lecture her children in another ten years: "What you're doing is stupid, useless—can't you understand? Like it or not, I'm the one in authority here—you have to play by my rules." At last, she'd tried reason: "Don't you see that you're eating the hand that feeds you? If I'm gone, how will you travel, where will you go? It's completely illogical—in nobody's interest, surely you must see that."

And then she'd refused all parley—they were no longer rebels, but an invading army. *Exterminate all the brutes!* They had been scalped, torched, drowned with chemicals. Five, three, perhaps only one escaped the assaults that poisoned her as well. Fleeing to unde-fended ground, pitching camp and recruiting forces, sending out van-guards to occupy still further reaches of a land lush, helpless as grass. That was the point at which her doctor had stopped joking, and her husband's hand had not seemed quite so firm when it grasped her own. Her children's clear and perfect faces became smudged when they looked at her; how could she help them, when she couldn't even save herself? She'd spoken one last time, not to rebels, or a victorious army, but to an unimaginable horde of travelers. "I see, now. You're not invading me; my body sent you, it has even kindly provided you with an itinerary. You may not even know that you're destroying yourselves by killing me—you may not even care. It's not you who are making me die. My body's committing suicide, and I'm given nothing at all to say in the matter. My body has simply stopped talking to me."

After the first operation he'd brought her home, put her in the spare bedroom, the one where they'd hung the old, bleached-out cur-tains with their tenuous patterns of gazebos, lovers, and gardens. She

was content. Here she could rest; here she could save something from
the wreckage, knit up the forces of something she could now call,
with all formality, her soul. This was the occasion to read Dante, to
listen to nothing but Bach. But the print scratched her eyes, the notes
blurred into one inchoate adagio. Very well, she would shut eyes,
shut ears, draw the curtains so that the lovers drowned in the muggy
light that struggled through the lining. She would lie in a square
white bed, enwomb herself, unfold the truth of everything she'd
wanted and hoped to be true. All the birthing and growing and cou-
pling for which the cells first joined themselves: whipcord sperm,
moon-faced egg—this counted for nothing. Only this malignant birth
was real, parthenogenesis of rebel cells. Born to die, this was the
truth her body uncovered under all its layers of skin, muscle, bone,
grown fragile as tissue paper.

Yet it meant nothing. Knowing brought no peace, no certainty,
no end of wanting. When her children came into her room she still
stretched out her arms to hold them. Holding them too long, too
tight, breathing in the bread-and-butter scents of their skin and hair.
They were very good, they let her hold them—they were afraid of
her. It was the truth, though her husband denied it. He wasn't concerned with what was true, only with the angles of belief, measured
by love's geometry. He was quite clear, quite confident in this; he
wasn't dying.

Everything she'd known and felt, watched and thought through;
everything she'd expected to have at hand, a rod, a staff to keep her
place, guarding whatever ground she'd gained—she'd lost it. And her
dying brought no revelation, only confirmation of obscurity. But she
wouldn't give in to it—if she'd lost control of what was happening
to her body, and why, she could at least dictate the how and where.
She would *not* be taken from her home, dragged over the border from
pain to stupor, dumped into a gleaming terminal where strangers
would speak to her only in charts and graphs, syringes, intravenous
bags. But in the end she was taken, dragged and dumped. Then *she*
was lectured to and reasoned with: *You need special drugs, special care.
Your husband can't cope anymore. It's become too hard on the children.* The

ambulance attendants were angels, substandard issue; they lifted her as clumsily as if they'd been using wings, not hands. She couldn't refuse them with her body, which had refused her orders for so long now; she couldn't refuse them with her mind, bumbling slow, soft circles round a wick of morphine.

Once out of nature I shall never take/ My bodily form from any natural thing. What made the poet think he'd be given any say in the matter? Metempsychosis, her soul sidling into the body of a dog, a cat, a rat —or perhaps just such another one as she, a body that will suddenly, and for no reason whatsoever, turn on itself after thirty years of working perfectly, the cells unfathomably obedient, so many of them reciting their messages word for word, relaying the codes through blood and tissue and across placental seas. Her children carry her body inside them the way she once carried theirs. Her body, and its switch, the mind, but not her soul, psyche, *pneuma,* whatever it is that lifts her onto the wooden plank—pull it back, back, and then release her into an arc of air. *Breathe out, breathe in.*

Those who hold that the soul perishes with the body are consigned to fire, on the authority of a great poet. And yet she could never acquiesce to an eternity of bliss, that potpourri of rose and fire. She cannot even think of angels except as white cockatiels, talons and tail feathers clipped, twisting their heads to the side of short, arthritic necks and croaking *holy, holy, holy.* She has read about accidental Lazari, expiring momentarily on operating tables, pacing vestibules of foggy light before their lives click on again. Do we at least get the afterlife we desire? Or does it depend on whether we perform our details the way we should? She is as nervous about this as she was about piano recitals, passing exams, taking off her clothes for her first lover. And yet it seems so simple—all she has to do, when the time comes, is to assume transparency. Her soul will weigh no more than a scrap of cellophane; than a breath on a mirror. It will float out of her body the way paper rushes up the flue of a chimney, the way children jump off a swing in full sail.

* * *

Breathe in, breathe out. . . . Her husband visits after work every day—he has stopped bringing the children; they are staying with their aunt in a different part of the city. He brings her their crayon drawings, stick figures drawn with the simplicity that certainty inspires: a circle and five lines = a body. Crayon lines cannot be erased, but only scratched away, and even if the color's gone, a line will remain, like a cut that's bled dry. She has held her daughters, sung to them, bathed them, scolded them for their four and two years of life; they will remember her, at worst, as a stick figure pinned to a square white bed; at best, as a temporary cradle of arms and breasts and lap. She told him, as soon as she knew, that he should remarry. They were drinking the bottle of Liebfraumilch he had bought on the way home from the doctor's (Chekhov's physician had ordered *him* champagne). "A wife for you, a mother for the children"—she'd said she didn't want him to play Heathcliff to her Cathy. He'd made a face that was not even a passable imitation of Olivier.

I am incomparably above and beyond you all. These will be her last words, if she has voice enough to speak them, and if anyone happens to be there to hear. Such things happen—everyone dies alone, though some are fortunate enough to have an audience. For it will be a show—of confidence, of unconcern, of panic or simply transformed energies; the effort her body now expends in crumpling and uncrumpling the paper bags of her lungs, sending her blood on its sluggish rounds, dispensing endless hospitality to footsore, hungry tumors, will go into lighting sure, slow fires of decay. Malignant cells and healthy—*All are punished.*

Breathe out, breathe in. She'd thought to go about her dying with a certain style. At first she'd entertained illusions the way you do the kind of guest you're certain to impress. But it came to nothing. She remembered a film she once saw, an image of a large, moon-faced woman cradling a death's-head in a muslin bonnet. But no *magna mater* has come to offer her the breast. Death and the maiden? He's stood her up—she hasn't caught so much as a glimpse of his spindleshanks, a twirl of his scythe. Perhaps because she has no flowers to give him, having twice rolled the stone away to bring her children out. They haven't yet learned to mourn the death of a pet—now they will be marked forever: "Their mother died when they were very young." A letter of introduction to Herr Angst.

Her husband holds her hands. They are an arrangement of bones—doesn't he fear they will fall apart in his hands, a game of pickup sticks? Her husband pays his calls and she knows his presence in the way she knows that Saturn and Jupiter orbit the sun: invisibly, at an incalculable distance. *Breathe out, breathe in, swing up, swing down, hold tight to the ropes, hold tight.* . . . He is holding her hands and bending his face toward her, eyes wide open, like the tulips she made him throw away. Murmurings, measurements, a jigger of morphine. Shaking out the long, fine hair she no longer has; running to the swings at the end of the park.

Incomparably above and beyond. He leans in over her, asking her what it is she wants, can he get her anything, is she in pain? How to tell him she feels nothing save the rush of air against her face as she swings higher, higher. She is somewhere between body and mind— it is too difficult to explain, and she has lost her voice, just as she's lost the ability to curl her fingers round even a child's hand, to return a pressure. *Breathe out, breathe in.* But she wants him to understand this being in between. It is something like looking at color transparencies whose outlines haven't quite meshed, so there's a gap between where the line is drawn and the color begins. A gap. Not absence, and certainly not an abyss, but just an unexpected space to slip through. Like that possibility, high up on a swing, of pumping so hard you go up and over the bars.

She'd never been able to do it, as a child, and she'd forbidden her own children to try. Because they would break bones, smash skulls, end up in hospital. *Swing up, swing down, swing harder, higher.* She's been so stupid to have left it behind her, left it so long, as if it were a shameful, a childish thing. When she'd taken her own children to the playground she'd avoided the swings, sitting instead on a corner of the sandbox, or patroling the rim of the paddling pool, trying not to get splashed. Now she doesn't care if anyone sees her like this, alone and free, head down and her long hair brushing the ground. The world turned upside down, a sky of packed earth, with stones for stars.

Swinging back and forth, higher and higher till the bars creak and groan. *Over the wall, and up in the trees/ Till I can see so far.* She can see everything now; the cracked ceiling over her head pulls back, like flesh from the sides of a wound. It shows whatever it is that lies in the gap between outline and color. Dante, Bach, *Mehr Licht,* but all that fills her head is a children's rhyme. *Out, in, out.* The swing coming up to its highest point; she's gripping the rope so tight it tears her hands. Something splits inside, a hairline crack; something fiery, clear as glass spills out. *In, out. Out.*

Over the bars

A Really Good Hotel

"Taxi, mum?"

Mrs. Paxton pursed her lips. Ordinarily, she would have swept past this sort of person—bearded, stooped, an emerald turban clenching an unfathomable mass of hair. Ordinarily, there would have been a car waiting for her, and a uniformed chauffeur: youngish, deferential, inoffensive. But this was intolerable—there hadn't even been a porter to help her with her luggage. Never mind that she was traveling unusually light this time. There were certain attentions she had come to expect, attentions due to elderly travelers who hadn't the vigor, the indiscriminate good humor of the young.

"You want a taxi, mum?"

Mrs. Paxton frowned. Why hadn't the hotel sent a car round? The doctor had assured her all details had been taken care of. As soon as she was shown to her room she'd sit down and fire off a letter of complaint to the manager. Outrageous, unheard of. . . . Little blots of light dribbled across her eyes, like rain on the windshield of a moving car. Nothing serious, the doctor had assured her, nothing to worry about. All the same, she would have to sit down somewhere, calm herself, set things back to rights.

"I take your bag, mum." He held the door open, gesturing with his hand to the waiting seat. The powder-blue upholstery was covered with indescribably dingy vinyl. Heaven knew how many bodies had slid in and out of this cab. She shouldn't get in, she knew she shouldn't—the fumes of patchouli would choke her long before she reached the hotel. This was an airport, not a bazaar—what were men with turbans doing driving taxicabs? What sort of man would condescend to wear a turban? He had shifty eyes, Mrs. Paxton decided —he looked like a thief. She shuddered, a small, violent shudder, then slid into the sweetened darkness of the cab.

Before the driver could turn the key in the ignition, Mrs. Paxton was leaning forward, clutching her collar tighter round her throat. "I want the Shady Nook Hotel. They were supposed to have sent a car. Can you tell me what the fare will be?"

The man nodded, then made a curious gesture with his hand, turning it palm downward and moving it from side to side, as if to indicate that there would be no charge, or at least that the regular fares did not apply. Perhaps, then, this was the driver sent by the hotel? Unthinkable. Yet before she could protest, the car had started up, and they were rolling out of the airport into a sunstruck afternoon, curiously like summer, though it was still the bleakest part of March. Trees on either side of the highway were in flagrant leaf—a perverse sort of evergreen, decided Mrs. Paxton, who'd always excelled at botany, though there were some who swore she couldn't tell parsley from poison ivy.

Trees in heavy, slumberous leaf, almost blocking out the sky. Several times the car arched over bridges—there seemed to be a remarkable quantity of rivers in this part of the country, Mrs. Paxton observed. She patted at her hair, tucking stray wisps under the hairnet which was her only adornment. She scorned any makeup other than fine, floury powder, and had the lowest opinion of women who painted their toe- and fingernails. In her prime, Mrs. Paxton hadn't needed to resort to tricks and feints. She'd been, in her husband's words, a "demmed fine gel" and it was generally acknowledged that she'd aged impressively.

The driver showed no signs of spying on her through his rearview mirror. His eyes were given over to the highway down which the cab was bearing with utmost gravity, if little speed. There was no sign of a meter, and he still hadn't given her any idea of the fare. Well, if it was excessive, she would simply refuse to pay. She'd no luggage in the trunk—she would just step out of the cab and into the hotel and have done with the whole unpleasant business. Mrs. Paxton licked lips that seemed to be dissolving, like rice paper, under her tongue. She could do, she decided, she could very well do with that glass of fortified wine that the doctor had prescribed to keep up her appetite.

Abruptly, the car turned a corner, and began, if possible, to slow. At first Mrs. Paxton thought the driver had realized he'd taken a wrong turning. Then, as the trees seemed to be thickening on either side of the car—white trunks on the right, black on the left, and everywhere that suffocating foliage—Mrs. Paxton's gloved hands went up to her mouth. Shutting her eyes, she recalled with distressing accuracy all those items on the front pages of the papers she disdained to read at the supermarket checkout counter—women raped down lonely country roads, bludgeoned in library stacks, assaulted in elevators. Women of advanced age producing miracle babies—often twins and sometimes quintuplets. Had she even checked the cab? Was it from a reliable company? She racked her brains for the name painted on the doors and on the triangular light perched over the car roof, but could only dredge up a handful of letters. S—was it an S? And somewhere an I and D—or was it a V? Whatever it was, the car had come to a complete halt. She was reaching for her shoe— not alas, a very high-heeled shoe—as the car door burst open—

"—the last time I take one a them goddamn intercontinental buses. Jeez, we came in fifty minutes late. *And* the service stinks. But the restrooms—let me tell ya—I swear there was snakes come creepin' outta the toilet. Holy smokes—excuse my Greek—but a girl could get bit but *good*."

The person sliding in beside Mrs. Paxton had the voice of Betty Boop and the carriage of the late Queen Mary. In fact, she was wearing a mourning veil and a severe black suit that reminded Mrs. Paxton of those photographs of the Dowager Queen that had so cowed her in childhood. Yet on a chain round her neck the woman wore the most ridiculous mess of ornaments: a Coptic cross, a Star of David, a tiny replica of the Koran, Nefertiti's profile, and a miniature cornucopia. "Ivy da Silva," the creature pronounced, offering Mrs. Paxton a lace-gloved hand.

Mrs. Paxton refused the hand but managed a vestigial nod.

Mrs. da Silva lifted her veil and grinned. "I guess you flew in. Me, I got this thing about airplanes. Bill, he went down with that 747 back in—oh, back a helluva long time ago. Almost as bad as the *Titanic*. Remember the *Titanic*?"

This time Mrs. Paxton didn't bother with civilities. She leaned away from the pungent cloud of her traveling companion's breath—gin? whiskey? Evening in Paris?—and spoke commandingly to the driver. "This is quite ludicrously far to go. I never agreed to sharing a cab, and I won't be held accountable—"

"Hotel round the next bend, mum. Sign on the left—you see?"

And indeed there was a sign. Under a painting of an old stone house with shuttered windows and a lake lapping at its walls she found the words, "The Shady Nook." "Sure to be damp," sniffed Mrs. Paxton, rather more relieved than she cared to show.

"Ca-rumba, I'll be glad ta get outta these clothes and inta a hot tub," screeched the da Silva woman. Mrs. Paxton couldn't help but silently agree, for the scents of gin and patchouli had impregnated the glazed linen of her suit, even the kid of her gloves. She would insist that her room be as many floors away as possible from this interloper's. Doubtless they would run into each other in the dining room, or on the grounds, but then a nod would suffice—there'd be scarcely any call for them to speak. At her time of life, Mrs. Paxton prized her privacy. Hell, she'd heard it said, was other people. She was not inclined to disagree.

As the taxi pulled up in front of the hotel, Mrs. Paxton drew to the extreme edge of the back seat, so decisively that the door handle cut into her side. But it didn't stop Ivy da Silva from leaning across and squeezing her companion's arm.

"Whatta ya say, Judy? Just what the doctor ordered, eh? Did ya know there's a lake out back? You betcha—I even brought my bikini."

To begin with, the bellhop was an albino. Mrs. Paxton had nothing against that particular deformity, but she thought it tactless of the management to present their guests with so visible a proof of what they'd come to the hotel to forget—namely, that all in all, life had rather less order and decorum than a rubbish bin. People were known to have been born with heads swollen to the size of beachballs, and without a trace of brain; in the course of one's daily business one could, with no warning at all, lose legs or eyes or life, as if legs and eyes and life were of no more account than a handbag or a pair of gloves. Gifted children perished in infancy; drooling idiots survived into the monstrosity of advanced old age, at which point they could not be distinguished from those who'd been the brightest and most beautiful among their peers. That was the reason Mrs. Paxton had never consented to have children. If it had been possible to pick out one's offspring from a display case or nursery, the way one did with bedding plants, then it might have been a different story. Incalculable, were children, and she'd never been one for gambling.

The bellhop was an albino, and the manager had not been at the desk, nor had his wife, who was presumably attending to some crisis in the kitchen, from what the chambermaid—a flittery, batlike creature—had been able to tell her. Nevertheless, the room was satisfactory; that had to be admitted at once. The furniture was white, quasi–French provincial, but not in any Sears catalog way. The vase of lilies on the desk turned out to be acrylic, to Mrs. Paxton's relief —she was allergic to pollen in all its forms. Later she would discover that the lacquered wood of bed and chair and desk was in fact a cunning form of plastic, and that even the luxurious wool carpet underfoot was nothing more than a *trompe-pied.* Ingenious things could be done with polyester these days, reflected Mrs. Paxton, folding her devastated linen suit into the bag marked *Laundry Services,* and entering the tub.

Judy, she had called her. No one had dared to address her as Judy since grade school; even Gilbert, on their wedding night, had permitted himself no greater liberty than, "Judith, my dear . . ." But however did the creature know her? How could a gin soak have been a former schoolfellow of Judith Paxton, née Dreedle? Preposterous. It only showed what good hotels were coming to these days. Mrs. Paxton began soaping herself energetically with the loofah she had brought from home. Would Wilson remember to water the geraniums? Should she have trusted her with forwarding the mail? Now that Gilbert was dead and the business closed down, now that she finally had a house of her own, why had she ever agreed to leave it? It was all her doctor's doing—he was responsible for sending her here, he was responsible for everything, and she would write to tell him so.

Climbing out of the tub, Mrs. Paxton wrapped her dressing gown tight as a shroud around her, and walked to the window. It was the old-fashioned kind, two panes that opened into the room, so as not to disturb the vine burdening the ledge outside. Mrs. Paxton leaned over the sill, breathing in great gulps of curiously cool and scented air—jasmine and nicotiana and mint, creasing the stillness. Overhead, in that shockingly blue sky, clouds like stray lambs browsed upon a light so clear it stung her eyes. Mrs. Paxton looked quickly down at the water licking the walls of the hotel. No sign, thank heavens, of that dreadful da Silva woman drifting by on an air mattress, martini in hand. No, the only thing to trouble the surface of the lake was a lighted window, rising like some great golden carp from the blackness of the water.

Mrs. Paxton took her morning coffee in the library. At least she assumed it was the morning—she seemed to have mislaid her watch, though she entertained suspicions vis à vis the chambermaid. Certainly Mrs. Paxton had lain down to sleep after her bath, having decided she'd dispense with dinner. And equally certainly, she'd risen from her bed after a most tiresome dream in which she'd been trekking across endless plains composed of either sand or snow. Wak-

ened by the barking of a pack of dogs—another item to be added to
the list of her complaints—she'd opened the window onto the same
azure sky, and had hurried to put on her coolest dress, only to find
all the lamps lit in the lobby; the dining room curtains drawn. She
was about to tug them open when a bearded man at a corner table
called out, "You mustn't. It's bad for them. They're imported, you
see." He was pointing to a huge vase of purplish flowers. "Rubbish,"
replied Mrs. Paxton, but all the same, she left the curtains be, and
made her way into the library.

It was a splendidly cavernous room, without any windows to let
light leak in and scald the bindings. Mrs. Paxton was a tireless reader,
not of novels but of educational works: histories of civilization, sur-
veys of philosophy, comparative studies of the world's great reli-
gions. Greedily, she homed in on one of the towering shelves. Really,
they ought to have a stepladder handy. How did they expect people
to reach the more interesting volumes, the ones with gold-embossed
and dust-embedded spines, promising revelations far beyond the facts
disgorged by mere encyclopedias? Right now she fancied something
weighty, something to settle the butterflies that capered in her stomach and beat blurry wings behind her eyes. She felt distinctly queasy.
This was to be expected, of course, this derangement of one's whole
being that traveling entailed: different time zones, parasites in the
water, disruption of one's personal schedule and physiological clock.
A history of the early church would be the very thing. On the top-
most shelf were stacked some ecclesiastical-looking volumes—she
would just reach up and see. . . .

"Kee-roust, I can't believe this one. All I want is a magazine—
you'd think that wouldn't be hard to get a hold of. They call this a
hotel? I'd like to see the manager, I'd just like to see him. You'd think
he was Harry Houdini or something. A hotel without a magazine
rack—I don't care how old a magazine, anything would do, even a
bunch of pictures—"

A startlingly high-heeled, abrasively crimson shoe, pumping from
the depths of a wing chair at right angles to Mrs. Paxton. A whiff of
some syrupy but not altogether offensive scent. It was to be hoped

that Ivy da Silva was talking to herself, that Mrs. Paxton in her gray piqué, her sensible shoes, would blend in with the books, but this was not to be. Ivy had heaved herself out of the wing chair and stomped across to her before Mrs. Paxton could grab her coffee and flee the room. Only this wasn't Ivy, or at least it wasn't the woman who had shared her taxi the night before, and who'd accosted her with such gross familiarity as "Judy." This woman was a good twenty years younger. Her hair was platinum blonde, whirled like cotton candy round her head, and she was wearing the most inappropriate of morning dresses: a red satin, sequin-studded bustière, even more outlandish than the skyscraper heels. Yet the sloppy diction, the petulant intonation could only belong to that aged creature with the lilac hair who had so precipitately clutched Mrs. Paxton's arm in the cab, and spoken of bikinis.

"Hey, let me help you with that. These heels got to be good for something besides slipping my discs. You want this one? What about a couple more?"

Mrs. Paxton gave the kind of grimace that can often be mistaken for a smile. "Thank you. I wouldn't dream of troubling you any further."

"Aw, don't mention it. Listen, sister, we've got to stick together —I mean, we're not going to let them sell us a bill of goods, right? And a hotel without a magazine— Aw, cripes, I'm going to go and find the manager. Right *now*."

Mrs. Paxton blinked as the red satin skin over the alarming breasts and buttocks bounced in the direction of the lobby. Her coffee was by now stone cold—the cream had formed cataracts inside the cup. There must be a bell somewhere to summon an attendant, though they seemed in singularly short supply here. Apart from the bellhop and chambermaid she'd seen on her first night, there seemed to be no staff at all. According to the brochure, the manager's wife did all the cooking—she grew her own fruit and vegetables in the gardens that were supposed to be at the back of the hotel, though Mrs. Paxton hadn't caught so much as a glimpse of them from any of the windows. "How irritating," she thought. Even though she deplored the vulgarity of the da Silva woman, she had to admit that it was an excellent idea to speak to the manager, an idea *she* ought to have acted upon, instead of leaving it to that tarty piece of goods. If one didn't make one's presence known, the staff would simply ride roughshod over one. Mrs. Paxton had stayed in innumerable hotels in the course of her seventy-odd years. She had been an equal partner in her husband's import-export business, and they had traveled wherever new markets presented themselves. What would Gilbert have made of this hotel? As if for an answer, Mrs. Paxton opened the tome that Ivy da Silva had got down from the shelf and that had looked indisputably like a work by one of the Nicaean Fathers.

"*A Treasury of Golden Hours for the Little Ones.* By Mrs Isabella St John Sims."

This simply would not do. Mrs. Paxton went back to the shelves, pulling out volumes at random, but all she could find were more children's books. Not even the classics, just dreary texts preached by writers named Lapwing and Ewer and Stodgson, sermons against dirtying one's pinafore, maiming one's cat, drowning one's brother. She would have to see the manager—no, better still, she would ring for a servant and have the manager fetched before her. After all, if she were spending her good money in this place for four, possibly six weeks (depending on what her doctor decided), then something would have to be done about the deplorable absence of reading matter. Were there no bookshops? Were there no lending libraries?

But before Mrs. Paxton could make her displeasure known, she was overcome by the clanging of what sounded unpleasantly like a churchbell. She rose to her feet, smoothed her collar, and strode out of the library into what ought to have been the lobby, but which turned out to be something different altogether.

"C'mon, sit by me, Jude. I'm an old hand at this. I'll show you what to do."

Ivy addressed her from behind a long plank that reminded Mrs. Paxton of the desks in country schoolrooms, in which four children sat to a row and memorized multiplication tables. This time she had no doubt it was Ivy speaking, though her head was shaved, all save a zigzag of stiff orange strips across her scalp. She was wearing a black leather jacket big enough for three, and a pair of satin trousers into which a child of ten could have barely squeezed. She had no shoes on, and her toenails, painted vermilion, were pierced through with little feathered rings.

"C'mon, or you'll miss the beginning—that's the most important part. He's such an asshole," continued Ivy. "He reminds me of Frankie, but then Frankie—"

"I presume you found the manager?" interrupted Mrs. Paxton, who'd decided, not long after her first youth, that reminiscence was a sign of weakness. Forget everything, and you will have no regrets, that was her credo. "The manager," she repeated, in a carrying voice. For answer, Ivy held up a finger to her lips, then tore a few sheets of paper off a writing pad embossed with the name of the hotel. "Jude, Jude—you mean you didn't even bring a pen?" Ivy's voice was surprisingly low and gentle. She didn't wait for Mrs. Paxton's reply, but broke her own pencil in half, dug a pocket knife out of the black leather jacket, and whittled the stub to a serviceable point. "Here," she whispered. "Now just keep your eyes peeled, and do like me—it's the only way."

"Only way to what?" demanded Mrs. Paxton, but Ivy's eyes were fixed on the exact center of the rotunda, to which a man with a top hat and black silk cape was striding. In one white-gloved hand he held a long, carved baton. He was no albino—his face was a deep, smoldering blue, like the flowers on the dining-room table. "That's the manager," Ivy ventured, chewing on a bit of fingernail. Not someone, thought Mrs. Paxton, to whom one would voice trifling complaints about the dishonesty of chambermaids, the dearth of anything but children's books in the recesses of the library.

The manager lifted his hands wearily, as though oppressed by the weight of rings he wore on every finger—gold and rubies, sapphires and silver, diamonds, emeralds, platinum. Light exploded from the jewels, reminding Mrs. Paxton of those little comets that no longer burned out over her eyes—perhaps there *was* something salubrious in the air of this country, perhaps her doctor had been right after all. Though it was the most curious hotel—how, for example, could so large and unusually shaped a room fit into the confines of The Shady Nook? Why hadn't she remarked the existence of a rotunda when she'd got out of the cab the night before? But then, she'd been exhausted, distressed. Sometimes the mind would simply not accept the evidence of the senses. Even now. . . . This room reminded her of a Roman basilica; indeed, the domed ceiling was paved entirely with golden tiles, except for the center, from which an enormous, unlidded blue eye stared down at them all. Where the pupil should have been painted, there seemed to be nothing but a hole. No, that would be impossible. How would one keep out the rain and the snow? Though it was, perhaps, a very little hole. . . .

"Ladies and gentlemen. We are ready to begin."

At first Mrs. Paxton thought they'd all been summoned to a gigantic bingo game. Indignantly, she started to her feet when suddenly she felt Ivy's hand upon her arm. It was the transparency of Ivy's hand, the waxy thinness of her face that arrested Mrs. Paxton, so that she fell back into her seat, grasping the pencil Ivy had given her. She wished that it were a candy, even a stick of chewing gum. She would have offered it to Ivy, who looked as though she hadn't eaten anything for the longest time, at least not since her arrival at The Shady Nook. Mrs. Paxton could understand her reluctance, of course. Breakfast had been appalling. Nothing but that mueslix business, burned toast, and something that may or may not have been scrambled eggs. She had contented herself with a spoonful of jelly—it was sour, mostly seeds, and a wretched shade of red.

"Try to remember," Ivy whispered, as the manager pulled a gigantic stopwatch out of his pocket. Slowly, deliberately, he scanned the circular rows of benches. People were hunched over papers, pencils raised expectantly in a silence Mrs. Paxton could only liken to the yellow roaring in one's ears before one is about to faint.

"Ready, steady—go!"

Suddenly the geometrical frieze along the rim of the dome pulsed and cracked. Jagged bits streamed up inside, where they became circles or sticks, remarkably, as Mrs. Paxton observed, like the letters of an alphabet. They were, in fact, an alphabet in a strangely familiar foreign tongue, swarming higgledy-piggledy over the golden tiles. But no sooner did the letters combine into something that looked like a word, an ordinary, pronounceable word, than they would break apart and recombine into some quite other arrangement. "If only one could pin them down," wailed Mrs. Paxton, but Ivy wasn't listening. Like everyone else, she was scribbling fractions of indecipherable words over her sheets of paper, one word across another and another on top of that, till the page looked like a verbal whirlwind.

Mrs. Paxton sat helplessly before her blank sheet, staring at the manager, who stood, stopwatch in hand, tapping the floor with his baton. She'd accustomed herself to the irregular color of his complexion—most likely a birth defect, a variation on a port-wine stain. She tried to catch his attention, but he looked right through her, as though she were merely another member of that scribbling mob. And so, Mrs. Paxton fixed her eyes on the dome, which looked like nothing so much as a gigantic pool of honey, heaving with flies. All these people madly writing, writing— Why on earth had they come here on holiday only to go back to school? What was the point in trying to fit the letters into some readable combination—what sort of message could they possibly convey. And to whom?

"What on earth—" began Mrs. Paxton, but before anyone could answer her a buzzer sounded. People dropped their pencils in panic, or else gripped them so tightly she thought the knuckle bones would pop straight through the skin. Ivy had let her pencil roll to the floor —she closed her black-lidded eyes and slumped in her seat, as if she had fainted. "Ivy," Mrs. Paxton shouted, groping with her hand in the direction of her neighbor. "Ivy, this is no time—"

"What? I can't hear you, speak louder." Ivy had jumped out of her seat, quite wide awake—even a little insolent. "Oh, it's no use, you'll only get us into trouble. Look, I'm going for a swim—why don't you join me?"

"I can't, you know that's quite out of the question." Mrs. Paxton had a fearful headache after the session in the rotunda. She muttered something about going to lie down in her room. Would Ivy be so good as to stop in after her swim? She had something rather important to ask her.

Ivy took Mrs. Paxton's arm and guided her to the elevator, an affair of swirling metal bars within a spiral shaft. Mrs. Paxton was loath to step inside but Ivy insisted, pushing her in and locking the gate. Mrs. Paxton stretched out her arms through the bars, calling Ivy's name.

"Don't do that—it's dangerous. You should know better than that by now," Ivy scolded. She pushed the button at the side of the shaft; Mrs. Paxton clung to the bars as the cage ascended. Except— she had the strangest feeling that instead of going up, the elevator was taking her slantwise down, around and around like a corkscrew into a stoppered bottle.

Her room was stuffy—of course the chambermaid had forgotten to air it out while making up the bed. Mrs. Paxton went directly to the window and fiddled with the latch. But it would not give. The wood must have swelled somehow—the window would not open. Maddening. She so wanted to put her head outside and find Ivy rippling through the moat, like some comic-strip Ophelia. For if she were to fill her eyes with Ivy, she wouldn't have to think of Gilbert, and it was necessary not to think of Gilbert because she thought— she couldn't be sure, everything was so confusing here—she thought she'd caught a glimpse of Gilbert in the crowd pushing its way out of the rotunda. She couldn't be sure—she hadn't seen anything so direct and deliberate as a face. It had been nothing more than the particular configuration of a bald patch, a certain hunch of the shoulders—the way his shoulders always hunched when she'd sent him away from her, when she'd refused him things for which he had no call to ask.

But no matter how closely she pressed her face to the glass, all she could see was a blue blaze overhead, an impenetrable gloom of leaves below, and in the moat encircling her, the multiplied reflections of a lighted window, an endless row of drowning lamps.

* * *

If only she could decide whether it was sand or snow through which she was trudging, Mrs. Paxton could have settled on an appropriate image of rescue. An oasis, or a log cabin with a friendly plume of smoke beckoning from the chimney. But she simply could not tell. It was most extraordinary, but for the first time in her life she could not seem to distinguish between what should have been black and white, chalk and cheese. Why was everything blurred and shifting here? Why in this hotel was nothing straight or sharply edged—why was the decor all arabesques and circles? Even the glass in the windows bulged out and in, even the stems of the artificial lilies spiraled in the crescents of their vases.

Would Wilson remember to water the geraniums? Why had she trusted Wilson? And how had she consented to this holiday, this forcible removal from the one place that was at last her own, after all those years in hotel suites and furnished rooms, and houses taken only for the summer. Of course she had agreed to go on the urging of her doctor, an obstreperous, an obtuse man, for all the diplomas and certificates on his office walls. Making her undress for the examination, as if that were necessary at her age. Strip to the skin, though drafts came pouring through the windows, a polar wind whirling in her veins. And yet how hot had been the lights over the examining table, probing her lungs and heart, and the gorge of her womb. . . . A most impertinent man. She would write a letter of complaint to the College of Physicians and Surgeons. She would do that straight away, instead of wasting her time in that awful rotunda place with the others. Sheep, that's what they were, nothing but a slaughterhouse of sheep.

Where was Ivy? She'd promised she would come to her. She would ask Ivy to explain what was going on—Ivy would know. Yet they'd been at the hotel for exactly the same amount of time—why should Ivy have got so far ahead of her, making herself so free? Dressing up, going for swims, stomping off to see that most distressing-looking manager. Where *was* Ivy? Mrs. Paxton sat up in her bed, waited for a few moments more, then pulled on her dressing gown. She hadn't any idea what time it could be. Since she had dreamed, she must have slept, but there was no way of knowing for how long. She should have reported the loss—the theft—of her watch that very morning. But had there been anyone to whom to report? Stealthily, Mrs. Paxton unbolted the door and ventured out along the corridor. Everywhere lights were burning—not lights, but torches, smoldering in the dark.

"Too much, this is simply too, too much," rasped Mrs. Paxton. "Why, I might be burned to a crisp in my bed. Torches indeed. I'll pack my things tonight. I won't even wait for Ivy, I'll call a cab right now and drive to the airport and take the first flight home."

When Mrs. Paxton returned to her room a breeze, half-mist, half-wind, was teasing the curtains. There on the window sill, swinging her legs, sat Ivy, in a cloud of a dress, her hair floating white and filmy all about her. She looked no older than a child, indeed, she was holding something in her arms that looked like a doll. Except that it wasn't a doll—it was a baby, and the baby was sucking at Ivy's small, pale breasts. "Oh, Judith," she called, "Judith, where have you been? I've waited as long as I could."

"Nonsense," declared Mrs. Paxton, shutting the door behind her, refusing to be flustered by this apparition in the window. Apparition indeed, for all round the cloudy hair and dress, even round the milk spurting from Ivy's breasts, hung a golden mist that made Mrs. Paxton think of pollen, of the mosaic tiles on the rotunda dome, the unbearable heat of the lamps on the doctor's examining table. Mists and contagion. She didn't like this, she didn't like it one little bit.

"Ivy!" commanded Mrs. Paxton. "Explain yourself! What exactly is going on here?"

"Exactly?" Ivy echoed. "Why, I don't know—exactly." She smiled, unlatching the baby from her breast. "Oh, Judith—just let go. You'll see. Everything will run on wheels."

"Run?" repeated Mrs. Paxton, folding her arms and digging her heels into the carpet. "Run where? My dear girl, do you realize I've been in this wretched hotel for—heaven knows how long—and I've never once been let outside? So how can you talk about wheels? Tell me, do—where will they run?"

Ivy smiled, dandling the baby in her arms. "Where? Why backwards, of course."

Mrs. Paxton took a long, measured step toward the window. "Ivy, Ivy, this is most unfair of you. I ask a simple question and you—"

"Backwards and over and away you go. Child's play, you see?"

Mrs. Paxton retreated a pace and stared. Ivy's voice sounded amazingly pure, as high and lilting as a child's. Indeed, it seemed as if it were no longer Ivy speaking, but the baby itself.

"Ivy!" Mrs. Paxton called again, but the name came out as no more than a whisper. "You have to tell me what to do. Ivy? Wherever are you going?"

Inside the line of golden fog the girl appeared to be trembling and fading, like an image on a distant screen. Heaven knew where the words came from, but Mrs. Paxton heard them quite distinctly:

"You forgot the driver, so I paid for both of us. Remember, Judith—just let go. *Addio.*"

Mrs. Paxton still hasn't been able to decide what happened next. One moment a woman transparent as gauze was sitting on a windowsill, holding an increasingly distinct and vigorous baby. The next moment both had vanished, exactly as if they'd done a backwards somersault. But there hadn't even been a splash from the water below. Mrs. Paxton had run to the window and leaned out as far as she dared. All she could see was a fine white ring that stung her eyes, exactly like a paper cut. And then it vanished into the water.

Mrs. Paxton hung down her head into the cool, tangled scents of mint, jasmine, and nicotiana. The sun beat upon her hair till she felt her whole head must be on fire. And she kept on calling out, impetuous, imploring:

"Sand or snow, Ivy? Tell me, sand or snow?"